THORNS

Best wishes
Fancy Band

THORNS

Frances Brand

Copyright © 2018 Frances Brand

All rights reserved.

ISBN:9781070647210

Imprint: Independently published

ACKNOWLEDGMENTS

The protagonists in this story and the specific events related are entirely fictitious and any resemblance to living people is unintended.

The background in Bosnia is based on what happened during the bitter civil war which racked that country in the 1990s affecting so many lives.

Some of the local gatherings actually took place in a Shropshire village well known for its outstanding community spirit.

My thanks to Howard Waters for his support and assistance and the design of the Thorns cover.
And to beautiful Cloudborne, 'Sonny', who is alive and well at the age of 28.

We were unable to attribute the base photograph but if anyone can claim copyright they should contact the author.

Chapter one

He leaned on the hurdle pen confining a small group of lambs and stared at them without seeing. They watched him, shifting nervously, crouched together, their fleeces stained and dark where the blowflies had struck. He looked away from them into the distance, seeing in his mind's eye another scene where maggots had played a part on two rotting human bodies heaped together beside a dusty road. That triggered another memory and took him back to the moment he'd walked along a stone-paved street searching anxiously for a cafe on the Alipasina. He found it eventually, through an ancient door surrounded by an arch worn smooth by centuries of human touch. Hesitant, he looked around and found himself facing a dark haired young woman with an apologetic smile.

"I'm sorry," she'd said in good English "but we have only one dish on the menu today. It's very hard now to offer a choice."

He shook his head. "I'm lost. They said to come here, you would be able to help me." He smiled back at her and asked if there was coffee. She nodded and said: "We still have a little." Returning with a jug she led him to a small table and sat down opposite. They talked. He could hear her voice and remembered so clearly the exquisite excitement she aroused in him from the first moment he saw her. That afternoon in Sarajevo changed his life.

He'd become hopelessly lost, taken too many wrong turnings in the city's old quarter trying to find the place he'd arranged to meet his photographer. He was sent to the cafe because someone there spoke fluent English and would be able to help him. She did. Her English was excellent with a soft, appealing intonation and for the rest of the day as he and Bob the cameraman worked he kept thinking about her, looking at him across the table. He was so preoccupied he messed up his interview with the UN commander who accused him of trivialising the situation. He lost his temper at the accusation and in doing so spoiled relations with a good contact.

"What the hell's got into you?" demanded Bob."You really fucked that up."

"Forget it. There are other stories," was all he'd said.

In the evening he went back, sure of the way this time, delighted to realise she was pleased to see him. He caught the way her eyes lit up as he approached the bar and she took him to the same table in the corner. He couldn't help watching every move as she went for wine and her easy, silky walk as she returned. Her eyes were large and very dark and he noticed the long, glossy lashes as she leaned forward. They talked over wine and slivovitz for hours.

She was twenty-two and a widow, her Muslim husband killed by the Serbs soon after the fighting started, three months after they were married. She'd had a child but the baby boy had died before he was a year old and, though a Croat, she'd stayed to help run the cafe owned by her husband's family. That marked her in Serb eyes as Muslim. It had never mattered before she said, she'd known her husband since they were children, mixed faith marriages were common in Bosnia and life was good for them. But that was before. Now their lives and the entire city had descended into chaos. They tried to maintain a semblance of normality but as the siege intensified and food, power and communications were cut off, staying alive became the only priority.

He shook his head to banish the thought of her and the pain it brought him. He studied the five lambs then reached down to grab one and began to snip away the dirty wool with the hand shears, revealing the writhing mass of fat grubs hidden in the fleece. He poured the thick oil and watched in satisfaction as the maggots began to squirm and drop out of the wool.

A wry smile lit his dirty face as he thought of his father and the constant rows and conflict all those years ago when he tried to make him understand that he had no interest in taking over the farm. He didn't want to be a farmer. Yet here he was doing one of the dirtiest tasks in the business. He attended to the other lambs then opened the pen to let them rejoin the flock. For the next few days he would keep an eye on them to ensure he had rid them totally of the maggots which, if not removed, would literally eat them alive.

He remembered his father's face, though he hadn't thought of him for ages. Strange to recall it now. The old man just wouldn't accept that he meant what he said but later the disbelief turned to anger. The rows, the endless arguments came flooding back into his mind -- his father wanted him to go to agricultural college, come back to the farm and eventually take over running the business — that was a son's role. But James wanted to get away from the cloying, narrow confines of his childhood. He meant to go to university and he did.

But it was hard, living on a minimal grant, because although the old man was well off he refused to help. He was so hard up it was ridiculous and without his mother's help he would never have got his degree. She gave him cash when she could, behind the old man's back. But stacking shelves and serving drinks in Sheffield was an education in itself. He found it hard going but enjoyed the city life after growing up in the country, it was busy and thrilling with people of all types coming into the bar where he worked. It opened his eyes to a totally different world. But back home it was always the same and even after he graduated his father still thought he would change his mind and come to his senses.

The crunch came when he announced at supper one night that he'd got a job on the local evening paper. His father was furious, swearing James would never get a penny from him, his mother had burst into tears and his sister left the room. Leaning on the fence, gazing uphill at his own modest acres he pictured the scene as he stood with his father on the crest of the downs. Arms held at length like a Bible prophet, he said: "All this will be yours, James."

"But I don't want it."

"You must want it! It's the family farm. What have I been doing all these years if not to build this up and pass it on to you? Land boy, land's in your blood, you must feel it. When you were born that was it, I had someone to carry on here. That's your job. Look at it."

He'd looked, rolling acres of Wiltshire downland stretched around him, huge empty acres. At that time of year near harvest, the land was golden with waving ranks of ripe corn, with scarcely a weed anywhere, let alone the scarlet splash of a poppy. To him they were barren acres, soulless, few trees in sight and no hedges.

Turning to his father he'd said: "How can you feel for this, dad, it's like a desert. No soul. You're not a farmer, you're a businessman. You're not in touch with the land, you simply ride over it in big machines. That's not farming. You don't even get your hands dirty."

"Don't be stupid. This is what modern farming's about. We've got to feed people, feed the world you're so worried about. You're right, it is a business and a damn good one."

"I'd be more interested if we had some livestock. All this arable is nothing to me, it's boring, it's not my idea of farming. And you know nothing will convince me that these enormous subsidies are right. Mountains of grain that make men like you wealthy."

"It gave you a bloody good education which has evidently only filled your head with romantic nonsense. Farming's like any other business, these crops give a good return, that's the way the system works."

"But it's not what I want."

That was years ago and now here he stood, setting up to be a farmer. He'd always liked sheep, there was something in their nature that appealed to him. He ran his eye over the rest of the flock, moving away from him as they settled to graze, his eyes seeking signs of lameness or lack of condition.

The young bitch Tess trotted at his heels. People laughed about her, she looked more like a jackal or a dingo -- he sometimes called her the dingo -- but in a very short time she had become a brilliant little working sheepdog. By a kelpie dog her mother was the most unprepossessing bitch he'd ever seen, a mistake. But he liked the pup and took her on to save her from being shot. She was very smart, her natural instinct for working the sheep apparent very early and she seemed to know at once what he wanted. Her sharp intelligent face had bright sweet eyes and she had pricked ears which turned over when she was worried and a bushy tail like a fox. Her hair was yellow, nothing like most people's idea of a sheepdog. But when it came to moving sheep she was a star. She stayed by his side as he crossed the yard to look over the valley. The sun was starting to sink behind the crag on Jagstone Hill and its rays glinted on the windscreen of a vehicle turning off the village road into his lane.

"Shit," he muttered, wondering who it might be. Across the valley, the church tower seemed very close in the evening light. He could pick out the copper beeches in the churchyard but the black and white pub was obscured behind oak trees. It was a mile away but often seemed closer, depending on the light.

He sighed, not eager for callers, ill at ease with most of the locals, not yet absorbed into the community and not likely to be, he knew, unless he made an effort. He waited by the wall and watched the Land Rover climb the last steep rise before his gate. He thought he recognised it as it pulled in and was relieved to see his neighbour Jack Wilson climb out. Jack was one of the few he had properly got to know, he'd helped him out several times over the winter and the farmer had returned the compliment. His daughter Pat was always ready if he needed a hand.

"I was close by so I thought I'll call up," he began. "Wondered if you might like a bit of shooting, that wheat stubble of mine is covered with woodies most mornings and it's good sport if you can bag a few."

James frowned then smiled awkwardly. "It's kind of you, Jack but I'm not into shooting much these days. Haven't had the gun out for years."

"Go on, give yourself a break. It's wonderful out there in the early morning, you'll enjoy it. Don't you like pigeon?"

"I do actually, they make a lovely hotpot. I used to shoot them at home."

"Well, think on it, you're very welcome if you fancy it"

"Thanks."

Jack eyed him. "Everything all right up here? Any problems?"

"Not really, maggots on a few lambs but I've dealt with that."

"Yeah, just the weather for 'em, warm and moist. Well, good to see you, I must get back for the milking. Don't forget, you're always welcome at our place if you fancy a chat."

James nodded and walked to the truck with Jack, waiting as he drove away, struck with a sudden spasm of emptiness, alone again with memories and too much thinking time. Indoors he looked at the whisky bottle handy on the kitchen top and fetched a glass from the cupboard.

The chatter of jackdaws busy on the roof roused him at first light. He snuggled deeper into the bed and drew the quilt over his head but the birds' noise was persistent and he lay frowning, dragging his senses together.

The unlined curtains revealed a sunny morning and the busy birds urged him to get up. A pair of wood pigeons cooed in their late summer courting, reminding him of Jack's invitation. A walk with his dog and the gun seemed a good thought. He opened the gun cabinet, unlocked against all the rules — and in his bedroom from necessity as the only place in the old stone walls sound enough to secure the bolts.

He sat on the bed, cradling the weapon across his bare thighs. He hadn't looked at it for months and not fired it for years. It had arrived with him in the cabinet but it was clean and well-oiled with both barrels spotless. Shooting had no great appeal for him but he enjoyed walking with the gun and taking a rabbit or bird when he could, something that could make a meal. He'd shot hares at home in Wiltshire but they'd become scarce in this hill country and he preferred to see them alive in the fields.

He'd never felt the same about killing hares since the day years ago on the downs. It was late May and out of season but he was a teenager with a gun, firing at anything that moved in the fields. To his dismay he realised the doe was heavily pregnant. Slitting open the belly he held his breath, dreading what he would find. The three leverets inside must have been only a day or two from birth. They lay on the table perfectly formed, bright dead eyes staring up at him, a silver sheen on their silky brown coats.

He cried, sick with shame and pity. He could not bear the thought of eating the hare and buried her with her young, telling no one what he'd done.

Bobbie the spaniel dashed around him eagerly when he appeared with the shotgun but he said: "No Tess," to the dingo. "You wait till later."

The late August morning already displayed a hint of autumn, with a heavy dew and in the sloping field above the house the climbing sun made a pathway of silver in the gossamer threads of spider webs across the grass. His leather boots were quickly soaked.

The pigeons congregated on a stubble field in the valley bottom, foraging for fallen grains, sometimes in numbers that turned the field grey. He could be lucky if he was there before them, in time to get into cover before they arrived. A brace of woodies would make a good supper.

With the gun broken over his arm, he trudged down the hill, the dog bounding near him or speeding off to explore the multitude of scents in the growing warmth. It would be scorching again later but at this time it was pleasantly cool. There were pigeon already on the stubble and careful as he was they flew up in alarm at his approach, wheeled and made for the trees around the field.

"Too late Bobbie," he laughed. But he carried on round the boundary on the other side of the hedge and settled himself into a place he'd noticed where several big round straw bales remained from a previous harvest, left as cover for just this purpose. He sat down to wait in the hope that the birds' hunger would be stronger than their wariness. Or some new arrivals might come, unaware of his presence.

He found it hard to sit and do nothing, restless in his own company, ill at ease with his thoughts. It was damp behind the bales which had lain for two years under the trees and the sodden straw had turned black and mouldy, sprouting weeds and shoots of corn, to create green mounds as if they had grown there, part of the scene. Jack would leave them till they rotted down to be ploughed back into the soil. The ground where they waited was littered with empty cartridges and idly he scraped some of them together with his foot meaning to gather them up when he left.

Patiently he waited, trying to keep his mind blank and concentrate on the bright morning. The pigeons which had flown up also waited and watched, perched alert in the trees. All was still, except for the distant sound of a tractor engine and the occasional sharp yaffle of a green woodpecker. He waited but his mind wouldn't stay blank and crept back always to the spot he wanted to keep buried. A sore spot inside that hurt when probed like the scar on his shoulder. He didn't want to think of her or of Sarajevo or the nightmare he'd lived there. He tried to bury it by recalling the happy time when they first met. Katya watching him across the table, her anxious eyes searching his. He needed to hold on to that, the way he'd felt then, the fascination she evoked, the attraction between them — he wanted to recall every detail and blank out the rest. If only he could.

Lulled by the stillness a fresh flock of pigeon flew in, joined by the watchers in the trees. James saw them and waited before loading his gun. He selected a bird as it flew in and squeezed the trigger. The other birds rose in panic and he fired again. They wheeled as one, heading again for the trees. He should have reloaded and shot again but the gun's blast shook him, he'd forgotten how loud a 12-bore sounded and he stood shaking behind the bale, holding his head as the noise repeated in his brain. Not the blast of the shotgun but the horrible, repetitive battering of the heavy guns the Serbs had used to bombard the city from the hills around Sarajevo.

The shock was that it still had the power to affect him, after all these months he couldn't rid himself of the horror. The spaniel trotted back with each bird in turn and dropped them at his feet. His contented whine recalled him to the warmth of the morning. "Well done, Bobbie. No more of that today. Good dog, we'll go home."

He picked up the birds, feeling their plump, well-fed breasts, young birds which would be tender, a pair of birds like this would have been manna from heaven in the siege. It haunted him still that he could do so little to make any difference, how he felt his failure to help at all because he'd got himself trapped there and couldn't even tell the world what was going on.   Images that haunted him at three in the morning when he woke sweaty and uncomfortable. He tried to blot out the burned bodies he'd seen in a Muslim village, two children and a woman huddled in the foetal pose clutching her tiny baby, around them cindered wood and blackened bricks.

He left the damp darkness of the trees to tramp uphill into the sunlight. Already it was hot and he sought somewhere cool; he changed course and headed for the rocks on Jagstone where he lay down in the brown dry grass and allowed himself to succumb to memory.

Katya, he wondered if the ache in him would ever be dulled, if only he had never gone there; if only he had never been a newsman, if he had stayed at home and run the farm, what an easy untroubled life he could have had. If, if, if. So many might-have-beens.

But that wasn't what he wanted, the easy life served up for him. At least he'd travelled and seen the world for what it was — which had seemed mostly a hard and awful place. Colleagues had told him more than once he would have been better off as a farmer. "You're too soft for this Jimmy, you take it too much to heart. Too sensitive, lad, you need a strong stomach for this bloody mess."

But because he'd been there, stuck in the siege because he'd got himself involved, he'd seen it from the inside and that was what he was doing here now, sitting on this hill in the middle of nowhere. Supposed to be writing about it. That was what it was all about, find a peaceful place, make a bit of income from the farm and write the book they were all waiting for.

He had a contract and been paid a good advance with a bigger cheque waiting. But the advance was spent and month after month nothing happened, he hadn't even made a start, just a few pages of notes. Every day he told himself, tomorrow, I'll start tomorrow.

But always he was side-tracked , by any physical task that demanded little from his brain, or someone to see or a place to go, anything but sit down and drag out the words. It was too raw, too fresh in his head, the images too close. He should never have agreed to do it but in the first gratitude of survival it seemed the right thing to do.

When his editor offered him the chance to cover the escalating conflict in Bosnia he'd jumped at it, he was ambitious, it could be the move that propelled him onto the next rung of his career — television, his aim from the start. He saw himself as the new Kate Adie, the face people recognised and trusted, knowing things must be really bad if he was there.

He'd seen more than his share of the world's conflicts — Somalia, Angola, India when the Hindu fundamentalists were killing Muslims and then on to Kashmir. But the developing crisis as Yugoslavia fell apart had drawn him like a magnet.

He loved the country — as children they'd had holidays there in the days when he and his father had fun together and Yugoslavia offered cheap trips to the sun with clear blue seas and spectacular landscapes. He recalled jumping off a jetty with his sister Louise into a pellucid depth of water where they could see fish and crabs swimming. He had more recent happy memories with two different girlfriends, bathing and sailing with plenty of cheap wine.

Now it was blown apart and the country become a battlefield, a shattered land that no one seemed to care about. There was coverage on the news from the beginning as Slovenia, then Croatia clawed their way to independence.

International politicians talked interminably but the situation wasn't seen as warranting intervention — it seemed to be working itself out. Until the Bosnian Serbs decided on a campaign of ethnic cleansing. James was stunned that neighbours in a European country, just a few hours away by plane, were murdering each other in the name of religion. As one united country under Tito they'd lived together in peace and apparent contentment with growing prosperity. But now the centuries-old epithet 'Turk' was heard again as part of the population embarked on what was nothing less than genocide.

He couldn't understand why people he knew and worked with weren't more troubled by the violence as if it concerned an alien people, far away and unimportant.

He realised how naive he'd been, arrogant even, to think that he, just another journalist in the war zone, could make a difference to the global perception of the crisis. The fact that many others had done the same was not the point. Somehow he, James Lambert would be the man to make a difference and open the eyes of the world. He'd failed of course. It was only now that the scale of his hubris hit him. He sent back brilliant copy with graphic and harrowing photographs, he did television pieces and live coverage from some of the worst-hit areas. It didn't take long to understand the futility of his efforts but by then he'd met Katya and his world had changed.

His help then was more practical, keeping people alive by ferrying food and other supplies through the dangerous routes into the city or dragging them off the streets as the shells landed. Too often it was women and children with dreadful injuries.

He looked down at the pigeons, lying with bloodied beaks and marks where the pellets had hit, reminded of his first discovery of how much blood was contained in a human body. And how far it could spread.

At least he was helping— that kept him there, that and the young widow who mattered to him more than anything else in his life.

She wasn't beautiful, not as people might understand the word. She had a calm radiance and a vulnerability that entranced him. It was easy to fall in love with her. They talked together in hurried, gasping snatches, there seemed to be so much to say. She'd been to London once and loved it — the atmosphere, the theatres and restaurants of the West End had particularly impressed but she said she could never live there because it was too far from the mountains.

He laughed at that and told her about the mountains and hills in Britain, places where she might feel at home. He knew Shropshire hardly at all then, only from driving through on the way to somewhere else. But he told her about Wales and the red kites and the battle to bring them back from near extinction. Sitting there in Sarajevo where human life was so cheap it seemed nonsense to talk about saving birds of prey.

But Katya thought it was wonderful, that people had time to think such things could matter. He told her about the different people that made up Britain and some of the battles in the past.

"But that was a long time ago," she said. "You all live together now in peace."

"Apart from the rugby," he said. "And don't forget our friends the IRA. See what they say about that in northern Ireland. That's the nearest thing we have to what's happening here — and that's down to religion as well."

"But it's not genocide is it? They don't hate each other just because they're there. Neighbours don't suddenly begin killing each other. People you've known all your life, children you played with when you were a child."

"No, it's not as bad as that." He looked at her and said: "I can't believe you had the Olympics here not so long ago. None of it makes any sense."

"That was a wonderful time for Sarajevo, showing off to the whole world. All the excitement, the glamour, people thought we had a wonderful city and we did. Now look at us." She sighed, reaching across to touch his hand.

"That's why your red birds are so important — the kites. It matters because it's civilised, things like that are the layers of concern that set us above the animals. Because we're human we can make it happen. Here humanity is a rare commodity."

He began to tell her about his childhood and they compared notes on what they'd seen and done. She'd been brought up around Sarajevo and for her Bosnia was the centre of the world, a land she loved. But it was hard to be light-hearted because down every track they tried they hit on something changed or wrecked by the war.

He stayed with her till two in the morning and the journey back across the city to the Holiday Inn was punctuated by the crack of gunfire and the rumble of heavy weapons. It never stopped, even through the night there was no let-up from the firing.

The plaintive mewing of buzzards roused him from his reverie, reminding him of kites, the sound so similar — and for always now kites would remind him of her. He opened his eyes and gazed into the blue sky, searching for the soaring birds. It was the kind of day they loved — warm and clear with thermals lifting their wings.

He counted five, each gliding in its chosen sweep, gradually moving across the valley as they hunted at leisure. Their appeal never palled and as he watched the easy grace of their flight the flash of pale under-barring on the wings of the nearest bird was caught in the sunlight as it banked away from him. The birds were coming lower and he lay still. They knew he was there but he sensed his presence wouldn't alarm them. One came down and settled on the rocks nearest him. Slowly he turned his head towards it and the bird swivelled its own head to gaze at him. Neither moved, the sharp eyes above the strong, curved beak looked directly at him. He returned the stare until the buzzard took off and flapped unhurriedly away to a further rock. It was not alarmed, just discomforted.

Chapter two

Luck was on his side and he caught the lunch time ferry at Southampton, driving on just before the ramp went up. The mid-week sailing was only half full and comfortably quiet on board, no shouting teenagers which had been his last experience. It was a decision taken on impulse as he lay in bed that morning wondering what to do with himself

Out of bed at half past four he'd made up his mind — a trip to France, get a new perspective. He left home without breakfast but when he went below to find a restaurant his appetite disappeared as his usual queasiness at sea began to make his stomach churn. The day was hot but windy and the waves rolled up a rough swell as the ferry headed out into the Channel. He bought a coffee and found a bench where he could stretch out. He was very tired and with his head down he fell asleep and stayed there through the voyage, waking as a French voice informed passengers they would be landing in ten minutes.

He went out on deck to watch the little port approaching, seeing bathers enjoying the late afternoon sun on the beach at Ouistreham. He still felt tired and very hungry and now dejected. Early in the morning it had seemed a good idea but as he waited to go down to the car deck it seemed a stupid thing to do. The idea was to drive south to visit his friend Paul who'd bought and renovated a little farm in the Lot Valley near Villeneuve. It was a long way and he didn't even know if the family would be there.

"Come any time," they'd said but dropping in on spec after a 700 mile journey was a bit crazy. Better find somewhere to eat and stay the night, he told himself and get hold of Paul. If it was no good he could have a day or two in Normandy and head back home.

The course of action decided he felt better and eager to be off the ferry and as he waited for the giant doors to open he grew impatient to be away. Being at the wheel of the MG again was good. He hadn't driven it since before Bosnia but it had been his pride and joy, left over from the time when such things mattered. He loved its dark green colour. One of the last MGBs to be made, it had sat under wraps at the farm for more than a year and before that in a London garage.

By now early evening and with the hour difference beginning to darken the sky, he opted to stay in Caen and booked into a small hotel. In the shabby restaurant waiting for his food he drank a large glass of red wine.

It took the edge off the meal which was better than expected, young rabbit cooked with prunes and shallots and a pile of frites alongside. After the first glass he ordered a carafe, the house wine, a light red from the top end of the Loire which he would never find in England. It went well with cheese which cheered him, one of the main delights of France, and he ate a large piece of the soft goat cheese. Too much. When the carafe was empty he finished off with Armagnac and then felt desperately tired and queasy. He remembered he still hadn't contacted Paul. In the morning, he thought.

He was almost alone in the restaurant, just a couple in the corner engrossed in each other. He had only his thoughts for company but the wine relaxed his mind and he wondered what had made him order rabbit. That took him back to the day in the cornfield and he remembered the pigeons and the hare from years before.

He'd given the pigeons to the dogs, not caring to eat them himself, recalling the sound of the gun and the impact it had. He was startled and almost frightened by the way it affected him and his excitement at travelling had dissipated into a growing aimlessness and depression, the bleakness he had come to know too well. He'd been on a high in the morning but all the memories that flooded back on the hill had plunged him into a darker mood.

That was why he got stoned in a cheap French hotel and struggled to sleep in a small, scruffy bedroom.

He thought about the sunny day with the dog. In the evening he'd gone to the pub, tired of being alone. He wasn't a regular but liked a pint sometimes and the beer at the Fox was well kept. Listening to the farmers and other locals could be entertaining, although there were never many in until late in the evening. At seven o'clock as expected there was just old Bert from Longstone and a young couple he didn't know. Well past eighty, Bert's daily five pints of bitter were what kept him going, or so he said. He sat always in the same corner, grunting his way through any conversation and sometimes dropping loud and often embarrassing comments about any strangers in the pub.

Nursing a pint in cupped hands James perched on a stool at the bar to chat with the landlord, Richard, a keen photographer and bit of an artist. He wasn't actually very good at running a pub, lacking the bonhomie of a real host and the locals thought him miserable. James had the impression that for Richard the customers were really a bit of a nuisance, interfering with the real business of life. But he liked him and in return Richard enjoyed talking with the man from the hill -- some said the fool on the hill -- as they'd taken to calling him, because his conversation extended beyond farming, sport and sex.

Several times he tried to ask about Bosnia, from a professional point of view, he said, being interested in the photographic aspects of war coverage.

James said he wasn't a photographer, just a words man and they would move on to other things. He listened without too much attention as Richard went into detail about sketches he'd done for a series of watercolours he'd planned of harvest scenes. Then he was off to pull pints for half a dozen farmers who entered noisily in a group.

The place sparked into life especially as two of them were nearly black with dust from combining and the rest were taking the piss at the state of them. They had come straight from the wheat, the skin around their eyes like pale goggles from the masks they'd worn.

"Don't sit down, you two," Richard said plonking their drinks on the bar. "You know I don't like you here in that state."

"Oh come on man, give us a break, we need to wash the dust down. We won't sit on your nice upholstery, don't worry."

The landlord frowned but those two were part of the mainstay of his trade through the year. They all nodded at James, friendly but cautious in the way they always treated him, nobody quite sure what to make of him. They considered him a townie and had no inkling of the inheritance he'd rejected, a farm which would have bought most of them twice over.

He listened to the farming talk and some offensive remarks from a noisy groups of youths about some girl. He had a malt whisky and bought a round for his immediate neighbours at the bar and soon after ten made a move to go.

They would be going strong until at least midnight, later if Richard didn't get fed up but James had had enough. The outsider — it was more than being a newcomer, he was always the onlooker. The job, he supposed, always observing, never taking part.

But it had always been like that, since he was little. Only in Sarajevo — he'd been part of it there, too much a part, and his involvement had nearly destroyed him. He shook his head, emptied his glass and slipped quietly away.

The evening's wine had made his guts uncomfortable so he left without breakfast, only coffee inside him, aiming to cross the Loire at Tours and on into Perigord. He stayed off the motorway, loving the long straight tree-lined French roads. The MG's suspension registered every bump in the tarmac but that was part of the fun and for a while as he headed south with the sun roof open through that particular brightness of the northern French plains his depression eased. On either side were massive fields of sunflowers, their huge yellow heads starting to turn brown as they waved in the breeze. Sunflowers or wide acres of maize, still green and filling the cobs but the roads led on with the age-old lure of the south. He thought of himself in the speedy green sports car following the same pattern as generations of English down the centuries, galloping south on horseback or in carriages heading for the sun on missions of conquest or delight.

Late in the morning he remembered he hadn't called Paul. He'd taken a detour south of Alencon to avoid the busy area around Le Mans and driving along the pretty valley of Le Loir he found a phone box in the little town of La Fleche, sleepy in the noon sun. The telephone rang for ages but at last he heard Paul's voice. "James!"

His friend was surprised but sounded wary if pleased.

"Where are you?" he asked and then: "Whatever you doing there? It's miles out of the way."

"You know me. I like meandering, so much to look at on the way."

"You'll have to drive like hell to make it by tonight."

"I shan't try. I'll stay near Limoges or wherever I land and be with you tomorrow -- if that's all right. Expect me some time from lunch onwards. Shall I bring anything? Other than wine, that is."

"No, just wine. It'll be good to see you again. I mean that."

"Thanks. Till tomorrow then." Paul's warmth made him feel better and glad he'd come. Ambling into the cafe near the grey phone box he returned the laconic greetings of the four Frenchmen lounging there. He was in no hurry to leave the sun-warmed town, just the same few customers in the shabby bar and most of the inhabitants concealed behind closed shutters. He smiled as he thought of them, sleeping or eating or making love in that sensible French habit which gave them a long rest in the middle of the day. They would emerge in mid-afternoon, fed and refreshed, ready to resume the day's business.

The decision to bypass Le Mans had put him further west so he forgot Tours and headed south to cross the Loire at Saumur. The river was low in its summer state, the gently sloping sandy beaches inviting. The great river that effectively divided France in two, flowed slowly here. Crossing the bridge he looked up at the massive chateau dominating the river and beckoning him south.

But his thoughts turned too easily to war and he remembered the tragedies of another war. He looked to either side at the river, seeing how low the water flowed, the sandbanks well clear of the current and imagined the German tanks surging effortlessly across, ignoring the valiant young cavalry cadets of the Cadre Noir. Horse soldiers with sabres charging the Panzers and dying in a Loire turned red with their blood.

At this rate he'd be lucky to make Paul's tomorrow but in the small town of Bellac he noticed the signpost for Oradour-sur-Glane — a few kilometres off his way. He knew the name and tried to recall its significance but couldn't remember why it was on his list of places to visit. So close — he couldn't resist turning off the main road onto country lanes running through woods and fields. He remembered the story before he reached the village, ruins enclosed by the original high walls.

Oradour, scene of one of the worst acts of infamy perpetrated by the German army — he considered turning back, unsure if he really wanted to face it. But now so close he felt compelled to go and approached the wall and gateway knowing he must see it all. He sat in the car and looked at the entrance for several minutes before parking in the allocated place beneath the walls. It was a bad time to see it — or appropriate, depending how you looked at it — evening, the sun going down, casting long shadows on the silent streets.

He paused beneath the gate arch to read the plaque, which recorded the fact that on a June day in 1944 the village of Oradour as a living community had ceased to exist. The Germans were in disarray, falling back ahead of the allied invasion of Normandy and a division of Panzers was racing north to reinforce the defence. Oradour was on their way and the commander decided to make an example of the village, to show others what to expect if they defied the Reich.

No other living soul was around as James walked slowly up the street, towards the shell of the church where the women and children were forced inside, more than 300 of them. The doors were secured and the building set alight as German soldiers waited outside, ready to shoot any who tried to escape the fire.

Only a few survived. He stared at the tower and went in, running his fingers along the blackened stone, clammy to the touch. He shivered in the cold interior, conscious of a perceptible sense of the dead around him. Above him the dusking sky gave no breath of the warm evening. All had been left exactly as it was fifty years before on the day the village died.

He hurried out and wandered on along the ruined streets, pausing to look through broken windows and doors into roofless rooms, once home to happy families. On some cottages there were inscriptions to tell how many died there and how. A wrecked car stood parked in a yard as it was before that afternoon of horror and in one room a sewing machine still waited on a shelf, beside a ravaged doll, mute testimony to the abrupt end to a way of life.

Behind a wall, among ancient fruit trees he found the graves where the victims lay at peace. The village was empty but for him and he was alone with its ghosts whose anguish was palpable. The aura of the place pressed on him like a burden of guilt that he should be alive and they were dead. Walking the grass-tufted streets he felt a familiar constriction in the throat and tears filled his eyes, continually drawn to the power lines. The concrete pylons and wooden posts with their broken cables sagging in loops only underlined the tragedy. They were so ordinary, like the power lines in any other small French town and their survival seemed to stress the dreadful implacability of that day. He took himself away, moved more than he could bear. It was all too real, too much like the ruins and the deaths he'd witnessed in another land. In one way he wished he hadn't been there yet it seemed meant to be.

The village was not rebuilt but abandoned as the Germans had left it, alone with its ghosts who watched in peace while time completed the work of fire and dynamite. After the war a new Oradour was created just a few miles up the road.

His mood of euphoria was gone and he kept his eyes stolidly on the road ahead, missing the scenery and villages he passed. He couldn't stop thinking of the desolate streets in the dead village which merged with others he'd seen and filled his head again with dark images of war.

He didn't notice the name of the town he drove into, watching for a chambres sign. He tried the first place he spotted with adequate parking, a small hotel in a side street, with a notice showing the tariff and demanding payment in advance.

As he fumbled for the correct amount of francs Madame smiled at him: "Non, Monsieur, it does not apply to you."

"Oh, merci madame," he said, confused.

She saw his confusion and smiled again with a knowing shrug.

"Monsieur is English and alone. You can pay in the morning."

"Ah, I understand."

Annoyed by his own naivety he realised the hotel was a maison de passe and hesitated, considering whether to try somewhere else. But the woman seemed kind and anxious to please and he decided the girls and their clients shouldn't inconvenience him.

She saw his confusion, asking: "You will stay?"

When he nodded she beamed at him, reaching for a key. "I will show you your room. You will take breakfast?"

He was still uncertain but she seemed so pleased to have a guest who might actually stay for breakfast that he thought: "What the hell! What did it matter?"

Not at all and he'd slept in places far worse than this.

Further down the street he found a small bistro with little on its menu that he fancied but he needed to eat and ordered a ham and cheese pancake and frites with a carafe of house wine. He'd drunk that before the meal arrived and ordered another. He toyed with the savoury plateful but left half of it and with a litre of rough wine inside him returned to the hotel where Madame offered him coffee and cognac.

He was the only customer except for a wrinkled man of uncertain age who seemed oblivious to everything around him and a youngish woman, fair-haired and slim, trying to catch his eye.

He looked firmly away but she continued to eye him, smoking languidly and sipping a beer.

Madame chatted to him in a mixture of French and English; her English was good and they chatted easily, though the conversation was sometimes disjointed. He told her where he was headed and she told him how hot it had been in the south and about the storms they'd had two weeks before. He half listened, his speech becoming slurred and several times he said: "I must get to bed."

When he finally got uncertainly to his feet Madame came round the bar, laid her arm across his back and whispered: "Would you like some company? Shall I introduce you to Jeanne?"

She motioned with her head to the fair-haired girl who stubbed out her cigarette in anticipation. James glanced at her and shook his head.

"Not tonight!" he grinned as Jeanne met his eyes.

"Quel dommage — what a pity," she murmured.

Fatigue reinforced by alcohol sent him to sleep almost at once. He'd shut the window to deaden the noise from the street but the night was hot and he woke up bathed in sweat after what seemed only a moment. He'd slept for nearly two hours but was roused not just by the hot room but the sound of voices murmuring close by, words heard clearly through the thin walls.

He groped his way across the landing to the toilet and realised how drunk he was when he splashed the paper seat cover, noting the wall-held dispenser for the covers. He dropped back on the bed, his sweaty body throbbing with discomfort and listened to the progress of the love-making next door. The murmurs became more insistent, the bed creaked critically and try as he would to bury his head in the pillow, the sounds of orgasm penetrated his consciousness.

As it quietened he slept again, a deeper sleep with dreams of Katya. He was waiting in her bed when she came in, laying her sleek body close to him. He stroked the soft skin and kissed her beseeching mouth and groaned and rolled as the sound of heavy gunfire echoed through the city. He took her in his arms and saw her eyes bright in the flashes which lit the room as shells exploded. She kissed him in turn, his mouth and his eyes and his belly and his penis which grew at the touch but all he could hear as they clung together was the guns like thunder, crashing around them in a roaring crescendo. He stared down into her dark eyes, his face a grimace of passion and saw a momentary touch of fear. He couldn't help himself and ground deeper into her so that she cried out but the cries changed to ecstasy and she came soon after him, the sounds buried in the greater violence of the shell that burst in the street outside.

The earth moved for them that night, the street shook and the window blew in, showering the bed with glass. Small shards peppered his naked back as he lay on top and sheltered her with his body. Jesus, yes, the earth moved — rocked by high explosives — and the crater in the street filled with water from the broken main. Every window in the house was smashed and half the wall had gone in the cafe downstairs, every glass and piece of crockery destroyed and now there was no water to add to the lack of gas and power.

She wiped the blood from his back with a towel from the shattered bathroom and they lay together quivering from fear and spent passion. For him it had been the worst and the best, overwhelming intensity with the horrid intrusion of the war and the proximity of death.

He awoke trembling, crying her name and heard the noise of the guns still banging overhead. He lay listening in terror to the sounds of the night and gradually came to the reality that he was in France and the banging was a thunderstorm. He got up to open the window and watched the lightning move further away with every flash, the loud cracks of thunder which had entered his dream fading into a distant rumble. It had rained heavily during the storm and the street smelt pleasantly fresh. Steam rose from the pavement in the light of the street lamps gleaming on the wet leaves of a plane tree. He felt sad and drained and filled with longing for Katya. He went back to bed wondering if there would ever be a day when he didn't think of her.

On the other side of the wall monsieur was getting his money's worth with more groans and creaking and laughter this time. James smiled for them. There were worse things than screwing a prostitute and who knew what reasons they both had for being in that room. After a while he heard the door bang and there were no more noises of the night, just a mournful cat in the street.

When he slept again there were no dreams and he didn't wake easily. Madame came to rouse him after nine with a small very strong black coffee. Seeing his anxious expression she explained this was not her normal service but she was worried for him and hoped he would eat before he left.

Her pleasure in serving him was poignant and he was happy to please her by inviting her to sit with him and join him in more coffee while he made a mess on the table with the croissants. He complimented her on the cherry confiture and she explained it was home-made and told him she loved to cook and use the skills she knew from her youth as a farmer's daughter.

He realised her shame in the seedy place and its clients and how she longed to cook for guests in a proper hotel. Circumstances again, twists of life that led down the wrong track. James smiled at her over the crumbs and the lined, elderly face lit up with pleasure. When he left she pressed a loaf and pate into his hands — for his lunch. Her concern cheered him and he hoped he'd given her something in return, if only his smile.

He crossed the Lot in late afternoon. The countryside reminded him of home, narrow lanes through fields with acres of sunflower and lucerne in place of wheat and barley. The MG roared up a steep wooded hillside to come out on a plateau with several little farms at the head of the escarpment overlooking the valley with the woods at their back. Paul's La Belle was down the second track he came to, forking to two properties. He sounded the horn as he drew in and saw them all gathered round the pool, Paul, his wife Jenny, two small boys and an older girl, the children all brown and nearly naked. The youngsters rushed to greet him, their excitement triggered by the car rather than him who they didn't know. It was hot, the storms hadn't broken the heatwave and the afternoon heat was shimmering off the stone as he leaned against the house wall answering their questions.

"James! It's great to see you." Paul hadn't changed, born to be a father, expansive with pride as he displayed his little empire. "I'll get you a drink."

"No, no!" screamed the children. "Come and swim."

"Drink first please."

The infinity pool was superb, its walls built like the farmhouse in the local pale golden limestone.

"It's fantastic, must have cost you a fortune," he said hanging onto the edge after six lengths, blowing hard as he clutched the far end wall with the wide vista of the valley revealed behind him. "I haven't swum for ages, getting unfit."

"That's what holidays are for," Jenny said, eyeing the scar, prominent on his wet skin. She lifted her hand to touch it but stopped as she saw his frown. "Sorry, that was rude."

Their eyes met and she blushed. "It's all right," he said.

"What is it, Uncle James? How did you get it?" Two young voices clamoured together.

"It's a war wound," Paul told them which only brought more questions.

"Maybe tell you later," he evaded their eager shouts. "I'm going back in."

As he dived he felt Jenny's eyes on him, watching him do another five lengths and realised from her avid attention that his visit was a mistake. She disappeared as he stood drying himself and came back with a tray of glasses, pink and fizzy.

"Celebration!" she laughed.

Standing close she gave him a glass. "Kir royale for a special guest."

She smiled and he could do nothing else but kiss her cheek. "That's wonderful," he said, "it's so good to see you both again." Paul came forward and helped himself.

Dinner was crayfish, messily delicious with butter and garlic chicken cooked in a large heavy casserole. Paul seemed put out by something but Jenny showed no awareness of his mood, with eyes only for James who ignored her, asking more questions about the place.

Paul looked at his wife but shrugged and started to talk about the district and what he was doing with the place. Most of their income came from letting two holiday cottages down the lane.

"No guests here right now or we couldn't be so free with the pool -- they have the use of it. You can't let a place easily these days without a pool. People expect it." His manner relaxed as he talked about the locals and the friends they'd made, both French and English and when they started musing about old times he refilled the glasses with a rueful smile.

It was nearly eleven before the children were ready for bed and he watched them troop away. But a few minutes later Jenny called from an upper window for James to go up. "They all want to say good night," she said.

He stayed put, carrying on his conversation with Paul but she called again. "Are you coming?"

He rose with a sigh asking Paul: "Do you mind?"

"Not at all, they can have you instead of me."

The boys were sitting up in their bunks, Tom up top and little Edward, only five, determined to stay awake long enough. He sat on Edward's bed while Tom climbed down and demanded: "Tomorrow, Uncle James, will you tell us about the war?"

"I'm not a soldier, Tom."

"No, but you've been places and seen lots of fighting."

"Some."

"Will you tell us, please!"

"We'll see, but now you must keep quiet and go to sleep." He ruffled the hair on both boys' heads. "Okay?"

Outside the room he frowned at Jenny: "What have you told them?"

"Not much really. But they know you're a newsman like Paul used to be and you've been in Bosnia. They don't really know where that is but Paul told them you were injured in the bombing and they think you're a hero."

"Well I'm not."

"You are a bit whether you like it or not. Come and see Jane. She's very shy of you but desperate to say good night."

Jane at ten was a small version of her mother with no trace of Paul about her. She looked up hesitantly from her reading. She'd been quiet all evening but had joined in the horseplay, following Tom's lead. James sat on the bed and she showed him her book.

"You like Tolkien?"

She nodded. "I finished The Hobbit last week, this is a bit more grown up."

"Yes," he opened The Fellowship of the Ring where she'd marked it. "The Flight to the Ford -- exciting, isn't it? I love these books. Do you know I've read them probably four times. You always want to come back to them."

"Have you really read them so many times?"

He nodded and she went on: "The black riders frighten me but I know Gandalf and Strider and the elf will look after Frodo."

James smiled at her. "It's a wonderful story."

She took the book, marked her place and closed it, laying it carefully on the bedside table before snuggling down into bed. "You remind me a bit of Strider, Uncle James."

"Why?"

"Because I don't know where you come from."

"Ah. We'll talk some more about that. You go to sleep now and tomorrow perhaps I'll take you out in the MG. Would you like that?"

"Can I sit in the front?"

"I don't see why not," he kissed the top of her head and went out with Jenny. "She has such beautiful eyes," he said.

"They're very like yours."

"What do you mean? She's not…"

"No, she's not yours — but she could have been. She's not Paul's either."

He grabbed her arm as she started to go downstairs and looked hard at her.

"Does he know?"

"Of course he knows but it doesn't matter now. He loves her and he's a great dad."

"But who?"

"I was in such a state when you left — I ought to hate you."

"Maybe. But you always knew I'd go."

"But I thought you'd come back, to me, I mean."

"I didn't say I would."

"Oh James." She threw herself against him with an urgency which appalled him.

He put out his arms to support her but held her away as she tried to kiss him. He flushed with anger and pulled away, trying not to shout. "Stop it Jenny, for Christ's sake. What you doing?"

"Don't push me away — please."

"Stop it."

She tried to kiss him again but he shoved her away with some force.

She gasped: "It's been awful since you rang. I've so longed to see you."

Shaking his head he hurried passed her and went downstairs.

He slept late the next day and they left him alone till the middle of the morning when Jenny knocked softly on the door and entered to leave a mug of coffee by his bed. He stirred at the movement asking drowsily: "What time is it?"

"Nearly 11:30," she said. "But it doesn't matter, we're not in a hurry about anything."

"Thanks for the coffee, I'll get up soon."

He wondered why his body ached so much but blamed the long journey in the MG which made a hard ride for serious travelling. A long hot shower should help.

The hot streams of water felt good and he twisted the muscles in his neck and shoulders, feeling the heat soothe them. He didn't hear the door open and had his back to the room so the touch on his bum made him jump in alarm — a hand stroking his lower back and buttocks. He spun round to find Jenny in the shower with him, clad only in bra and pants.

"What you doing? Get out of here."

She moved in, water cascading over both of them, her hands clutched his buttocks, trying to draw him close.

"You used to love me doing this," she said, reaching up to kiss him.

"That was then — get out Jenny, stop this." But she threw her arms around his neck, missing the fury in his face. He wrenched her arms away, shoved her to one side and fled from the shower, grabbing a towel to cover himself.

"Get out, Jenny. You're not going to do this."

"Paul's gone to the village, we've got time — nobody will know."

"I'm not going to fuck you in his house, even if I wanted to, which I don't."

"You don't mean that."

"Believe me — I do."

Jenny slumped on the bed, making no move to leave. Ignoring her, he dried his wet legs and pulled on the same clothes from the previous day, still dumped on the floor.

"Where are you going?" she demanded.

"Out."

Downstairs the children were waiting for him. "Okay — who wants a ride in my car?"

They rushed for the MG and piled in. As they headed down the lane he called out: "You'll have to tell me where to go. I don't know where I am."

The boys, squeezed together on the dickie seat behind were laughing with excitement. "Head for Agen," Tom said. "It's a good road, you can open her up."

Jane sat quietly beside him, her hair blowing in the wind as they gathered speed but he sensed the suppressed excitement bubbling inside her.

For the children it was a wonderful day, he bought them lunch, sitting outside in the street in the sunshine protected by a bright red awning, drinking like grown-ups. He watched them lapping up the atmosphere of the little town where they hadn't been before. It was late afternoon when they got back, met by a frowning father and Jenny pretending it was all planned. All shouting at once he heard them telling Paul about the day while he went up to his room.

He lay on the bed reading but heard light footsteps on the wooden stairs and sat up in irritation. After a quick tap the door opened and he saw it was Jane, sent with a message.

"Daddy says supper will be about seven but come down soon for a drink."

"Thanks, tell him I won't be long." The little girl stood near him twirling her long hair between her fingers. "You okay?" he asked.

"Mmm. I just wanted to say" she hesitated. "I love your car — we had a brilliant day, thank you."

He grinned. "That's all right sweetheart, I enjoyed it too, you were all great company."

A smile lit her face, so innocent and loving he had to look away. He reached for her hand and drew her closer, touching the delicate fingers to his lips.

"There, a proper salute for a proper lady. Off you go, I'll be right down."

Paul appeared unruffled during the meal but Jenny hardly spoke, while the children prattled on about the day. Later the two men sat together in the courtyard when Jenny took the children to bed. Across the valley lights gradually appeared as the dusk deepened. The evening air held a sudden sharpness that in England could have meant frost. The stars were very bright in the clear sky and the only sound was the cicadas and cattle calling somewhere.

"It's beautiful here," James said. "You're lucky you found this place. Do you miss England and the job?"

"Sometimes but I always said this was what I wanted."

"I remember."

Paul lit the brazier and the smell of wood smoke jerked James back to the scent of the pine wood fire on that last night in the forest. He shivered.

"Are you cold?"

"I'm fine."

Their talk grew strained, both struggling to make conversation though Paul listened with interest to the description of the farm, including the sheep.

He laughed: "So after everything that happened with your dad, you've turned into a farmer."

"For now anyway, the future remains to be seen. It's quiet, you'd probably find it boring but I like it."

"Why should I find it boring?"

They drifted into silence. Paul fiddled with the fire, poking and riddling the base to make it burn brighter and adding more logs. They were small logs and very dry and burned down quickly. There was no sign of Jenny. Then he disappeared, returning with a bottle of Armagnac and two glasses. Without asking he poured the brandy and handed one to James, looking down at him. As he gave him the glass he said: "Why did you come?"

"I needed a break, you said come any time. But maybe it wasn't such a good idea."

Paul grunted and sat down. "She couldn't wait to get you alone, could she? She was so obvious."

"I'd no idea she still felt that way or I wouldn't have come. It was over long ago, you know all that."

"Yes. But she's still lugging this bloody great torch about."

"She loves you."

"Maybe," Paul hesitated. "But not the way she felt about you. She's been in a state since you rang. She must think I'm stupid."

"Paul, believe me. It never was a big deal for me. When I went off to India that was it."

"You didn't love her?"

James shook his head. "No. Fond of her."

"You know about being in love, do you?"

He glanced at Paul catching the look of resentment. He thought before answering then said: "Yes, I think I do." Then: "I'll leave tomorrow."

"No, not yet. You need to make her understand."

"What?"

"That you don't care about her. Talk to her. Just one thing — don't screw her in my house."

Wincing, James said: "I hoped you thought better of me than that. Do you really think I'd do that?"

"That was a bit crude. You've got someone, have you?"

"Not now."

"But there was someone?"

"Yes."

"Someone who mattered?"

"Yes." He paused, then said: "Paul I promise you, there's nothing between Jenny and me but what's in her mind."

"It hurt — a lot — when it happened. But we're good together. It works and the children are wonderful. It works as long as you stay away."

"Right. How about I take Jenny out in the car tomorrow — have a chat? Would that be okay with you?"

"Do that." Paul played with the fire again, hiding his face, then turned back and smiled. "Drink up and we'll finish the bottle." He grinned at his friend: "The trouble with you, you bastard, you're too easy to forgive."

After breakfast he looked for Jenny in the kitchen. "How long will you be?" he asked.

She looked up eagerly: "Why?"

"You and I are going for a drive."

"Are we? Does Paul know?"

"It was his idea."

"Oh."

"So — how long?"

"Give me half an hour."

"I'll be outside."

He waited for her by the pool, watching the children pick figs in the garden, one fig eaten for each one dropped into the flat willow basket. Paul came out to help, stretching up for the high ones beyond their reach. They brought some for James to try, giggling when the juice from the luscious fruit trickled down his chin. He wiped his mouth and laughed with them.

"There's nothing like them straight off the tree," Paul said. "You must take some with you."

It was a long half-hour and he was annoyed when she finally came and he let it show in his abrupt: "Let's go."

"Where to?" she asked, settling in the seat beside him.

"We'll go up to Penne, get a coffee."

He drove up the steep hill, slowing to take in the panorama of the Lot winding its wide, sluggish way through the valley, the trees along its banks already tinged with the first colours of autumn. Above them the white basilica of the huge ornate church in Penne shone in the sunshine.

Jenny said quietly: "If you want to stop there are quiet places in the woods further on."

"I'm not stopping, just admiring the view."

She was quiet while he parked in the square and followed him to a table outside the bar. Two Frenchmen sat smoking with small glasses of liqueur in front of them and a trio of English women chatted noisily, planning the evening's meal.

He ordered coffee and studied her, trying to recall what he'd seen in her. Nine years on she was still attractive but with an edge he didn't remember, perhaps motherhood had released elements he'd never noticed. And the years change people, he thought. They'd both changed. He found it hard to imagine they'd shared a house and then a bed for nearly a year.

She broke the silence, growing anxious under his gaze. "What are you thinking?"

He switched his stare to the vista of river, hills and trees and said: "At times like this I wish I could paint. Such a beautiful valley and photos never capture it."

Still absorbing the view he asked: "What's the matter? Is there a problem with you and Paul?"

She shrugged. "No special problem, we get along. But it's not the same."

A girl brought their coffee and he poured milk into his, stirring slowly. "What's not the same?"

"Like you and me. There's no tingle."

He laughed. "Things do cool a bit after eight years and three children."

"No. It was never there. He doesn't do it for me, like you do."

He was surprised and saw her blush. "Did," he corrected. He didn't remember it being that good, not like the girl whose image came when he thought about sex. Being with Jenny seemed an intrusion.

"It wasn't that good," he frowned.

"For me it was."

"If you say so. But it was a long time ago and you have a husband and kids. You owe Paul a lot. If he's not Jane's father that makes him a pretty decent guy. And I can't have meant so much if you went straight off with someone else."

"Classic rebound."

"Why didn't you go to Paul? He'd loved you all along before I came on the scene. I always felt guilty — I didn't know how he felt about you until we were shacked up. You kept that very quiet."

"I wanted you," she reached across the table to put her hand on his but he snatched it away.

"And that made it all right?"

"It's not black and white, is it? Nothing ever is."

"But you married him and forgot me."

"No, I didn't, not the way you made me feel."

"For Christ's sake, it's only a chemical reaction, there's more to life than fucking!"

He spoke too loudly and the English women went quiet, listening with raised eyebrows.

Her expression of hurt softened him and he leaned closer. "I don't mean to upset you but it was years ago and I never said I loved you. We never thought it was going anywhere, did we?"

She met his eyes for an instant. "I did think you cared."

"I did care, I was fond of you. We had good times, didn't we? Good fun together. But I didn't think I was the love of your life. You always knew I'd be off somewhere."

She sighed, seeing his attention again fixed on something in the distance. "Do you see how those trees on the far ridge catch the light, they look pure gold in the sun. I wish I could capture scenes like that."

She tried to see what he found so fascinating but to her it was only rocks and trees and sky. "Is there someone who matters?" she asked, her voice soft.

"There was."

"But not now?"

"No."

"Didn't it work out?"

"I left her in Bosnia — she's dead."

Chapter three

He hurried eagerly across the fields to fetch the dogs from Jack's, where he'd left them in the rush of his sudden decision to go. They were ecstatic when they heard his voice, a chorus of barking which went on until they were let out to jump all over him. Tess looked thinner and Jack said she hadn't eaten well but Bobbie was just the same.

He'd brought wine to thank Jack, not knowing if the family were keen but he knew at least it would come in for Christmas. When he put the box on the kitchen table Pat's eyes lit up and she flashed a cheeky, knowing smile at him.

"Do you like wine?"

"Yes," she said. "That'll liven up Sunday dinner, won't it Dad?" she grinned.

"Good. I hope you enjoy it," he said.

He was glad to be back, surprised how much. As he'd driven up the hill and seen the handsome stone front of the farmhouse greeting him he had the sensation of coming home, an emotion he hadn't known for years. The first evening with the dogs around him he felt almost content, reflecting on how much he'd improved the place. He hadn't written much but the year hadn't been entirely wasted. He'd transformed a dreary untidy house into somewhere warm and inviting and the money he'd spent on the aga was worth every penny.

He'd laughed at the idea when his sister Louise had looked around and pronounced: "God what a hole. There's only one thing for this kitchen. It needs an aga."

He'd laughed, protesting about the price but she was emphatic: "I tell you Jamie, you've got to do it. Trust me, it'll transform the place."

And she was right, as usual — it was a different house.

The darkening evenings of September brought shorter days and some mornings a light mist hung over the fields bringing a chill of autumn and he noted the first tinge of yellow in the trees and felt glad of the warm kitchen.

He thought about Louise who had called that afternoon to ask about Christmas. "You're well ahead," he'd said cautiously.

"Yes but I know you and you'll be off somewhere if I don't get in early."

He was surprised and said nothing for so long she asked if he was still there. "It doesn't matter," she said, "if you've got other plans. We just thought it would be nice for the girls to get to know their uncle. They never see you."

"No, it's a great idea," he said hastily.

"I'm just surprised, Christmas in Shropshire. Do you really want to come? It's not usually your sort of thing."

"Well, your house is comfortable now and the girls will love a real country Christmas. So it's okay?"

"Of course. It'll be good." He paused. "What about mother?"

"She'll come, if you'll have her."

"Of course. Why wouldn't I?"

"She's not sure how things stand. You never go and she says you hardly ever ring. She thinks you still blame her."

"No, it's not that. Life's been difficult these last few years. I'm not good company. You understand a bit, don't you. But I never blamed her for the way it was before. It was Dad. No, please come, all of you. I'll make an effort."

December seemed a long time away but it was something to look forward to. He hardly knew his little nieces and children in the house would bring it alive. He enjoyed the thought of them opening parcels by the Christmas tree.

Louise, eight years younger, had done all the right things, married well and produced the grandchildren just in time before their father died. At least he had lived to see them both. He was fond of his sister although they'd grown apart and was grateful she hadn't tried to discourage him from buying the farm, just advised him on improving it.

He came down from checking the sheep next day to see an unknown car in the yard. His heart sank but he relaxed when he saw the figure of a girl looking at the view from his wall. She turned as the dogs ran ahead of him, and appeared disconcerted at his approach.

"Oh, Mr Lambert, I'm glad you're back — from France I mean," she said.

He noted her dark hair and pretty features but frowned, wondering how she knew he'd been away. He waited for her to speak.

When she hesitated he said: "What do you want?"

"I wondered if you could help me."

She looked even more uncomfortable. "Go on," he said.

"Well I — it's an awful cheek to ask you."

"Is it? Until you ask I can't say no, can I?"

"You might be the answer to my problem."

He smiled: "Might I? But if you don't say what it is, we shan't know, shall we?"

"My friend Pat -- you know, Jack's daughter -- she said it was worth asking you. I'm trying to find somewhere to keep my horse."

"And Pat thought I might help?"

The girl nodded. "She said there are some old loose boxes you don't use."

"Did she."

"He wouldn't be any trouble, honestly. I'd keep everything tidy, it wouldn't involve you at all and I won't be obtrusive."

The choice of words made him smile at the implication he didn't want people around. "Have you just bought him?" he asked.

"No, I've had him from a foal."

"Where do you keep him now?"

"On a farm." She seemed embarrassed, unwilling to say too much. "But I need to move him."

"Right." He took it at face value, asking no questions but recalled seeing a girl riding in the lanes. Without the crash cap it was difficult to recognise her.

"Who are you?" he asked.

"Kate Patterson, from Sedge Farm."

"Let's go and look at the building," he said, trying to recall a connection. Then he remembered, the night in the pub before he went away, he'd heard some young roughnecks talking about a girl. A story to be told, he thought.

The old stone building was earmarked as a future project, a job to tackle when he had time, used so far only briefly for separating ewes and lambs. The roof leaked, patched with corrugated iron to make one section serviceable but dark and in need of cleaning out. The other side was full of junk. "It's on my list of things to do."

"Pat and I could soon clear it out."

"I don't know. I'm not sure the roof is safe and the door's broken."

"We can fix it."

"It sounds urgent."

She blushed and took a deep breath: "Actually I'm desperate," she said.

"Like that, is it?"

She said nothing under his searching gaze and looked away. But when she raised her head he saw the incipient tears and gave her the chance to recover by walking away to peer inside the old stable. He said sharply. "I'll want to know more about this but you can bring him here, for a while at least."

Her face changed into a smile with an appealing warmth which charmed him. "Thanks. You don't know what it means to me."

He stood musing by the wall and watched her car go down the hill, his interest piqued, the newsman scenting a story.

"Interesting," he murmured aloud, very odd, turning up like that, pretty girl, slender, fit from the riding — and those eyes. He needed to know more and Pat was the one to tell him.

But she wasn't about when he drove over, just her father in the milking parlour. It wasn't the best time for conversation and his questions were answered with shrugs and grunts as Jack worked his way along the line of udders, moving the milking clusters from cow to cow.

"Friend of Pat's — at school together — some trouble with the boyfriend, I don't know much about it, you'll have to ask Pat."

"That's why I came but she's not here."

"You'll have to wait then. Kate's all right though, I can tell you that much. Lovely girl."

He didn't expect things to happen so soon but they were there next morning, hard at it removing the accumulated trash of half a century. Pat had brought a trailer towed with her dad's pick-up and he was amazed at the collection they lugged onto it. Not just farm junk such as old syringes and feed bottles, bits of rope and dead tyres but shoes, odd boots, even an ancient once-pink pair of corsets. A car engine had them stumped till he fetched the tractor to drag it out and hoisted it with the bucket. The rubbish included dozens of motor parts, wads of baler twine, electrical wire, light fittings, mouldy books and magazines, an old oven. Pat went off to the tip with one load and they filled the trailer again. He watched them mend the door and fit a new bolt. He was tempted to help but refrained and left them to it. After they'd gone he inspected the work and saw how they'd supported the roof beams with three well-placed lengths of four by two timber to prevent it falling in. He was impressed.

He waited for an opportunity to question Pat but when he'd been twice more to the Wilsons' without finding her he realised it was deliberate; she was definitely avoiding him.

He was puzzled by the apparent frantic haste to move the horse. It seemed unlikely that she could be kicked out of a livery place without some notice but Harry arrived only three days later. He turned out to be a handsome grey gelding who James liked at first sight. He knew about horses and this one brought back instant memories of his own grey pony and long boyhood rides over the downs. That was years ago and he wondered if he could still ride, deciding it was probably like riding a bicycle, you never really lost the knack. He thought about it while he offered the horse a carrot over the stable door and Harry's soft muzzle snuffled at his face.

People around the farm, girls, driving in and out two or three times a day. He wasn't sure if he liked it or not. He feared for his privacy and the interruption to his writing — but that was nonsense because he wasn't doing any.

On the other hand he lived a solitary life and a bit of company might be welcome. And he'd been thinking about the pretty girl and discovered a frisson of excitement when he saw her, though it was always at a distance. He thought it was coincidence but it was obvious they were both deliberately avoiding him. He didn't think he was that intimidating. But Kate came each morning, very early to muck out and exercise Harry and then she was gone. Pat came in the middle of the day to top up the hay but always managed to miss him, just leaving as he appeared, waving but not waiting.

He wondered what would happen as the days got shorter; he guessed she had a job and she'd soon find it hard to ride so much. She'd asked him only for a stable and paid rent a month up front for that but there was no mention of turn out or grazing. Knowing how it worked he expected very soon she'd be looking for another favour.

Two weeks on he'd barely spoken to either of them but as dawn came later each morning he waited for her and would watch from the bathroom window as she set off. One morning he opened the window and leaned out with shaving foam on his face to call: "Good morning."

Startled, she turned looking really nervous, gave him a quick wave and kicked Harry to trot away. Another day she arrived in a smart tweed jacket and cream breeches to go cubbing with the hunt. He decided he would go too, eager to watch the hounds at work and followed her to the meet in the Land Rover. But she made no attempt to speak to him or even acknowledge his presence.

His resentment grew as he thought about it — he'd done his best to help the girl yet she avoided him. It made him angry but more determined to get answers. Before all this he hadn't thought about loneliness, he was as he was, alone at the farm with a purpose. But already she had made him lonely.

Sometimes he went to the pub for supper, to chat with Richard if it was quiet. But often he sat alone at the bar, excluded from the animated conversations around him, because he'd made no effort to make friends in the village and people thought him aloof and left him to himself. Sometimes Jack and Sheila were there and he would join them but most were reluctant to approach him.

As the October days shortened he resumed long walks with the dogs. On his way down the hill, damp from a sudden shower, he paused to look at the sunset, changing fast as the clouds shifted. The sky to the north was a glowering grey, holding more rain, swathing the long shoulder of Bow Hill in darkness. But the lie of the land meant both valleys were in view and in the other direction the sinking sun illuminated all the land under the Edge right to the russet slopes of Clee Hill, picking out in gold and brown the ordered lines of a larch plantation four miles away. Sunlight glinted on the hilltop mast and flushed the fleeing clouds. He gazed transfixed at the skyscape altering to rays of deepening red as the sun sank below the horizon. This simple glory, if for nothing else, was why he loved the place. The landscape changing with the season was a constant consolation, the craggy hills were like friends. Their splendour under the sun massaged his very soul. He stayed until the colour faded into dusk and called his dogs for home.

Behind him the sound of hooves disturbed his reverie and he looked round as the spaniel barked and danced away. It was Kate and Harry. He waited for them to draw level, a spark of gladness springing in him as he called to control the dog. "Stop it, Bobbie, you'll scare him."

She said: "It's okay, he's used to dogs."

"Did you see the sunset?" he asked. "It lit the whole valley?"

"Yes," she smiled, shy and sweet. "I saw it from higher up — beautiful."

The horse walked fast and he didn't try to keep up. But he hurried to get back before she left. She had the horse unsaddled as he strolled across to say: "You're out late today."

"I met a friend for a long ride. Brilliant, best time of the year for riding, now and the spring."

He nodded: "No flies, I suppose."

"They've been bad this summer,"

"Yes. They were bad on the sheep." He hesitated. "Fancy a brew?"

She shook her head. "I'm fine, thanks. I don't want to be a nuisance."

He felt cross. "If it was a nuisance I wouldn't offer — just thought you might like a drink if you've been out so long. You must be thirsty."

"I am a bit."

"Well then."

"You've been so kind about the horse."

Exasperated he raised his voice: "It's only a cup of tea."

She grinned. "Okay then, thanks. No sugar."

He knew she wouldn't come to the house without an invitation so he carried the mug of tea out for her and put it on the wall without a word. As he walked away she called after him: "Thanks. It's kind of you."

He turned back. "You are allowed to speak to me. Am I such an ogre?"

"Of course not." She blushed. "But there's nothing worse than being bothered when you want to be left alone."

"Who said I want to be left alone? Anyway, if there's anything you need when you're here, a drink, whatever, just ask. Will you be hunting next month?"

"Only the closer meets. No transport now."

"Haven't you got a trailer?"

She looked away and said slowly: "Yes but nothing to pull it. Not any more."

In the weeks before Christmas he watched her leave three times, hacking up to an hour to meets. It pleased him in an oddly proprietorial way to see horse and rider smartly turned out. He noted her stock wasn't white but cream with a sheen that was almost certainly silk. He admired her taste.

On a bitterly cold afternoon in mid December he realised she hadn't returned. Early darkness brought a murky chill typical of the year's fag end. A cold wind was blowing from the east, bringing short biting showers of sharp icy drops not quite hail. The early winter had been mild but worse weather was forecast. He found himself looking out for her, keen to see her, if only to shout a greeting across the yard. The girl and her horse were nothing to him but he was concerned for their welfare. He'd finished his chores with only the dogs to feed and wanted to be in with a drink by the fire. He stood for several minutes by the gate, listening for the sound of hooves on the road but all he heard was the wind and a distant car. It was nearly dark and the fog was closing in, visibility deteriorating fast.

He longed to go in and forget about them but he couldn't. He had no contact number for her home and by the sound of it they wouldn't welcome a call from him. So he rang Jack's. They might know more of her movements but Sheila could only tell him where the meet had been.

"But if hounds went the other way, towards Ludlow," she said, "she'll have a long ride home."

"Which way would they come?" he asked.

"Who knows, depends where they are, dear. I shouldn't worry".

"But it's dark and foggy, she shouldn't be out in it."

"Well, that's hunting," she said and repeated: "I shouldn't worry."

But he was worried. It was gone five and very dark, the icy rain slanting down. He pictured the state she would be in, jacket drenched and hands chilled in soaking gloves. He climbed into the Land Rover with no idea which road to take and tried the lane she would have followed to the meet and one of two ways she would have to come from the south. He found nothing between the village and the main road so returned to try the other road. A mile beyond the next village his headlights picked them out in the fog, trotting along the edge of the verge, the horse's head down like her own against the battering rain. He passed her, turned and came alongside, window down. The horse shied at the lights shining on tarmac.

"Who is it?" she asked warily."

"James. I was worried about you.

"I didn't mean to be so late."

"I've got a coat, stop and put it on."

He pulled up ahead and grabbed his waxed coat from behind the seat. "Can you get it on without dismounting?"

"I think so. If you could hold his head, he's pretty good." She shivered and her hands shook as she struggled into the coat.

Harry sidled nervously, ill at ease and cold but he let James hold him.

"Pull the hood up," he said. "It'll take you nearly an hour from here. Shall I stay with you?"

"It's all right."

"It's not. It's dangerous with the rain and the dark. If something comes along here fast they won't even see you. I'm going to stay with you, keep you in my lights. In front or behind?"

She thought a moment while the rain fell more heavily and he was soaked waiting.

"Perhaps if you drive slowly behind so I'm in the lights. It's lucky you came along."

"Not luck. I came looking."

"Oh."

He crawled along behind the horse who accepted the beams of light and seemed reassured. It was tedious but when a 12-wheeler lorry came fast round a bend, creating waves of water as it ploughed through a puddle, he realised what might have been. The driver saw the horse and rider in the lights and slowed down to pass.

At last he saw the corner light of his house on the hill, a mile away as they crested the opposite bank — down this hill, then up and home.

When Kate rode in Pat ran out of the stable, where she'd been waiting.

"Mum said you'd rung and sounded worried. I thought I'd better come over."

Kate climbed stiffly off the horse wincing as her feet touched the ground. "Oh that hurts. My feet are so cold."

"Let me take him," Pat said.

"Thanks." Kate tried to smile but her face was numb. James watched them both and she met his worried gaze. The state of her troubled him, dark wet hair sticking to her face, wide eyes tired and forlorn; she reminded him of someone else, someone also cold and afraid. She reminded him of Katya.

"Thank you," she mumbled through cold lips. "It was stupid — I didn't realise how far we'd gone. I should have left them earlier but the hounds were going full blast — it was a brilliant run. But when we stopped I realised how far back it was. It was so cold."

"I'm glad you're okay. But you need to change and get warm."

"I must see to Harry."

Pat came out carrying Harry's mud spattered tack: "Come back with me and change before you go home. But we must do Harry first."

"I'll do that, I know about horses. Get her home, Pat and leave the horse to me."

The girls stood in awkward hesitation and Kate began to thank him again.

He interrupted, cold and irritated: "I know, you don't want to be a nuisance. Well let me tell you something. Today you've been a bloody nuisance, so bugger off and let's all get warm."

He grabbed a bucket and headed indoors for warm water. They'd gone when he came back and entered the dark stable. Harry drank the whole bucket of tepid water and in the torchlight he removed the rugs from the trembling animal and saw his legs were thick with wet mud. He washed them with cold water, hands stinging, then carefully wrapped them in woollen bandages. The horse still shivered as he piled straw along his back with a sweat rug and two stable blankets on top. The long ears were cold and he stood massaging them until they began to feel warmer to his touch. The horse stood quietly, head down, exhausted and James remembered the old groom teaching him as a boy in Wiltshire. The little man was an ex-jockey who worked as a stable hand for a big chasing yard in Lambourn.

"If a horse's ears are cold, then he's cold," he'd said. Rubbing the soft grey clipped ears, he recalled happy days doing the same to his pony in a warm sweet-smelling stable at home.

"Well Harry," he whispered. "Look's like I've got a good job on with you. We'll have to rug you up properly later, old boy." The horse moved to nose the empty bucket, seeking another drink.

"You'll have to wait, you don't want too much at once."

With his back and hands warming against the aga he thought about the two girls, sorry he'd sworn at them. He hadn't meant to and the sight of Kate's pinched face looking at him with something close to fright when he shouted made it worse. He was glad he'd gone to find her but frowned when he considered that nobody except Pat had shown the slightest concern.

He poured a whisky and slumped in a chair to puzzle over it and soon fell asleep. He woke up feeling muzzy with the phone ringing and his answer was bad-tempered. It was her, ringing to thank him again and ask about Harry: "I didn't want to bother you but I was worried."

He said something sarcastic about bothering him all the time, told her the horse was fine and he was about to rug him up for the night.

There was silence and he heard a choking sound. Her voice came back, faltering: "I'm so sorry for all this. I'll move him if you want me to but it might take —."

"No," he felt a shit. "I was glad to help, really."

Silence again but she was still there and he suspected she was crying.

"Don't get upset," he said, the image of her bedraggled body in his head. "Are you warm now?"

"Yes."

"Were your parents worried?"

"Angry."

"Was it worth it?"

She hesitated: "Yes. It was a great day till the rain started."

"That makes it all right then."

"I suppose so. I'd better go."

"Hang on. Give me your number."

"It's the main farm number."

"Okay."

He caught the hesitation. "Try not to ring me —"

"What?"

"It's difficult, ring Pat if you need to get me."

"I see. Why difficult? It's your home isn't?"

"I will explain."

"Well, give it me anyway, in case."

"All right."

He wrote it down. "Harry's fine for the night. Don't worry about him."

The rain was still siling down when he went back but the horse heard him and nickered a greeting in the darkness. He stayed beside Harry as he ate, stroking the glossy neck and checking the ears were warm.

In the morning she didn't come. He saw the barrow in Harry's open door and hurried across to say cheerfully: "How are you this morning?"

Pat's voice said: "Fine thanks." Shocked by his own disappointment he looked in at the horse and asked: "Is something wrong with Kate?"

Pat's reply was non-committal: "She couldn't make it this morning."

"Is she okay?"

"Yeah. She asked me to thank you for looking after Harry. It was good of you."

"No problem."

He was tempted to question Pat but her body language told him she was in a hurry and would find an excuse not to stay talking to him. He went in and watched her drive away then cursed himself for not making her talk. He thought about the number business, why shouldn't he call Kate at home?

He didn't see either of them for three days, somehow he missed whoever came, wasn't sure who, if it was her or Pat. But someone kept the horse fed and groomed. But not ridden.

He'd got used to seeing her around, even if only from a distance and realised he missed her. He told himself it was only because she brought back memories. But when she didn't come he felt deflated and had to admit he was drawn to her.

He tried the pub for company to lift his spirits, Richard was always glad of a chat at quiet times. After nine it filled up with the drinkers including a group of lads, noisy from starting their evening elsewhere, five of them, recognised from previous loud comments. He assumed they were young farmers and didn't look their way. But they were taking an interest in him and he heard the name of his farm. He ignored them but when more customers came in and Richard was busy serving, they came over and gathered round him. One stood arrogantly close, in his space, a tall boy with fair wavy hair. James was drinking wine and the youth knocked him hard enough so he dropped the glass. No apology and James spoke sharply: "Watch yourself, you've spilled my drink."

"Careless of me," the lad said, moving in closer, putting an arm round James's shoulder, as if they were old friends. He smelled of beer and his face was flushed as he spoke softly.

"A bit of advice, Mr Lambert. You need to be careful how you meddle in other people's business."

"What!" James pushed him away. "Who are you? What're you on about?" He grabbed the boy's arm, saying: "You owe me a drink."

The others crowded closer and suddenly the atmosphere in the quiet English pub changed to an insidious sense of menace. They meant business. The glass was rolling about the floor under the stool and the lad stamped his foot down hard on it, crushing it to tiny pieces. "Get your own fucking drink," he said.

Richard came round the bar in a hurry and the group moved away to the far end of the room, laughing and looking back at him.

"What's going on?" the landlord asked, calling his wife to bring a dustpan.

"You saw what happened?"

"I heard him swear at you, not what caused it."

"He spilled my drink on purpose. Who is he?"

"Steve Sterling, Bill Sterling's son, from Bishton. The big place on the right as you go down the lane."

"Nasty bit of work, is he?"

Richard hesitated: "Well, I suppose so -- can be. He's a bully and big headed because his dad's loaded. Those friends all toady round him."

"Like a gang?"

Richard nodded.

"I can imagine. But what's he got against me?"

"Don't you know?"

James looked blank: "Should I?"

"Kate Patterson's his girlfriend -- or was. It's about the horse -- she kept it at their place and couldn't dump him without losing the horse. But now you've given her the chance to get away from him."

"By renting her a stable?"

"You didn't know?" Richard seemed incredulous.

"No — but now it all begins to make sense."

Chapter four

His sister and her two little girls arrived on Christmas Eve bringing with them an instant bustle and happy confusion. The husband came too, Alec, an accountant, a pleasantly complacent man who to James seemed very dull. He saw him as an extension to Louise, who initiated all the ideas in their relationship. But he was glad to see them all and when his mother came later in the day he kissed and hugged her for a long moment and she said simply: "It's lovely to see you, darling."

That was all but it carried a whole story of forgiveness and new understanding and he was relieved to see her there in his home. She'd aged. He knew his father's death had hit her hard yet he sensed relief in her too, she appeared more relaxed about life. She looked older but happy in spite of everything and Louise at least had done what was expected of her and produced children for a granny to dote on.

He watched in amusement as his sister took over the house, she'd told him not to worry, just provide a turkey, a tree and some alcohol and she would do the rest. He'd bought a tree, a tall good-shaped one with thick needles, knowing how choosy Louise could be but when they arrived it was still in a tub by the back door. He'd found a holly tree with dense clusters of berries and cut enough two weeks ago before the redwings and fieldfares flew in from northern Europe to strip them. Louise arrived with silver baubles for the tree. She and the girls spent the afternoon decorating it and decking the house with greenery. The children argued for many minutes over whether a fairy doll or a golden star should top the tree. With their mother and granny they began to create Christmas.

Kate came in the afternoon to do Harry. Since the day of the hunt he had spoken to her only once, after he'd wired up a light in the stable. She'd come to the door to thank him but looked edgy and hurried away as he was about to ask her in. He watched her go, disappointed, and thought ruefully that his good Samaritan act seemed have made her even more wary of him. He thought also of the incident in the pub -- he had, after all, been threatened.

The girls, Sarah and Charlotte had spotted her as soon as she arrived and demanded to know all about her. Then they had their coats on and were off out to meet her before he could say anything. Louise followed as they were being introduced to Harry while James stood watching at the kitchen window. Louise, who'd sold her own horse when she got pregnant looked at Harry in admiration, saying: "What a super horse. Do you hunt him?"

Kate nodded and Louise continued the inquisition. "Are you going out on Boxing Day?"

"No, I can't. The meet's too far away and I've nothing to tow the trailer with."

"That's a shame. We could all have gone to the meet," said Louise, organising again. Then she said: "James could take you. I'll ask him."

"Oh no, I couldn't let him. Please don't mention it."

"Don't be silly, he won't mind. And the girls will love it, won't you," she said to them. "That's what Boxing Day's all about."

Louise called her brother and he came out to them. He saw at once Kate's deep embarrassment, she looked trapped and started to apologise as Louise said: "You'll take her to the meet, won't you Jamie?"

Startled he hesitated. "Er, I suppose I can. Do you want to go?" he asked Kate.

"Well yes, but —"

"That's settled," Louise said. Then Kate mumbled something about fetching the trailer at once, ready for Boxing Day.

"You might as well go now," said Louise to James, who'd forgotten how bossy she could be, but he shrugged and fetched the keys for the Land Rover.

Kate huddled on the seat beside him in silence, her expression tense. He'd hoped to question her but felt too sorry for her as they drove to her home.

He said: "My sister has a habit of taking things over. I'm sorry if she's upset you."

"No. It's very kind of her, of you. But I wouldn't have dreamed of asking you. — And it's difficult."

The trailer was away from the house, parked among the farm buildings. He backed up to it and she jumped out and hitched it almost before the vehicle stopped. He nearly said: "What's the hurry?" but kept quiet. As they drove away he saw there was just one car near the house.

"Are your parents out?" he asked and she nodded: "Posh lunch."

The house looked beautiful, transformed, with lights twinkling among the holly placed strategically around the hall and sitting room. He flopped smiling into a chair to admire their work. He talked and played with his nieces and enjoyed it enough to wonder if he would ever have children of his own. Doubtful now, he thought, drifting back to the trailer business. He must corner Pat and make her answer him.

When Louise asked him to check the time of the midnight service he said: "Are you thinking of going?"

"Of course," she said. "You'll come I hope."

"No, not for me."

"But we always went."

"A long time ago."

"But you must come," she insisted.

"I really don't want to, I don't feel the same about it now. Take Alec, I'll stay here and babysit."

"Alec won't come. And Mum says she's too tired to stay up." She planted herself in front of him, arms around his neck and pulled his face towards her. "Please Jamie, I can't go on my own. Please come."

Smiling at her intensity he weakened: "Okay, if I must. But I warn you it'll be cold in that church."

Out in the crisp starlit night the bells summoned them clearly from across the valley but it brought no Christmas joy for him. The sound took him straight back to Bosnia — bells ringing in icy air meant sorrow or alarm, tolling for death or a warning.

"Hurry up." His sister's voice urged him to the car but in the crowded church as he knelt surrounded by whispers and giggles from the fidgeting congregation his thoughts were far away. In another church, one wall open to let the snow blow in, soft flakes settling on the bloodstained floor, red as they melted.

That was where they were taken after another series of mortar and heavy artillery shells had hit the market and the church, wreaking a dreadful toll among shoppers desperate for whatever was available to eat. Black-robed monks helped the medics and James had stared through the shattered wall at ruined buildings as he cradled Katya in his arms and so missed the instant when her life slipped away. He sat with her on the broken mosaic floor, split deep across the golden halo of the saint, the fissure collecting blood from the dead and dying.

Groans and crying filled the church as helpers moved among the broken bodies, many with ripped and missing limbs, sorting the living from the dead. His hands and clothes were soaked in her blood and her body grew cold in his arms.

When the time came Louise had to nudge him three times before, shaking his head, he rose and followed her to the communion rail. He stared at the big cross above the altar, remembering her. The vicar had to take his hand to give him the wafer but he held it clenched in his palm. Katya's sympathies had been with her Muslim husband's family yet her life had ended in a church. The irony sickened him, she hadn't cared about religion but it had cost her life. And the bearded priest had come to do what he could which was little enough.

Kate sat three pews behind them through the service but he didn't notice her as they trooped out, met by an icy wind with the bells ringing again to herald Christmas morning.

"Why did you make the sign of the cross?" Louise asked as they drove home. "We never did that."

"What? Oh, something from Sarajevo. Did it bother you?"

"No, just unusual. It doesn't matter."

"The vicar won't care, he's high church anyway."

The family had gone to bed but he poured himself a large tumbler of whisky and crouched close by the fire. "Told you the church would be cold," he said when Louise came to sit beside him.

"You okay, Jamie?"

"Mm? Haven't been called that for a long time." He looked up at her. "I'm sorry, Lou."

"You're not okay are you?"

"Not really."

"Can I help?"

He shook his head.

She leaned over and kissed his cheek. "Sarajevo? You never did tell me what happened out there? Do you want to?"

Again he shook his head. "No, I can't. I can't talk about it, not yet anyway. But I can't get it out of my mind."

His sister took his hand and whispered: "Oh Jamie, I wish there was more I could do to help you."

"You can't," he said. "But having you here with the girls is good and brings back a little bit of the magic."

The room was lit only by the fire and the pale lights of the Christmas tree. He looked at it and murmured: "I love the tree in a half light, it's the only thing that brings Christmas alive for me. It looks wonderful. Thank you for coming." He smiled at her. "I remember the good Christmases, with you Lou, you were always a light spot in the gloom."

She knelt and took his face in her hands, surprised that he still shuddered with cold.

"You need your bed Jamie, you're so cold."

"I'll go when I've finished my drink. Sorry, I didn't get you one."

"I don't need any more tonight." She stroked the hair back from his face: "You had someone there didn't you, someone that mattered?"

"Yes." He whispered: "I can't get rid of it, the image in my head, this awful vision of blood, so much blood, Lou. There was blood everywhere."

"Oh Jamie." She kissed his cold face: "I wish I could help."

"D'you know the worst thing? We stood by and let it all happen — nobody did anything to stop it. And we've learned nothing."

The family stayed four days. He felt better on Christmas Day watching the children open their presents. Their happy excited faces made him realise how lonely he would have been if they hadn't come. He'd made an effort and bought an elegant gold rope necklace for his sister, rewarded by her loving smile. Gifts too for his mother and even for Alec who sat back and let it all happen around him.

He was especially pleased with the turkey, from the butcher he preferred in Ludlow and Louise watched him consume a large helping. Later they had a cake she'd made and a light supper . Much later after the children were in bed she went into the kitchen for a clean glass and found her brother with the turkey out on the work top, gnawing on a drumstick.

Startled, he faced her with a grin of pure satisfaction which changed to guilt as he met her eyes.

"James!" she laughed. "Didn't you have enough earlier? But you needn't look so guilty."

He laughed. "That's one thing about being grown up. If I want to pick at the turkey, I can. I always got my hand smacked as a kid if I was caught."

"It's your turkey," she said.

"Yes and remember, I spent a Christmas in Sarajevo — there wasn't much to eat at the Holiday Inn. We were on starvation rations. The only thing there was plenty of was the local red wine. This is a real treat."

Kate appeared early on Boxing Day morning in her jeans but by ten o'clock was in hunting kit which showed no sign of the mud smears from that wild day. Harry went into the trailer, ready saddled, his mane in nine neat plaits. The family followed in the car and the girls and Louise stood beside Harry chatting eagerly to Kate before the master blew the horn to move off. She'd hardly spoken to him on the way but when he gave her the Land Rover keys she'd looked at him with such gratitude he had to turn away. They followed for a while until the hunt entered a large field of stubble and let rip. He watched the galloping horses until he could no longer pick her out among the throng.

In the evening Louise found a bottle of whisky and an envelope with the keys on the doorstep. She brought them to him wondering why the girl hadn't knocked and come in. "She seems very shy — or she's frightened of you, Jamie."

"I don't see why she should be, I hardly see her."

Three days before new year he woke to an unaccustomed stillness and looked out on a silent world of glistening ice. Freezing rain the previous evening had continued through the night and soon after midnight a wind blew up which beat the tiny drops of cold against the window panes. By morning the north facing windows were opaque with a thick layer of dimpling and from the rear of the house he surveyed a scene of desolation.

He eyed his still-warm bed and wondered if he could allow himself longer there but forced himself to dress, dreading the feel of the cold outside and the arduous effort of thawing taps to fill buckets to replace frozen drinkers. He pulled on extra socks, thick scarf and the woolly hat he kept for bad weather. Not pretty but it prevented a headache from the bitter wind. In a way the black ice was fascinating but he swore when he couldn't pull back the feed room door bolt without fetching a hammer to shatter the glassy film which had sealed it. As if a mighty hand had been spraying, a lacquer-like coat covered everything, gate posts, barn walls — anything which faced north shone with ice. Every twig on the trees was exquisitely outlined, encased in a transparent shell, tinkling constantly as they shook in the wind. The grey trunk of the ash tree was polished steel, gleaming like a gun barrel.

The cold wasn't as severe as he expected, the sky was clearing and a pale sun trying to get through. Its delicate rays made everything shine and each stone in the yard wall was highlighted, the natural colours showing through the ice. It wasn't so bad and be began to feel better when the sheep rushed to the fence, knowing fodder was on its way.

The tractor box lugged the hay most of the way but he had to carry it up a slope to the feeders, wading through the sheep who pushed round him, desperate to feed. When he opened the first long lid and lowered it back it was twice its usual weight with the crust of ice wrapping each corrugation. He dumped the hay in and went back for a second bale. The sheep looked heavier, their fleeces stiff and thickened with frost but they were content once they got their mouths into the hay. He brought two more bales for the other feeder and returned for the corn. They were all heavily in lamb and he needed to up their daily ration.

A pheasant's call made him look up in time to catch a pale shaft of sunlight on the church clock and that made him think of Kate. He fed the barn sheep, ewes due to lamb early that he'd brought inside, gave the horse a wad of hay and fed the dogs. What excuse could he find today not to work on the manuscript? It wasn't a conscious thought, just his brain seeking other priorities. But it was too cold to be outside for long and indoors there was the keyboard and the room he avoided like a prison cell.

Just then the sun succeeded in shaking itself free of the encumbering cloud and burst out in a triumphant blaze, lighting the frost-whitened farm in glory. The trees sparkled and the icicles on the buildings felt the warmth and began to drip after only a few moments. He knew it wouldn't last but it was time enough to take the dogs for a run. Calling them he set off up the fields to make the round of water troughs. Tess and Bobbie loved it, the frost under their feet made them run for excitement in the sun. The spaniel bounded round him, bouncing against his legs and nearly knocked him over on the icy field. The grass was crystallised and the earth hard as iron, set in the indented pattern of sheep's feet.

In the top pasture the air was bitter and the wind cut into the skin, stinging his face and snatching his breath. The sun was soon defeated by the gathering clouds, darkening to gloom, a heavy stillness that meant snow. The bright morning closed down into winter and the wind chill factor went up. He'd soon had enough of the cold and turned for home.

The dogs ran ahead and he found them bustling round Kate as she mucked out. The spaniel was eager to gobble the fresh dung and she shouted at him, trying to avoid catching him with the fork each time she swung towards the barrow

He was glad she was there. "Did you have to walk?" he asked.

"Only the last bit, I got most of the way. The car's good in ice to say it's not four wheel drive. But it's very nasty on the hill. I shan't be able to ride."

The horse looked content in his box. "I gave him hay in case you were late," he said.

"Thanks."

"It's nothing."

"Do you think this weather will last?" she asked.

"The forecast's not good and it feels like snow."

"I hope not," she said.

"Look how heavy the sky is. I'm sure it'll snow."

"I won't be able to exercise him. It's not safe on the hill." She faced him, anxious and he knew what was coming. "Is there anywhere I could turn him out if it lasts?"

He laughed at her. "They've warned me about you horse people. Give you an inch and you'll take a mile." She blushed scarlet and he wished he hadn't teased her.

"It's all right. I'm only teasing. Will he bother the sheep, do you think?"

"I don't know, I doubt it but I'd watch him at first."

"You could let him out in that patch beyond the barn. He can't do much harm there and if it snows it won't mark."

She smiled that smile. "You've been so kind about it. I'm really grateful."

This was his opportunity. "Were you really that stuck for somewhere to take the horse?" he asked. "He must mean a lot to you."

"He does. I'd have had to sell him and I got him as a foal. It's a long story, I don't want to bore you with it."

"I'd like to hear it if you want to tell me," shivering as he spoke. "It's cold. I'm going in for coffee. Would you like one when you've finished?"

"Please. I won't be long."

The dogs rushed to the house, waiting by the door. Tess wasn't supposed to come indoors, the experts all told him it ruined a sheepdog to be coddled. But in weather like this he wouldn't see her left out in the barn, she deserved a little comfort. The pair of them dashed in, vying for the best spot on the rug by the aga. They got in his way every night and he had to toe them aside to start cooking.

He picked up the instant coffee then put it down and hunted for his coffee grinder. Dusty and unused since the days of Paula he blew on it to clear the dust, wiped it quickly and opened a packet of beans. The scent of fresh-ground coffee filled the kitchen and she knocked at the door as he was pouring the water.

"What a lovely smell. I've never had proper coffee. Instant would have done."

"I don't often have company, so I thought we'd treat ourselves. Sit down or have a warm by the aga."

She held her hands on the rail then turned to rest her bum against the hot surface. "It's very cold out there," she said. "You do catch the wind up here but it's a beautiful spot."

"Everything has its price," he said. "Get the view and get the wind. Milk?"

He put her mug on the cooker beside her and sat at the table to study her. The dark, straight hair hung in a child's bob about her neck but he'd already noted the way it swung when she moved. She wasn't so much pretty as striking, a strong face with dark eyes that returned his gaze with that now familiar diffidence.

With his most gentle smile he asked: "Why do you always seem anxious with me?"

"Do I?"

"You know you do."

"I suppose I don't want to upset you."

"I would like to know why your horse is here."

"I will tell you — when we've got more time."

"Plenty of time this morning," he said. "My schedule's very flexible."

"But I can't stay long, I have to get back." She looked at the table as if its wooden grain was fascinating.

"I see."

She peered at him from beneath dark lashes and muttered: "I saw you in church on Christmas Eve."

"I didn't see you."

"No, we were a few pews back."

"Oh."

"You looked in a sort of daze."

"Did I?"

"You seemed very unhappy, not much Christmas spirit."

Frowning he said: "How could you see my face if you were sitting behind?"

She mumbled something and he told her brusquely to speak up.

"It was the way you sat there, all kind of hunched up and your sister — "

"What about her?"

"I watched her. She had a job to rouse you for communion."

"I was tired, probably a bit drunk, it was nothing."

"Right." She met his gaze. "When you walked down the aisle I thought you'd been crying."

He looked down and the silence dragged into embarrassment. She broke it, saying: "I'm sorry, none of my business, I shouldn't have said that."

Eyeing her again he said slowly: "No, you shouldn't."

She stood up: "I'll go. The coffee was great, thanks."

He didn't move but said: "You're very perceptive and you had better go."

She hesitated: "You're not cross, are you?"

He shook his head: "No, not cross." He didn't get up.

She started for the door, stopped and came back to him.

"Thanks for everything," she said, leaning close and with a hand on his shoulder bent to brush his cheek with her lips, barely a kiss. A thrill shot through him and his hand flew to the spot, staring at her in surprise. She hurried to the door without looking back and was gone.

He nursed his mug of coffee and poured another, musing on that unexpected moment. Why would she do that? She'd kissed him, only a brief touch against his cold cheek, not sensuous and he too startled to react — but still a kiss.

He recalled the smell of her, suddenly close to him — a touch of the stable but something else, something indefinable — a warm, musky scent that was her, the delicious woman smell of her skin. He hadn't noticed at the time but it came back as a shock.

He smiled, it meant nothing, he told himself. It was gratitude for having Harry. But the idea stayed with him and the memory of her touch brought the first pang of physical hunger he'd felt for months, since Paula had been banished. And he hadn't missed it, the dreams of Katya and his desire for her were cerebral with the long-nursed misery of loss that he cradled to himself, no longer a physical hurt but something his mind sought constantly. That was it, about the girl, the smell of her. Katya's scent had stayed with him for so long, the strangest things would bring it back. But he realised now he couldn't recall it any more. He'd lost it.

Lying awake he thought about the horse mystery, frustrated by the lack of information, the sense of being kept out of the loop and made up his mind soon after midnight. He would make Pat tell him — it was her idea in the first place, he knew the threat of kicking Harry out would make her tell.

He drove the Land Rover carefully on the icy road and reached Jack's soon after nine hoping to catch them at breakfast after milking. He knew their routine, he'd had breakfast with them a few times when he'd helped out.

He went to the kitchen door, knocked and went straight in, expecting to find them all at the table but the room was empty. He called but there was no response. The cars were in the yard so they must be somewhere about.

From the direction of the barn he heard a loud crack like a gun. He followed the sound and went in, calling hello in a cautious voice. Jack's voice answered: "Okay, Jim, come in, nothing to worry about."

The farmer was on his knees beside a large swollen ewe, obviously dead with a bloody hole in her head. "Too old," Jack responded to the unasked question. "She shouldn't have been tupped this time but she got back in with the flock. She went right down overnight, this was the only thing to do."

"Didn't know you had one of these," James gestured at the bolt gun in Jack's hand.

"It was dad's, been in the family for years. Kindest way to do it, saves a lot of trouble, we'll drop her in the dead hole later."

He stood up. "What can I do for you, lad?"

"I was looking for Pat. I need some answers — they keep fobbing me off. I want to know what's really going on with that girl."

"She's gone up the hill to fetch some lambs down, she shouldn't be long. Go indoors. Sheila'll make you a drink. I'll send Pat in."

"I couldn't find anyone in the house," James said.

"Expect she was busy upstairs — go in and put the kettle on."

When Pat appeared she was red in the face from running after the lambs who'd been spooked by the young dog, over enthusiastic in his work.

"Dad said you were here but I'm very busy. Haven't really got time to speak to you."

"I need to talk to you."

"Well, not now." She headed for the door but her father was just coming in. She turned to face James but avoided his eyes. "I need to get on," she said. "Lots to do."

"Nothing that won't keep," said her father. "If he's come over special you'd better talk to him."

The girl sighed but said. "All right, but we'll have to talk while I'm working."

He followed her out to where the group of lambs were penned ready for sorting. "I need to get the ewe lambs out, dad wants to take the tups to market tomorrow," she explained. "Look, Mr Lambert, I'm sorry I've been avoiding you but it's difficult."

"I just want to know what I'm getting into. I need some answers."

"You're right."

"Why's she so desperate about the horse? You told me she had to move him due to a misunderstanding but that could mean anything. Where did she keep him before?"

"At her boyfriend's farm, well, his father's. The Sterlings."

"Okay," he said. "Has she fallen out with him?"

"Not exactly. It wasn't a row, nothing so simple. She told him she doesn't want to see him any more."

"But the family are farmers — why doesn't she keep the horse at home? She dumped him. Nothing unusual in that."

"It's more than that, they've known each other all their lives and it's always been the thing with both families that Kate and Steve would marry."

"Does that still happen?"

Pat nodded: "You'd be surprised. It's not easy round here to find partners, a lot of farmers don't marry till they're nearly middle-aged."

"Right. So Kate has grown up and decided she wants something better."

"More than that. She can't stand him."

"I can believe that, I met him in the pub — unpleasant guy. He kind of threatened me."

"Nasty's the word," Pat said. "Didn't know you'd come across him." She eyed him with concern. "They keep on at her, telling her she's crazy, she shouldn't throw it all away — but she can't bear to be with him. Her father wouldn't have the horse at home and Bill Sterling told her straight to move the horse or make it up with Steve."

"Blackmail, I see."

"That horse means so much to her and he's just getting to the stage where he's ready to do a real job. She wants to event him, he's six in the spring and he should be great."

James was opening and closing the hurdles for her, letting the lambs through into different sections. She stopped what she was doing and looked at him.

"She didn't know what to do but you can't marry someone just to keep a horse.

"She wouldn't be the first," he said dryly.

"Well that's not Kate. They all think she'll change her mind but she won't. She's been in an awful state — she really has — but then I had an idea."

"You thought of me."

She smiled at him, a kind appealing smile. "Yes. It was worth a try."

"I thought it might be something like this after that oaf was so aggressive in the pub."

"I'm sorry, we didn't mean to make things awkward for you."

"It's okay."

"You won't kick Harry out, will you?"

He glanced at Pat, her earnest gaze now fixed on him, anxious for his reaction. "No, I wouldn't do that." He smiled at her. "She's got a good friend in you, she's lucky."

"We've always been friends."

"Thanks for telling me but it doesn't really say much more than I got from Richard in the pub." Frowning he said: "What really puzzles me is her parents' attitude. Why aren't they backing her up? If she doesn't like the guy, what's the point? Is there something more?"

Pat nodded: "You're no fool, are you? It's like everything round here, it's all about land. I'm not sure exactly but there's some sort of deal involved."

Chapter five

The threatened snow had not arrived and the roads were safe enough for Kate to resume Harry's exercise though there was never an opportunity to speak to her. But the weather was only delayed. Large goose feather snowflakes drifting down on a Saturday afternoon made him hope he might see her and he watched as the snow began to settle and deepen. The difficulties the weather created were to him a challenge and he found a perverse pleasure in the harsh conditions.

Since she'd spoken to him about Christmas Eve he'd thought about her often, more often than he wanted to and he couldn't any longer deny his desire to know her better. When she arrived on foot, cold and breathless it was the excuse he needed to ask her in for a hot drink. This time she didn't argue but came in gratefully, drank the tea as soon as it was cool enough and returned to the horse. He waited for a while then went after her, watching her change Harry's rug. She brushed the horse's back and quarters with long firm strokes then replaced the rug. Her strong fingers buckling the straps were quick and efficient and he wondered how they would feel on his own skin.

"Have you left the car at the bottom?" he asked.

"I knew I wouldn't get up in this."

"Sensible. You'd better hurry, you don't want to be stranded up here all night."

"I wouldn't mind. It's pretty grim at home. I hate weekends."

Avoiding her eyes he said: "You'd better go. The road will be bad in the morning even if Geoff gets round. I'll do Harry to save you struggling up here. Don't worry about him, he'll be fine. I assume he'll only need hay if he's not going out?"

"Yes. How d'you know that?"

"I told you before, I know about horses, had one as a boy. Don't reckon they've changed much."

Outside the stable the air was thick, the wind already driving the fallen snow. "This looks nasty," he said. "Might get some bad drifts." Then half to himself: "It was like this in Sarajevo the last two days before we got away."

"What?"

"Nothing. I'll walk down with you to the car."

"There's no need. I'll be fine," she protested.

"Maybe, but I'm coming anyway."

They trudged down the lane, speech impossible in the wind. On the steep bend she slipped and he caught her arm to steady her. She looked sideways at him and kept walking. The car was already covered with snow and he cleared the windscreen with his gloved hand. Before she drove away she opened the window to thank him, letting the swirling snow blow in.

"Stop talking and close the window."

She persisted: "I'm glad you came to Derrington."

"Just get going and take care. Don't worry about the horse."

The blizzard conditions persisted on and off for three days, the sky would clear for a while but then dark clouds swept in again and more snow was added to the white-out. A vicious wind howled round the farm whipping the snow into cones and deep drifts against walls and hedges. The cones were crisp and brittle with ice, frozen into shape by the north east wind.

Kate rang in a panic about Harry but he was warm and fed in his box and James told her not to come. The road was blocked by a wide drift on the bend which would be there until

Geoff, the farmer contracted by the council to clear roads, could get round to it. She couldn't get up and James had to stay put on the hill. He walked down to see if the Land Rover could get through but the drift was too deep and black ice beneath the snow made it treacherous.

For those three days he fed the stock and worked indoors, forcing himself to sit and dredge his brain for the memories he wanted to bury, reliving the awful days when it was impossible to get out of the city.

The snow round the farm recalled that time, the biting, wicked cold of Sarajevo, water frozen, power cut off, food scarce and little hope of respite.

He persevered, laying out the political and military aspects as they had seemed to him at the time, not as the outside world had seen it but as he and the people he was close to had lived it day by day. He made no time for food, just mugs of tea or coffee with chocolate biscuits, wanting to progress the project. Once he began to write he dared not stop, hitting the keyboard with a ferocity that left a trail of literals which he had to go back and correct. He couldn't type it quick enough to keep pace with his seething brain.

He wrote forty thousand words in a frenzied intensity of effort but when he came to the part about Katya and how she died, it stopped. Inspiration flew away and the sun came out to melt the snow. It was the third day and he was hungry, tired and defeated.

He thought about food, knowing how little he had in the house to eat.

The freezer was empty, only a few tired, unlabelled packs lying in crumbled ice at the bottom. He picked the first he found which turned out to be lamb neck chops. They were tipped half-thawed into his large green casserole pot with the last of the carrots, an onion and some herbs. He found two large potatoes which went into the oven to bake. He was suddenly very hungry and cursed himself for not stocking up before the bad weather.

He looked up from cooking and saw Kate had come. He tried to ignore the turning-over sensation in his stomach but pulled on his boots in a hurry to be out there. He'd done the best he could for Harry though it was difficult wheeling muck away through the snow. She was creating a pile outside the box and looked defensive when she saw him.

"I'll move it as soon as the snow's gone but it's hard work getting to the muck heap. I'm sorry, I hope you don't mind — " she tailed off, seeing him look as if he hadn't heard what she was saying.

Sunlight was catching an auburn tint in her hair and his eyes were fixed on it. He studied her, face flushed with effort from the work, slender figure thickened by warm clothes. He said sharply: "How did you get here?"

"I walked. It was fun, the drifts have gone but the road's still slippery — it's like walking through a tunnel on the corner."

He didn't respond and she found his prolonged gaze uncomfortable. "About the muck, I'm not going to leave it here."

"What? No, it's fine. I'll shift it with the tractor when the snow's gone."

He left her abruptly. She sighed as she watched him hurry away, wondering why he'd bothered to come out.

He couldn't stay by her, the sun on the hair was so like the other Kate. He remembered once he'd called her Katie and she'd said: "No, Katya, my name is Katya."

He walked out beyond the barn to scan the valley, glaring white in the sun, so bright it hurt his eyes. He leaned on the fence to crush his face against his arm, to block the image which had made her seem so close, he felt he could touch her. The love and loss came flooding back and he cursed the girl with her bloody horse and wished he'd never seen her.

When Harry was done she looked for James but couldn't find him until she spotted him by the fence staring into the sky. Following his gaze she saw a pair of buzzards wheeling overhead, their plaintive calls loud in the still air. The birds circled closer, gradually lower, revealing the pattern beneath their wings.

He turned and smiled at her. "It's the first chance they've had to get up since the snow. Not much fun being a bird in bad weather."

She smiled back and said: "They're beautiful. I know the farmers don't like them but I love to see them. There's so many more since I was little, you hardly ever saw one then."

"At home we never saw them, there aren't many now, though they are spreading. Dad used too many chemicals — not good for birds."

That surprised her, the reference to a family farm but she didn't ask the questions that came into her head, fearful of his strange mood.

But she did dare to ask: "Are you all right? Have I offended you again."

He met her troubled eyes. "I'm fine, really. Just ghosts, that's all. Come on in, I'll make some tea."

"You don't have to."

He laughed, dismissive and jerked his head in a gesture she couldn't fail to understand. She followed him and sat quietly waiting for the tea while he knew he'd made a fool of himself and felt awkward but the kitchen's cosy warmth thawed their mutual discomfort. And it was enhanced by a savoury aroma from the casserole.

She sniffed in appreciation and said lightly: "Something smells good!"

"Yes. It was a sort of lucky dip."

"It's very inviting. Are you a good cook?"

"Not really but I like to cook. It's relaxing."

A happy thought occurred to him and he turned to her with an invitation. "Stay and have some if you like, it should be ready by half past six."

"I don't know," she hesitated. "It's kind of you — "

"Another time maybe," he shrugged.

"No. I'd like to stay. But I walked up and — "

"I'll take you home, I should get down okay. It's up to you — no big deal." He passed her the tea and she glanced through the window, wanting to stay. The sun had gone and the lengthening January afternoon was over. Hesitant she asked: "Is there enough?".

"Oh forget it. It's only a bit of stew. Don't make a drama out of it."

She frowned at his tone and flushed. "Thank you. If you'll run me home I'd like to stay. It's good to talk to someone who doesn't keep telling me what I should do."

"Good. I'll finish outside and feed the dogs. Make yourself at home. TV through there, bathroom upstairs or cloakroom over there." He pointed across the kitchen and went out.

She wandered into the sitting room. Unfamiliar with the tastes and habits of a man living alone, she expected disorder at the least, knowing only how her father and brother behaved.

The tidy room with its atmosphere of homely comfort was a surprise, especially when she looked at the eclectic mixture of tapes and CDs varying from the Stones to Mozart. Serious music was not an option she was used to.

The room conveyed a suggestion of elegance, plain walls and plain carpet but it had three oriental rugs which lifted it above the mundane. But it was the pictures that drew her, mostly watercolours and a pair of numbered prints, one showing red kites and the other a buzzard in flight. She fastened on one particular painting, in pastel, fascinated by the story it might tell, just an old man alone, eating his supper. Not much in itself but as she studied it, the empty chair opposite across the table, the watching cat and the ancient dog, she pondered why he was alone. She stood before it, entranced, realising that the artist, whoever he was, had achieved his aim, grabbing her imagination and involving her in the old man's life.

She was still looking at it when James came into the room. "Fascinating, isn't it," he said.

"Yes. It grabs you. You want to know more about him."

"It was my grandmother's, that and the barometer in the hall were all I had from her. But they were all I wanted. The old man was a watchman, we think. — The meal won't be long. Would you like a drink?"

"Oh, yes, why not?" She looked back at him with such a smile he gasped. For once she seemed relaxed. "I haven't made it to the bathroom yet, too busy admiring the pictures."

He showed her the way and turned on the TV to catch the news. The third item was another suspected massacre in Bosnia, shots of men at gunpoint, taken into "protective custody." He watched for a while till they showed a child's body, face down in the street like a broken doll, blood pooled around the head. He switched off, fists clenched and retreated to the kitchen, angry with himself that it still mattered so much, that it could still hurt to see it when all he wanted was to forget about it.

That was it, that was the point, why he didn't want to write it — he just wanted to forget. He reached for the whisky, ready on the kitchen top near the aga, poured a large tot and gulped it down, guilty because the good malt deserved better treatment. Shuddering as the liquor hit his empty stomach he thought about Katya and her sweet breasts above him in the half light of her room. He shuddered again and the idea of Kate with that lovely hair tumbling about her face came to confuse him. He steadied himself against the aga as she strolled into the kitchen and he had to deal with reality. He dredged up a smile and asked: "What would you like to drink?"

She'd seen his strained expression and was back on her guard.

"Anything."

"What do you usually drink?"

"Whatever's going," she said.

"Do you like wine?"

"A glass of wine would be great — white if you have it, not too dry."

He wondered what to give her, doubting if she'd ever had the chance to choose. Good wine was a passion with him and he thought sometimes he'd gone wrong in life and should have tried the wine trade. Now that was a career his father would have approved.

He opened a Sauvignon Blanc from the Loire, another purchase on his trip, and passed her the glass. She sipped it cautiously. He poured another whisky and asked: "Is that okay for you?"

"It's lovely, thanks. I don't know much about wine, I expect you can tell."

"Perhaps but you can learn. — I saw Pat," he said. "She told me about your problem. I guess you're still getting a lot of pressure?"

"Pressure. You could say that."

"I know all about pressure. Been there, done that."

She smiled at him.

"Do you have wine at home?" he asked.

"Sometimes but only with special meals."

"And what about your boyfriend?"

"If you mean Steve Sterling, he's a lager man — but he's not my boyfriend."

"No?"

"No."

"Sure?"

"Quite sure. You seem to know about it. I've done the right thing -- I know I have -- but nobody will accept it."

He left it alone and handed her the cutlery to set two places at the kitchen table while he lifted the big green casserole pot from the bottom oven.

"That looks brilliant," she said as he ladled out meat and vegetables and added the slightly blackened jacket potatoes.

He was hungry but his effort was better than anticipated, tender from the long slow heat and the melding of flavours.

"Good peasant food," he laughed, offering her bread. "I would have made dumplings but there's no suet."

"It's great," she said through a mouthful.

They laughed together and he was glad he'd asked her to stay.

When they'd finished eating she returned to the subject of Steve Sterling, suddenly anxious to talk about it. "They never let up, as soon as I get in, mum starts on me. Meals are a misery and he keeps ringing. He just won't take it in. Won't take no for an answer. What else can I say?"

"It's hard to stay firm," he said. "I know."

"Yes, that's why it's good to be here, out of it for once."

"Will they be worried? Do you want to ring?"

"No! Let them worry. That sounds bad but if you knew what it's been like. I get no peace."

"I can imagine."

"He keeps ringing or coming round as if nothing's happened. He's convinced I don't mean it."

"Can't you leave home, get away?" She frowned at him as if he was mad, made bolder by the wine he thought, anger waiting to get out.

"You've no idea, have you?" She sighed. "I have a job but I've got no money. Where would I go? And there's Harry."

"Yes," he smiled. "We mustn't forget Harry."

"He matters to me."

"A lot more than Steve I guess."

"Steve never mattered, not to me."

"What happened, was it a row?"

"No, we didn't have rows, that made it worse."

"No spark, you mean," he said

She looked at him eagerly. "That's right. There was nothing, it was boring." She twirled her empty glass and he refilled it and went on listening. "We were supposed to get married this year, in June, between first and second cuts of silage."

"You're joking." He laughed out loud but saw the look on her face and remembered the scene in the pub. "You're not joking are you."

"No, that was when it fitted in. He's never asked me, it's always been assumed. — I've always been taken for granted, by him, his parents, my family, everyone."

"And now you've decided to make a point?"

"No." Her fingers were playing with the bread, crumbling it to tiny pieces on the table.

"Much more than that. I don't know why I'm telling you all this. I don't know you, perhaps that's why and nobody else will even try to understand. Even Pat has doubts, though she knows what he is. They keep telling me not to be stupid. Mum nearly had hysterics when I told her, she was really upset as if it was her who was so unhappy." She paused, twisting her hands together and looked up into his face: "I just can't bear him near me and the prospect of a lifetime with him — it's impossible."

He saw her anguish and realised what it had taken to tell him. Perhaps it was easier because they were strangers, or had been.

He ventured to say: "He doesn't come over as a good guy."

Her laugh at that was bitter and her eyes glistened; he said nothing hoping she wasn't about to cry.

When she had control of herself again she whispered: "No, he isn't a good guy. He's pretty much anything bad you can think of, unkind, no — cruel, selfish, arrogant. I could go on. There's something in him, James," the first time she said his name. "It's almost evil — I really think that's the word for it."

"That's a strong word."

"I know."

He thought about that, unsure how to respond, then said: "Do you mind me asking, what sort of relationship was it? Did you go out much?"

"How d'you mean?"

"Did he take you out?"

"Sometimes. Mostly Young Farmers stuff."

"Didn't you go places just the two of you? Dinner, pubs, cinemas, theatre, holidays?"

"Pubs yes. We went to the cinema once because I particularly wanted to see a film and he thought it was wet. He took me for a meal on my birthday once."

"Did he buy you flowers?"

She laughed at that. "He's a farmer."

"So what did you do all the time?"

"Just met in the evenings at his house or mine and watched TV or went for a drink. We were supposed to go on holiday last year, to Tenerife but it didn't happen."

"Why?"

"He kept making excuses and in the end I think he was afraid of flying."

He stretched his arm across the table to touch her hand. She started but left the hand where it was so he kept his hold. He spoke gently to her. "Sounds like you've had a bad time. You can do better than him."

She said nothing, then peered at him: "You ask a lot of questions."

"Sorry. It's the job. You get so you can't help it. You can ask me stuff."

She met his eyes and hers were troubled but beautiful. It was he who looked away, unable to stop himself asking, mumbling the next thing. "Did you sleep with Steve?"

His directness shocked her and she blushed and gasped.

"Sorry, that was very rude," his voice sounded thick.

"It doesn't matter."

"Forget I said that."

She avoided the intensity of his gaze and he realised how much he wanted to know.

"Once. I let him stay one night when mum and dad were away. I didn't want to do it but he forced me. He'd done it with other girls, a lot."

"Did he rape you?" James had to know.

"Not quite but I had to let him. He frightened me — had his hands round my neck. It was awful, he was so rough and it hurt."

"Did you tell your mother?"

She shook her head. "I told her something years ago, something much worse but nobody listened, nobody wanted to know."

He tried to think what might be worse and it dawned on him that the story was altogether darker than he'd imagined. Her young face showed pain from the past and pain within her now.

"Do you want to tell me?"

"No, I've told you enough. Perhaps some time but I want to forget it all."

Then she looked straight at him. "I think the whole sex thing is horrible, I can't understand all the fuss. If that's it, I don't want to know."

He smiled then, couldn't help it, with a delighted sensation of triumph. As if it mattered whether or not she'd had regular sex with the awful youth. But it did and he was so happy she'd hated it.

"Why are you smiling?" she demanded. "It wasn't funny."

"I'm just pleased you hated it. Listen Kate, that's not what it's about. Don't give up on men because of him. The world is full of men like that but there's much more to it."

He paused. "Was that it? That once?"

She nodded. "I couldn't bear him to touch me after that."

"And was he happy with that?"

"No but I made sure there was no opportunity and said we ought to wait."

"That's a good one, these days."

"Virgins aren't so rare, you know," she said.

"Maybe you're right. And it looks like you're as good as one yourself."

"I wish you wouldn't make fun of me," she protested.

"I'm not. I'm — " he was stuck for words. "I'm charmed to find such innocence remains in the world."

She thought he was being facetious and he let her think it. But he meant it, exactly what he'd said. He released her hand to offer her cheese and coffee. "Then I'd better take you home."

"I'll stay a bit longer. The less time I spend there the better. Let them worry."

"It's your family. Stay as long as you like but don't make more trouble than you need."

"I know you don't want to get involved — it'd be embarrassing in the village."

"I don't give a shit what the village thinks. You've already got the horse here. But it matters to you what people think, it's your home. I may not stay here."

"Oh." Her eyes scanned the room. "But you've done so much."

"I'm not upping sticks right now. But who knows in the long term? Things change."

"This was always an untidy hole. You've made such a difference, the place looks cared for."

"I love it," he said. "It's a good house in a grand position with some decent land. It deserved a bit of care. Besides," he added, "I've had plenty of time to give it."

He thought a moment, then seemed to make up his mind: "Go on through, make yourself at home. I'll bring the coffee. Put on some music if you like."

She looked very comfortable on his sofa, feet tucked up and he flopped down opposite in his favourite armchair, at ease as they chatted, answering some of her cautious questions about his life.

He contemplated moving to sit beside her but after what she'd told him it seemed crude to try so obvious a seduction. The last thing he wanted was to scare her. About ten he said: "I really think you should go home now. They may deserve a lesson but this is probably enough."

"I am twenty-three."

"Yes but you live with them and the weather's bad." How pompous that sounded when he recalled how he'd behaved to his parents at the same age.

Outside it was freezing hard and he had to clear ice from the Land Rover before they could move. She shivered beside him and he put an arm round her for a moment pushing her to get in out of the cold. "I'll do Harry in the morning," he said. "You needn't come up but with luck the road will be clear by tea time."

He drove carefully down the icy hill, it was very dark, the crescent moon obscured by cloud moving from the west which might raise the temperature. At the bottom of the hill she said: "Thanks for this evening, it's good to talk and the pot luck was brilliant."

They passed the first house in the village and she suddenly touched his arm. "Don't drive up to the farm," she said. "Drop me in the lane."

"What? Ah, I get it."

"Sorry."

"It's okay, I understand."

As she climbed out he caught her hand and leaned over to raise it to his lips. The way her eyes lit up enchanted him, grabbed at his heart as she said: "No one ever kissed my hand before.

Chapter six

He'd kissed her hand on impulse and couldn't forget the look of delight it produced. He'd enjoyed her company and watched with misgivings as she set off along the dark lane towards home, the beam from the torch he lent her bobbing as she walked, undaunted by the darkness. He admired her courage but knew she saw greater danger in being seen with him than she might meet in the winter night. He couldn't stop thinking of her and all they'd talked about, eager to see her again.

But he'd told her not to come while the road was bad, so he didn't expect her and contented himself looking after the horse, taking him out to the paddock each day while Pat came on the tractor to muck out.

The snow had retreated to long streaks across the hillsides and dirty piles beside the roads and his lane was clear for traffic but she didn't come. He continued Harry's routine and Pat came to ride him but of Kate there was no sign. At first he was annoyed and felt taken for granted but when he thought about what she'd told him he began to worry, especially about what she hadn't said.

Pat said nothing about her friend but he caught up with her after she'd ridden. Before he spoke Pat said: "Kate isn't well."

"What's wrong?" he asked. "She told me stuff that evening and since then I've heard nothing from her. She could call me."

She didn't look up from mixing Harry's feed. "It's difficult."

"How? Come on, tell me what's happened."

"She told you about her and Steve, didn't she?"

"Yes. You seem to be the only one on her side,"

"Well, Steve's a bastard. I've never liked him." From her expression it was obvious she too knew bad things about him but he resisted the temptation to ask and let her continue.

"When she told me she wanted out I said I'd help. But he won't leave her alone. He came round the other night and they had an awful scene. She sprained her wrist. I think she fell."

"When was this?"

Another look from Pat, this time quizzical as she said: "Day after she stayed for supper with you. Her mother says it was an accident but I doubt that. He got angry, he's got a really nasty temper. He grabbed her, shouting and that, and she fell."

"Christ. Why do her parents allow it?" Then he said: "Have you seen her?"

"Yes, I called yesterday but Mrs Patterson wouldn't leave me alone with her. Kate was in bed. She had a mark on her face too, not quite a black eye but ..."

"I can't believe I'm hearing this. They let him get away with it. Why didn't they call the police?"

"Oh they wouldn't do that."

"But this intimidation can't go on. If she's packed the guy in, that's it."

"They won't accept it, none of them."

"I'll phone her," said James.

"No, don't," Pat shook her head. "It might make things worse."

"Why?"

"Come on Mr Lambert, you must realise. They don't like Harry being here anyway and you took her to the Boxing Day meet. They were well steamed up about that."

"She's twenty-three years old. She's not a child. Why do

they treat her like one?"

Pat shrugged. "Her mum's making a fuss about the wrist. I think they're keeping her off sick as long as possible to make it more difficult. They hope you'll get cross and tell her to move him. That's why I'm here."

"Well I shan't do that. They sound a fucking awful family — I can't believe it."

Fists clenched he walked away cursing but then came back to Pat: "You don't have to keep coming up, I'll see to Harry till she's back. Tell her not to worry — and give her my love."

He went to the pub that evening hoping to hear any gossip which might be going round about the Pattersons.

Richard leaned over the bar, his head on one side like a pirate in a pantomime speaking in a loud whisper: "All I know is there was a big row. Word is young Steve lost it and thumped her. They say she's in a real mess. They're keeping a very low profile."

"Were the police involved?"

The landlord shook his head. "No, all between the families, you see."

"Not really," James muttered. "I don't understand it."

"You will, when you've bin 'ere a bit longer." The old man standing along the bar from James had been listening. "It's the land, you see," he said. "It's all about the land, 'nother one if you please, Richard."

"What land?" The old boy winked at James and supped his beer.

He moved to the fireplace, though the snow had gone it was still cold and Richard kept a good blaze.

He stood before it, warming the back of his legs. The pub's fireplace was always a focal point, visitors attracted by the photograph of the young royal seated there having his lunch after an outdoor visit several years before. The fire threw out a lot of heat but if the wind was in the wrong direction it sometimes flickered and smoked. Its awkward angled chimney regularly caught fire. He failed to notice the group of regulars at the nearest table get up and move away without speaking to him.

He'd passed the Pattersons' farm many times without interest but when he stopped outside and sat in the dark to study it he was impressed. The handsome stone-built house was lit by spotlights on the corners and when he started to walk across the forecourt bright security lights flashed onto the three expensive cars parked there.

He hesitated but approached the front door where he knocked and waited. It took a few minutes for the door to open and if Elizabeth Patterson was surprised to see him she gave no sign of it. She appeared tired and middle-aged, with hair showing tinges of grey but he thought she must once have been an attractive woman. He'd only seen her in church and around the village — but she knew him,

"Mr Lambert, how are you?" The woman was charm itself.

"I'm fine thank you. I came to ask how Kate is. I heard she had an accident, with your neighbour's son was it?"

"Yes, she tripped on a rug. But it's nothing. She'll be fine."

He gave her his most charming smile and said: "That's good. Well, tell her Harry's absolutely fine and I'm happy to take care of him till she's better."

Mrs Patterson's face didn't falter but smiling she said: "That's kind. But it shouldn't be long before she can move him back. She's a silly girl, letting a trivial quarrel spoil everything for her."

He took a deep breath and ventured: "I understood it was more than a trivial quarrel. She told me she can't bear him."

"She didn't mean that."

"Really?" He made his doubts clear. "Can I see her?"

"I think she's asleep," said the mother. "It's all been a bit much for her. It was good of you to come. Goodbye."

She made a move to close the door but James stood his ground: "From what I've seen she could do with a bit of support from her parents."

She stood by the half-closed door and sighed. "Mr Lambert, I can see you don't understand the situation, it's not as simple as you think."

"Isn't it? If the girl's ditched him that should be the end of it."

"Whatever gave you that idea?"

"She did."

"They'll work it out, you'll see. You don't understand, that's all."

"No, I don't understand. You're right about that. You'll tell Kate I called?"

"Of course."

He hesitated but left -- there was nothing else he could do short of barging into the house to find Kate's room. But the short exchange had unsettled him and unwilling to go straight home he returned to the pub. Among his guest beers Richard currently had a strong ale from a small, local brewery which James enjoyed. As he sipped the second pint the landlord had time to talk: "That's a good pint, it's very popular."

James nodded: "Yes, I like it, if you kept it all the time you might see more of me."

"I've sold a lot of it but I like to ring the changes. Maybe I will think about keeping this one as a regular. Without being nosey —" he leaned over the bar to speak quietly. "I suppose I am being nosey but where did you go just now? You weren't away long. I thought you'd gone home."

James smiled. "I went to the Pattersons to ask about Kate — to leave a message about the horse."

"I hope you know what you're getting into."

"What's the big deal, Richard? Why all this fuss about where she keeps the horse. She's packed in her boyfriend, so what? It happens all the time."

"That's not the way they see it."

"Strange way to go on, it's like they're telling her who she should marry."

"You got it. That's exactly what they're doing," said Richard. "Both families expect them to marry."

"Right," he frowned "but now they've grown up and she doesn't want to. That's not unusual, childhood friendships often fall apart, people change. It's no big deal."

"You haven't lived here long, you don't know the background. I'm an outsider too but I've been here long enough to know it's best not to meddle with the Sterlings."

One of the girls was helping to serve and Richard left her to it and came round from behind the bar beckoning James to a quieter spot. In a low voice he carried on: "They're nice enough as long as everything goes smooth — but you cross them — it's a different story. Bill Sterling always gets his own way, that's how he got where he is. Land. That's the problem. They're all the same, these farmers. Land hungry."

James nodded muttering: "I know all about that."

"I expect you do," James had told him something of his own farming background. "They must have it, no matter what they've got already — they all want more. When land comes on the market they compete like enemies, it often causes trouble. But Bill's the man that usually gets it, people are afraid of him."

James gave a sceptical laugh but Richard said sharply: "You think I'm exaggerating but I'm not. They won't cross him, he's got a vile temper — that's where the boy gets it from."

"A picture of seething rural drama! You should mind what you tell me. I'm a journalist, remember. Sounds a good story."

"Just be careful. Excuse me."

There were customers waiting and he left James to muse into his beer. Behind him in the corner sat three farmers he knew by sight, heads together over the table engrossed in deep conversation. He guessed they were discussing the same topic and as he glanced round one of them smiled uncertainly and he knew he was part of their interest.

When Richard came back James resumed, saying: "I understand the land greed — my father was the same — but we're talking about the future of two young people. What does it matter if Kate and this Steve don't marry?"

"As I said, they don't see it like that. Steve wants the girl, he sees her as his property and to the old man it's a snub. And the bottom line is that Ted Patterson's a weak man who's afraid of Sterling and, more than that, he owes him."

"Is that it?"

"Yes — except they all think you're after her."

"What?"

"She spends a lot of time at your place, people are bound to talk. I shouldn't repeat what I hear over the bar but you should know what's being said."

"All I've done is find a place for the horse. She came to me and said she was stuck. I could've said no, I suppose but the building was empty. There's no more to it than that."

"Pretty girl though," Richard winked.

"Yes, she's attractive — and intelligent, too good for that lout."

"I'm just saying be careful." He reached for another glass to dry and whispered as if to himself: "People think nothing happens in the country, they don't know the half of it. Feelings run deep and farmers have a lot of time for brooding. It's bloody lonely on those great tractors all day, with just a radio and the sat nav to look at. Those big cabs are like spaceships with acres of land in front, behind and either side — lonely and monotonous. Modern equipment makes the work quick and efficient but it's taken the heart out of farming. There's no time for companionship and joy in the land."

James looked at him in surprise, he'd never heard the mundane Richard show so much feeling. "I didn't know you thought so much about it and I didn't think it was like that round here, not like where I come from."

"I've seen a lot of farmers in despair over the years, here and elsewhere, I worked as a feed rep at one time. It can be a very hard life. I've known two shoot themselves and one of them had nearly a thousand acres. But it didn't make him happy. He was lonely at home and lonely at work. No, modern farming's no joke. There's no romance in it, I can tell you."

James thought back to his own fights with his father and the huge farm in Wiltshire, certainly his father hadn't died a happy man. He built an empire but for what? And now he was playing at it — that's what the locals called it. He knew what they thought but he didn't care. But he enjoyed it and there was satisfaction in hands-on contact with the livestock, at least he'd rediscovered his feeling for the land.

The pub was filling up with late drinkers and he looked around for someone to talk to but none of the chattering groups showed any invitation, only backs turned against him. He finished his pint and drove slowly up the hill, staying outside to look at the valley and up to the sky where Orion's three-starred belt and the dog star Sirius were prominent in the clear night; the first constellation he learned, easy to recognise in the winter sky. On the horizon an orange glow hovered above the town.

Dark skies were another reason for his attachment to the place. The nearest light pollution was far enough away to let the stars show brightly and he was learning to pick out more constellations visible at different seasons. As a boy on the downs the stars were pale spectres, barely visible in a sky contaminated by light from the motorway and the conurbations it connected.

Countless stars in an infinite sky emphasised his loneliness, his insignificance but he admired them just the same. Neck cricked back he wondered what they said in the village, perhaps people imagined much more in his relationship with the girl. He would like it to be more. Her coming had woken him again to what life could bring and the shell he'd built around himself was cracking — and in the cracks he saw the reality of his isolation.

He couldn't help thinking about her, wondering what she might see in him and despite her initial reticence it did seem she liked his company. She wanted to talk, maybe just because he was someone from a different kind of world with a new perspective. For him she was more than a pretty girl, she was young and attractive but with something more which drew him and she trailed this stream of speculation, a puzzle he was only just beginning to unravel. Whatever else he felt about her she was greatly in need of support with only Pat on her side. He told himself he liked her because she seemed brave and sensible but when his thoughts strayed to her as they did too frequently his body told him there was more to it.

He knew the difference between sex and love and had always managed to keep them apart, knowing they were quite different — but Katya had changed that and now this girl too was getting under his skin.

He enjoyed sex like any man but he relished the seduction and the foreplay as much as the main event, generous with his attention and giving pleasure to the woman he was with added to his own satisfaction, a fact appreciated by several girls over the years. His love life had proceeded alongside his career, meeting girls and women where he happened to be and moving on, usually as friends. There'd been few complications — except Jenny, she'd given him a shock in France. Travelling on assignments made it easy to avoid involvement and generally he loved and left them. Until he met Katya. He'd never understood what made the difference, why suddenly he fell in love, almost the moment he saw her and he a man who didn't believe in love at first sight.

He just wanted to be with her in a way nothing in his life had prepared him for and when he left her dead in the ruined church he thought no woman would ever move him again. But now this girl with the horse had stirred him, the mere idea of her excited him. Her innocence was part of the appeal and he felt guilt for that but excused himself by saying she's not a child.

He would lie in bed or in the bath picturing her, imagining how it would feel to stroke her thigh and trying not to think beyond -- the idea of his fingers on her bare skin was exquisite. He would groan and try to stop himself but the ache she generated in his groin was unbearable. But she wasn't a child and he longed to know her better, maybe introduce her to the joys her body might bring. But despite the ache she induced he wanted to protect her, she was vulnerable, trapped in some family nightmare. The day he went to find her after the hunt, he'd been afraid for her yet he hardly knew her. Perhaps it was because no one else seemed to care.

Since the night they had supper he was afraid of frightening her and wanted any move to come from her. He told himself he wouldn't touch her unless she wanted him. That turned him on, the fantasy of her begging him for love. But he might have to wait a long time for that.

Chapter seven

She turned up on a wet and blustery evening when he'd already gone in to warm up. He lit the fire and sat beside it to watch the flames licking at the dry wood, waiting to be sure it would keep going. With the wind in this direction the chimney sometimes created a backdraught which filled the room with smoke, making the fire sluggish and slow to heat.

He watched her arrive and could see her in the stable, over the half door, one arm over Harry's neck. He wondered what soft words of nonsense she was confiding to the horse, closer to her than her family. She might be telling the sleepy horse how hard and unfair life was. Harry would rather have a carrot or more hay but he might appreciate the attention. He resisted the temptation to go out, hoping to learn something from whatever she did next.

Harry was already fed and settled for the night, a task he'd done daily for nearly two weeks, so there was really nothing for her to do but he watched her fetch the skip and bring out a pile of droppings. She stood a long time by the door, looking at Harry, leaning her head on it in a way which made him think she was crying.

This spying made him uncomfortable but he couldn't help himself, it was impossible to leave the window and do anything else. He wanted to see her and willed her to come to him. At the very least she would surely come to thank him. He watched as she looked about the yard and then at the house.

He fancied he saw a determined shake of the shoulders as she came his way.

Perhaps she was expecting anger but the way she approached told him she was ready to face whatever might come. He paused after her knock, long enough to make her wait and to conceal his eagerness. She knocked again before he opened the door and smiled at her, pretending surprise. He noted the look of relief in her face. Her answering smile encouraged him. "Hello stranger, how are you?"

She didn't answer.

"Coming in?" He held the door for her and she passed him hurriedly, head down.

She stood awkwardly in the middle of the kitchen and watched him put the warm kettle back on the aga. He waited for her to speak and handed her the mug of tea in silence. She blew on the hot drink and tried to take a mouthful but gave up and put it down on the table. He waited until she finally looked at him.

"I've come to thank you. I've been worried about Harry and though Pat said it was all right, I didn't know how long you'd put up with it."

"I told your mother it was okay. Didn't she tell you?"

"No. You rang the house?"

"I called and had a conversation with your mother."

"Really? She didn't tell me."

"Why am I not surprised?"

"Pat told you what happened?"

He nodded.

"It was awful."

"Why did it take so long?"

"Mum made a fuss, didn't want anyone to see me."

"I suppose that's understandable."

"There was more to it," she said angrily. "They were hoping you'd get pissed off and make me move him. This is my first day back at work — my first chance to get away."

"How's the wrist?"

"Okay but it still hurts, no strength in it yet."

He looked at her thoughtfully: "Your parents have a strange attitude, Kate. I take it they do care about you."

"I suppose so."

"You'll forgive me asking. They seem to have strange priorities."

"There are problems, it's difficult. They were upset about Steve."

"I can see that but I don't understand why they're trying to force you to make it up with him. They don't seem on your side at all, especially when the guy starts knocking you about."

"He didn't," she said with indignation.

"No? So how did you get the marks on your face? Pat told me — and a damaged wrist."

"It was an accident."

"He lost his temper, I bet?"

She slumped onto a chair and hid her face. He continued: "It's not my business, you don't have to tell me but I was worried. What happens now?"

"I don't know."

"You haven't gone back to him, have you?" He asked urgently, a spasm in his gut as he stared at her. His intensity startled her but he resisted the impulse to take her hand.

She shook her head. "I don't know what to do."

He sat down and faced her across the table. "Drink your tea," he said gently. "Talk about it if you want to, if it helps."

"I need to talk to someone," she whispered.

"He did hit you, didn't he? I can see where the bruises have been. It wasn't an accident — why can't you admit it?"

"I don't know." She drew breath in a long sigh then said softly: "Probably because I'm so ashamed of myself and my family being in this situation."

"Come through and be comfortable." He led her into the sitting room where the fire was going strong, roaring up the chimney. She hurried to it and stood close to the blaze murmuring: "This is such a welcoming room."

"Shall I open some wine? Would you like that?"

"Oh yes. You don't know how good it feels to be treated like an adult. And it helps me relax a bit."

He grinned at her: "You look more cheerful now, anyway."

He left her by the fire and went away for the wine.

She waited for him to speak, answering questions was easier than trying to explain. But he didn't want to prompt her, needing to hear it her way. He sat back and looked at her by the fire, sipping the red wine. Eventually she had to speak: "It seems easy here when I'm with you, straight forward. It's all so sane. Down there they make me feel ungrateful — unkind— as if Steve had been hurt by me, as if it's my fault. It's not like that."

Gaining confidence she met his insistent gaze and said: "I don't really know you. But I feel you're a friend — well — you've been so kind about Harry. It's good to have someone who's -- what's the word?"

"Objective?"

"Yes. "

"I may not be entirely objective," he said. "But I hope I'm your friend — you seem to need one." She didn't speak so he went on: "So — where are you at?"

"Where I was before. I can't get rid of him. There's so much pressure, from him and my family."

"You've got to get out, get away from them."

"Easier said."

In the silence they both became conscious of the rising wind, blowing up hard into a gale. Somewhere a door banged and a small cloud of smoke belched into the room as a gust hit the chimney. James laughed: "It's going to be a rough night, typical March."

"I hate the wind," she said.

"Do you? I love it, well, that's not quite true. It's a pain up here when you've got to work in it but I love the power of it. The fact you can't see it but only feel it and see what it does. It's so elemental."

She stared at him in astonishment and he shut up, feeling foolish.

She said: "It scares me. When I was little I used to hide from the wind. A tree blew down one night. The noise was terrifying — like a demon coming for me."

He frowned, wondering about her, and said: "It's just a natural force, dangerous if you get in its way, doors banging and things falling and stuff blown about, but it's something to respect not be afraid of."

As he spoke the hood over the fireplace shuddered and produced an echoing rumble. She looked nervous but he said: "It does that if it's coming from the north. It runs up the valley and hits this place head on."

He held out his hand: "Come and sit down, enjoy the wine in comfort. You needn't be afraid, of the wind or me."

"Don't make fun of me! I couldn't bear it from you as well."

"I'm not." He moved to the chair near her, saying: "I wouldn't tease you about it, it sounds as if you had a real fright."

"I did. It was silly, I suppose — but at the time I was terrified. I'm claustrophobic -- you know, fear of being shut in small spaces. I was only about eight, playing with some of the others, children from the village. In the Easter holidays. It was a windy day and we were playing hide and seek — I was hiding. There was a little cupboard place for the dustbins, next to the coal shed and I went in there and squatted down behind the bins. But they were ages looking for me and it got more windy and the door slammed shut. There was no catch on the inside and I was trapped in there. I shouted and shouted but they didn't seem to hear."

"How long were you in there?"

"Not that long, maybe half an hour but it felt like for ever. They came back to the yard and heard me. I think I was hysterical. I panicked, I thought I couldn't breathe. It was horrible."

"I don't like being shut in, it's a nasty feeling."

She faced him and said: "Yes but the worst bit was, I heard someone outside, footsteps and breathing. It was Steve. I heard him laugh, then he went away. He knew I was in there — I was calling out, so frightened, but he laughed and walked away. How could he do that? He said something about it later and I've never forgiven him."

"So — he has a cruel streak as well."

"As well as what?"

"He more or less warned me off in the pub."

"What!"

"I'd no idea what he was talking about."

"Did he threaten you'?"

James considered: "I suppose he did."

He smiled: "Don't look so worried!"

"You don't know him."

"I can't understand why your parents are so keen."

Kate sighed and drew her feet up into the chair. He liked that. "It's a long story, but basically Dad owes the Sterlings. It was about some land, Mum and Dad don't want to upset Bill."

"Well, I think you're going to upset him aren't you? Because you won't marry his son, will you?"

"Never."

He couldn't help staring, the wine did relax her, as she said, made her speak more freely and he wondered what she was thinking. "Would you like something to eat?" he asked.

"I'd like to stay but I'd better not. If I'm late tonight it'll only make things worse."

"Have another glass before you go, give you courage," he laughed.

"I wish I never had to go home. I wish I could stay here."

He didn't answer and they were both quiet, listening to the wind. He made up his mind and said: "Kate, if you need somewhere to stay, you could always come here. There's a room you could have, no strings, no problems, as a friend."

"Is that all?"

"How d'you mean?"

"Don't you fancy me?" she asked. He stared, eyebrows raised, then laughed and got up shaking his head. "That's cheeky. You must be feeling better."

"Sorry — but I thought you might. When you kissed my hand, it felt as if you did."

"You kissed me first, remember."

"That was only being friendly, you looked like you needed a kiss."

He was standing behind her chair and leaned forward: "That's what I thought, I didn't think you wanted my hand in your knickers."

She gasped and jumped up, face flushed with embarrassment. He couldn't stop himself saying softly: "Or maybe you do?"

She seemed so shocked he knew he'd blundered: "Sorry, shouldn't have said that. It's okay, I wouldn't do anything you didn't want me to."

"I couldn't bear Steve doing that," she said violently. "He was always trying to put his hand up my skirt or down my jeans. Nasty creepy fingers, it was horrible, it made my skin crawl. I couldn't bear it and he wanted me to play with him." She caught his eye and looked away.

"You don't have to tell me," he said. "Only if it helps."

"I've avoided all that for ages." She found the courage to face him: "It isn't always like that, is it?"

"No. I've told you before, it shouldn't be like that."

Standing close to her he said gently: "But you have to want someone. It's chemistry, simple physical attraction."

"I never fancied him. Never wanted to be with him — as," she hesitated — "as I want to be here. I do feel so relaxed here."

"Ah," he said with amusement, "it's just the ambience of my home and because Harry's happy here. Nothing to do with me."

"You know that's not what I mean." His hand rested on her shoulder now, and he allowed his fingers to quest across her neck .

"To answer your question," he said softly. "Of course I fancy you — what man wouldn't — but you're quite safe and I meant what I said. You could stay here with no strings of any sort, just as a friend." He kissed her neck lightly and headed for the kitchen, returning with her coat. "If you're going you'd better go."

The wind howled into the kitchen when they opened the door and she shuddered. "It's dreadful," she said.

"You'll soon be home. I'll come to the car with you." Again he put an arm lightly around her, shielding her from the wind. He opened the car door but she stayed close to him asking: "Why are you so kind to me?"

"I'm a kind person. All I've done is talk to you and look after your horse. I'd do that for anybody."

"I'm glad you came here. I needed someone like you," she whispered, cringing as a boisterous gust whirled across the yard sending buckets and a stray plastic sack flying. The horse whinnied and he felt her shake.

"It won't hurt you," he said and held her tighter. Trembling she tucked her head against his chest and he cuddled her like a child. She nestled against him and reached up to kiss his cheek before she found his lips. He kissed her gladly in return, delighted by her eagerness. When he forced her lips apart she responded and he felt the familiar surge of lust. Wind howled around them and he said: "Bloody hell, Kate! You pick your moments."

He kissed her again and put his hand on her breast, for a second she recoiled then pressed against his touch. Encouraged he found his way inside her coat to bare skin. His eyes widened when his fingers lingered on a nipple, hard to his touch. The expected protest didn't come and he stroked quietly, waves of heat and desire washing through him. He was getting hard and to his delight she pressed against him with the wind forgotten.

He pulled back, though reluctant to break the moment. "We can't stay here. Either get in the car and go or come back to the house."

"I'm frightened," she said.

"Then go home. You mustn't be afraid, of the wind or me."

"Kiss me again, James."

He kissed her forehead and pushed her firmly into the car.

"Go straight home and forget the wind. I'll be here when you come again."

That was next day and he saw at once a change in her. It wasn't in the way she looked, though she'd plainly taken extra trouble with her appearance, there was fresh lipstick which he'd never seen before and there was perfume, subtle but definite. She came towards the house first, without going to Harry and when he opened the door she walked straight in without hesitation. To his experienced eye the body language had changed, the head a little higher and something in the way she walked indicated a new assurance, even determination.

"You look good," he said watching her move. "Nice scent."

"You noticed — I don't usually bother. "

"I'm honoured."

She laughed: "Thought I'd better come in first because you might not notice after I've done Harry. Eau de horse muck instead."

Eyebrows twitching he smiled back at her: "You always smell good."

He kept away from her but asked: "Do you want a drink?"

She shook her head: "Better do Harry first — won't be long."

Waiting by the fire for her return an idea came to him and when she came in he said: "Are you free for the evening?"

"I'm here, depends what you mean."

"I had a thought, how about we go out and get a meal somewhere."

Her face screwed up into a frown and he watched the new-found assurance disappear. "Oh, I don't know. I'd love to but—"

"But? Don't you like eating out?"

"Don't do it very often. I'd love to go out with you but someone might see us and I couldn't stand all the hassle. It would spoil everything."

He studied her, she looked hesitant again, back to contemplating the floor. Without a word he poured a glass of wine and gave it to her. "Have a drink," he said kissing her on the forehead as he would a child.

"It was just a thought, it doesn't matter, we can go another time but I thought you might be hungry.'

"I am."

"Well, you have a choice of cheese on toast or baked beans."

"Oh, cheese on toast — great."

"Cheese it is." He raised his glass: "Here's to you."

She edged closer to him and tipped her glass against his, eyes brighter as she whispered: "Thanks."

Later he was glad they'd stayed in, it was intimately comfortable, just the two of them eating a simple meal by the fire and he watched her visibly unwind as she began to talk again. He listened with only an occasional comment and realised his instincts about her were correct, there was much more to Kate than he'd seen so far. He understood how the prospect of a future with someone like Steve would be a life sentence. Her quick intelligent mind was under-used in her desk-bound job and her thirst for knowledge enthralled him. He smiled to himself as she talked, imagining her as a clean page waiting to be written on. Her life had been narrowly confined with few options and she grasped with real hunger at the knowledge he offered of a wider, more fulfilling world.

Something had been unleashed in her and she rattled on in a torrent of words, as if a dam had been breached. He studied her as he listened, the way she gesticulated with both hands when she made a point or searched for the right words to express herself. Her cheeks were flushed with the wine and the warmth from the fire, she'd pushed the dark hair back from her face which made her prettier than ever and he wanted to touch her. Longed to brush that hair back as she had done and hold her face very close to him. Distracted by his desire he lost track of what she was saying and was slow to realise she'd gone quiet.

"You okay?" he asked.

"I think I'm boring you," she said.

"No, not at all — I just enjoy looking at you."

"That's kind but you must think I'm very silly," she said.

"Why should I?"

"Because I'm so ignorant."

"You're not ignorant but you haven't had much chance to do anything, go anywhere. Why didn't you go to uni?"

"University. You're joking. Why go to uni to be a farmer's wife?"

"But most parents want their kids to do well, you could have gone to agricultural college. Did you want to go?"

"I thought about it, it would've got me away from Steve. We did talk about it once, but my father said 'what can they teach you there that you can't get here'." She laughed — an unhappy laugh of derision and frustration. "How can you answer that?"

He said: "I've heard comments like that before."

She went on: "I'm the daughter, a girl. It never occurred to them I might have a brain or ideas of my own. And of course Steve's family were dead against it, worried I'd meet someone else. It was never a serious option."

"It's not too late Kate. There's a big world out there waiting for you."

She'd left her chair by the fire to wander round the room looking at his paintings again. She stood before the old man eating his supper and glanced round at James who was pouring coffee. She said: "Yes, I have a lot to learn — art, politics, the ways of the world — so much." She paused then said, in a strong, firm voice: "And sex, I need to know about sex — will you teach me?"

He spilled coffee on the carpet. "Jesus! That's the sort of invitation men dream of."

"Will you?"

"You want to learn about sex? — Would that be theory or practical?" The flippancy was an effort to conceal the conflicting sensations ripping through his body.

"Both maybe. But I think I know the theory."

"And when do you want to begin these lessons, madam?" He tried to keep his voice steady.

"This evening maybe," she said. "I like being close to you so I suppose that means the chemistry must be right between us."

"I think it could be," he said. Then in a serious voice: "Do you know what you're saying. It's not that simple, we could both get hurt. I'm a lot older than you, is it really a good idea?"

"Yes," she crossed the room and put her arms around his neck. "Last night when you touched me, it felt so good. I didn't want it to stop, I had a sort of need. Never had that before."

He pulled her arms down and clasped her hands together in his own, frowning at her, confused by his own feelings. "Kate, you're wonderful and I can't think of anything better than exploring your body. But you mustn't rush ahead so fast."

"But I feel safe with you. It just seems right."

He breathed in deeply. "Does it?" He struggled to control his longing to touch her and dropped her hands to draw her close. "I won't do anything you don't want but I will do this."

He swept the hair off her face and tilted her head, kissing her throat before pressing his mouth hard on hers. She stiffened and he thought she would pull away but the fleeting hesitation passed and her arms were around his neck again, opening her mouth eagerly against his.

He murmured: "I hope you don't expect me to be detached about this."

"No, it wouldn't work."

Her pale silk sweater was soft to the touch as he pulled it over her head and pressed it against his face to catch the scent of her. She raised her arms to help him and stood quietly as he undid the bra and dropped it on the floor.

"It starts with these," he said, kissing each breast in turn and nuzzling against them. He felt her tremble. "That should give you pleasure, so you want more and more of me and that makes it good for me you see."

"Yes," she whispered.

He stepped back to gaze at the half naked girl — undressed she was slighter than he expected, small sharp breasts with wide dark aureoles around the nipples, hard now in anticipation of his touch.

"You're very lovely," he whispered and the intensity of his gaze made her blush. "You're beautiful."

"I'm not. I'm very ordinary."

"You're not ordinary, you're young and unspoilt and healthy and just gorgeous."

"Steve never said anything like that."

"Let's not talk about him," he said but couldn't stop himself asking: "Did he often see you naked?"

"No, probably twice and that was ages ago. He didn't seem to notice what I looked like, he just wanted to grope me."

"We won't mention him again. I don't want to know what you did with him. Let's forget it."

"Very little — believe me."

"I do and I'm glad. But the thought of it puts me off."

Anger at the thought of her with someone else made him want to crush her against his body and kiss her savagely. But that would ruin everything. Instead he said: "You'd better put your sweater on, you'll get cold."

"Why? Don't you want me?" He saw tears welling in her eyes.

"Of course I want you. For fuck's sake, what d'you think? But the mood's gone, the moment's passed. It's all right. Come here by me," he beckoned her as he sat down.

He put an arm round her, snuggling her against him, stroking her hair and face. Gently he kissed her on the cheek, saying: "This is all a bit sudden and a bit dodgy. I need time to think what I'm doing. What we're both doing. It's bound to cause a lot of trouble."

"I know," she whispered. "I understand if you can't be bothered with me. But I feel good with you, I can't help it."

"I know and that's what worries me, but I don't know if I'm ready for all that — and I'm not really free."

She looked miserable as she said: "I didn't realise you had someone."

"I haven't. Not really," he paused.

She moved away, peering at him to discover his meaning and said softly: "I know you were in Bosnia — everyone knows that much about you. It must have been awful. Was it someone you knew there?"

He nodded. "She died, you see. Her name was Katya." He reached for her hand and stared at her: "You're like her in some ways, that's what makes it so unsettling."

"Can you tell me about it?"

"Not sure, I haven't told anyone but maybe I can tell you."

With an arm around her and his lips against her hair, his voice at times hardly audible, he began to talk about Sarajevo.

Chapter eight

The snow lay almost a foot deep, the city at the mercy of guns embedded on the surrounding hills and the howling wind gusting through boards on shattered windows. There was no power -- the supply main destroyed weeks before by the shelling. James had a torch but they used it sparingly to conserve the battery and for hours at a time the family huddled with a candle in the wreckage of the kitchen. The cafe at the front was open to the elements and Katya's valiant mother-in-law Esma, had given up trying to keep tables ready for customers who never came. Staying alive was the main preoccupation of everyone in the city, no one had time for coffee and a chat and anyway coffee was almost unobtainable.

As protection from the winter cold and for cooking they had an open fire, their only source of warmth, fed by whatever wood could be found among bombed-out buildings. But that was getting harder to find, since so many of the population had the same quest each day. They had a small store of paraffin which provided dim light from an ancient lamp but most of the time they used candles because the cafe had always kept a good stock for the tables.

James no longer did his job — he should have been with the rest of the press corps, holed up in the Holiday Inn but he had moved in to be with Katya and sending despatches from the battered street was impossible. With bitter cynicism he knew that whatever he told the world would make no difference and he was too close to the issues. He'd become part of it, in danger every day of injury or death. He'd gone there to find out about the misery of Bosnia and he knew it now at first hand, all the grim details, pinned down for weeks by the Serb artillery which commanded the heights around the city. Even the heavy snow had not interrupted the murderous intensity or the determination of the troops to batter their erstwhile neighbours into submission.

The cafe was in the mainly Muslim quarter, where fewer Serbs or Croats lived and the big guns were concentrated on that area. The snipers too trained their telescopic sights on any pedestrian out in the streets, knowing there was a good chance it wouldn't be 'one of theirs'.

The TV crew had lost touch with him, they'd given up on him when he went native as they put it, retreating to the comparative safety of the hotel. He couldn't bring himself to join them and the last instruction he'd been given was to pack up and go home. He should've left months ago but he wouldn't leave Katya. He couldn't bear the thought that if he left her, he might never see her again.

Pledging to return after the war was pointless, with the future of the whole region in doubt and nothing was certain in that turmoil. To leave her would be to lose her. And in those harrowing months she had come to mean everything to him, a beautiful, gentle, loyal woman who by an accident of marriage was on the wrong side. Knowing her and the family brought home to him the awful stupidity of the whole conflict, comparing it with Ulster, only so much worse. You couldn't tell by looking at someone if they were Catholic or Protestant — and here in the Balkans the racial differences were so slight that it was impossible for him as an outsider to know who was a Muslim and who an Orthodox Christian or a Catholic. When he'd first met her in the cafe he hadn't considered who she was or might be, she was simply an attractive woman who spoke excellent English.

Religion meant little to him — if he thought about it at all, it was that all the major doctrines of the world — Islam, Christianity, Judaism were essentially the same in owning one god and teaching principles of humanity and caring. That was how he saw it. So he found it impossible to understand the hatred ripping apart a nation which had been at peace for so long and in the same cause murdered young soldiers and innocent bystanders in the streets and fields of Ireland.

Arif, the father of the young volunteer who had briefly been Katya's husband, tried to explain the deep differences which had surfaced so tragically in the Balkans. He listened as the dark-haired man, now grey in middle-age but still strong and vigorous, spoke proudly of his country and its mixed heritage and he realised the fierce independence that drove them. He marvelled again how Tito had held it all together for so long.

He had plenty of time to ponder on the tragedy and wonder if it was simply repression like all communist states or did the man himself give them something more, a pride perhaps, a belief in the concept of Yugoslavia. Long gone now. And as in Ireland, it was history that counted, the Serbs and Croats mouthing the word Turk about their Muslim neighbours, animosity from the old days when the Turkish empire ruled the Balkans. Dislike that turned into hatred.

He understood the hatred spawned in the war when the Croatian Catholics had backed the Nazis. Black deeds on all sides were hard to forget and bitterness lingered. But what he couldn't comprehend was how a man who'd lived by his neighbours all his life, maybe shared their table and seen their children grow, could suddenly set fire to their home and watch them burn to death or cut them down as they tried to escape. In this conflict people murdered each other without pity or compunction.

He'd been in Sarajevo for the winter Olympics, a young reporter, keen and idealistic and he remembered the thrill of it, the excitement, the brilliant snow for the skiers and the magnificent ice stadium where Torville and Dean's magical skating held the world enthralled. He'd walked out with Katya in the summer to look at it, a weed-strewn wreckage of twisted metal.

Now as they sat trying to keep warm, hungry but not yet starving, that all seemed a dream, another distant world and he found it impossible to balance those scenes of pleasure and international sociability with the carnage and bloodshed he'd witnessed in the city.

"We've got to get out," he was saying as he'd been saying for weeks to Arif and Esma as much as to Katya.

And always the answer was the same. "This is our home, if we leave we lose everything, we may never be able to come back. You should go James, use the tunnel, they will let you through, you have only to say who you are."

"Not without Katya."

"But she cannot go without paying, the army wants dollars for civilians and we have no dollars."

Exasperated James would say: "I'll go to the hotel, one of them will give me the money, my credit's good."

But they wouldn't listen, they were determined to stay and he wouldn't leave without Katya. "Come with me to England, forget all this, there's nothing here for you, your parents, your child, your husband, all gone, why stay? Come back with me and start a new life," he said but she would shake her head and murmur: "This is my country, my home."

Or as they lay together, on a mattress at the back of the kitchen, with the old couple not far away, he would whisper to her: "What is it? Don't you love me? I love you Katya, I want to marry you. This life is a lost cause for you, in England you could be happy. Don't you want to be with me?"

"Yes, of course. But how can I leave them, I am all they have now. Mirko was their last son, the other three are all dead too. We have only each other."

The argument had gone on like this for more than a month, since the night the cafe had been blasted by a shell landing in the street outside. They were lucky, two houses in the same block had been demolished and most of the people killed. Windows were shattered and frontages wrecked all down the street and the inhabitants retreated to the kitchens and cellars. The constant shelling from the Serbs meant everyone lived in the knowledge that a direct hit would kill them all.

He surprised himself by the way he adjusted to this simple fact, not especially brave, he just accepted it as reality and his life had never been so good that he should be afraid to lose it if his name was on the shell. He wondered at his own stoicism but that helped him understand the resilience of the people, how they found the courage to carry on. Not just courage but a bloody-minded determination not to be beaten. That was why Arif and Esma would not leave, it was their property and when it was all over they would rebuild it into a thriving cafe, or die trying.

He thought often about the tunnel, the idea that once through it they would be out of the Serbs' reach and among Bosnian and UN troops made him determined to keep trying to persuade Katya, if not her parents. He made up his mind to visit the hotel to borrow the cash he needed.

The journey on foot held real danger and he hurried through the streets, avoiding wrecked cars and running people, seeing what little traffic there was swerving or screeching to a halt when a shell landed ahead of them.

The international media guests at the Holiday Inn were surprised to see him, his friend Josh, correspondent for a leading US paper, hurried forward to grab his hand. "Jim boy, how're you doing? We all thought you'd gone home. What you doing, why aren't you here with us?"

"I've got a place down in the city, it's rough now but it's okay."

"Why're you there? It's not safe. Mind, it ain't that safe here."

"No. But there's someone —"

"Oh, I get it! You got a girl down there."

James nodded. "Listen Josh, I need some help, I wanna get out — with her. I need dollars."

Josh stepped back with a sharp intake of breath which made James' heart sink.

"That's not so easy now," his friend said. "We're all running low on dollars, plenty of local."

"They want dollars for the tunnel."

"I know. How much d'you need?"

"I don't know, I'm told it depends who's in charge — even what day it is."

The others in the group had gathered round to listen. Someone said: "They won't charge you, just show them your press pass."

"I need the money for her, for Katya."

"She must be something special."

"She is."

"Oh, Jim boy, you shouldn't have got involved, not in this city, not right now."

"I know. It just happened."

"Like it always does," Josh said.

"Oh come on, guys, you gotta help me. You know you'll get it back and they'll surely send money in on one of the drops."

Josh glanced around: "I haven't got enough on my own." He looked hard at the others. "Can we do a whip-round? Help the guy get his girl back home?"

The room went quiet with hesitation, then hands rustled in pockets and handbags opened. Josh went round collecting the proffered notes but got only shaking heads from three of the Brits. Anita, a woman he'd known very well in London, went to him and took his hand saying: "I'm really sorry, I've only got sterling — you know I'd help if I could."

"Thanks. It's got to be dollars."

"Right, what we got," Josh counted the dollar bills. "There you go, Jim, one hundred and fifteen bucks. That's the best we can do, just hope it's enough for you."

"That's brilliant. I can surely persuade them with that. Thanks guys, I owe you."

"You sure do," Josh said grinning. "Good luck to you, Jim, you're gonna need it."

That night, as they lay together listening to the wind whine like a voice of despair, James whispered: "I've got the money, the dollars. We must go, it's getting worse by the day. What's the point of staying here to die?"

She was sleepy and murmured: "Leave me alone, we'll talk about it tomorrow."

But he'd already told Arif he had the money and in the morning as they were talking her father-in-law suddenly said: "You should go with him. Get out while you can."

"But dada, how can I leave you?"

"You should go. If the Serbs take the city we could all die or at least lose everything. He's right, there's nothing for you here. If you love him, go with him to Britain. It makes sense."

Katya said nothing. She looked at James who waited in silence. She turned to her mother-in-law. "Esma, what do you say?"

"You should go. Arif talked to Berin this morning. His cousin got through from Tuzla, the Serbs are tightening their grip, nothing can stop them. The foreigners seem powerless and they say the butcher Mladic has sworn to wipe us out. He says he will cleanse Sarajevo of Muslims."

"What have you heard?" asked James quietly.

"Just that," said Arif. "Your UN can do nothing — or will not — and Karadic defies them all. He says let them bomb, these mountains are his friend, they hide so much.

"Why were the partisans so effective against the Germans? You know why — it is guerrilla country, every tree and rock makes it hard for an ordinary army. The Serbs cannot lose unless we get arms to fight them on their own terms."

James listened, catching the despairing acceptance in the old man's voice.

"But surely the UN and the rest of Europe won't let that happen? They're negotiating, they've sent troops."

"Huh!" Arif's laugh was bitter. "Troops. With their blue helmets, they look pretty but they do nothing. And this talking — it's just talk. Why won't they give us guns? We need weapons to defend ourselves."

"Yes," said James. "We need to fight."

"There are worse things," Arif went on, "rumours of massacre. It's hard to get the facts but there may be many hundreds dead, buried in the woods and fields. And Mladic's men are raping too, taking young women to their barracks and to hotels — and some are shot. It gets worse by the day. No, my child," he drew Katya to him. "Get out with James while you still can. Much as we love you as our daughter, we must part. Get out and be happy with him."

Esma said: "Go tomorrow, before the snow gets worse, it's bad now but it will get colder."

"The snow may be your friend," said Arif. "The blizzard will make it harder for the Serbs to find their targets."

James listened and asked Katya: "I don't mind tramping through the snow but what about you?"

"I'm tough enough, James. D'you think a little snow will stop me. But with luck we won't need to walk far, the group from Tuzla are going back, we'll get a lift in their truck. Dada, will you find out?"

He looked at her with delight. "So you'll come?" he said.

She nodded and smiled. "You think it is so easy to get out — you know we may die trying."

Smiling he began to dismiss her words as unnecessary fears but was stopped, chilled by the look on their faces. Arif said softly: "She's right."

"But I'm British! Why would they kill me?"

"You might not get the chance to tell them who you are. In that thick local jacket and hat, you look Bosnian and they'd shoot you before they found out. "

"But surely they wouldn't shoot innocent people, women or children, just on sight?"

"Have you learned nothing? You came here to cover our war. Do you still not understand? If they think you are Muslim they will kill you — no matter what they tell the UN. Out there in the snow where no one can see, you'll be just one less piece of rubbish. When they find your British passport they'll be very sorry and say it was an accident — but you'll be dead just the same. "

"But even war has rules," James said weakly.

Arif laughed. "Not this war. Too personal, too much hatred on both sides. Kill or be killed. The mountains are full of dead, some buried, some left to rot where they fell, little massacres all over this country. And when it's over, the world will find out and be shocked and call for retribution and trials for atrocities. But the dead will still be dead."

Shaken, James stared at him. "But surely — " he began but Arif went on: "Have I shocked you? You reporters, even you, who live with us — you don't understand. It's not just the Serbs, my people too do dreadful things, people burned in their homes, children battered against walls. If you get out, tell them, tell them what is really happening here. But it will make no difference."

Through the night he couldn't sleep, lying close to Katya but with Arif's words churning in his head. They'd not talked much in the past and the man's eloquence surprised him, though it shouldn't, he was well-educated and in business all his life. But he hadn't expected it, relying on the image of

Bosnians as peasant farmers which was maybe true in rural areas but not in the modern sophisticated city that Sarajevo had become — until so recently.

Arif's talk made him afraid in a way that all the months of horror in the city had not affected him. For the first time the reality of the war and the guns made him fear the journey which he'd been so keen to start. Not fear of death itself but of dying in pain and indignity — and a greater fear for Katya. Towards morning he slept a little and woke in the dark dawn, his mind full of dread for the night ahead.

Arif returned with news that the Tuzla group weren't leaving till next day. They were to meet the truck two streets away on the Alipasina, it couldn't get nearer through the uncleared rubble and dead cars blocking the way. It would pick them up as soon as darkness came and drop them where the tunnel began.

Afterwards he couldn't remember many details of the truck journey, except crouching in a doorway in a dark street then helping Katya into the back of the old-fashioned canvas screened vehicle like an army lorry, very high off the street for her to climb in. The city was quiet, the guns still for a while, with more snow falling as Esma had predicted, not heavy but steady — tiny, biting particles of ice which stung as they hit his face. Always in the future he could recall Arif hugging him, telling him they would meet again in better times.

Esma kissed him and could hardly speak as she held back tears and clung to Katya and he had to pull her away as the men in the lorry urged them to hurry, then he was gazing back at the couple standing together in the snow until the truck turned a corner.

Huddling close to Katya in the dark truck he had no idea how far it was they travelled but the journey seemed slow, with several halts and some reversing to get round obstacles. When they stopped he heard urgent voices talking quietly and gunfire in the distance. The canvas back lifted and a man spoke to Katya but he couldn't catch the meaning and looked at her for explanation. He flashed his torch as she spoke and saw the anxiety in her face. "What's wrong?" he asked.

"We can't go this way, the tunnel is closed."

"Why?"

The man with her spoke in English: "Water — tunnel is flooded. Must be pumped, no good tonight."

"How long before it's open?" he asked.

Katya spoke to him in Bosnian, looking devastated as she listened to the reply. "He says it could be three days, the flooding is bad and the pumps take a long time to clear it."

She sighed: "He says we must go back. They will turn off and try to get through on a hill track to bypass the Serbs. If not they will wait in Sarajevo until the tunnel is open. He says we can wait and try again in three days."

Frowning James said: "Then let's do that. We should go back and wait with them."

"No. We have begun, now we have decided we should go on. It is bad luck to go back."

"But Katya, you've said no for so long, another three days won't matter."

"No! I won't go back. We've started the journey, we'll go over the mountain."

"In this snow?"

"We'll manage. If the truck can't get through we'll go on foot. I know a path that leads up from the stadium, we'll follow that."

"On foot?"

She smiled at him: "It's not a steep mountain and at night, in the snow under the trees we'll have plenty of cover."

As they debated their options the men grew restless, anxious to move. Every delay made the journey less safe and even without lights on the parked truck the shelling began again into the darkness. Their hold on the city had created a pervasive climate of fear and even these tough young fighters were jumpy and ill at ease.

When the truck's engine started James lifted the tarpaulin to peer at the bleak landscape as they reversed and started the journey back into the city. Snow covered the road and the marks of the truck's wheels were already filling with fine snow that hadn't ceased since they were picked up. They headed eastward branching off on the Alipasina again as it turned north, climbing towards the mountains and passing two of the Olympic stadiums.

The truck began to struggle on the slope, losing grip as the tyres slithered in the snow then James and Katya were thrown together as the vehicle slid back. The driver tried reversing out of the track and restarting in lowest gear but the engine whined and the tyres found no traction. A voice from the cab said in Bosnian: "It's no good, we'll have to go back. You can come back with us or we'll leave you here to try it on foot."

Katya answered in his own language and told James: "Get out, we'll go on foot."

"She was determined to do it," he said, bringing his thoughts back to the girl beside him. "That was when it all began to go wrong."

James stopped speaking, silent for several minutes staring into the fire and Kate, hardly daring to breathe, waited until he remembered she was with him.

He shook his head and looked at her, his face screwed into a frown. "That's when it all went wrong."

"We should have gone back but she wouldn't. She wouldn't listen. I'd tried all those weeks to persuade her but once she'd decided, that was it. She wouldn't go back."

Chapter nine

The wind made its presence known in an incessant moaning as they climbed from the truck and said their farewells and it increased to screaming pitch when it caught the overhead cables running up the hillside. The truck driver clasped James' arm and kissed him roughly on both cheeks saying: "Good luck." He and the other men saluted and echoed the call. The driver watched them move off before climbing back into his cab.

When the engine restarted James felt an unpleasant twinge in his guts and as the truck moved off he drew Katya closer to him. They watched the dark shape without lights grow gradually smaller and disappear into the snow. Then they stood alone on the path, silence around them except for the wind which seemed to gather strength now they were no longer sheltered by the truck.

He looked at her. "Right, no good standing here, which way do we go?"

"They said follow the road a little way and there's an opening in the trees. There's a grit dump there and the path leads up from that."

"Right, let's do it."

He kissed her warm forehead and held out his hand. She clasped it firmly and together they trudged up the road. Within half a kilometre they found the opening in the trees and the dump as promised and passing snow-hidden heaps of stone and grit, they headed on upwards. At the top of a bank was the path, leading steeply uphill.

James was depressed. "I thought you said it wasn't steep."

"It gets easier," Katya said, leading the way. But it was steep and rocky and in the darkness and snow, hard to see where they were going. He swore as he stumbled along. Katya seemed to find it easier, she went more slowly but steadily.

"Try to feel with your foot before you put it down each time," she said. "Then you will be more sure and stumble less."

He tried, following her footsteps in the deepening snow. They saw the darkness of a tree line ahead and he wondered how they would get on with even less light. "If the snow would stop and the sky cleared there would be a moon," he said pointlessly. "We'll have to use the torch."

"We should save it until we really need it," was all she said.

The snow made every step an effort and as the path climbed his ankles began to ache and his chest hurt with the heavy breathing. It was not a mighty climb, his memories of maps of the area told him these were not big mountains, little more than hills and he had done several gruelling treks in Cumbria and Scotland — but not trudging in deep snow, under-nourished and in fear of his life.

Katya seemed undaunted and as the trees closed round them he was grateful for her courage to boost his. He accepted they were on the mountain for the night at least — he had earlier supposed they would find somewhere to stay — but every step emphasised the stark reality of their situation. Increasingly he thought they should have waited, gone back to Arif's to wait for the tunnel and he called to Katya: "Wait. This is crazy, let's go back."

But she just said: "Going back will be as hard as going on."

He couldn't understand her sudden determination to press on through the snow. Nothing he had visualised before coming to the Balkans had prepared him for this. There was no breath for talking and when after an hour Katya sank onto an icy rock to rest, they just looked at each in silence.

Shivering he checked his watch: "It's nearly midnight. What do we do? Carry on? I feel useless. I haven't the remotest idea where we are or where we're heading. I just hope we were right to trust your friends."

"They wouldn't mislead us. Why would they? They say this track will take us above the Serb bunkers and down towards a UN base. We just have to keep going."

"That's all."

"At least there's a path."

"It's very narrow. Are you sure it's not just a goat track?"

"Yes, there is a way here over the mountain. Have faith. We will get through."

He could barely make out what she said, her words distorted through numb lips and her body shaking with cold as they huddled closer together for comfort but she whispered: "We shouldn't stop, we stay warmer if we keep going."

"Shall we eat something," he asked — they had a little food, bread and cheese and some biscuits but he longed for hot coffee. He'd lost his flask, smashed early on in the bombing.

Katya shook her head. "Let's wait, it's not so long since we ate."

"Long enough and that wasn't much. But you're right, we should move on, the snow's getting thicker."

They struggled upright and faced the hill. The snow was heavy now, falling in large flakes driven at an angle by the wind which rose in volume as they started to walk again. When people spoke or wrote of the howling wind it was just words, he thought, but as it rushed through the pine trees it sounded like some demented creature. Ahead the trees ended and the path curved and dipped. As they rounded the turn the land fell away sharply before their feet and they saw the track lead on, clinging to a cliff face for several hundred yards.

Katya gasped, for the first time showing anxiety but he said firmly: "It won't be as bad as it looks, it's quite wide but we must be careful not to slip."

With the change of direction and without the shelter of the trees they felt the full ferocity of the wind strafing their skin. James touched his cheek but couldn't feel it, just the repeated blasting effect of the blizzard. The driving snow reduced the visibility to a few yards and he switched on the torch but its tiny beam couldn't penetrate the curtain of white. A stumble on this path could send them plunging down into the darkness. It looked as if a whole section of the hill had slid away, leaving a slice missing because very soon they saw the dark shape of a rock formation on their left and the path ran back into sheltering trees.

"Thank God," he said though the cold was no less intense and he wondered how long they could go on like this. Katya didn't speak, she was following now, putting one foot before the other with a stoical determination but he could tell from the way her neck was bent that it was becoming a greater effort every moment.

"Maybe we should rest again," he called through the wind.

"If we stop we could die," she said huskily, her throat dry and sore from cold.

"We must find shelter," James said, hearing how pointless it sounded. Where on this wind blasted mountain was there shelter? The trees were too slender to provide protection, probably there might be rocks somewhere which might help, but where? He knew they dare not leave the path, the snow filled their footsteps within minutes. If they became lost in the forest they would not survive.

Katya caught up with him as he waited but wouldn't stop. He tried supporting her but it was little help. Her breath came in heaving gulps but she managed to say between gasps: "I've been here before. I remember the rock slip back there. We came here years ago, Mirko and me, in summer. It was beautiful then," she added. "If it's the same track there was a hut somewhere, for the goat boys."

He stared at her, hoping her memory was correct. "That would save us."

"If we haven't missed it, we must look carefully, it was a short way off the path."

"Oh God! Surely we would've noticed a building."

"It was just a hut and several years ago. It may've gone."

"Please God it's still there," he said.

His mind whirled with strange emotions — he'd grown used to the fear of a freezing death on this mountain. If it happened, it happened and there was nothing he could do but accept the inevitable without panic or horror. But now the thought of shelter, of a hut, however poor, somewhere ahead of them, created a terrible fear. If it wasn't there, if they'd passed it already in the dark. The thoughts brought him near to panic and he found himself trying to move faster, ploughing ahead, peering from side to side along the path.

Only Katya's pleading brought him back to reality — for a moment he'd forgotten her. Her voice behind him: "James! Wait for me, I can't keep up with that pace."

Turning he waited. She was moving so slowly now, each step dragged by force of will alone, each foot placed in the snow before the next, her mind concentrated entirely on achieving that one step and the next beyond that. He knew she wouldn't get much further, only a matter of time before she collapsed. And he doubted his ability to carry her, he'd try; but he imagined them huddled together in the snow, while cold and exhaustion overcame them and fresh snow, falling thicker than ever, quickly covered them to become another lump in the landscape. Watching her, pitying her struggle, he wondered how long it would be before their bodies were found, perhaps not for years as this war went on. They would probably be eaten by some wild creature, bears still roamed in Bosnia and there were wolves and foxes, crows or birds of prey.

Curiously he didn't mind that, it seemed a clean way of death. He didn't consider these as black thoughts but simply facts of life — or death as it would soon be. He'd feared death as all men do but he had seen so much of it in his short life that it was just another statistic, even his own death. And it seemed to him, hard and cold as it was on the mountain, that it was a gentle way of dying and there were many worse.

He held out his hand to Katya, clasped it in his sodden glove and said: "Never mind my love, not much further to go, it'll soon be over."

Slowly they pushed on, side by side, step by step, his arm around her, walking awkwardly together, as she leaned on him and found it easier but made it more difficult for him. He was sinking into stupor, if he lost his senses that would be it; once he lost consciousness, that would be the end. He didn't care, it was finished and the snow would cover them. Stumbling on into the wind that blew still harder he thought with longing of English tea and hot toast.

When they came to the clearing it didn't register at first, he passed stacked lengths of pine trunks without noticing. They were half way across the open space before he realised there were no trees. He glanced to his right and looked again. It was there, they'd found it. A little way up the cleared slope was the shape of a hut, the goatherd's hut.

"It's there, the hut. You were right."

Katya mumbled something but didn't raise her head and he saw she was barely conscious. He half carried her the short distance to the hut and tried the door. If it was locked he didn't think he had the strength to force it. But it opened and he went in without a thought off caution. If there were an enemy within it could be no worse than the deadly foe outside. Total darkness stunned his eyes after the snow, he fumbled for the torch and his numb fingers struggled to switch it on. The light flashed round the room and showed him a bare space with a bench down one side and a rough table. He carried Katya to the bench and set her down. She blinked and asked where they were. It was cold in the hut but the sudden cessation of wind and snow made it feel like comfort. He smiled at her in the torch light.

"We made it," he whispered, kissing her cold face. "Now we can eat."

She was too tired and cold for hunger but he made her eat and the effort revived her. Now they were safe for a while he felt more confident, able to cope and after food he looked round to see what was in the building. Not much, a few cups and beakers but nothing to put in them and a pile of blankets and sacks. They were musty and damp to the touch and in the torchlight he saw they weren't clean. He didn't care how dirty they were, they meant warmth. The hut had a basic fireplace at one side with a rough stone chimney up through the wooden roof, beside it a stack of wood but he was so cold he couldn't tell if it was damp or dry.

"There's wood here, shall I try to light a fire," he asked.

"No one could see the smoke in this storm," she said. "It should be safe but can you light it?"

"I'll try."

He had a lighter in his pocket and there was an old magazine under the bench. He rumpled it up with pages from his notebook to build a pyramid of logs. He lit the paper and the flames roared up in a cheerful brightness. But they didn't last and sank away, unable to catch hold on the damp wood. The logs smouldered and grew black but wouldn't burn. He knelt and blew to fan the sparks but little happened. He swore in frustration then noticed a candle stub on a stone ledge near the fireplace.

"What do we need most, heat or light?"

"Heat," she said without hesitation.

"Right."

He tore out more of his notebook and relaid the logs — they were at least warmed now — with the candle strategically placed in the heart of the pile. Then he tried again. This time the blaze lasted longer and with joy he heard the hiss as the candle melted, the flames flared higher fed by the wax and he heard the first ecstatic crackle of burning wood.

The fire was small and gave little heat but by kneeling close it was sufficient to warm their numbed hands and faces.

When he felt thawed enough to speak he looked at her crouched close to him and said slowly: "We should have waited, three more days wouldn't have mattered. It was a mistake to come this way."

She didn't look at him but muttered: "It had to be this way, I didn't want to go back."

"I don't understand, Katya. All those weeks I was trying to persuade you, why couldn't we return and wait for the tunnel."

She groaned. "I can't explain. But I knew if we went back I couldn't bear to leave again. It seemed so unfair to them, Arif and Esma."

"But three days — just three more days and we would've been safe. We had the money, it was so simple."

"It'll be all right James, we'll get through, I know we will."

"I wish I could be so sure — we may not survive this, you know that."

"We're here, safe in the hut, the worst is over. Trust me, James."

He sighed and stared at the miserable fire.

Then he remembered the slivovitz. He'd kept one of the whisky miniatures from the flight when he first came out and refilled it before they left from the big jar Esma kept in the kitchen.

Tucked in the inside pocket of his padded jacket he'd forgotten about it, so small, wrapped in a handkerchief for protection. They'd swallowed snow to quench their thirsts after the bread and cheese but the spirit would revive them. Katya sipped the fiery liquid and grimaced as it hit her throat. She handed it back to him with a shudder. "It's rough," she said. "I've never liked it but now I've never tasted anything better."

He took a swig and held his wrist near the fire, the watch showed well after two.

"Shall we try to sleep?" he asked. "We'd be crazy to go on tonight."

"Yes," she agreed. "It won't be so bad in daylight."

"I'll make up the fire, try to keep it going. We'll sleep better if we can stay warm."

The relative warmth of the hut made it almost cosy and he piled more logs on and around the little fire to keep it burning low but steady.

They both coughed in the damp dust as he shook out the musty blankets and laid the sacks on the bench to make a bed. They huddled together in the narrow space, under the three blankets and Katya tucked her head against his chest with her hand between his thighs. The scent of her hair in his nostrils masked the damp odours of the hut, more evident in the growing warmth.

He thought he'd never sleep, troubled by aimless memories. When he whispered: "Are you awake?" there was no reply but he listened happily to her breathing. He moved to get comfortable and relaxed against her, the shape unfamiliar in the rough outdoor clothes. He felt his way inside her jacket, nestling his hand there, drifting gradually into sleep.

Something tickling his nose made him open his eyes to find her smiling as she trailed a piece of dried grass across his face.

"Wake up, sleepy. It's morning and look, the sun is shining." He sat up and peered through the grimy window to see that indeed the snow was bright with sunlight, glistening in the winter rays .

"We are warm now and rested and the snow has stopped so all we have to do is get up and walk down the mountain."

She laughed at his glum face. "Come on, where's your British optimism, your stiff lip?"

"Stiff upper lip you mean. It was stiff all right last night, frozen stiff. We may have to go higher yet before we come down and I'm so hungry."

"It's not so bad. It can't be far now and even if we have to walk all day, we shall make it. I know we shall and then we can eat all we want. I think, from before, that the path goes no higher. It winds round the mountain and then down the other side. I hope my memory is right but we should soon start downhill."

"Let's hope so." He looked at her. "You look remarkably good for a girl who's just spent a night in a grubby hut under dirty blankets."

"I had a good sleep and I know all will be well. Suddenly I am happy. I was unsure about leaving but now I think it is the right thing and I will come with you to England and perhaps get a job and maybe we'll stay together?

"Of course we'll stay together. You'll be my wife." He looked at her uncertainly realising what he'd said: "That is, if you want to marry me?

She laughed again and asked: "Do you think I'll make an English wife? Will I be suitable?"

"Very suitable." He kissed her, feeling the familiar desire as he held her close. She kissed him back but pushed him away saying: "No, no, we have no time for that now."

"But you have not said."

"Said what?"

"Well, I have proposed to you, as we call it, and you haven't given me an answer."

The look she gave him then, filled with such love and longing, he would remember all down the years, her eyes fixed on his, all laughter gone as she leaned to him and kissed his mouth and whispered: "You are my life, how could I refuse you anything?"

In silence they gazed at each other, before he took her hand, saying: "Till now I hadn't realised how much I love you. I never thought I'd love someone, not really be in love. It's not given to everyone, mostly make do. I didn't think I'd be so lucky. Thank you for loving me. We'll survive and we'll be happy and you'll like Britain, I know you will."

As he spoke they heard, quite near, the plaintive cry of an eagle, calling in the clear blue air, hunting while it had the chance after the snow and wind. They went out into the snow brightness and looked up to watch the bird wheeling overhead.

"James, when we are in England, will you take me to see the kites?"

He laughed and kissed her. "They're mostly in Wales."

"But that's not difficult is it, you have no border controls there?"

"No." He laughed again. "No visa needed for Wales, not yet anyway. Yes, we'll go and see the kites and think of this and the eagle. Do you think he's come to wish us luck?"

She nodded. "Yes."

He hugged her and they took the last of the biscuits from his pocket and set off munching them, back to the forest path which in daylight with the clean, fresh snow and the sunlight, looked almost inviting. The path seemed wider as they walked hand in hand, going slightly uphill to a crest where they looked out on a vista of forest and white hills. The sky was incredibly blue, azure, like a dome above the wilderness which seemed to stretch for miles. But in the distance they saw the flash of sun on metal, cars, the road, the road that meant escape. They smiled at each other and Katya said: "This is the right path, if we follow it'll bring us through. It looks so peaceful, it's hard to believe what's happening here."

Listening in the silent landscape they heard the eagle call again but another sound they knew too well. The boom of heavy guns, Serb artillery and with it the crackle of small arms fire, rifle fire — how far off they couldn't tell. They waited in the shelter of the trees as the big guns rumbled but he judged they must be several miles distant. There were Serb bunkers all over these hills but they had no way of knowing how close they might be.

"We must go on," he said. "We don't know how far we have to go. We can't spend another night in the open."

She nodded and gripped his hand, the mood of happiness spoiled by the gunfire. She clung to his hand as a child does, for security, trusting that together they would get through. The trees thinned out and the path led downhill, though he still wondered if there might be another mountain to climb. But the going was easier, the snow less deep on this side and they made good progress. They began to talk again, about Britain — he told her of his father's farm in Wiltshire that he should be running now. She asked a lot of questions about livestock in Britain, she couldn't believe that some of the farms milked 300 or more cows a day. He told her what he knew about dairying in Britain, which wasn't much but she was fascinated.

"You don't want to be a farmer's wife, do you?" he asked laughing. "I had a mighty fight to get away from farming, I don't want to go back to it. Still, with you I suppose it could be fun."

He was watching her happy face, now relaxed with the thought of safety; he smiled and she half turned to him. It was so sudden, the noise just a snapping sound, not even a crack but he saw the shock and pain as she stumbled and he fell with her headlong into the snow. He heard the second shot, sensed it whistle above them. Hugging her to him he rolled a little way from the path and lay still. Glancing back he saw their broad trail in the snow, stained with blood. That was when he knew it was bad.

She groaned and moved against him. "What was it?"

"Sniper."

His hand at her back was wet with blood, he pulled away to look, the bullet had hit her below the ribs and gone straight through. The hole in her back was gaping, he'd seen wounds like that before and was amazed she was conscious. He felt numb but clear-headed, thinking what to do. He laid her down in the snow and she whispered: "I think you must go on alone, I can't walk any further. I shall die here."

She was so calm. "Does it hurt much?" he asked foolishly.

She shook her head "You must leave me and go."

"No, I can't leave you."

He tried to concentrate. His scant knowledge of First Aid told him the wound was bad, very bad but if he could staunch it for a while and get her to help there might be a chance. He took off his coat, struck by the cold but stripped his sweater as well. Gently he turned her and somehow contrived to staunch the hole, tying the sweater around her by the sleeves and buttoning the coat round her shoulders. It was little enough and a poor effort but he could think of nothing else. He knew he shouldn't move her but he had to.

Part of him knew it was hopeless but he weighed up the chances. She couldn't stay there, it was already afternoon and soon the short day would be gone and the temperature which was hovering around freezing, would plummet with darkness. She would die there, of the cold or the injury, whichever got her first. So there was only one decision, he had to get her somewhere for help.

He whispered: "Katya, can you hear me?" She didn't answer but when he shook her gently she murmured: "James."

She was barely conscious, a mercy for her, he thought, the pain must be bad, unless the shock had dulled it.

Then he thought of the marksman out there somewhere and they highly visible among the thinning trees. If they moved they could be hit again. But if he waited for darkness there was no chance for her. Crawling back towards the path he studied the terrain but saw nothing except snow and trees and the eagle wheeling in the distance.

In so much cover the sniper could be anywhere but maybe on the far ridge between them and the road. It was not that far to the road — and yet so far. The path went down into thicker trees, he estimated about half a mile. But half a mile was a long way running the gauntlet of sniper fire carrying an injured woman. But he had no choice.

He was cold without his coat yet sweating in raw fear at the knowledge that at any moment he too could have a bloody hole in him letting his life pump out into the snow. His bowels churned and he crawled away from Katya to crouch behind a snowy bush. His stomach had been upset with a bout of dysentery through the last days in Sarajevo but this was pure nerves. The thought of death was bad enough but the indignity of shitting himself was unbearable. At least let it be a clean death.

He cleansed himself with the snow and crawled back to Katya. She lay very still and he thought she might be dead but she whispered as he came back: "You must go without me." He ignored the words, trying to think what to do, whether to somehow crawl with her down the path or get to his feet and carry her as best he could.

He decided to stand up. Crawling and dragging her would take too long. He couldn't believe she was still conscious but when he lifted and held her upright she took her own weight. He pulled her arm across his neck and held her round the waist. "Do you think you can move a little like this?" he asked.

She nodded. "I'll try. Is it far to the road, do you think?"
"Not far."

Slowly they moved down the path towards the trees, every second anticipating the thud of a bullet. She drooped against him, placing each foot like an automaton, each step slower as she got heavier and he supported her more and more. But they made it to the trees and he set her down and flopped with a groan beside her. She lay propped with her back against a snow bank and he watched it redden around her.

"Oh God," he whispered. "How far is it?"

He doubted his own strength to carry on and when he went to lift her she was unconscious. Her heart was still beating and the breath gasping but steady. He'd have to carry her. He got to his feet and somehow managed to raise her, staggering forward with her in his arms.

When he thought about it later he couldn't imagine how he did it, perhaps his tortured brain wouldn't let him recall summoning the strength to carry her through the snow. But he did. He reached the road and laid her down beside it, careless of who might come, whether Serb, Bosniak or UN. At least face to face he could tell them he was British and then maybe they wouldn't shoot him.

It was French UN troops who stopped, surprised to find them in that particular spot. Katya was placed on a stretcher, covered with a blanket and lifted into the back of the truck. James sat beside her, shuddering with cold as he held her hand while outside it began to snow again.

"I think it is very serious, Monsieur," the French captain said and he just nodded. Explanations and answers were for later.

They drove into a small town he didn't know and halted at a church. The Frenchman explained they were using it as a treatment centre because part of the hospital was damaged but the church too showed the impact of war. She was carried in and laid on the broken floor, an intricate mosaic depicting a saint with a golden halo. He noticed the pattern of each tiny stone and couldn't take his eyes from it, even as the priest was saying, with a hand on his shoulder: "This woman is dead, my son."

"No," he said. "She has a wound in her back, a bullet hole, it went right through but she was all right."

The doctor came and glanced at Katya before covering her face with the blanket. "I'm sorry," he said.

"A wound like that, in a decent hospital with proper equipment, if we'd seen it sooner, maybe she would've lived. But she lost too much blood — and the cold and the journey. I'm sorry."

James frowned in disbelief and uncovered her face, holding his hand over her mouth to feel breath that wasn't there. He knew they were right. He kissed her but the lips were pale and cold and though he tried to breath life into her, no answering breath responded. He stroked the hair back from her face, kissing the closed eyes in turn and gripping her hand until the priest came again to say: "You must leave her, you can do no more."

He drew the blanket back to cover her face and left her, lying on the mosaic with an icon of an infant Christ and his mother gazing down from the wall. Dazed he walked out into the street where a UN soldier was waiting for him in the fading light.

Chapter ten

His speech had become very slow, each word an effort and Kate leaned close to catch what he said. At last he ceased talking and sat hunched beside her.

She said nothing, waiting in silence until he recovered himself. When he looked at her again his eyes were bright with tears.

"Do you know what was worst? I didn't feel it, not then. She was dead but I went sort of numb and it became like any other story. It didn't seem to involve me. It wasn't till I got out in the street that it hit me and I realised I was on my own, she wasn't with me. As if it'd all been unreal and I'd just carry on with her beside me. But it wasn't like that — she wasn't there."

Kate didn't move but he took her hands and held on, gripping hard as if to a lifeline.

"I had to leave her. The soldiers took me out to the UN base, they wanted me away, to get rid of me. I tried to get a message to Arif and Esma, but it was hopeless. Not until I got back and contacted the guys at The Holiday Inn, they sent someone to the cafe. At least they said they would. I had to leave and I don't even know where she's buried."

"I'm so sorry — I had no idea —"

"Why would you? I haven't told anyone."

He clung to her hand and drew her close, leaning his head against hers. "Don't know why I'm telling you, but you're kind and you might understand." He sighed: "You deserve honesty from me if nothing else."

"What does that mean? You're saying you couldn't love anyone again? I can understand that," she said though her voice trembled.

But he answered quickly: "No, I'm not saying that — I don't know what I might feel in the future. I need to explain — why I might be difficult to be with."

"I only want a friend."

"No Kate, you want more than that. And so do I."

He hesitated, looking at her sharply: "I want you, and you know what I mean by that. But I don't want to hurt you, I like you too much for that."

She shook her head. "I'm not a child and I'm starting to know myself and what I want. I think I want you. I didn't realise what that meant, I've never felt anything like that." She kissed his cheek and with her free hand turned his face to brush his lips with hers. "I know what we're doing, James, if it goes wrong, so be it."

"Perhaps." He cuddled her to him and kissed her forehead. "It's very late, you should go home."

"I could stay."

"No, not yet, too many questions to answer."

He couldn't tell her how he really felt — drained and desolate, torn between wanting her, so vibrant in flesh and blood and painful ideas of disloyalty to the other he'd left in that church. He needed time to work it out.

He hadn't realised how the hours had flown, it was almost one o'clock. He asked: "Where will you say you've been?"

"Out. You keep telling me I'm not a child. I have to stand up for myself. It's the only way they'll accept I've finished with Steve."

"Brave words. But it won't be easy."

"I don't expect it to be."

She left with a kiss and he went to bed alone thinking of Katya. Telling the story brought it all back, memories so sharp it seemed like yesterday; the intense blue of the sky and the eagle crying overhead just before the bullet struck.

The grey spring dawn matched his mood, bleak and blustering outdoors and inside him that familiar emptiness, the physical result of a restless night and a brain that wouldn't shut down, leaving him exhausted to face the day. His thoughts lingered in Sarajevo with the images of them together that night on the mountain. He contemplated the hostile morning and took a long time to rouse himself. He rinsed his face with tepid water and thought of Kate hanging on his words. The implications of what they'd begun troubled him, given all the baggage she trailed.

He was glad it had gone no further, too easy to take advantage but she was worth more than that. She was going into it with her eyes open, asking him to teach her — what an offer. But she was vulnerable — sex lessons were fine in theory but that didn't allow for emotion.

That didn't stop him thinking about her and the parts of her he hadn't yet discovered and once downstairs he caught himself again watching for her car. It was Saturday and she would come to ride Harry.

The ewes were due to lamb any time and he was busy preparing the barn, setting up pens so that each unit of mother and lambs could be properly bonded before going out to pasture. Being a novice at the job he preferred to lamb inside, easier to handle problems and the spring weather could never be relied on not to change to bitter winds and hail that could destroy a newborn before it even breathed.

When the car came he saw she had Pat with her and scowled in disappointment.

They came across to the barn and she called. "Pat's come to help with Harry, she's going to exercise him while I do a thorough clean up."

He nodded, not pausing in his work, maintaining a pretence of indifference in front of Pat. She waited for him to speak but he ignored her.

"I had to bring her," she explained when Pat left. "She called round so it was easier to get away with her."

"So much for making a stand," he said.

She kissed his cheek, grinning: "You're very grumpy, you don't seem pleased to see me."

He put down the spanner he was holding. "Has she gone to saddle up?"

"Yes."

He leaned over the wooden wall between them and pulled her to him, kissing her roughly on the mouth. She began to pull away, her body tense with alarm for a moment before she kissed him back. He thrust a grubby hand inside her jacket to squeeze a handful of clothes and breast. It hurt and she flinched. He softened his grip and smiled, kissing her gently, deliberate, testing.

"Pass me that other spanner," he said.

She watched in silence while he bolted the pen together, ignoring her till he'd finished when he looked up into troubled eyes studying him.

He smiled: "Have I upset you, too rough?"

"I didn't mind." She sounded uncertain.

"But you didn't like it?"

"I didn't say that."

"Did it turn you on?"

"What do you mean?"

"What do I mean?" He spoke in jerks as he tightened bolts and fitted hurdles together. "I mean, did you want me to stop or go on? Were you sorry when I let go?"

"I'm not sure,"

"Was it horrible?"

"No. Because I wanted to kiss you."

"Could you feel it all the way down?"

She considered before nodding and he laughed delightedly, confusing her even more.

The change in his mood from last night troubled her. "You're teasing me," she said.

He didn't answer until he'd tightened the last bolt. "I must get this finished today, they'll start any time. But I need a drink."

She followed him to the house, her pride pricked by his behaviour. While the kettle boiled he beckoned her to him and she obeyed and stood close to him. Without a word he unzipped her jacket and reached behind to undo her bra. She gasped and tried to back away as he pulled up her sweater and bared her chest but he held her firmly, bending to mouth each nipple in turn. Squirming she protested: "I don't want to do this now."

"But I do," he murmured. She struggled a moment then gasped and went still as he spun her round and pushed his hand inside her jeans, fingers probing until she groaned and leaned back on him. "Kettle's boiling," he laughed and pushed her away. "And so will you be soon."

He studied her flushed face and the surprised eyes.

"You're very wet," he said quietly but she looked about to cry.

"Why are you being like this? Don't you care — it seems to have no effect on you."

"No? You can see what it does to me."

"'You can't treat me this way, I'm not your property to grab when you feel like it." He watched her, unsure if the deep blush suffusing her face and neck was desire or indignation.

He said: "Were you sorry when I took my hand away?"

"No! Well, that is — I don't know "

He made the coffee. "Kate, you're gorgeous and I'm longing to fuck you but I'm not going to, not till you really want me."

"You're so direct," she said,. "You frighten me when you're like this."

"Grown-up games. Now tell me — were you sorry when I took my hand away?"

"Yes," she whispered.

He smiled: "Come here." But she hesitated. "I won't hurt you. I won't do anything you don't want." He stroked her face and kissed her gently. "There — you're a sweet child and you've never had an orgasm, have you?"

"I don't think so."

"I think you'd know."

"Sex isn't Steve and his groping but it isn't all gentle and sweet either, it's hard and adult and sometimes close to pain. Can you cope with that?"

"I'm not a child."

"No indeed you're not. Drink the coffee, I must get on."

"Shall I stay and help?"

"If you want to — I can manage. What about your chaperone?"

"Pat'll go home when she gets back."

"Up to you, I could do with a hand but you don't have to. Its's okay, I won't grab you again."

"I might grab you," she said.

She helped him finish the pens and they did the stable together, finding the effort of work created an insouciance between them. This time when he suggested they go out for supper she agreed. She went home to change and he arranged to meet her in the lane at seven.

He waited with growing anxiety as the minutes ticked by but she didn't come. He knew she wouldn't stand him up, there would be a reason

By eight thirty he realised she wouldn't be coming and drove to the pub for a sandwich, with no appetite for anything more. The group he'd seen before was in the corner making a commotion, rowdy laughter and coarse jokes but Kate's would-be lover wasn't there. They were eating steak and chips, girls and young men swilling pints, smoking while they ate. He looked away in disgust but heard someone say: "Wonder how Steve's getting on" and a comment drowned in laughter — then something like "with his in-laws".

He felt the shock in his guts and strained to hear more but the pub was noisy with a background blur of conversation. He couldn't tell what was being said until one of the youths came to the bar, turning to shout something in response, "give her a bloody good one, more like."

He saw James listening and scowled: "What's your problem?"

He stared the boy down and carried on drinking. He couldn't believe the Pattersons would encourage their daughter to be among such people. He finished his beer, left the sandwich uneaten and went to his car where he sat drumming his fingers on the wheel, wondering what to do. "Sod it," he said and headed out of the village.

He drove slowly past her home. All the outside lights were blazing and among several vehicles lined up on the forecourt, he recognised Bill Sterling's Range Rover. He watched the house for nearly ten minutes but nothing moved and he forced himself to drive away.

At home three ewes were lambing. They were managing without him but it took time to settle them with the lambs, swabbing navels with iodine and upending each ewe to check the milk was coming through. Others showed signs of imminent birth, their heads back and straining up. Tired and despondent he knew he fussed and probably could have left them to it but hated to leave them struggling.

He'd learned the hard lesson of letting nature take its course the first year, wasting hours on a lamb with a deformed backbone.The swaybacked lamb — caused by copper deficiency, eventually managed to stand and he bottle reared it when the ewe wouldn't have it. He called it Wobbly and it would totter round the yard bleating after him. It grew on well but after its poor start he'd neglected to castrate it with a rubber band. In late summer when the ewes were set for tupping poor Wobbly tried his luck and James found him dead on his back in the field. The little ram had fallen backwards off the ewe and with his deformity couldn't right himself.

He was out with them again around midnight and just as he decided to attempt a few hours in bed another started. It was well past two before he left them to get some sleep.

When he woke after ten he saw someone had been to feed Harry and both dogs were dashing around the barn, the spaniel scavenging for afterbirths and upsetting the sheep. But Kate wasn't there.

Twice during a long day the phone rang and he rushed to answer it but it wasn't her. In the afternoon he saw Pat's car and hurried out to find her doing Harry.

"Where is she?" he demanded, past worrying what she thought.

"Hello, how's the lambing?"

"Fine. Where is she? What's happened?"

"Nothing as far as I know. Don't look so worried, she asked me to come up. Her mum had a lunch do today and Kate was supposed to help."

"She never mentioned it.

"Probably forgot."

"Did you feed him this morning?"

"What? No, she did, she just asked me to do the evening. What's wrong?"

"You're her friend, you know the situation, we were going out last night but she didn't turn up. That dreadful family were at the house last night — and Steve."

Pat eyed him with interest — it sounded as if the rumours were true. "Well done Kate," she thought. "Are you two getting it together?" she asked.

"What d'you mean?" He was instantly defensive.

"You know — she likes you."

"Does she?"

"You must know she does."

"I thought she was afraid of me."

"That too. But she likes you all right. Well?"

James was surprised her question didn't annoy him but he wanted to talk about Kate. He said: "We've become friends, no more than that but I like her very much."

"Is that all?" Pat asked, pushing her luck.

"She's got enough problems already."

She looked away before saying: "They're an odd lot, the Pattersons, they have some strange ideas." She looked him hard in the eye and said: "You will look after her, won't you?"

"Of course, if I can. I wanted to see her today or at least speak to her, to know she's okay. I can't ring the house." Pat brightened: "I'll call her, tell her you're worried. But I'm sure it's all right."

She nodded towards the barn. "Do you want a hand there? It looks busy."

"I can manage, I expect you've got plenty at home."

"I can spare an hour, you've done a lot for Harry, fair exchange. I can do the hay and water if nothing else."

"Thanks. But listen, go indoors and ring her now, set my mind at rest."

He watched her go to the house, anxious when she was quickly back.

"Well."

"She's okay, she'll try and see you later."

"Oh."

"Cheer up .You've got me."

Later as she waved goodbye she glanced back in the mirror and saw the desolation in his face. Reversing towards him she thrust her head through the window to say: "It's not that bad, she said she'll come." His smile was bleak.

"You do care about her," she said, "more than you realise."

Hour by hour he waited but by evening the let-down had brought depression and he began to doubt her. Maybe all she'd told him about Steve was lies, just to get somewhere for the horse. But that didn't make sense. He couldn't eat though he expected to be in the barn most of the night with lambs coming fast. He lay on the sofa watching television, listening for the phone or a knock at the door. He was angry about his own feelings, it shouldn't matter so much. The idea of her with Steve tormented him, he'd never been jealous but the thought of that bully touching her was intolerable.

When the phone rang he grabbed it eagerly but it was only Louise, on her routine sisterly call. "And how's that lovely girl with the horse?"

"They're both fine, as far as I know, I thought it might be her on the phone."

"Have you got to know her any better? She seemed shy."

"She is," he said and Louise asked no more.

Restless he went out to the sheep and spent long minutes by the wall gazing at the lights in the village. It was well after eleven — she wouldn't come now.

One ewe had triplets and when he went back a fourth had arrived. He groaned, she was a big ewe with plenty of milk but she'd never rear four. She was bleating in confusion as the tiny lambs nuzzled around her. He left them to help a maiden ewe who looked in trouble but wouldn't be caught. He realised how tired he was when it took him so long to get her cornered and down. The lamb's swollen head was out but the front legs were turned back with little room for his hand inside the young ewe. It was hard to hold her down, reach the lubricating fluid, get in position and grope in her tight vagina to catch a tiny hoof and draw the leg forward.

He couldn't get the second leg through the pelvis so pulled hard on one leg until the lamb slid out in a yellow, slimy mess into the straw, its tongue lolling limp. He dragged it in front of the ewe and slapped it harshly, probing with his finger in the mouth. He thought it was gone but he swung it heavily to clear the lungs and dropped it again by the ewe who licked and nickered to it. It looked hopeless but he slapped it again as a last chance and saw its rib-cage heave. Then its eyes and mouth opened to snatch a first breath and the ewe struggled to her feet invigorated by the sign of life. She increased the pace of her licking while he slumped down to massage his bruised hand, numbed by the pressure of her pelvic bones.

But the lamb was alive, a big strong single, the reason it had struggled to be born. He wondered if the young ewe would take one of the quads but the size disparity was too much.

The night was very still with a frost setting firm outside and stars bright above the farm. He shivered, chilled from struggling in damp straw and went in to make coffee, conscious of two more ewes showing the tell-tale signs. He made a flask and was frustrated to find a ewe had given birth in his absence — and the lamb was dead. Whether born dead or lost from lack of attention he couldn't be sure but he was angry to miss it. She was having another, maybe she would foster one to go with it.

The second lamb was small but lively, shaking its head to break free of the membranes, trying from the start to get on its feet. He moved them to a pen, dangling both dead and live lambs before the ewe to make her follow. She allowed herself to be settled in the small triangular pen he'd built for adoptions and fetched one of the quads — the strongest, which he'd seen butting its mother's bag eagerly for milk. He laid it next to the dead lamb and smeared yellow birth slime and blood from the body over the head, back and tail of the wriggling baby and pushed it under the ewe. The surest way was to skin the dead one and dress the live lamb. But it was a tricky job and he hadn't the skill. He'd had success with this simpler way, especially if the lamb was persistent.

The ewe had plenty of milk and with her own lamb sucking well the foster child kept at the other teat. The ewe knew something wasn't right and kept butting it away. But she wasn't vicious and he thought within a day she'd accept it as her own. She nuzzled first one bottom, then the other, trying to work it out before turning again on the fosterling. But he stuck at it, darting under her to grab a teat as she turned. He left them to it and sat down on dry straw with his back against the bales to drink. All was peaceful, only lambs bleating and rustling in the straw and low answering calls from the ewes, over all the steady sound of munching hay. He told himself he'd go in soon and risk an hour in bed — but for now he'd close his eyes a moment.

In his sleep he heard Bobbie barking and felt the dog nuzzling his face. Drowsily he pushed him away and nestled deeper into the straw but the touch on his face was insistent and someone was shaking his arm.

"James, wake up." He opened his eyes and took a while to realise Kate was tugging at him.

"What time is it?"

"Nearly three. You'll get chilled lying there, there's another ewe starting."

He sat up. "What are you doing here at this time?"

"I said I'd come. Couldn't get away earlier but I'm here now." Sitting on the bale above him she said: "You can see your barn lights from our place so I knew where you were. I've walked up."

"At this time of night?"

"If I'd brought the car they'd have heard me. This way no one knows I'm not in bed." She shivered: "It's cold in here and you don't seem pleased to see me."

"Oh Kate," he smiled. "I am, very. I've been thinking about you all day. There's trouble again, I suppose."

"You could say that." Her eyes showed signs of weeping. "I don't know what to do." She began to cry, deep gulping sobs that shook her and he got up in haste to sit beside her. "Hey, come on. That won't help. It can't be that bad."

He wrapped his arm round her and pulled her close.

"You shouldn't have walked up here in the middle of the night."

"It was safe enough. It's not likely someone would hang around on these roads on the off-chance of a victim — my biggest danger's at home."

He kissed her, a gentle touch of reassurance. "You're going to have to decide soon. Come on, let's sort the ewe and go indoors and talk about it."

Another pair or twins, strong without problems — they settled them and checked the rest. "It's been a busy night but I reckon I can leave them for a while."

"You need rest," she said.

"Not much chance of that now you're here."

"I'm sorry."

"Don't be."

Inside he made more coffee and flopped in a chair saying: "I'll have to lie down, I'm knackered. What d'you want to do? Shall I drive you back?"

"No, I don't want to go back."

"But you said they think you're in bed. If you're not around in the morning they'll know anyway."

"If I'm not there they can't get at me." She studied his face. "You look exhausted."

"I am. Can't keep my eyes open, I must get to bed. Come with me," he grinned. "I don't mean that — I haven't the energy right now. The bed's made up in the middle room, you can go in there — it's up to you."

He led her upstairs and into the room she could use. When he'd gone she sat on the bed wondering about him and what she was doing in his house — a man she was only just starting to know. Yet she felt so right with him as if she'd known him for years. She wanted to be near him, that was why she'd come but in this empty spare room in the darkest hours of the night she was cold and nervous. She went out to the landing and saw his door ajar. She crept in to look. He was fast asleep, his dirty jeans and quilted jacket in a pile by the bed but he still wore his mucky shirt.

She frowned, reluctant to go back, shivering and wracked by indecision. She had to get into one of the beds or walk back home. She made up her mind. Smiling she went to the other side and crept in under the quilt, snuggling close to his back, in his aura of warmth. She lay still, afraid to wake him. She relaxed and felt better, her nostrils assailed by the pungent smell of sheep. Softly she laughed, thinking she wouldn't forget the first time they slept together.

He stirred at dawn, turning over for the first time since he'd fallen into exhausted oblivion, shocked into wakefulness as his arm met soft skin. He raised himself on an elbow to look at her, lying half towards him, almost on her stomach, one hand under the pillow. She wore a T-shirt which didn't cover a dark area of bruising on her upper arm. He lifted the quilt, examined the smooth slender legs and put out a tentative hand to stroke her bare thigh. She murmured sleepily and he asked softly: "What are you doing in my bed?"

"Sleeping." She was awake now and looked up at him anxiously.

"You're very bold, invading a man's bed."

"I was cold and lonely — I'll go if you want."

"No." He stroked her face then got a whiff of himself. "Hell, I stink! Sorry Kate."

"It's only sheep and I am a farmer's daughter. It'll wash off."

He laughed: "I must see what's happening out there."

He started to get out of bed but she was quicker. "I'll go. Stay and rest while you can, you've only had a couple of hours. I'll go check and fetch you if I can't cope."

As soon as she'd gone he was up and into the shower, he couldn't get close to her smelling like an old tup and he was back in the bedroom with a towel round him when she came upstairs with two mugs of tea.

"You needn't get up yet, another one's got twins but she's fine. Get back into bed — I need to talk to you."

"Aren't you going to join me?"

She sat on the bed beside him, eyeing his body.

His skin had a natural dark smoothness which held the effects of sun for a long time but it emphasised the livid puckered scar about four inches long at the top of his chest, just below the right shoulder.

"What did that?"

"Part of a shell."

"Bosnia? You didn't tell me about that."

"It was nothing really, a lump of shrapnel from the shelling."

"It looks nasty."

"Could've been worse, the medical treatment wasn't the best of course."

"Does it hurt?"

"Not now. It's nothing — does it put you off?"

She shook her head and kissed the place and he took the moment, pulling her close in what turned into a long, exciting cuddle.

He sighed saying: "This isn't a good idea. I'm here naked in bed with a hard on, tired as I am and you at my mercy. But it's not time for that yet — you need to decide what's happening."

She nodded, smiling: "I know you're right but I do like you kissing me."

"So tell me, what happened the other night when you didn't meet me and what caused the bruise?"

"What bruise?"

"On your arm. Take off your sweater, let me see."

Obediently she pulled the sweater over her head and he leaned forward and whipped off the T-shirt with it.

"Don't!" she cried and jumped up. He caught her hand and pulled her back. "Let me look."

His eyes weren't scanning her breasts but the unmistakable marks of violent hands on both upper arms.

"Steve I suppose." She didn't answer. "What happened? I'll swing for that bastard before I'm done."

"Mum invited Steve's parents for supper on Saturday — she hadn't told me. He came too. I said I was going out but Dad said if I did I could stay out. I didn't know what to do, I needed to think. So I stayed. It was all a con of course, a set-up. After supper they kindly left us together — to talk things over as Mrs Sterling put it. What a joke. Nothing's changed, least of all him."

"And the bruises?"

"He grabbed me, shook me — trying to make his point."

"He didn't hit you?"

"No. It could have been worse, like your shoulder."

"That was war. This is a guy who's supposed to care about you."

"Well, that's what happened."

"And yesterday? Did your mother have this lunch thing?"

"Yes. I did know about that and I'd promised to help her. I didn't mind but they kept finding more for me to do."

"And now you're here and soon they're going to know you're not there. What then?"

"I haven't much choice, James. Either I stay at home and give in and marry Steve or I get out."

"What's the matter with your parents, can't they see what he's like? If he does this now what will he be like when you're married?"

"They've got a blind spot, they don't understand, they think it'll work out but it won't."

"No, he's a nasty bully and I pity any girl that marries him."

He pitied her, torn with loyalty to parents who didn't deserve it. He wished he knew what was really behind it, powerful reasons must dictate such behaviour. But he forgot all that because her silky breasts with those dark centres were beginning to disturb him and he couldn't help but kiss them before saying hurriedly: "Cover yourself, Kate, my good intentions are disappearing fast."

That seemed to cheer her as she dressed. "You have a lot of willpower or you don't fancy me that much. I was nervous being here like this."

He cupped her chin in his hand and stared at her a moment saying softly: "I think you know how I feel and I won't always be so restrained but first we need to sort you out."

"It all depends on you. If I get a flat or something that's the end of Harry, I couldn't afford to keep him in livery and run a flat or cottage. You did offer me a room here, for a while — is that still on?"

"If that's what you want," he hesitated. "I also said there'd be no strings, you can have a room here and it's your room. Moving in doesn't mean you have to be in here." He patted the bed. "No strings."

"Don't you want me?"

He just smiled and she laughed. "When word gets round everyone will think the worst anyway, so it might as well be true."

"That's up to you. But I'll change the sheets before you get in here again, too much sheep."

She had it all worked out. She'd go home on foot, say she'd been for a walk and give no hint of her intentions until she had time and opportunity to move her stuff. She'd already arranged time off and planned to do it when her father was out on the tractor and her mother at the WI. As long as there wasn't heavy rain which would stop him sowing corn and keep him near the house.

"Not that there's much to bring," she said, "just my clothes, books and CDs and a few oddments from around the house. I've a lovely old chest of drawers granny left me but I suppose I'll have to leave that."

She said it wistfully. "It's the only thing in the house I really care about. I wish granny was still alive, she'd have stood up for me."

"Your father's mum?" he asked, curious.

She shook her head. "Granny Patterson was awful. Mum used to be more like granny. But it all changed."

Her face crinkled and she looked away. "I'm going now. Wish me luck. Pat will come later for Harry. I'll see you soon."

"Maybe she could help you with the chest," he said to cheer her but she didn't answer.

Chapter eleven

He tried hard to suppress his growing excitement at the prospect of her moving in. He'd said no strings but couldn't avoid the hope that she might become more than just a tenant in his house. He could no longer pretend to himself that he wasn't interested.

He spent the day impatiently waiting for the afternoon but she didn't turn up. When Pat arrived to do Harry his disappointment was obvious and she couldn't help laughing at his anxious face as he hurried across the yard.

"It's all right," she said at once. "She's still coming but not today."

He was surprised. "Oh, you know what she's planning?"

"She got the day wrong for the WI meeting, it's tomorrow."

"But you're doing the horse."

"She needed to make time up at work so I'm here — you missed me this morning, I was early. But she said to tell you it's still on."

"She could have called from the office," he said in an injured tone.

"It's open plan, too many nosey ears and there's a girl who knows the family."

"Can't she trust anyone — it's like a conspiracy."

Pat frowned. "Only me, but you're right, it is a bit like that. It's very difficult at home."

"I'd go there myself but it'd only makes things worse."

"Don't do that. She's got tomorrow afternoon off and she plans to get her stuff out and come up as normal to Harry — and not go back."

"Let's hope it works out," he said.

Another broken night he spent partly with the sheep and more hours in fitful sleep thinking about Kate. He couldn't believe the strength of his eagerness and when she arrived at last he held himself back from rushing out. The car was full, both back and front passenger seats piled high. He went to give her a welcoming hug but was deterred by her expression. She looked miserable and distant — unapproachable.

"You made it then, got everything out okay."

"Mm."

He thrust out his hand to pull her to him and bent to kiss her but she jerked away. "Please don't."

He winced and sucked in a deep reluctant breath but moved back. "It's all right Kate, what's wrong?"

"I don't know, it felt so sneaky, though it had to be like that. And I feel guilty about lying to mum."

"Why?"

"It's not her fault."

"But she doesn't stand up for you."

"That's because she's scared of Dad, she daren't cross him and they're both afraid of the Sterlings."

"What's the matter with them all?"

"When there's time, I will tell you about it."

"I wish you would."

She turned abruptly and he watched her pull on rubber boots to fetch Harry from the paddock.

He was stunned by the disturbing body language and her apparent rejection, was this the same girl he'd invited into his home? He frowned but shrugged and began to unpack the car.

He put her suitcase in the spare room but she came upstairs and passed him without a word, almost shutting the door in his face. He knocked once with no response and he was left to stare at the door in frustration. For a moment he considered going in but turned away, puzzled and disappointed, on the point of resentment. Was this the girl who'd climbed into his bed only a few nights before?

He assumed she'd be down for supper and opened a wine he thought she would enjoy but he waited in vain for her to appear and got through the bottle on his own. He'd also put a bottle of champagne to chill, just in case— he'd bought it specially and he wondered ruefully when it might be drunk. The alcohol stoked his growing indignation at her behaviour, she was acting like a stranger and whatever he'd expected it wasn't this.

There was a lull in the lambing and he sat alone all evening, churning bitter thoughts.

In the morning she left without breakfast after a brief greeting, climbed into the car and was gone. He stared after the departing vehicle, his face puckered in an angry frown.

She avoided him again in the evening and he contemplated confrontation but allowed her to go upstairs without comment. His confusion had turned into anger and later when a loud knocking at the door disturbed him he let it show to the tall, well-built young man who stood there.

"What do you want?" he asked, his tone belligerent and unwelcoming. He assumed the caller must be connected with Kate and tried to assess whether he could prevent it if this person attempted to physically remove her from the premises. The stranger in turn looked him up and down but asked in a mild voice: "Is my sister here?"

"Your sister?"

"Kate Patterson."

James studied him carefully before answering. The man was good looking, an element of Kate in him and an open expression with a trace of anxiety.

"What makes you think she might be here?"

"That's the horse, Harry, isn't it -- in the box over there?"

"Yes, that's Kate's horse."

"Well, is she here?"

"Why do you want to know?"

"She's my sister, isn't that enough?"

There was no aggression in the answer but James said: "No."

The other man frowned. "Is she here or not? If she is I need to see her."

"What makes you think she might be here?"

"Because I'm not stupid. You can't stop me seeing her, it's nothing to do with you."

"True – in some ways. But it is my business to stop the girl being coerced and bullied. She is here – I've let her a room for as long as she needs it."

To his surprise the younger man relaxed and half smiled.

"Is she in now?"

"I don't know."

"Look – Mr Lambert – James – I don't want to make her go home. I just want to be sure she's all right. I haven't come from them -- my parents I mean."

"That's something." He made a decision: "You'd better come in."

"William." Kate appeared on the stairs and rushed to the door as James ushered him in and brother and sister embraced in a way that put his doubts at rest.

"So you have a brother, Miss Patterson. You never mentioned it."

"There was never time. But this is William. Oh, I'm so glad to see you."

She hugged him and James watching, saw two shoots from the same stock. He felt surplus to their needs and disappeared into the kitchen. When he came back William stood up and said: "Look James, I want you to know I'm totally against my parents in this. I never could bear that nasty little prick."

He grunted: "Good. At least that's one more on her side."

William went on: "I wanted her to come to London, I'd found her a good job and she'd have lived with me but she won't leave the bloody horse."

They all smiled: "Harry has a lot to answer for," said James.

"I just came to make sure you're okay," William said, an arm around his sister.

"How did you know?" she asked.

"Mum rang, trying to get me to talk sense into you. I told her what I thought."

"So that's fine," said James sarcastically. "But what's she supposed to do now? What's wrong with your parents? Can't they see what an arsehole that guy is?"

"There are reasons -- it's a long story."

"People keep saying that but nobody tells me the long story."

"It isn't very nice, no credit to anyone involved but let me warn you, the Sterlings don't like being crossed. Watch yourself."

"Hell -- this is now, we're not talking Victorian."

"You've been in Bosnia, I've read your stuff. You know what happened there. People are the same wherever. Jealousy, greed, it's everywhere. Don't forget that."

James stared at him. "That's why I went to London, to get away from it. I'm an accountant, I could've practised here in the Midlands but I needed to get away. And Dad always wanted me to farm and I just couldn't.

"That I understand."

"But you're farming here."

"There's farming and farming. They laugh at me round here but I suit myself."

They smiled at each other, an unlikely bond discovered. When he left, James walked with him to the car. Before he got in William asked: "Are you two together?"

"You mean am I shagging your sister?"

"That's just what I mean."

James hesitated but went for the truth. "No but I'd like to."

"That's honest."

"She's here with no strings. Everyone will think the worst of course but she has the room, that's all -- at the moment. We've become quite close — at least I thought we had, though she's been like a stranger since she moved in. But I care about her and she's very innocent."

"I know. I'm glad she kept that wanker at arm's length."

"Would you mind if she was sharing my bed?"

"Why should I? You seem a decent bloke, you'd probably be good for her. But please look after her, she's a great kid."

"I'll try."

He watched the car's lights disappear down the lane and stayed outside to think, wondering again about the story he never got to hear.

He expected she'd disappeared back upstairs but she was waiting for him and he said at once: "Why didn't you tell me you had a brother?"

"It never came up."

"Are you sure it wasn't because if I knew about him I'd make you go to London instead of staying here and dragging me into all your problems?"

"It just never came up and I hate talking about my family."

"But he's the good bit." He glared at her: "You haven't been straight with me."

He scowled in growing anger, the temper he tried so hard to keep under control welled up, unreasoning and unreasonable. It swept over him like a wave and he turned away and left her, not trusting himself to stay.

He made sure not to meet her in the morning and was beginning to think he wanted to be rid of her — though the thought of her going, back to her home, back to Steve, was hard to bear.

In the evening she appeared in the sitting room where he was attempting to relax. She didn't come near, as if wanting space between them. "Do you want me to leave?" she asked.

"Not especially," he didn't look up.

"Please. I must talk to you, the thing about William — I honestly didn't think to mention him. He's away in London, I don't see much of him."

He turned his eyes on her and said: "What's the matter, why are you keeping away from me? It seems ungrateful when I'm trying to help you. You seem afraid, I thought you liked me."

"I do. I'm nervous — about what I said to you. Maybe I went too far — but I'm so lonely."

"We're all lonely."

"Be kind to me."

He got up and put a log on the fire. "I thought I was being kind to you." She stood just inside the room as if poised for escape. "Come in if you're going to, there's a draught with the door open and it's cold tonight. Come and sit."

She came nearer and sat on the floor by the fire, half turned to him.

"Well what is it? What do you want to say?" he asked.

"It's so stupid. What I said about teaching me — look — can you forget I said it."

He laughed: "It was an unusual thing to say but I'll take it as a joke and yes, I can forget it."

"It wasn't a joke, not really. I meant it when I said it but I'm scared."

"Scared? You didn't seem scared when you climbed into my bed the other night."

"That was different, but sometimes, like when you grabbed me in the barn, I don't know how to react."

"I remember, I was just trying to make a point." He reached out to touch her lightly on the cheek. "Do you want to stay or are you thinking better of it?"

"I don't want to go back, not now I've got out. James, I'm sorry the way I behaved, you've been so kind."

"Kind, is that what I am? Come here." He leaned across and caught her arm, pulling her near enough to touch, cupping his hands under her chin to tilt her face towards him. She drew in a sharp breath, tensing but he laughed and kissed her lightly on the forehead.

"Right miss, here's what we do."

She waited, wondering what he was going to say.

"I said you could have a room here, no strings and that's what I meant. From now on I won't come near you, I won't touch you. We'll be strangers."

Her face wrinkled in alarm as she said: "Oh I don't want that, we're friends aren't we?"

"I hope so but for now just friends. I think it's safer that way. And Kate, if you want to change that, if you want to go further then you must make the move. Do you understand?"

"I think so, it's down to me."

"Correct. Right now I'm going out to the barn and then I'm going to make some supper, is it for one or two?"

"I can do that," she said hurriedly. "Eating together should be safe enough."

He smiled, a slow sardonic smile and she felt like a foolish child.

The spring had been a long time coming but in the cold bright morning he saw signs everywhere of new life, frantic birds clutching twigs and clumps of sheep's wool, leaf buds touched with green poised to burst open and tiny spikes of grass pushing through the dull brown winter sward.

Above him the sky was deep blue where two buzzards called and circled. He took his mug of tea to sit on the wall and watch them soar across the valley. In the clear light the village looked closer and fields of winter barley on the far slopes rippled in the breeze. He looked again for the buzzards and spotted them moving back towards the farm and as he watched, two more large dark birds plunged down the sky, in an aerial game of tag. The distinctive kronk, kronk call as they passed was unmistakable. Ravens. He thought he'd heard them in February, uncertain, but there was no mistaking these two.

He tracked them as they flew towards the copse of Scots pines at the valley's western end. He thought they were gone but minutes later they were back, flying in formation like aircraft, round the valley and back in a perfect flypast. They moved in sequence, calling, somersaulting together, sailing down the wind, in the rush of the cold clear air.

"They must be nesting in the pines," he said aloud to himself. They were rare in the area, not seen in the valley before, so he was thrilled to watch them, something good to tell Kate. His thoughts curled back to her, trying to work out what was happening.

Her hostility or fear, he wasn't sure which, had evaporated and their relationship as friends settled into routine as she got accustomed to being around him. The lengthening spring evenings gave her more time outside, schooling Harry several nights a week but she also began to tackle his neglected garden. He was pleased when she came home with a selection of shrubs and flowering perennials in the car and set about planting them. She chatted eagerly about bulbs she would buy and where she would place them in the autumn.

They waited for reaction from her family but their anxiety eased when there was no word from anyone other than William and Pat had heard nothing from the village. James was surprised but relieved, not relishing the prospect of confrontation with her family or the odious Steve.

Despite his brave words that night he found it hard to resist the temptation to reach out and touch her when she was near; he'd said no strings but hoped after all she'd said that she would want the comfort of his body as much as he longed for hers. Having her in the house was tough and after a chaste goodnight he would lie awake with his loins aching.

On his way to the bathroom in only his underpants one morning he met her on the landing. "Oops, sorry," he said and she laughed easily, unconcerned. He saw her focus on his scar and while he waited for her to pass she reached out and ran her fingers across the rough tissue before hurrying to her room.

The touch ran through him like electric shock and he stepped towards her closed door. But it was firmly shut. Shaking his head to regain control he sighed; it was his own fault, he must remember to wear a dressing gown.

When they'd finished supper that evening, chatting at the table she fell silent as he topped up her glass with red wine. He noticed it at once, beginning to know and anticipate her moods, wondering what was coming next. "What is it?" he asked.

"Your scar," she said. "Will it heal any more, will the skin soften and settle?"

"I don't know, it may. Does it bother you?"

"No, of course not — it's just — "

"What?"

"I wish you'd tell me, how it happened, how you got it."

"I told you, a lump of metal from a shell."

"But what were you doing? I want to understand how it was out there."

"I told you about Katya — how she died."

"I know but how did that happen?" She added quickly. "If it's not too painful to tell me."

She feared she shouldn't have asked, he looked far away as if he'd forgotten her, back in the beleaguered city. But he met her eyes and smiled. "If you want to know I'll tell you," he said

"We were shopping — been to the market to look for bread — when the siren went off. We started running down the street, a whole crowd of us looking for cover." He spoke slowly as if dragging the incident back into his mind. "A child was in front of us, with her mother, a tiny girl with dark curls, maybe two years old. The mother held her by the arm half carrying, half pulling her and the kid had a job to keep up. I remember her chubby little legs pounding the road as they ran. I was holding Katya's hand."

His gaze was on something elsewhere but he paused to glance at Kate. "Are you sure you want to hear this, it's not pleasant."

She took his hand across the table. "If you can bear to tell it I can stand listening."

His soft voice went on: "The noise of shells was all round us and not far ahead a car blew up as it was hit, showering metal across the street. We kept running and I heard an awful whining sound and another shell passed just above us.

"The mother and the kid were about forty yards in front and they caught the full blast as the shell exploded. I stopped, didn't know where to go but we got into a shop doorway. I told Katya to stay there and went to see if I could do anything. I ran across to them, there was an awful lot of blood, streaming out of them. They were both dead, there was nothing I could do. What was left of the child lay half covered by her mother, her little head had rolled into the gutter. The mother was more or less intact but her guts were all trailed over the remnants of the child. It was a horrible shock and next thing I was being sick. I couldn't control it at all.

"That was when I caught it. I'd stayed too long in the open street and another shell landed by a car and blew a wide arc of metal towards me. I felt this awful thump in my shoulder and hit the ground. I thought I'd had it. I clamped my hand over the wound and blood oozed through my fingers. But I didn't pass out and got back to Katya — she was down, huddled in the doorway watching me. She used her scarf to stop the bleeding. I remember saying: 'I think it's just a splinter. I'll be all right but Christ, it does hurt.' She looked so terrified for me and she couldn't stop crying.

"That was it, that's what happened. I got patched up and it was only a splinter, though quite a big one, but it looked and felt much worse than it was."

He finished the story and looked for her reaction. "Satisfied?" he asked.

"Thanks for telling me, it's hard to imagine all that, it's like some scene from a war film."

"That's what it was like, a dreadful civil war and it's still going on."

"You were very brave."

"Not really, I didn't do much. That was what finally made me want to get out, it was very scary. I was afraid and I wanted to get out with Katya, bring her back to England and safety. But I failed."

He stopped speaking and sighed. "And now you're here and I'll probably make a mess of things with you as well, let you down as I did her. Don't worry about my scar, it doesn't bother me — it itches sometimes."

That seemed a dismissal and she had no notion what to say next but just mumbled: "I'd better go to bed."

He nodded as she left but at the foot of the stairs she hesitated and came back to kiss his cheek, her hand on his shoulder. Startled he touched his face where she'd kissed and smiled. "I'm glad I told you," he said.

He watched her go up and heard the door close. Resigned to being alone again he poured a shot of whisky, musing on her kiss as he added a splash of water. He wished she wouldn't do that and began to think she did it deliberately, leading him on, but that seemed so out of character. He sank unhappily into his armchair and sipped the whisky.

The bedroom was cold and she hesitated before undressing, listening for him to come up. She wanted to be with him but the remnants of fear held her back from the final step. When she heard no sound she knew he must be still down there and pictured him frowning at the fire -- he did a lot of frowning.

She went down, her shoeless feet making no noise on the stairs, anxious he shouldn't hear. The sitting room door was open and she crept across the hall and peered into the room, dimly lit with only one lamp and the dying glow of the fire. His head was flung back on the chair, his eyes apparently closed. He was muttering something and she strained to catch his words. She heard him say her name and what sounded like: "Oh Kate, what the hell have you done to me?"

She padded across the carpet to his chair and stood behind him waiting until he sensed her presence. It felt like an age before he moved, to lean forward and grasp the whisky. He sipped it and sat back and she bent to kiss him on the nape of the neck.

He sprang from the chair and the whisky went flying as he spun to face her. "What the fuck? What you playing at?"

His angry glare was intimidating and she shrank away in alarm.

"I didn't mean to startle you."

"Well you did. What is it with you? One minute you're kissing me, the next you shut the door in my face. I never had you as a prick teaser."

"I'm not! I just — I'm so confused." She started to cry but he didn't care. Let her.

"Why're you here? I thought you'd gone to bed."

"I wanted to be with you but you change so quick, I don't how to deal with it."

"I change! That's rich from you. You're confused! What d'you think I am? I don't know what you want from me, except a home for your damned horse."

"Please James," she spluttered through tears. "I came down to be with you."

"What does that mean?"

She grimaced as if afraid to speak.

He stooped to retrieve the whisky glass and stood up, his face stern as he eyed her. "Come here."

She moved close to him and before she could speak smothered her words with his mouth pressed hard on hers. He paused asking harshly: "Is this what you want?" and kissed her again. She was so tense and unresponsive it made his anger burst out and he crushed her against him. She struggled, her hands pushing at him and he almost released her but she yielded and kissed him in return

"Don't say anything," he said, running his hands up inside her sweater, feeling the bones of her back as he freed her breasts. She stiffened as he lifted the sweater and stroked and kissed each in turn.

He pulled her down onto the carpet and fast fingers unfastened her jeans while she gazed at him with an odd fearful longing. He kissed her again, more gently and this time her reaction had an intensity which made him gasp.

He unzipped himself and she groped for his penis and wrapped her fingers around it feeling it rigid in her hand.

Urgently he pulled off her jeans, kissing her breast and stomach, stroking her pubic hair as his fingers found their way inside her.

He watched her face as he played, saw her eyes widen with pleasure, groaning quietly. He held back, stroking her, mouthing her face and neck, holding off the longed for moment.

"Is this what you want?" he asked.

"It's why I came."

"Are you sure?

"Do it, please do it," she whispered and he pushed into her, overwhelmed with a conflict of tenderness and lust.

When it was over she lay so still in his arms he was afraid to speak, fearing he'd hurt or disappointed her. He thought he could hear her heart beating against his chest but it was his own, thudding fast.

Chapter twelve

After that evening she became more sure around him but his expectation that she would start sharing his bed was disappointed. To his immense frustration she remained in her own room and though happy to kiss and be close to him it was as if they had not made love at all. She would let him touch her and played with him, satisfying his need but seemed unwilling to go further. She seemed afraid of the act itself which puzzled him but he didn't try to force her. The last thing he wanted was comparisons with Steve and rape was something way outside his comfort zone.

Harry's career became the main focus of attention as she prepared the horse for the eventing season. He was happy to see her so fired up at the prospect of at last getting the horse to do what he was destined for but hadn't reckoned on being so involved. He knew she planned to compete but was disconcerted when he discovered her programme for April and his role in it.

She needed his truck to pull the trailer so he felt obliged to go with her. He didn't want to spend his weekends and several evenings with horse people but she said it was exceptional and necessary to get Harry into a competitive pattern of dressage tests and show jumping leading up to his first official event at the end of the month. He didn't mind the dressage because that was timed precisely but the indoor show jumping was a bore. The waiting between classes seemed endless and on one long wet evening, they weren't home till the early hours. By then he was tired and irritable.

"I'm glad you're not really into show jumping," he said when she apologised for the third time. "I couldn't stick many nights like that."

The list included a local riding club one day event which was more enjoyable. It was a sunny day in an attractive wooded setting and an easy, straight forward course which meant Kate stayed relaxed. She and Harry were fourth in their section and the green rosette hung in the front of the Land Rover as they drove home. She kept fingering it with delight although James said: "Red would be better."

"You don't realise how hard it is to get any rosette in this sport. I can't afford to do it as I'd like to but you've no idea what that ribbon means to me. I've wanted to do it for so long but nobody was prepared to help me till I met you."

"I'm glad. I enjoyed today though I never thought I would. We'll settle him, feed the dogs and get cleaned up. Then I'm going to take you out for a celebration meal."

At the bistro he wanted to order champagne but she stopped him. "Let's wait till he gets his first affiliated ribbon, that'll be worth celebrating."

That achievement came a week later involving a much longer journey and a very early start. But it was worth it when Harry went clear in both show jumping and cross country and finished on his dressage score of 35. Kate had been one of the first to go in the section and had a long wait for the results.

"Surely you'll win this," he kept telling her but it was a good section with the winner on 28 so Harry was fourth again and his rider was ecstatic.

"That's brilliant," she danced round James and kissed him in delight.

But he wasn't impressed. "Only fourth again," he said.

"It's only his second event. He's just six and very green, some horses go for years and never get placed."

"Must be the rider," he smiled.

"No, I'm not that good but he is. I always knew he would be. He's clever, he picks it up so quickly and he's bold and his paces are super — "

"In fact he's just wonderful," he laughed. "Should I be jealous of that animal?"

He watched the prize giving. As she made her way through the crowd to collect the rosette and prize her eyes shone with happiness making all his doubts about their situation vanish. He was glad he'd given the horse a home. When she first turned up from nowhere he hadn't understood what it was about, thinking her just another horse-mad girl. But now he knew Harry's history, how she'd bought him as a foal in the face of opposition at home and stuck to her belief that the horse was a bit special.

She thought that because the old man who'd sold it to her had told her so, it was the last of his breeding and he'd waited years for a colt foal after a string of fillies. He said the mares were always headstrong and uncooperative but the males, once gelded, were brilliant. And she believed him and now Harry was coming good. He was proud of them both.

It was a long drive home and they picked up a takeaway on the way. Out of habit he lit the fire, more cosy than eating in the kitchen and welcome in the chilly later evening. She finished her meal and moved onto the floor nearer the heat, leaning back at ease against his chair and chattering about Harry's qualities as she reviewed the day's success. He stretched out a cautious hand and began to stroke her hair.

"It's like running my hand down Harry's neck," he said. "So glossy."

She glanced up at him but didn't move and he carried on caressing her as he might pet an animal. Finding he wasn't rebuffed he kissed the top of her head and the back of her neck and let his hands stray to her breasts.

She almost held her breath, passive as he touched her but when he unfastened the bra she became so tense he stopped at once.

"Relax."

She nodded and pulled his hand back in place, where the nipples were hard to his questing fingers. "Good?"

"Yes," she murmured." She tried to turn to him but he held her where she was, undoing her shirt and bending to kiss her neck and bare shoulders. He stood up and pulled her with him, kissing her hard on the mouth and she pushed against him and clung to him as his fingers explored her. When she touched him with hesitant hands he gasped in delight and laughed through the kisses. He drew her down, saying quietly: "Here we are back on the floor again. You seem to like it here."

"It's sort of snug. I feel easy here."

"Are you sure?"

He knew he was pleasing her because her eyes widened and then half closed as they had before and she was bolder with her hand at his waist undoing his jeans. Then she got up and pulled them off which made him laugh with delight and in a moment they were both naked.

Afterwards he looked at her uncertainly and said: "I didn't expect that — you've kept me away, I didn't think you wanted this."

She sighed. "Oh, I did, it seemed right."

"I'm glad. It seemed right to me too." He put the guard round the fire and offered his hand to help her up. "Let's go to bed, it's getting cold. Will you sleep with me tonight?"

She nodded and he started to lift her, thinking to carry her upstairs but she struggled, laughing. "I can walk."

He set her down with a kiss, strangely shy now and followed her up the stairs, watching the slim body walk into his room. She turned to stare at him and said: "I've never looked at a naked man."

"You were in bed with me before."

"I couldn't look at you properly then."

"You've got a brother."

"Oh, my family don't do nude."

"And do you like what you see?" He stood by the bed growing hard again under her scrutiny. She nodded and smiled: "Glad I have an effect on you, I was beginning to wonder."

"God, if you only knew!" He grinned and went back downstairs, naked as he was, through the sitting room where their clothes lay scattered. The bottle of champagne he'd bought when she moved in was still in the fridge and laughing with happiness he found two glasses and the bottle.

She was in bed with the duvet up to her waist as he entered the room and waved the champagne bottle. "I got this specially for when you moved in. Even more reason for it now."

He drew the cork and as the white froth spilled out he flicked it onto her breasts and leaned over to lick it off.

"Your health, sweetheart — and your freedom, in more ways than one."

"I've never had champagne."

"High time, then." His shyness vanished and he felt he'd known her for years and seeing her tilt the glass he thought how easily he could love her. He lay back on the pillow and asked: "Will you stay with me now?"

"What d'you mean?"

"In here, sleep with me — every night."

"Properly shacked up you mean?"

"If that's what you call it. I hope you will." He gazed at her. "Was it good? You did come, didn't you?"

She blushed. "Yes. At least, I never felt like that before. It was – I can't find the words -- beautiful, exhilarating, indescribable."

"Right over the top?"

She nodded. "I'm glad," he whispered. "That first time, I wasn't sure you enjoyed it. Tonight was fantastic for me —

you're so lovely." He pulled her down beside him. "But what I really want is you here, just to feel you close to me. You don't know how comforting that is.

"Mm, you need comforting. But am I enough?"

"No comparisons, Kate." A shadow crossed his face and for a moment he was serious. "You're here and she's dead. That's all there is."

He buried his face against her, hiding the unexpected rush of emotion, tears could come too easily to a man supposed to be tough. He hugged her tightly and she held him until she could raise his head to kiss him. She kissed his lips and eyes, lavishing caresses and love on him with all the fervour of new passion, drowning his sadness in an intoxicating lust.

She brought him joy -- that was it, so simple -- and a freshness and innocence to all the mundane aspects of living. And the bonus for him in the new relationship was a rejuvenating sensation of health and vigour. She found pleasure in all he did, the gradual awakening of her own body as he learned what pleased her was equalled by the fascination she found in him. Not just the sex but his way of life and attitudes were totally different, even the food he ate was a novelty. He was no chef but a reasonable cook because he enjoyed it, especially with the stimulus of someone to cook for. The fact of being able to please themselves was a major contrast for her, so they might just fancy something light, maybe a baked potato or an omelette. Diet had been another issue at home.

"It's always the same, so dull. Mum can cook but Dad won't eat anything but plain food, it has to be meat in some form. Meat and two veg — he won't touch fish, so restricted. And always at a set time and my job is — was — to lay the table."

"There's nothing wrong with that," he said. "Families should eat together when they can. It's one of the things that's gone wrong with modern life, the French see the meal as the most important thing in the day though they're starting to lose it too."

"Yes but it doesn't have to be set in stone."

He grinned. "It's fine, I won't make you lay the table every day." Then he added: "But I might lay you on it sometimes."

"Sounds uncomfortable," she laughed, never sure when he was serious.

"Maybe but very sexy." He looked across at her, stopped his chopping of vegetables for a stir fry, taken with an urgent desire to push her against the kitchen wall. He toyed momentarily with the notion and the thought had an immediate effect. But he dismissed it as crude folly, it might upset, even frighten her, she wasn't ready for the careless abandon of such unfettered sex. He hoped she would learn that sometimes it could be just fun. She saw his face and tried to read his thoughts.

"What are you thinking?"

He answered truthfully. "About all the things I'd like to do to you."

She blushed: "Such as?"

"You're not ready for it"

"Are they that bad?"

"Not bad, just not prim."

They laughed together and he kissed her, forcing her gently back towards the wall, just to see. "Won't you tell me what you were thinking? Shouldn't I know?"

"All in good time," he kissed her again and uncovered her breasts, kissing and fondling them.

He caught the awed look on her face as he knelt and heard the sharp breath when he unzipped her jeans. When he started kissing her stomach and probing between her legs she gasped: "Someone might see us."

"Who?" He stood up and to tease himself further let his fingers feel her again. "Oh Kate," he groaned. "I could eat you."

Her nervous half smile became a real one: "We could go upstairs."

So they went upstairs but afterwards she said: "You think I'm being coy, don't you?'

"No, but I don't want to do anything you don't like."

"Please tell me what it was in the kitchen, what you wanted."

He frowned. "Do you really want to know?"

"You'd better tell me or I might be thinking much worse."

"I was imagining what it would be like — what I wanted, was to pull down your jeans and have you up against the wall."

"Oh!"

"Shocked?"

She didn't tell him it was the sort of thing she expected Steve to say, he'd tried once but she'd ducked away from his reach. The idea had revolted her but now as James lay with a contrite expression the thought aroused her. She shook her head. "Is that all? I was wondering what you might ask me to do."

"I'm not some kind of pervert. I'm not into anything weird, just your body and mine, what pleases us both, no more than that. I just love the freedom, I couldn't bear to disgust you."

"I don't think anything you did could disgust me."

He looked at her leaning over him, her hair touching his cheek, tempted to say he loved her. Uncertainty stopped him and he said nothing, fearing it was mere infatuation. So easy to say the love word but cruel if not true.

She had said it one time at the peak of orgasm when her body was arched up under his hand in a paroxysm of ecstasy but he discounted it. But the way she stroked his body, as if she worshipped him, made him realise she was in love. That worried him, what he'd feared. He thought again that showing her the pleasures of the flesh was all very well but it played havoc with the emotions.

He found it hard to believe she was so untouched and her pleasure in it all enhanced his own. With Katya it was different, a widow for whom love had been no mystery. What they had together was intense and amidst the misery of Bosnia there was no time for games. But he knew from the start that he loved her and that it would endure; even if he'd foreseen the ending he would not have changed their time together
Isolated in their own world they paid little attention to local events but even James could not ignore the growing sense of anticipation about the VE Day anniversary celebration early in May -- to mark fifty years since the end of world war two.

The organisers had appealed for war time memorabilia, there would be a grand village tea and on the Caradoc a huge beacon was growing. In the last week in April the village blossomed with flags and for the first time since Kate moved in he went down for a beer in the Fox. Richard greeted him with his usual welcome, telling him his plans for the big day which was a Monday when the pub was usually closed.

"I shall be open all day," he said. "And in the evening after the beacon fire we're having live music. You must come down -- bring Kate," he added.

"You know about that?"

"Everybody knows. Not the sort of thing you can keep quiet, is it." He lowered his voice. "They're not in yet but I've been wanting to see you, I nearly rang, to warn you. Young Sterling and his cronies have been saying some nasty, wild things in here — about you and her. Mostly bravado I expect – I hope -- but you need to watch your back."

The weather was kind for the big day and he went to look at the exhibits in the village hall where flags fluttered in the breeze and the warm sun added a holiday atmosphere. The hall was the old school building, taken over when the primary school closed and now crucial to village life. The display amazed him, so much effort had gone into it -- helmets and uniforms, war-time posters, flags, even weapons. Touching photographs of men he knew, mostly now in their eighties, shown as proud youngsters in navy, army or RAF uniform. Old Tom Randall was pictured there, sepia-toned, young and handsome on his charger in Palestine. He had bought the vicarage for his retirement and was still at the centre of village life though his involvement would soon be cut short.

The celebration tea was buzzing as people laughed and enjoyed the mood. The women who served the teas were in character with their hair done in the scarf-wrapped mode of the forties — as if the peace was newly achieved and not fifty years ago. Fifty years – James watched three small boys examining a Bren gun and listened to its owner explaining that this was the gun that won the war along with the .303 Lee Enfield beside it. He wondered how he came to have such weapons. Fingering the Bren he thought -- fifty years and nothing had changed. He'd watched the news before he came out and there were nine more dead in Sarajevo that morning from the shelling — more bone and blood in the dust. Was it imagination that made his shoulder ache at the thought of it or just the knowledge of pain that came from clear memory.

He rubbed his shoulder and turned away from the guns, pushing through the crush to the impromptu bar where he wrapped his hands round a glass of wine and drank it quickly, before ordering another.

The alcohol helped. He knew he was drinking too much, though less since there was Kate and it was better than drugs. He turned away from the bar to survey the crowded room, a figure apart, out on his own. People spoke to him, friendly and welcoming but it was always the same. He wished he'd brought Kate, he wouldn't have been so alone then, on the outside looking in. All his life had been like that, the observer, looking on, never part of it.

"Are you coming up the hill tonight?" Jack Wilson had come across to stand beside him.

"Yes, I'd like to. It's not something to miss."

"Come with us, there's parking in the field below though they're taking the oldies up in trailers on the quad bikes. No point taking too many vehicles. Bring Kate, won't you, Pat'll be there."

"Thanks."

Chapter thirteen

In mid evening they trudged up the wide grassy track with the Wilsons. In front and behind little groups hurried upwards, some fit and quick, others struggling and panting on the steep path, everyone pushing on to be there before the appointed time for lighting the beacon at twenty minutes to nine. Jack's wife Sheila fell behind, telling them to go on, she would follow at her own pace. "I haven't been up here -- for nearly – 20 years," she said between gasps. "The last time -- was the silver -- jubilee."

He smiled at her and looked ahead at the sun sinking towards Wales. There'd been blue sky and warmth all day but on the hill the wind was cold and beginning to bite. As they walked he gazed at the landscape laid out all around. He sometimes took the dogs on the Caradoc as they called it. Caer Caradoc, one of several hills of the same name in the Marches and Wales but this one bore the distinctive outline of ramparts from an ancient British camp.

It had commanding views of the Shropshire hill country and from its summit it seemed only a stone's throw to the Wrekin, once next in the long sequence of warning beacons.

He watched the light fading towards the Wrekin until the bend of the track brought the hill between them and the view, on the last steep approach to the top where a large crowd waited around the huge pile of wooden pallets ready to be burned. The farmers had been busy for days ferrying loads up the slope and the scouts had finished the job that morning, assembling an imposing pile. From the valley the beacon had changed the outline of the hill, adding what looked like a newly-erupted rock formation.

More than three hundred people crowded the site, many with a drink in their hands and the sound of laughter and chatter increased every minute. Farmers along with the interesting mix which made up the community— a couple of bankers, one who commuted to New York, a whiz-kid solicitor, a computer expert who appeared to do very little for his money and the policeman from Birmingham who'd been stationed in the village and bought the police house so he could stay.

But as the time approached and the frail figure of the elderly parson was helped up on a box to speak, a gradual hush descended.

James liked this old parson who'd seen active service as an officer in the war and knew its realities. In his retirement living next to the church he took most of the village services to help the vicar-in-charge who found his parishioners in this corner of the four-church parish, too far out of line with his High Church views.

Now he stood, long dark coat fluttering, his voice almost carried away on the wind, to say a few simple words about the sacrifice of those who'd died that the life of those around him could be as it was.

The chattering went on at the back but gradually all went quiet as he repeated the familiar words of Laurence Binyon: "They shall grow not old as we that are left grow old, age shall not weary them nor the years condemn. At the going down of the sun and in the morning, we will remember them."

"We will remember them" came the vigorous response from the crowd while the old man checked his watch and bowed his head for two minutes of silence.

James looked at the sky, still clear but darkening by the minute, hearing again the sound of guns banging and screams from a more recent conflict with different priests trying to bring absolution before death came. He closed his eyes against the tears and bent his head to hide them. Beside him Kate squeezed his arm and he realised he'd forgotten she was there.

The two minutes seemed to go on and on before the old man said in a cheerful voice: "Right, lighting up time."

Two farmers pushed forward with a giant taper made of sacking and straw wrapped round a broom handle. A strong smell of diesel pervaded the hilltop and when they lit the taper and thrust it into the pile of wood, it took hold with a rush of fire.

As the blaze caught hold the dry pallets crackled and became a mass of flame leaping high into the evening sky. Faces were suddenly illuminated and people began to see who was next to them, greeting neighbours and friends; the excitement grew as cans of beer and bottles of wine were emptied in a toast to the beacon. Something primeval in the effect of the fire liberated emotions and swirled everyone on the hill into a sense of good humour and well-being, a fitting climax to the day.

They looked around for other fires but James could spot only one small blaze away to the south on the rim of hills towards Herefordshire. But then he looked more to the east where the Malverns could be seen in daylight on a clear day. Sure enough, there was the distant pinprick of dancing light which answered their own from forty miles away.

Jack thrust a can of beer into his hand and said: "Cheer up mate, it's supposed to be a celebration!"

He smiled and took the can, opening it and tipping back his head to drink. When he looked down it was into Kate's anxious eyes gazing up at him. "Are you all right?" she asked.

"Never better." He put his arm around her, pulling her in close to kiss the side of her head and she clung to him as if afraid he would vanish. He could feel her trembling. "What's up?"

"You looked so strange when John Wagstaff said the prayers. I thought you were in pain or something."

He bit his lip and smiled at her troubled face. "Yes – something, but it's gone now. Come on, let's enjoy ourselves. There's Pat over near the fire."

The beacon flames were still roaring high but began to drop away as the heat subsided and the watching crowd moved nearer for warmth. The May night was turning chilly and the festivities began to ebb as people shivered and thought of the pub and a late evening ahead.

In twos and threes the crowd drifted towards the homeward track, back towards the cars. Raucous shouts and laughter carried from near the fire, cries of excitement on the edge of intoxication.

"We'll have some fun and games later, when that lot get to the pub," said Jack. "It'll be a long night."

As they passed under the rim of the old encampment James felt a heavy blow on his shoulder and a can of beer rolled round his feet. He glanced up in time to see a rock the size of his head bouncing down the hillside towards them, he shouted a warning and pushed Kate to one side as Pat jumped the other way. They watched, shaken, as the rock tumbled on towards the valley. He picked up the can and looked towards the summit but there was nothing to see.

"That was close," said Pat, scrambling to her feet. "Someone should be more careful chucking stuff about up there."

"Yes," he rubbed his shoulder. "I'll have a bruise there, it caught me on the bone."

He'd seen Steve and his cronies on the hill but they'd kept well clear. A strange chance he thought and Kate looked worried as he opened the can.

"Waste not want not," he joked as the shaken lager fizzed out and he drank what was left.

But Kate took his hand as they walked down the hill in the darkness.

The pub was heaving and Richard behind the bar appeared unsure whether to be pleased or put out. His usual ambivalent attitude to his business showed in the perpetual fixed smile on his face along with an air of harassed irritation. Part of him was delighted to see a packed bar with customers struggling to reach the front to order drinks but another side rebelled at the intrusion into his easy, laid-back life. His wife Caro was helping to serve with the regular barmaid who carried on her accustomed unhurried pace regardless of the crush of faces demanding attention.

Jack was at the bar trying to get served and James, Kate, Pat and Mrs Wilson managed to grab the last empty space outside, a table alongside the stone wall which ran round the pub's small paved garden. Inside there was squeezing room only and as more people arrived from the beacon the garden too became a crush.

Inside the mournful singing of a Scottish ballad began as the musicians who got together every month in the pub, swung into their repertoire. They were enhanced by the voice of a Scots woman, new to the village, who specialised in the folk music of the far north. There was a violin, a guitar and someone with a flute plus a mixture of percussion from the local solicitor.

They were good together and provided music for frequent merry nights in the Fox but after half an hour of what seemed the same lament the music grated on James. The high, melancholy voice kept up the wailing dirge accompanied by the prominent violin and several voices started muttering loudly for a change of mood.

"Why don't they try a few Vera Lynn songs?" Jack asked. "That's what we want tonight, more appropriate -- White Cliffs of Dover or We'll Meet Again. Much better for the occasion."

His daughter agreed: "We need something a bit more lively, that's for sure."

"If it's all about VE Day then it should be Vera Lynn," said James. But the lament continued and he drank his pint in silence, watching Kate as she talked to Pat. It was the first time they'd been out together in public and he was uncomfortable after the rock incident, certain it was no coincidence. He finished his pint and offered to go for another round.

"I'll get a bottle of wine," he said to Kate. "I can't drink any more beer and we don't want to fight our way through that crush too often."

It took him twenty minutes to get served, returning with two bottles of wine and two pints for Jack to keep them going. He'd had enough and would gladly go home but he could see Kate was enjoying the atmosphere. Around him customers were jostling and impatient, Richard was now red in the face and his smile was drooping. As he went outside he saw Steve Sterling among the latest arrivals followed by the two boys they'd seen on the hill. He avoided passing Steve directly as he came in but knew the other had seen him. He couldn't help glance at him and their eyes met for an instant, Steve's showing blatant hostility.

Outside he said to Jack: "The Sterling boy's just come."

"I saw him," the older man said tersely. "Dunna worry. He won't start anything while we're here."

He said nothing, unsure how to take that, not liking the idea he needed Jack's protection. He said after a moment: "I'm not afraid of him."

"Never thought you were."

"But I don't want unpleasantness, especially in public, I've seen too much of it."

"You'll be a bit more, what's the word, about it than Steve, I daresay."

"Subtle?"

"Yes, that's the word."

"I certainly wouldn't pick a fight with him, if that's what you mean. But if needs be I can deal with it."

"Good, hope you're right," said Jack. "But I tell you, that boy's nasty."

"Everyone says that, but why and how come he gets away with it?"

"Born like it, I s'pose and he's a bully, like his dad. Folk find it easier to avoid a quarrel with them."

"Mmm. Letting bullies have their way usually leads to trouble."

"Ah, you mean in your job like, in all those bad places in the world . He's just a local lad throwing his weight about. It don't mean much. It's not like you mean."

"Isn't it?"

"This is Shropshire. We don't have wars here. The quietest place under the sun, that's what that poet chap said, wasn't it?"

"I think that was Clun."

"Maybe but it's all the same."

James laughed: "I expect you're right."

Continuing that train of thought Jack went on: "His dad's in there. Haven't seen him here for a long time, usually goes to the Tankerville, but it's a special night, I s'pose. I saw him when I went to the gents, over by the fireplace, with her dad," he gestured at Kate. "You maybe didn't pick a good night to come out."

"I'd like the chance to speak to Kate's father, try to sort things out, but I don't suppose tonight's the right time."

Jack shook his head. "Bad idea."

With the typical curiosity which he'd had got used to, Jack said to him: "Fond of her are you? Think you might make a go of it?"

"Who knows, Jack? As I told her brother, Kate's staying at the farm because life at home was unbearable. You know all about it ."

"Yeah, but people do talk, you know."

He nodded.

"But why will no one tell me what's behind it? Why are they so set on her marrying Steve? It's as if there's some sort of hold on them."

"Well there is."

"But what?"

"We don't talk about it. It's one of those things that everyone knows but nobody wants to admit."

"Well, for once, let's talk about it. I'm involved whether I like it or not because of that blasted horse, I think I ought to know."

"Ah, s'pose you should."

"Well?"

Jack took a long pull at his pint and said: "Don't you tell anyone where you heard it."

"Of course not. I'm a journalist, remember."

"Yes, and don't you write about it, neither."

"Jack! I won't write about it. Just tell me, for Christ's sake."

"There was a shooting see, nearly twenty years ago. Nasty business."

"Murder?"

"He wasn't killed -- but it didn't do him a lot of good."

"Who was this?"

"Chap called Graham Milburne. He had the farm next to Patterson's. Bit younger than Ted, good looking chap and not wed. He moved from mid Wales and bought that farm, Ted wanted it but he couldn't raise the cash. It didn't seem to bother him that much, not then. The family farm was 200 acres or more so he was all right. He married quite late, and they'd got William and little Kate. I suppose he wanted to expand, like we all do. There was the fuss about the water too, that caused a lot of trouble."

"Water? What water?"

"Bill and Ted had this idea to sell water, it was just getting going then, people mad for bottled water, long before the ministry began encouraging farmers to diversify and that. They didn't tell anybody, just got on with doing it but the lie of the land wasn't right on Bill's so they sunk the borehole at Sedge Farm." Jack paused and took another long sup of beer. He looked round the pub to see if anyone was listening before he went on.

"Lovely pure water they got, just the thing, so they applied for planning permission. That's when you know what hit the fan. A lot of people round here have a private supply, springs or boreholes and they reckoned this scheme would take their water. All on the same what d'you call it?"

"Aquifer?" prompted James.

"Yeah, that's it. So a right old campaign kicked off, stories in the paper, meetings and stuff and it was mostly led by Graham Milburne. It caused a lot of bad feeling, at the time. Anyway to cut a long story short the protesters won — they were right, mind, it would have left a lot of homes with no water — and Ted lost a lot of money. Bill as well but he's got deeper pockets. They reckon Ted was going bust but Bill bailed him out."

James frowned as he listened. "Surely a simple loan wouldn't give him that much of a hold?"

"I haven't finished yet. It was the land thing that really did it."

"Land?"

"You know, that's how you got your place, farms and parcels of land come up for sale from time to time. Round here it's usually Bill Sterling buys them. But Milburne started buying as well, don't know where he got the money but he always seemed able to raise it. He made his farm a lot bigger and then this forty acres came up for auction, adjoining his farm and Ted's. Ted wanted it because it would give him access to land he had a mile or two away. But Milburne wanted it too and at the auction he seemed determined to have it and he just kept on bidding. He paid nearly £2,000 an acre which was a lot then, but he got it and Ted was that mad. He was in the pub cussing about it and going on that he'd get his own back."

He looked up, the pub was still throbbing and the Scottish voice still wailed.

"Get's on your nerves after a while doesn't it?' he said.

"Yes," James nodded. "He surely didn't shoot him over a bit of land."

"No," Jack looked at him and winked. "It was more persomal than that."

"Go on, none of this explains what I want to know."

"Hang on, I'm getting there! Ted's wife Elizabeth, Kate's mum, was a cracker when she were young. She and I and Ted were all in Young Farmers together, a lot of the lads liked her, you know, fancied her but most of us didn't have the money or weren't good enough. Anyway she and Ted got together, perfect couple and all.

"But I reckon she got bored with Ted, he was always pretty dull. Nobody was ever sure what did or didn't happen or how far it went, but she started seeing this Milburne – he wasn't married see — it happens, doesn't it? Ted'd be at market and she'd meet him somewhere, it may have been harmless, no one knows. He was certainly a ladies man, nice looking and a lot to say for himself, interesting if you're a woman, talked about more than farming. Bit like you I s'pose in some ways, that'd be why Ted don't like you."

"Thanks."

"Anyway, whether they were having it away or just a bit of social fun like, we never knew. But Ted got to know something was going on and he must've told her to stop it. Remember, she'd got two little ones to think about and she did stop. If they'd been older I reckon it would've been different. But it seems Ted didn't believe her or she carried on with it, whatever. It must have built up in him, like it does and he was always on about this chap, if you talked to him it always got round to that. Like he was obsessed. It's understandable but he shouldn't have let it get that bad. He should have told her to bugger off if that's what she wanted."

Jack emptied his glass and sat staring at it a while. "It went on, nothing sorted and it got round to the shooting season. Ted and Bill and some of the other farmers had a small shoot, they still do but it's a lot bigger now. They put birds down but it was mostly rough shooting, walking them up yourself, no beaters like they have now. They were on that patch at the edge of Ted's land, a bit of woodland next to the forty acres that Milburne'd bought. No one knows what happened, probably never will but Milburne got shot. He wasn't on the shoot, he was on his own land near them. He had red hair, you see."

"Red hair? What was that to do with it?" James was puzzled.

"They thought it was a fox. Don't you see. Ted reckons they saw this flash of russet through the bushes and thought it was a fox. There'd been a lot of fox trouble that spring, taking lambs and that. So he blasted off -- or that's what he says."

"You're joking."

"No, that's what happened."

"And the police believed that?"

"That's the point. Ted maintained it was a fox he shot at and Bill backed him. He swore he'd seen it, brush and all. The three other guns were too far off to see what happened, first they knew was Bill running for the Land Rover to get an ambulance."

"Was he badly hurt?"

Jack nodded: "Bad enough. He got the cartridge in the head at fairly short range, a miracle he wasn't killed, specially as Ted fired both barrels."

"What!"

"Only one shot hit him, like. But it caught his cheek and eye, and there were pellets in his head, in his brain they said. Mind you, folk do exaggerate."

"What did he say about it?"

"He was unconscious for a few days and when the police asked him he just said he remembered getting off the tractor to make sure they weren't on his land and walking through the wood. After that, nothing."

"And that was it?"

"Difficult for the police you see. Everyone knew what had happened about the land and Elizabeth thought Ted had done it deliberately. We all thought it -- still do -- but nobody talks about it. Ted swore it was a fox he shot at, they might have broken him down on that. But with Bill saying he'd seen the fox and sticking to it they couldn't prove it."

"So he got away with attempted murder?"

"Yes. Things'd be different now — they've tightened up on guns and that but farmers and shooting then -- and two men's word -- well -- they couldn't make a case, could they."

"So he wasn't charged at all?"

Jack shook his head.

"You obviously think it was deliberate. Bad thing in a community like this."

"Mm, 'tis. We don't want any more of it."

"So that's why Kate's dad owes the Sterlings."

"Yes. That and the fact that when Graham Milburne's farm came on the market Bill lent him the money to buy half of it. He bought the rest himself and that forty acre went a damned sight cheaper second time round."

"What happened to Milburne?"

"He was in hospital quite a while. He had plastic surgery but it made a real mess of him. He lost the sight in one eye and it sort of pulled his face down."

"Like a stroke?"

Jack nodded: "Yes, like a stroke and his cheek was badly scarred, it spoiled his nice looks. It changed him. I never saw him – I'm only telling you what they said. He was popular, it was a wicked shame because he was a good bloke. But it changed his personality."

"Brain damage?"

"Not exactly."

"So he sold up?"

"Yes, they got rid of him and profited from the bargain. Hey up." Jack looked up. "Best change the subject."

James looked round to see Steve standing in the pub doorway, pint glass in hand.

"Where did he go?"

"They reckon he went up to Scotland to live with a sister, his family came from there originally -- leave it now," he said, anxiety in his tone.

James leaned forward and said softly: "Would he know about all this?" indicating the glowering figure.

"I'd be surprised if he didn't."

"And what about her?" He nodded at Kate who was still chatting happily to Pat, oblivious of their conversation.

"She might know something but I doubt it. Her mum will've kept the details quiet and like I said folk don't talk about it."

James shivered, the wall where he sat felt clammy in the cool night as he stared into the darkness and then across at the malignant figure of Steve. "Bury it deep and it might be forgotten," he whispered to Jack. "Is that the way?"

"It's about the size of it. If you can't do anything, best forget it. Violence isn't just in towns you know, there's plenty of scope for it out here -- the quiet and peace of the countryside — huh, folk don't know the half of it. People still give those two a wide berth but they dunna care. Ted's done okay from his dealings with Bill."

James was shocked more than he expected and he looked again at Kate, wondering how much she knew, wishing suddenly he'd never met her or come to the village. He didn't need all this, wanted a quiet life. But he watched her animated face and smiling eyes and the dark hair moving as she spoke and imagined her as she looked down at him in bed.

Then he glanced at Steve, holding an empty glass, still in the doorway – Steve watching Kate — and thought of him and her together and why he'd got involved. The music had stopped but the pub was still packed. He felt Steve was waiting for something, maybe a chance to do or say something to cause trouble. He wanted to leave before anything could happen.

"Will you be much longer, Jack?" he asked.

"No, I've had enough, it's gone midnight and I'm milking in the morning. It's late enough for me."

He left the wall and went to Kate, putting an arm round her shoulder. "Come on, you two've gossiped long enough. Jack and I are making tracks, are you ready?"

She turned to him with the sweet smile that wrenched his heart each time she did it. "Yes, I'm ready. It's been a great evening, I'm so glad we went to the beacon."

"We've only sat here talking."

"Yes but relaxed and doing what I wanted to do. Pleasing myself."

"I'm glad you're so easy to please."

To leave the garden they had to go close to the pub door or jump over the wall which was four foot above the road. Steve had moved to the end of the wall so they had to walk past him.

"Don't you even speak to me now, Kate?" he said to her.

"Hello Steve, you all right?" she responded.

"As if you care!" He grabbed her arm. "How long you going to muck about with that prick?"

His voice was thick with drink and she tried to shake him off but he held on. James' heart sank but he turned back and said: "Let go of her, Sterling. You're committing an assault."

"Arseholes! You gonna make me?"

"If necessary."

Jack was behind them and said: "Don't start anything, Steve. It'll end in trouble."

"What's it to you?"

Before anything more was said Pat took a hand, hitting his wrist with a beer glass and shouting in his face: "Piss off Steve!" as she pulled Kate away. They hurried to the car park but James, bringing up the rear, heard Steve's angry voice call after them.

"I'll get you Kate, you wait."

James spun round to face him, to catch the glowering sneer on his face. Before he could speak Steve lunged at him with the beer glass but he flicked his head away and the heavy glass went wide of his chin. In fury he started forward but Jack was beside him. Steve stared at them both, pure hatred in his eyes. He hesitated then said: "You're lucky Lambert, too many people about. But there'll be another time and then we'll have you."

Then he was gone. Jack had his hand on James' shoulder and could feel him trembling. "He's a real bastard that one, don't let him worry you, he's all talk."

"I wish I could believe you."

Chapter fourteen

He stood in the porch of the Pattersons' house wondering what his reception might be. He could hear the bell ringing somewhere inside but no sound of answering footsteps. He pressed it again, wishing he was somewhere else but now he knew the story he had something to say to Kate's mother.

It was several minutes before he heard the sound of someone coming and the door opened. Mrs Patterson said nothing at first, her look of surprise turning to anger and then concern as she said: "What are you doing here, what do you want?"

He said. "I don't want to be here but there's something I need to say. Shall I say it on the doorstep or will you ask me in?"

She sighed, paused and looked into the yard. "Ted won't be back for a while so you'd better come in. It's lucky he isn't here."

"I knew he'd be out or I wouldn't have come. I don't want to see him."

He followed her into the house and she led him, not into the kitchen as he thought but into a sitting room, more homely, better furnished and inviting than he'd expected, showing taste and a touch of elegance. He glanced around and then at the woman waiting for him to speak, greying hair, slightly stooped with an air of defeat but with bone structure and a certain stamp which told him she'd been an attractive woman. She could be still, he thought, if things were different and it flashed through his mind what a waste it all was — a set of lives caught in a web from which they couldn't escape.

It struck him that he was caught in the same web and for a moment of near panic he thought he should leave the farm, leave Kate and get away before something happened that he could not retrieve. He shivered at the notion of something bad to come.

"Well," she said. "What do you want?"

No niceties here, he thought, no offer of refreshment.

As if she read his mind she said: "I won't offer you a drink, there's no point prolonging this interview."

"I came," he said "to try to understand why you are so determined to ruin Kate's life. She's living at my house because she feels she can't stay here. She needs to make her own decisions and work out her own life. I must tell you also that I know the story about you, your lover and what happened."

Her face changed when he said that, her eyes widened with shock. She looked at him as if he'd hit her. He saw she must have loved the man and realised her life too had been ruined.

He said more gently: "If you cared about him I'm very sorry."

She stared at him and sank down onto a chair as if her legs wouldn't support her and suddenly he felt sorry for her and understood why Kate was so torn.

"I didn't mean to upset you. Perhaps I was too blunt. We haven't had the best of introductions, have we? It was a long time ago, I know, but it must have been very painful. It's just that I can't understand why you have this obsession with Kate marrying such a wanker who'll ruin her life and bully her and -- "

She interrupted him: "And her life will be like mine -- yes I know." She pulled out a handkerchief to dab her eyes. "It's all about power, you see, that's the point. If she marries Steve, it's all in the family, all the nasty secrets kept together and no one need be sure or know."

"Blackmail."

"Not exactly but it is a hold. I know Ted tried to kill Graham. He might as well have killed him because he destroyed him just the same. Jealousy is a terrible thing, Mr Lambert."

She eyed him and asked: "Do you love Kate?"

He looked away and didn't answer at once, hesitating before he said: "I've given her somewhere to stay while she sorts things out. I think a great deal of her – I'm fond of her but that's all it is for now. She's a wonderful girl who could do so much with her life. She has a great talent with the horse as well and I've helped her with that."

He moved away to think a moment then said: "If you love your daughter how could you condemn her to life with that thug? I know I can't hope for your support but I thought I might at least get some understanding."

She stared at him in silence, considering his words. Then she smiled and some of the years fell away, launching in him a fresh surge of sympathy.

"She could have gone to London with William," she said, "out of it, away from here, that would have solved it. But when she bought that foal from the old boy it was fatal." She stopped and sighed: "If only it were Ted who was shot in that wood."

She paused again. "What am I saying? How awful — but he's been a miserable husband and he's a selfish and greedy man, utterly thoughtless. Why I was ever attracted to him I don't know. The other one -- my life would have been so different with him, he thought about things as you obviously do. You remind me of Graham, you have the same attitude, you can talk about things. In this family we never talk, nobody speaks openly about anything -- it's all sliding round the edge, nothing ever out in the open."

He looked at her in amazement at such an outpouring. But she went on.

"You seem a kind man, Mr Lambert, give Kate my love, — because I do love her. I want her to be happy. I don't want her to marry Steve but I have to go along with the idea. I wish you and she could get away from here, right away. But now you've bought that farm." She was almost musing now, then she said almost eagerly: "But you could sell it couldn't you? — Couldn't you? And go somewhere else?"

"That's very drastic. Are things so bad?"

"Steve is vicious. There's something basically bad in him and now he's jealous and angry and he doesn't like anything in his way. You're in his way -- don't ever turn your back on him."

"Literally or metaphorically?"

"Literally or any other way -- never trust him."

"What a recommendation for a son-in-law," he said.

"Indeed." Then she rose from the chair and took his hand -- startling him again. She said: "Thank you for coming, I'm glad you did."

Then she repeated anxiously: "Please tell Kate I care about her, you will, won't you. I'll try to call up and see her when I know Ted's well away. It's difficult — or if you don't mind me ringing I could meet her in town some time. That would be better."

"I don't mind you ringing, call any time. "

"If I do and it turns into a strange call you'll know why, because I've been interrupted."

"I'll understand," he said. "Glad I came.

Kate was astonished when he told her about the visit. " M u m spoke to you like that?" she said. "I don't believe you."

"I'm not making it up," he said. "Why would I?

"But she never speaks like that, she never says anything."

"No, that's what she said. She's all bottled up in there, isn't she?" he mused.

"You've no idea what's going on inside her head. I felt sorry for her, Kate. She's had a rotten life and I don't think she wants it to happen to you. You'll see her, won't you, if she calls?"

"Can we trust her do you think?"

"She's your mother."

"Yes, and he's my father and look what's happened so far."

"If she wants to see you, you must. You should make it up with her if you can. She seems frightened. She said she wishes we'd sell up and move away."

Kate shook her head, impatient to change the subject. "I don't want to talk about it any more, I must get Harry out. He needs a gallop on the hill if he's going to do any good on Saturday. He needs fast work today and again on Thursday."

It was early evening and she'd rushed home from the office to ride. James had brought him in and begun grooming the horse, almost without thinking. He hadn't ridden Harry yet but had offered to exercise him if she was short of time. She'd looked at him as if doubting his ability and that had annoyed him but now he hurried after her as she went out.

"Where are you going?" he asked.

"Up the top hill on the green gallop, he needs a good pipe opener."

"How long will you be?"

"Only about an hour."

"Take care," he said, watching her ride away.

That was around six. She wasn't back by seven thirty and he stood anxiously in the yard gazing down the lane, expecting her to have come down off the hill and round by the village and be back about seven. He looked towards the hill where he could see the far crest but there was just the outline of several walkers on the skyline. He got in the Land Rover and drove up the near slope to where the fence met the open hill but saw no sign of her. He drove back to find her coming up the lane, the horse wet with sweat and her face smeared with dirt, her light blue T-shirt soiled with grass and mud stains.

"What happened?" he called. "Are you all right?"

"There were lads with bikes on the hill -- trial bikes -- they startled him."

"Deliberately?"

"I don't know. We were cantering up the green slope and they just appeared, we met them right on the brow. I can't blame Harry, he's usually so good. It was so unexpected, he swerved to the left and I came off. I couldn't stick on. They just roared off and then they all came back, three of them and by then he was galloping up the hill. They turned off the track and went after him. I thought they were trying to catch him at first but they were just being silly and didn't realise they were making it worse but -- "

"But what?"

"Oh, I'm not sure but I think they did it on purpose."

"Did you know them?"

"I'm not sure," she repeated. "I think two of them were those friends of Steve's."

"Shit. Is the horse all right — are you all right?"

"A bit bruised, I came off on my arm and almost got dragged but I got my foot free. I think he's okay but he's very hot. It really upset him. I caught him eventually, he went right up the hill and then poor love, he came half way back toward me and just stood there and let me catch him. They'd vanished by then."

"I don't like you going up there on your own, it's too far out. Another time I'll come with you in the Land Rover or meet you up there — something."

"You can't be everywhere with me."

"It's too much of a coincidence. Let's have a look at Harry. You go in, I'll see to him."

"No, I want to wash him off. I only hope he hasn't done a leg. Saturday matters, I so much want to do this one -- it's important."

While she unsaddled he fetched two buckets of warm water to sluice Harry down and scrape the sweat from his neck, flanks and legs. She felt each leg in turn and he helped her apply cooling gel to the front legs which were hot, all the veins distended. She threw a sweat rug over him with a light blanket on top. "He was in a real state," she said.

"What about you? Were you frightened?"

"A bit, it all happened so quickly. It could've been an accident, maybe they just happened to be there and it was an unlucky coincidence."

"Yeah," said James "like the beer can and the rock. I wish I could believe it was an accident but I doubt it."

Later she pulled off the long-sleeved T-shirt to reveal a patch off raw skin in a wide red graze on her arm.

"I got scraped on a rocky bit."

"You're lucky it wasn't worse, that'll be sore."

"It's nothing. I scraped my bum as well," she said, grinning.

"You're taking it very lightly."

"It could have been much worse. If he'd bolted down the steep side it could have killed him, he was very scared."

By morning Harry's foreleg had swollen and she was in tears. With only three days to the competition she was desperate to get him right.

"Why don't you put him in the paddock, let him walk it off," said James while she debated staying at home.

"You go to work, I'll deal with it."

"But he needs cold poulticing and hosing."

"Take my advice and put him out. It's the quickest way to shift the swelling, let him relax and move around. It's a warm night, he'll be fine. If you leave him in he'll stiffen up and the swelling will get worse."

"But will he be fit for Saturday?"

"You'll have to wait and see. I'll bring him in later and hose the leg but you could bandage it with the ice pack and turn him out like that. I'll do it if you like."

"No, I'll do it before I go."

"I do know something about horses you know."

"I always forget that," she said.

By the next evening when he should have been galloping again, the leg was normal but Kate decided not to work him hard and instead set off on a hack round the village. Without telling her James followed in the Land Rover, keeping a few hundred yards behind. T

They met nobody apart from old Mr Randall who stopped and complimented Kate on the horse, saying he'd always liked greys.

She smiled and thanked him and when James passed him the old man said: "They make a grand pair, those two -- that must be the best animal around here for a long way."

"You like horses?" James asked.

He smiled: "I haven't ridden since my army days but I used to love them."

The weekend turned into disaster. It began well enough with near perfect conditions for the dressage. The arena's turf was smooth and bouncy, not too short, on a perfectly flat field well away from the rest of the event.

The setting among majestic oaks in the Capability Brown parkland of a Northamptonshire estate created a perfect atmosphere of calm for the horses. The hand of the master working with nature was clearly visible in the rolling landscape.

James was delighted. "What a great place," he remarked as she was waiting to go in. "At least you get to visit some lovely places with this sport."

"You're a snob," she said.

"Not at all. But if I'm going to walk a cross country course it might as well be a nice walk."

Harry did a good test but she was anxious.

"Do you think he was sound," she asked.

"He's completely sound. Don't worry."

But when they walked the course he was surprised at the size of some of the obstacles.

"This is known as one of the most challenging of the novice courses," she said. "It's big but inviting but the coffin's a bit tricky."

"What about that water?" he said

"Oh that's simple enough, it won't bother him."

"You have to jump in."

"That shouldn't be a problem."

"It's quite a pop coming out."

"I tell you, no problem."

"You think he's fit enough?"

"Of course, why, don't you?"

"Yes," he laughed. "I think he's fine -- just stop worrying."

She smiled uncertainly and said: "You shouldn't tease me."

"You take it so seriously."

"It matters."

"Okay, it matters."

In the show jumping she had a pole down which added penalties to the dressage score of 31.

"I thought I'd done better than that."

"Judging by the other marks I think they were marking hard, you're in the top ten. It's very consistent, the best so far is 28," he said as they looked at the scoreboard.

She seemed nervous before the cross country, more than usual and he said: "Look, if you're not happy, just pull him up."

"I will."

He positioned himself where he could see some of the course but from the rising ground in the middle only the valley was visible and he relied on the commentator to follow her progress.

"Kate Patterson on Sir Harry clear of the water," -- "clear at the coffin" then a double bounce fence, in and out, not big but the striding was awkward and then he heard the words:

"Ah, Sir Harry and Kate Patterson in trouble. They've pulled up, something wrong there." A long pause, then: "Sir Harry retires after the bounce."

"Shit," he said aloud as he hurried to meet her.

"What's wrong?"

"He's not right, he feels lame."

"He looks all right."

"Maybe but he wasn't happy."

He felt the bruised leg. "There's some heat but nothing much."

"Look at the sweat on him, he never gets like that."

She was in tears and struggling to get her breath back, collapsing on the grass when he took Harry.

"Fuck you, Sterling," he thought. He knew the incident on the hill was deliberate, somehow they'd known she'd be up there. How they had managed to time it so well was hard to imagine but he knew it was no accident.

The leg needed time to heal and it took two weeks before Kate could begin the slow process of getting Harry back to competition fitness. On a Sunday morning she took him out past the church and met several people she knew on their way to the service, pleased by their friendly greetings.

She'd put things into perspective after the disappointment and agreed to meet her mother for lunch. They'd done that twice now and it had cheered her, removing one complication from life. As the horse walked briskly along the lane she thought happily about her mother who'd given her money to buy equipment for Harry. A brand new Jeep passed them slowly. She didn't notice the driver but waved her hand in thanks for his consideration. Two bends further down the lane she saw the same dark blue vehicle parked in the passing place. She thought nothing of it until as she rode up the door opened and Steve got out. As she came up to him he smiled and said pleasantly: "Well Kate, it's good to see you. How you doing?"

"Fine thanks." She kicked Harry on but Steve said: "Hang on a minute," and grabbed the rein just behind the bit. The horse threw up his head in alarm and Kate spoke quietly to soothe him. "Let go of his bridle," she said. "You're upsetting him."

"I only wanted to speak to you a moment. Is that too much to ask?"

"I suppose not. What about?"

Still holding the rein he said: "What do you think of this? Smart eh? Top of the range Cherokee, go anywhere. I thought you might fancy coming for a drive with me, try it out."

"I don't think so."

"It's a great motor."

"I'm sure it is."

"Look Kate, you're gonna miss out. Dad's making me a partner in the farm end of year. I'll have loads more money, you and me can do anything we like, go anywhere."

"What d'you mean? You never want to go anywhere."

"Things can be different. I know I've been a bit rotten to you sometimes but I can change — things'll be different. And when we're married you'll wonder what this was all about. Me and you were always meant for each other, you know that."

"Not by my choice."

"Oh come on Kate, you can't stay with that soft guy, can't even stand the sound of a gun. We've heard all about him, he knows bugger all about farming or anything else."

"He knows more than you'll ever know, about farming and about life."

"Does he fuck! Half-baked writing type. He's no good for you. You need a proper man."

His words stung her into saying what she should have left unsaid. "What, like you? You haven't a clue about what I need."

"What d'you mean?"

"The fact is Steve, I can't bear you near me. I never could. I don't fancy you -- you don't do anything for me."

"And he does?"

Defiant, she shouted: "Yes."

His face changed as she spoke, contorting with the rage she knew so well. "You admit he's screwing you then!"

"I don't admit anything. It's none of your business."

"Don't you! Watch out, you fucking bitch, you might get more than you expect!"

"You and your vile language — let go of my horse."

She kicked Harry to urge him on and Steve made a grab for the other rein hauling on both to hang onto the horse. The jagged pressure on his mouth hurt and Harry snorted, stepped back and reared. Steve was forced to let go, and, losing his balance made another grab, this time catching Kate's leg. She was angry too and swiped her whip down hard across his neck, at the same time kicking the horse into a canter. Steve bawled more filth after her and she could still hear him half a mile up the road. She knew and loathed his cruel rages, had seen too many of them, just wanted to get away and didn't see him standing in the road, the fury turned to icy menace, the voice quieter, speaking to himself.

"You'll regret that, Kate. You'll pay for that. You and that cocky wanker you've latched onto. He'll wish he'd never seen you. You wait. I'll have you, one way or another you'll get what's coming."

She didn't tell James what had happened. It was only when he was making love to her, as he tried to kiss her, she turned away her head and said: "Do you still like screwing me?"

The way she spoke turned him cold and stopped it dead, he rolled away and stared at her. "What's the matter? Have I done something?" She was silent so he went on. "Screwing isn't a word I'd use about us. Screwing is just getting it away -- for the sake of it."

"Is there a difference?"

"What's brought this on, what's the matter?"

"It's what he said."

"Steve?" Then she told him.

When she finished he asked: "He threatened you?"

"Yes. He's so foul-mouthed and he's cruel, you know. I'm sure he would have hurt me and Harry there in the road if he could've got away with it."

"He's a vile bastard from what I've seen."

"He is. I grew up with him, I know him. He did some horrible things as a boy."

"What sort of things?"

"You know, the nasty things some boys get up to but he was always worse and took such a delight in it. I remember him throwing hedgehogs into a bonfire. Baby ones, we found a nest of them and dad had a fire going, burning up old baler band and rubbish after the winter. Steve caught these little hedgehogs and started throwing them into the fire. Dad stopped him -- it must be the only time he's ever stood up to the Sterlings.

"Another time it was kittens, there were too many cats on the farm and his dad wanted them gone – I know it has to be done sometimes -- but there are proper ways to do it. Steve put the whole lot in a sack, mother and all, and drove the tractor over them. He said it was quick — maybe it was — but it was horrible and the point is, he enjoyed it, made jokes about it."

"Some boys are like that, cruel without thinking, they usually grow out of it."

"But he did think about it. It was all deliberate." She stopped and said slowly. "He caught a rat one day, in a cage trap. He lit a fire specially and dangled it by the tail over the flames till it roasted and died. Its screams were terrible. I was screaming too and crying, he did it to upset me I think. It was so deliberate, so cruel. He did other things too, much worse than that."

"Do you want to tell me?"

"No, I want to forget it all."

"Whatever you like." James lay still beside her, visions of other cruelties in his mind, all thoughts of sex forgotten. Soon, at a loss what else to say or do he went down for a drink.

Kate followed, wanting to be near him, at two in the morning the world looked very bleak to her.

"I'm afraid of him, James, I wish we could get away. I think you were right, it was deliberate with those bikers, they meant to frighten Harry. Steve must've put them up to it, he's capable of anything, to get back at me through the horse."

"I don't know what we can do Kate, I don't want to leave here. I suppose we could take your mother's advice and move but it takes time. You don't think we should move Harry, put him in livery?"

"I can't afford it.'

"Well no, but I could -- for a while anyway."

"I can't let you do that."

"We may have to. I'm afraid for the horse and for you. What's going to happen next?"

She turned her miserable face to him: "I don't understand why it has to be like this? I don't want much, just to ride the horse in peace and do my job and be with you. It's not much to ask, I'm not hurting anybody else."

"Steve thinks you're hurting him."

"But I'm not."

"You're something he thinks is his and he's lost it. That's what bugs him."

Chapter fifteen

He stood upright to ease his aching back when the rain began, enjoying the soft, gentle drops on his bare skin after the heat. He was digging in the vegetable garden beyond the barn, a patch of land he'd fenced off from the field and ploughed and just beginning to look as if it belonged there. The digging was hard because the stones were near the surface and however many he removed more seemed to work up through the earth. But the soil was good, light, free-draining and fertile and properly nurtured it had already repaid him with a few vegetables.

He'd tried a cultivator but its blades cut too deep and only brought up more stone and a gravelly sub soil. So he worked by hand -- and enjoyed it. Digging made his mind go pleasantly blank, smothering problems, working off frustrations, taking pleasure in simple physical effort. Now he surveyed the sky dominated by a rainbow shining through the shafts of sunlight while the rain was still soaking him. The shower was heavy but ceased as soon as the cloud had passed. He felt charged with a wild delight as he saw the heavy grey mass like a drooping curtain, drifting away down the valley and he gloried in the moisture glistening on his brown skin.

It had been dry for three weeks and they'd made a fine crop of hay which would be enough for Harry and the sheep with a bit to sell. He was grateful for the sunshine but had looked for rain to bring on new grass on his close cropped fields. This hill land with the rock not far below the surface soon burned off in the sun and he needed grass.

While he watched the retreating clouds, Kate came up behind him, calling in concern but he said without turning: "Rain like this never hurt anyone."

When she was beside him he kissed her with such vehemence she drew back in awe. "I'm sorry, did I frighten you?"

"No, of course not. I was worried you might catch cold."

He laughed. "After that heat. It'll thunder later, brilliant."

She stared at him. "Sometimes you scare me, some of the stuff you say is a bit weird."

"What? Enjoying storms? So much power there, Kate. Raw nature. Sorry. You don't know me that well yet. Rain like this -- it's God's gift. Look on the bright side -- you won't have to water the plants tonight. We don't want sun all the time or we'd die."

He stared at her in sheer lust, part of his mood. "Come here." His voice was husky with desire and she hesitated but he caught her wrist and held her, kissing her again, almost savagely. Then he hauled her after him, heading for the barn.

"Hold me," he ordered and she touched him fearfully, so he pulled open his jeans and shoved her hand against him. "Don't be coy Kate, you know enough by now."

He fondled her breasts in hasty greed and pulled her down, urgently tugging at her jeans as he pushed her across a bale of hay. "Not here, please," she protested. "Someone might come."

"Let them," he said as he continued. She cried out a little and struggled but he stroked her breasts to quieten her.

When it was done she was frightened. He rolled over and lay very still face down on the barn floor. She wondered what was coming next but he turned and grinned at her.

"That was wicked, wasn't it? But wonderful." He gave her his little boy gaze and said: "Did you mind? It probably didn't do much for you. Sorry, did I hurt you?"

"A little at first, you haven't done that before. I didn't exactly mind, when I relaxed it was good. I just have trouble letting go. But I'm getting better," she said laughing. "You can please me later."

"Now if you like," he kissed her gently, quiet, sated, back to the lover she trusted.

"It's no good now, I couldn't relax out here — but you can spread me out later if you will."

"Mm, you are learning," he smiled, kissing her again, wooing now and trying to please. "You're sure you didn't mind?"

"No. It was good, better than I thought and I felt you a long way inside me."

He touched her face. "You're so lovely, you stir me up, I can't help going over the top sometimes." Then he looked outside. "The sun's back, come on, I must finish the digging."

"I don't know why you bother."

"I want that extra bit of garden to grow more beans next year and I want to put some in this autumn."

"You could buy them instead."

"I know. But I like growing my own and you know how I feel about supermarkets."

"But the ground must be like rock."

"It's not so bad and I didn't have time before with the research and hay making."

"I think you're a masochist."

"Perhaps. But it's satisfying to grow stuff, a simple pleasure that's hard to explain — very therapeutic. Basic — takes us back to what we should be."

"Here we go, Lambert lecture number fifty-five!"

At least he could laugh now, sometimes he'd got cross with her when he talked about things that mattered to him. She couldn't comprehend why he didn't buy everything at the supermarket or his aversion to big companies.

"But everyone shops there, it's so easy."

"Yes, that's why they've got so much power. Don't you see the damage they've done. They make shopping easy but they rip us off on prices as customers and hold farmers to ransom and they're killing off the small shops. That's not right."

They'd argued about it many times and she was starting to see his point but she liked to tease him about the garden.

He laughed: "If you don't stop arguing I shall put you over that bale and do it again. I could just manage it." He pretended to grab at her and she darted away.

The horse plans were on hold until the ground eased in the autumn and Harry's leg was properly healed. It suited him not to have Harry as priority because he'd begun to write again. He'd still found no way round his block on the Bosnia book but he'd taken a commission for a series of articles on the current boom in farming. He'd made several visits to big arable farms in East Anglia as well as dairy units in Cheshire and Shropshire and it made interesting copy.

Farm incomes that year were at an all time high particularly because Euro subsidies were out of line with actual prices giving British farmers a big advantage. The 'never had it so good factor' was being bandied about in the media. But some, James included, with his own experience and knowledge of big-scale farming through his father, were only too aware of the cyclical nature of agriculture and that a trough could very easily -- and quickly -- follow the current peak.

He and Kate followed an easy pattern of life, she had her job at the building society which left him the days free for writing and farm work. She turned out to be a good housekeeper now she had the chance to do things her way and she enjoyed it. Having someone to iron his shirts was a novelty, not that he used many, but it was a task he hated. But Kate doing some of the domestic jobs removed one of his excuses for not working.

He thought about her frequently when they were apart, how she'd changed since she came to him, now more mature and less the child. The age difference bothered him, nearly fifteen years was a lot but it was more than years. Her naivety troubled him plus her original request to be taught about sex. He'd certainly done that, giving him the chance to indulge his fantasies, pushing back the borders of her acceptance. But he wasted a lot of time in reverie, contemplating aspects of her body and just the thought of lying beside her was enough to turn him on. Sometimes it was so strong he couldn't wait to be with her. He retained his boyhood guilt about that and would never admit to her what he did, still seeing it as shameful.

He worried also about the whole picture, her family, the threat from the Sterlings, wondering if it had been blown out of proportion. Nothing more had happened since the incident on the hill and Steve accosting her in the lane. She was in contact with her mother and things seemed to be working out. But looking into the future he couldn't put aside the thought of what might happen once the initial heat had dulled. Though they had a lot in common the novelty of acting as her mentor could pall in time and he might need someone on equal terms. It was then the thoughts of Katya would come, she who'd always met his ideas half way or been there ahead of him. He wondered if he was simply besotted with Kate's body.

When she came home she would hurry to find him, wherever he was. She had to kiss him, she couldn't get enough of him or keep her hands from touching him. It was flattering and he sank his doubts into the pleasure of being with her.

They were outside having breakfast which she loved -- alfresco eating was another thing her father hated. Meals at home were a matter of consuming food, not for enjoyment. She'd done scrambled eggs and bacon, though the eggs were over cooked to his taste. He'd taught her how to do them but she hadn't quite mastered the light fluffiness he liked. The limits of her culinary skills surprised him in a farmer's daughter but she was improving and he refrained from criticising the rubbery eggs.

It was pleasant to relax on the stone paved terrace and take life at a slower pace. He read yesterday's paper while she watched the raven duo performing overhead. Since he'd drawn her attention to them she was fascinated by their aerial dances and if she heard them call would leave what she was doing to scan the sky.

That morning it was a dome of azure blue, promising heat later. She stretched her head back and closed her eyes in the sun. "It'll be a great day for the fete. Shall we go?"

"What fete?"

"You know, the church fete in the village, it'll fun."

"Can you see me at a fete?"

"Not most, no, but this is different, it really is."

"How?"

"They fire a cannon to open it. Don't you know about it?"

"Someone did mention it. The first summer I heard a loud bang — but you know guns aren't my favourite."

"No but Derrington fete is different and it's such a lovely day. Now Tom's dead it'll probably be the last time they have it there."

He agreed, smiling, happy to please her. "I suppose it'll cost me."

"Not much — take plenty of change."

Changing his clothes at lunch time he thought about the old man who'd been the backbone of the village for so long. He'd got to know him enough to recognise the depth of character although Tom revealed very little of himself. Modest about his considerable war exploits he'd been known chiefly in later years for his love of gardening and his zeal for the Conservative party. When he discovered James was a journalist he became wary of what he said but the two had hit it off and the old man looked forward to the occasional visits, listening fascinated to stories of his travels. He was sad when Tom died suddenly in the spring. But it was a good death for the old man who at 93 had been afraid of becoming a burden to his family.

He had a heart attack while cooking supper but managed to call his neighbours who got him to hospital where he died just after midnight.

It wasn't the perfect death he'd wanted because, as he was conscious enough to say as he felt the end approach: "I always wanted to die in the garden."

He pressed the button on the radio to catch the news headlines, still thinking about Tom and enjoying drinks with him. But his mind moved sharply to the present when Bosnia was mentioned. He turned up the volume and listened to the BBC reporting accounts of an alleged massacre at a place called Srebrenica. He'd never been there but knew it was to the north east of Sarajevo, supposedly a safe area under the control of the UN but in a Serb dominated part of the country. The reports were sketchy but told of men and boys being separated and taken away to slaughter -- early figures suggested the toll might run to thousands.

He shivered as he heard it and glanced out at the bright English summer realising he hadn't thought about Bosnia for more than a week. He felt guilty because he was enjoying life again while they were still dying.

The garden at the Old Rectory was a bit special.

It was why Tom bought the place and once when James sat with him in the warmth of a summer evening enjoying a gin beside a glorious red rose, he'd gone into lengthy details about it.

"You know what these old houses were like in the seventies," he said. "Nobody wanted them, nor the work they needed -- all the effort such a place took to maintain, especially the garden. But I'd left behind a beautiful garden in Cheshire and needed a new challenge."

"I always needed a project," he said, "have another drink." And James listened happily as he described what he'd found.

"It was a wilderness, that bottom area," waving his arm to indicate the lovely pond with pink and white lilies dappled by the evening light and the brilliant emerald of dragonflies. "That was a bog, a swampy tangled ravel of rushes and overgrown grass. It had been a pond but the stream that fed it was blocked and over the years it backed up and turned into thick mud.

"The courtyard at the front was weedy but you could get to the door. Out here it was a jungle of nettles and foxgloves, brambles, even some bracken right up to the windows. Ivy was growing through the bedroom windows and lifting tiles off the roof.

"My wife said 'we can't live in that' -- but we did. What you see now is what I did, all on my own with just a spade and my mini tractor. I'm not boasting -- it was my project, I loved every minute. My son bought that cannon at Sothebys and set it up here and I built the little fort for the grandchildren. Over the years it's brought endless fun for the family and the village."

The fort was a medieval castle in miniature, about eighteen inches at its towers, complete with barbican, battlements, two baileys surrounded by a curtain wall, a twin portcullis and a drawbridge quietly rotting.

At his funeral his grandson, now a young army officer, had recalled the fort and others made of sand on Welsh beaches.

"Holidays with grandpa were something else. Not for us the bucket and plastic spade — Tom was there with a foot of steel, glistening clean from plenty of garden use and we set to work to build an edifice in moist sand.

"We constructed castles that were the envy of the beach, other children gave up on theirs to gather round and marvel at the turrets and battlements Tom created. His structures were built to withstand the onslaught of the tide and it was a challenge to build ever stronger ones that would last longer.

"And survive they did, sometimes for as long as an hour, turned into islands by the rising water until finally overcome by the insidious waves."

That was the man himself, he would not be overcome, not by age nor encroaching poor sight, nor the gradual loss of hearing. Slowly day by day the years had worn him down but he'd never bowed -- only two days before his death he chaired a meeting at his house -- and at the end, which came mercifully unexpected, he was still himself, old but the same individual he'd always been.

And now the old boy was gone. While the vicar spoke a few pompous words to open the fete, he wondered if Tom's spirit hovered in the garden to ensure all was in order for the day. The house was sold, the contract waiting to be signed after fete day, the cannon was moving to the home of Tom's son -- it was the end of an era.

As they waited, keyed up for the moment when the cannon would sound for the last time in that garden, he realised what a gift the old man had given to the community for all those years.

He gave his garden for all to share, the flower beds and the lawns full of stalls and trestles of sweets, bottles, cakes and preserves and in the centre, a mighty chestnut tree, gnarled by age, which anchored a swinging tractor tyre for the children.

When the vicar spoke of the old man's dedication the village listened in approval and all those months after his death tears glistened in many eyes.

The loudness of the blast surprised him and despite expecting it he couldn't suppress a shudder. Kate looked at him in surprise saying quietly: "You really do hate it, don't you?"

He didn't tell her about the news report and only said: "I have reason."

Later they discovered Tom's son had put in an extra large charge to make the final bang the best ever and certainly the cloud of smoke hung over the lawn for several minutes before dispersing. It was very hot in the sun but most of the stalls were shaded and they did the rounds, spending several pounds in change.

He collected a £10 prize for guessing nearest to the weight of two fat Suffolk lambs and donated it back to the funds. As he rejoined Kate he heard someone say: "That was a bloody fluke, he knows fuck all about sheep." He looked towards a knot of people and recognised Bill Sterling standing with Kate's father and others -- the two men making no effort to conceal their ill will. He looked at Sterling long enough to let the man know he'd heard and smiled with satisfaction when he dropped his gaze. He noted the absence of the younger Sterling.

After the fete they were blessed with five hot dry weeks stretching into September. Kate had holiday to take and his farming features were finished and published. But their ideas of going away turned into a long weekend at the coast with one happy day on the beach and another sailing with a friend of William's.

The sea wind and sunshine away from the village worked on his anxiety and he felt free and happy and would have stayed longer. But there was Harry to consider. So they spent the long hot days doing as little as possible and when he should have been writing he lay in the garden and soaked up the sun. She lay next to him, naked except for briefs, trying to get her breasts brown to match the rest of her. Sometimes she would play her fingers across his scar and that light touch and the proximity of her bare skin sent him beyond resistance. Then he would get up and lead her indoors, into the coolness of the stone-walled house, laying her down on the carpet, windows open, oblivious of who might come by. Afterwards they would drink beer or wine and the days passed in a pleasant dream and he began to think that life could be good after all.

The long spell without rain had frizzled the fields to brown and what was left of the grass was crisp as he walked, burnt off in the drought. But the sheep seemed happy in the sun.

He began to look anxiously at the sky, repeating the same mantra each time: "It's got to break soon, it can't go on like this."

Late in the afternoon a breeze began to cool their bare skin and flutter the leaves, gently at first, blowing up from the west into a busy storm wind that tumbled wisps of hay across the yard and snatched the paper he'd been reading to scatter its pages. In the house a door banged shut and heavy black clouds loomed in from Wales. They listened for thunder and heard it in the distance moving rapidly closer. When the first drops fell, Kate rushed to grab the garden cushions and washing from the line before the downpour arrived. He stood unmoved, face upturned to the rain. Across the valley lightning flashed, forking in vivid scars down the darkening sky. She hurried in to watch from the window but ventured back out to huddle close.

"We'll be soaked," she protested.

He laughed and said: "It's not raining much, it's going round. Look."

Where he pointed she saw cloud billowing low over the opposite ridge, lightning flickered and the thunder banged in a continuous rumble well away from them. The deluge fell from scud clouds reaching down like leaden fingers but where they stood the rain was gentle until it began to bounce around their legs and they were driven indoors.

"You're crazy!" she laughed.

"You know I like rain. Trouble is now we'll get too much and be sick of it."

The morning air held an exhilarating freshness and the fields wore a flush of green to soften the parched turf. In the field above the house he spotted the first tiny white beads of developing fungi. Bobbie was chomping something and he saw the spaniel had found his first mushroom of the season.

The sight cheered him. He'd come out with the dog in low spirits after a radio bulletin had brought more awful news from Bosnia. A Serb mortar had fallen on a busy market in Sarajevo, killing thirty-eight people and injuring more than eighty. He thought at once of Esma, she could have been shopping there and he had no way of knowing if she was among the victims. He frowned as he watched the dog foraging and wondered if she and Arif were still alive in the struggling city.

Bobbie always went for whatever he was picking, blackberries, the few strawberries he'd managed to grow, mushrooms in the field or potatoes from the vegetable garden. He knew if it went in master's mouth it was good to eat. Last year he had to leave him behind on a mushroom hunt because the dog got there before him, grabbing the white caps as he bent to cut the stipe.

He put on a brave face for Kate and came back, bare-chested, carrying a cluster of fungi in his T-shirt, white or coffee coloured caps with gills of pink or light brown. She was delighted.

"These are just the first few — there's masses coming," he said. "They're early because it's been so dry. We must take the basket and knife tomorrow. You should cut them, you know," he explained earnestly. "Then you don't damage the mycelium and it keeps them going."

"Is there no end to your knowledge?" she said, amused, watching him slice his treasure to fry in butter for breakfast with bacon.

"We'll take some over to Jack and Sheila tomorrow." He was pleased about the mushrooms, he loved them, one of the compensations for the way he farmed. He knew they laughed at him for his sparing use of bagged fertilisers but excessive nitrogen killed the delicate mycelium.

It became his morning ritual, going out while the Septembes dew was sparkling wet on the grass with a basket and small sharp knife to cut the white, delicate fungi -- horse and field mushrooms. He picked them by the pound and they became embarrassed what to do with them. Some she took to work, some went to the Wilsons and Richard added new mushroom specials to the pub menu.

Their sudden profusion was a source of fascination. In the spring he'd power harrowed that field, reseeding into the existing turf with a small dressing of potash and phosphate to help the young grass. It must have suited the mushrooms and the mycelium tentacles which spread thinner than a spider's web beneath the surface in long curving runs and fairy rings.

"You're obsessed by mushrooms," Kate accused.

"They're fascinating -- don't you understand?" Katya would have understood, he knew that. "There's something so sensuous about picking them, spotting their white innocent heads, waiting to be plucked -- tumescent -- like you," he said to her.

"You bring sex into everything."

"Do I? Do you mind?"

"Of course I don't. But James -- " she looked at him anxiously.

"What?"

"You will be careful what you say when Mum's here. I'd be so embarrassed if you said something like that in front of her."

"What do you take me for? What we say to each other is between us. Don't worry, I'll behave."

William and Annie were expected that day for the weekend and they were to collect Mrs Patterson for lunch.

She was nervous about it but he was relaxed. Bring her to the farm, nice easy lunch, no fuss, plenty of wine and act naturally.

"You make it sound easy."

"It is. Look, that day, I told you, I felt sorry for her. She's trapped as you were. The fact she wants to come says it all. She may even talk your father round."

"No – she'll never do that. He's too far in with Bill."

"We'll see. I just get the feeling your mother's had enough of all this. Who knows, they might agree to forget about Steve and then you could go home."

"What do you mean?"

He kept a straight face: "Well, you wouldn't be forced to stay here then."

"I thought you wanted me here."

"Joke, sweetheart. Course I want you here, I'd have a permanent ache in the balls if you left."

Dismayed, her lip trembled and her eyes glistened on the edge of tears.

"Oh Kate! Don't look like that, I was joking."

"I know your jokes," she said. "Is that all I mean to you — a good shag?"

"Kate love, don't think that. You know that's not it. You mean such a lot to me, I'm very fond of you – I -- "

"But you don't love me."

"I didn't say that."

"You never say anything."

He tried to kiss her but she turned her face away and pulled free. All laughter gone he sighed and saw her desperate not to cry. Her mother's visit was an ordeal to face and she feared his joking had an edge of reality. She went upstairs and he found her in the room she'd used at first, where her things were kept, where William and Annie were to sleep.

"Kate! Don't be upset. I care about you, I want to look after you. It may be love, I'm just not sure. Does that one word make so much difference?"

She faced him wearily. "You tell me I've changed a lot but you still treat me like a little girl. I'm so unsure of you and with mum coming and William I'd feel so much safer if I knew you cared."

"I do care." He sat beside her and held out his arms. "Come here."

"No, I don't want that."

"I was only going to kiss you, stroke you."

"I'm not a pet."

She tried to rise but he caught her wrist and held her tightly. "No, you're not, you're wonderful. And I want you here, believe me, and I'd do a lot to make you happy." He lifted her hand to kiss the palm. "Darling Kate, what would I do if you left me?"

William had brought his mother for Saturday lunch on the pretext of taking her to a pub while Ted took cattle to market. He'd been instructed to bring her in by the kitchen door so she would find him cooking. As they came in he put down his chopping knife and wiped his hands before greeting her with his most charming smile.

"Kate will be here soon, she's busy with Harry. Let me get you a drink."

William and Annie sat at the kitchen table and she followed suit as James produced wine and glasses. They all observed her as she looked curiously around the kitchen, obviously slightly on edge. "You've made a difference to this place. It used to be an awful hole ."

"Yes, there was plenty to clear up. But it suits me and Kate likes it."

"It's comfortable."

"You won't mind if I work while we talk – I'm cook today."

He continued preparing lunch, making a show of being busy while William promoted a three-way conversation. Then James chipped in, changing the subject: "By the way, I'm very glad you could come."

She studied his back a moment before saying: "It was time."

William smiled. "Have some more wine, mum."

The door opened and Kate entered, halting when she saw them gathered at the table but she tossed her head and met her mother's eyes, glanced at the others and kissed her on the cheek. Elizabeth Patterson stood up and held her daughter an instant, returning the kiss gladly.

A brief but awkward silence was ended by William saying: "That's all right, then." And everyone laughed.

She lingered for tea. When her son asked if she wanted to get home she shook her head. "No, I won't go back yet. I'd like Kate to show me what she and James have done outside here."

In the warm air of early evening they wandered together around the small farm, looked at Harry and the garden, the older woman listening as her daughter talked about James and his work and Harry's progress. But it always came back to James and how he'd made it possible. As they walked back to the house she said: "This man's really got under your skin. Are you sure he's right for you?"

Her frankness startled Kate after years of non-communication on anything but trivialities, stunned by the apparent concern.

"I don't know. He's changed my life. He's taught me so much, about so many things. Oh Mum, it's just all different."

"I can see that," she paused. "Are you living with him, like — well — you know what I mean?"

Kate flushed and lowered her eyes but she said firmly: "I know what you mean and yes, I am. He's taught me about that too, that side of life can be wonderful. He's wonderful."

"I expect he is."

"You like him, don't you?" asked Kate.

"Does that matter?"

"It didn't — till just now but with us talking like this — yes it does matter. There, you see, he's done that. He's brought us together in a way we've never been. You were always like Dad, not talking or seeming to care, you seem a different person today."

"Do I?" She stared across the valley where the sun was sinking behind the hill and mused: "You see much more of the sunset from here." Then: "Your man must be very special, he's unlocked something in me. I know we never talked, Katie and if we never do again, at least we have today.

"The answer to your question is yes, I do like him. It's difficult not to and he reminds me of Graham." She peered at her daughter. "You know who Graham was?"

Kate nodded.

"He has the same approach to life, unfettered, open."

"Oh Mum I'm glad you came. You do understand about Steve, please tell me you do."

"Of course I do, I've always understood. I know what a nasty bastard he is but I've had to go along with it. But your James has made me see there's more to it all and I've been hiding it from myself all these years."

She stopped and said sadly: "I wish I could get away like you. If only I could leave him."

"Can't you?"

"Where would I go, Kate, at my age? No, I must stick it out but I shall tell him I won't support them in trying to make you marry Steve."

James, watching from the window saw them in deep conversation and prevented William from going out. "Leave them — let them talk while they can."

As they walked to the car for William to take her home, she waited for James to open the door and when he was beside her swiftly reached up to kiss his cheek. "I have to thank you," she said. "You've made me see."

"I have to thank you," she said. "You've made me see."

Chapter sixteen

Pat drew the short straw as the one who had to break the news. She tried to make her father go but he wouldn't do it, nor would her mother. It took them a day to realise Kate didn't know, all assumed her mother would tell her -- although Mrs Patterson was very mute in her grief -- or that William, the brother, would come from London to deal with things. But William didn't know. It was only when Pat saw Kate on the horse, waving as she passed by, appearing to be quite unaware, that she realised the girl didn't know her father had been dead for two days.

She braced herself to tell them, relieved to find James on his own though Kate soon came in when she saw the car — but he heard the tale first.

"How do you think she'll take it?"

"Don't know, after all that's happened — but he was her father."

Kate listened in silence with no sign of emotion then said: "We must go to mum."

It was he who asked where Ted Patterson was found. "Down near the river, in the lower fields by that high stile -- looks as if he was shooting pigeons in the maize crop. They think he must've tripped but he was carrying the gun closed. It caught him in the head."

Pat didn't repeat what she'd heard, that the blast from the 12-bore had blown his face away. A messy unpleasant way to die but hard to tell if it were accident or intent. Already the village was saying he'd been too clever to do it that way, so they couldn't be sure — which meant no problem with the life insurance.

"Thank you, Pat, I'm sorry it had to be you who told us. It's strange nobody else let us know."

"They all thought Kate's mum would've rung you. I thought things were better with her."

"They are."

When she'd gone he looked at Kate who said again: "We must go to mum."

"Better ring William first."

William, at his office, asked quietly: "How come you're telling me?"

"We've only just found out -- from Pat."

"Strange, I hope mother's all right."

"We're going there now," said James.

"I'll come down soon as I can."

Elizabeth Patterson was in the easy chair in the kitchen, looking through the window. When they entered she said: "You know then."

"Why didn't you tell me?" Kate went to her, took her hand and kissed her. "Are you all right?"

The woman looked vague and distant and it seemed an effort to drag herself to the reality of what they were saying. She almost shook herself as her eyes focussed on Kate's face. She smiled, a funny, bitter little smile, more a grimace and said: "He made a better job of it this time."

"What d'you mean?" Kate said. But he knew exactly what she meant.

"Leave it," he said. "I'll make some tea." Kate brought another chair and sat holding her mother's hand, unable to think of anything to say.

He watched them for a while and soon realised Mrs Patterson was incapable of doing anything of her own volition. He pulled Kate away and said quietly: "You'd better do something about a meal, I doubt if she's eaten today. And ring William's flat, find out when he left."

He took Kate's place in the chair, taking the empty cup from her hands. He said: "William will be here soon."

She looked up at him. "James -- you and Katie, I'm glad you're here. It's all right now, you can come when you like."

He nodded, wanting to keep her talking. But it stopped again.

"Mrs Patterson, have you made any arrangements yet, the funeral or anything. I suppose there'll be an inquest."

"Inquest? Yes, I suppose so. They'll want to know why he shot himself -- won't they?"

"Shot himself? Why d'you say that? Do you think he did?"

She looked hard at him, as if struggling to come to terms with the reality of his question. "Of course."

"Are you sure?"

She nodded but answered his earlier question. "The police took him away, I've done nothing else."

She retreated into reverie and he took her hand. "I know it's hard," he said, "but the grief will pass, life goes on." He heard the platitudes issuing from his mouth but could think of nothing else.

"Grief?" she turned to him, looking at his hand on hers. "Kate's James -- you can come here now whenever you like. I can do what I like. You think I'm grieving? No, I'm free. Kate's free. He's gone."

Her words shocked him but he told himself it was her shock which made her speak in such a way. He stroked her hand absently wondering what to say.

"Graham used to do that," she said.

"What?"

"Stroke me like that."

"Oh," he snatched his hand away.

"Do you think I could find Graham?"

"Christ," he thought. "I hope she hasn't lost it." Aloud he said: "Do you know where he is?"

"I did have an address, for his sister."

"It was a long time ago," he said slowly. "He may be dead."

"I know that. You needn't fret, I'm not going balmy."

"I never thought you were."

He started to rise but she caught his arm and leaned her head against him saying: "I know why Kate cares for you. You listen." She looked at him with a depth of sorrow in her eyes which made him want to comfort her. Not sorrow for the husband taken violently from her life but sorrow for the wasted years and the other life she'd missed. Without thinking he put an arm round her shoulders.

"Talk away Mrs Patterson, say what you like."

"My name's Elizabeth, please call me that — that's what he called me — not missus, like Ted. All these years I wanted to write to him, go to him, try to help him. And I didn't."

"You could have written."

"I didn't have the courage. I went along with all this, here, and the years slipped by. Do you think it's too late?"

"I don't know. You could try, after the funeral."

"Yes, there'll have to be a funeral, I suppose. Will they bury him in the churchyard, d'you think? They didn't used to let suicides be buried in sacred ground -- that's right, isn't it."

"Yes, I think so — but it may not be suicide. You shouldn't keep saying that."

"Oh, let's have some honesty for once. At long last. He shot himself and I'm to blame. And I don't care — I don't care. Do you want to know the truth? The real truth?"

He was silent. "Do you?" she insisted

"Only if you want to tell me."

"I do. You see I'm glad he's dead. Glad! Because I'm free and Kate's free."

Kate, trying hard the other side of the kitchen to ignore what was being said, gasped and spun round but James motioned her to stay quiet. He missed the expression of surprise when she saw his arm around her mother but he shook his head and went to her. "She's very shocked, she probably needs a doctor," he said quietly. "Did you get hold of Annie?"

"Yes, William left around three. He should be here soon."

"Good, I think we need him." He began to open cupboard doors "Is there any drink in this house?"

"Not much but there'll be whisky and sherry in the sitting room."

"Bring some. It can only help. We need to know what happened before she speaks to the police again."

He took two glasses and returned to the woman in the chair, sitting close to her again. He offered her a glass but she shook her head. "Drink it," he said. "I'll join you. It'll do us both good."

She sipped the whisky and he drank his quickly, glad of it. He kept talking softly to her, trying to piece together what had happened.

"Why do you think it was your fault?"

"Because of what I told him."

"What about?"

"After I came to see you, that day, when William brought me for lunch."

"That was more than two months ago."

"Seems longer."

She leaned back in the chair and rested her head wearily, looking up at the ceiling.

"I told him I'd had enough of it all, enough of the lies and pretence -- the bullying and greed. I told him I was sick of his toadying to the Sterlings. And I told him there was no way I'd let Kate marry Steve."

"I see. How did he take it?"

"He went potty. We had an awful row and he hit me and then he calmed down and said if I cared about him I'd not stand in his way because I knew what would happen."

"Then I said I didn't care about him, not at all and -- maybe I went too far -- but I said I'd be glad if the truth came out and they put him in prison because he ought to pay for what he'd done."

"What did he mean, you knew what would happen?"

"Bill Sterling. It's been a kind of blackmail all these years. Ted plays along with whatever Bill and Steve want, that way Bill stays quiet. If he told the police the truth about what happened in the wood that day, they could still charge Ted with attempted murder. It's been hanging over him all these years, that and the guilt of doing it in the first place."

"So you think Ted was afraid of going to prison and killed himself rather than face it. But Sterling might have kept quiet."

"Not him."

"And you wouldn't have stopped it?"

"Not any more."

He pictured the scene as the couple rowed and she said that finally he would have to pay for what he'd done.

"I know what he did," she said, "and I know why he did it."

He watched her face as she spoke, saw all the pent-up, raw emotion spilling out. "He knew I loved Graham and he couldn't bear that. And worse, he knew I'd never loved him."

He gave her another drink, wondering how to proceed when the phone rang in the hall and Kate hurried in: "It's the police, they're waiting for an answer — they want to interview mum again. What shall I say?"

"Stall them," he said. "Tell them she's gone to bed with a sedative, ask them to come tomorrow. Put them off."

He strained to hear the conversation and heard the phone go down and Kate returning. He met her at the door, with a finger across his mouth for caution. She said quietly: "They're coming at ten in the morning."

"Well done. We have to get her to understand that she needs to be, let's say, economical with the truth. There's no point saying she thinks he shot himself. An open verdict would be better for everyone."

"You're quite a fixer, aren't you." Kate grinned at him.

"It's not that, better to keep an open mind, things are rarely black and white and your mother might be wrong."

"But I'm not," came a voice from the chair.

"Ah."

"Neither am I deaf."

"It's just -- " he began.

"I see no point in lying," she said forcefully. "Why shouldn't I tell everyone the truth at last?"

"Because the truth can sometimes do more harm than good, it could hurt Kate and William and yourself. After all, you've kept quiet all these years as well as the Sterlings."

William didn't arrive till early evening and was at his mother's side next day when the police came. They wanted to know about Ted Patterson's movements on the day he was found dead and about his mood on that day and on previous days.

"Was your husband usually a careful man with his gun?" asked the sergeant.

"As far as I know but I didn't get involved with his shooting arrangements. He was usually careful about handling it and always walked with it broken."

"It seems strange he should have tried to climb the stile with his gun closed ready for firing. Doesn't that sound odd to you?"

"Perhaps he saw something he wanted to shoot while he was on the stile," put in William "and maybe he lost his balance and fell."

"That's quite possible, sir, we've considered that."

"What are you trying to discover?"

"Just need the facts, sir. Assuming he shot himself, was it an accident or did he kill himself deliberately."

"I see."

"We're fairly happy no one else was involved. There were no other fingerprints on the gun and it was definitely the one that killed him."

"What do you think about it?" asked William.

"I don't know, sir, that's for the coroner to decide. But it seems to me we may never know the truth."

Which was exactly what the coroner said at the inquest. It was a surprisingly short affair as the Shrewsbury coroner inquired into the circumstances of Ted Patterson's death before returning an open verdict.

There was an awkward moment when he asked the widow if anything particular had been troubling her husband -- or if she knew of any reason why he would take his own life. James had his eyes fixed firmly on Elizabeth's face as she stood there and hesitated but she met his gaze steadily before saying: "Nothing unusual that I was aware of."

He breathed out and glanced at Kate, who sat subdued, beside him.

After the hearing William, looking tall and competent, took his mother's arm and led her away before Bill Sterling, who'd been sitting at the rear of the court, could get near her.

But the verdict didn't satisfy the village and the gossip continued, with a consensus that he'd shot himself but, as always with Ted, he'd managed it well enough to cast doubt on the outcome.

All the old story about Graham and the other shooting was revived and gone over from every angle and it was generally agreed Ted's guilty conscience had finally become too heavy to bear.

And then the funeral – William arranged it all and it was only later in the evening that he told James of the trouble with Bill Sterling. He'd been to see Elizabeth, demanding to read a lesson at the service. She'd refused point blank and he had tried to bully and threaten her. William had come in during the exchange and heard his mother say, in a voice of total control but with a venom that astounded him: "You and he have ruled my life for years but not any more. He's dead and nothing you can say or do matters to me now. Right or wrong, he's dead and you're not going to carry on your bullying beyond the grave. We'll bury him -- and you and yours will stay away."

William watched the anger change to surprise on the blustering man's face. "I think you'd better leave, Mr Sterling."

Then Sterling had said: "But I need to talk to you about that land by the river. Ted always promised me...."

"We haven't decided anything about the farm, there's a lot to think about. But if my mother decides to sell it will go on the market for tender."

Sterling opened his mouth to speak but William had said: "And Mr Sterling – whatever the price it will be too high for you."

James had listened in admiration at their stance, mixed with fascination about the story. William said: "There's no way he's going to get one foot of that land. His greed and my father's have done so much damage over the years. Now it stops."

They buried him near his parents in the churchyard, given the benefit of the doubt in death as he had been in life. Kate cried at the graveside, not for the bullying father he'd become but for someone she dimly remembered from years before when he had been daddy and she his little treasure.

"I don't suppose he was really a bad man, James but I think I grew to hate him."

"Circumstances, Kate, it's what life makes of people. They get twisted by things that happen and it depends how they react. He was probably a weak man, too easily swayed. William doesn't seem at all like him."

"No, he's not -- but he got away."

William had indeed got away, he stayed long enough to sort out the initial family affairs but then London called him back. Mrs Patterson seemed unable to decide anything and there was still a farm to run and the main man gone. James was forced to take a hand in running things until she made some decisions. There were more than a hundred cows to be milked and although the farm had the dairyman, Rod and Tommy, the young farmhand, both needed time off. For the first time in his life he found himself milking, at first under Jack Wilson's tutelage, until they could find a relief manager. Once he got the hang of the machinery, which was modern and computerised, the cows followed their diurnal pattern, only rolling their eyes and huffing at the stranger if he came too close. Kate helped when she could but against his will he was dragged deeper into the family's affairs and soon began to resent the intrusion.

He was in effect managing the farm. There was grain to be sold, ploughing and autumn planting to be done -- or arranged -- and in the middle of it all Elizabeth Patterson announced she was going to Scotland.

She'd found Graham. The day after Ted's death she'd contacted a detective agency and from the details she gave them they'd found her damaged lover. James could only admire her determination. The man's sister had died and he was living on his own in a croft somewhere near the coast in Galloway. The news brought William hurrying from London.

"Mother you can't just go off up there on your own, it's twenty years or more. He may not want to see you. I don't think you should go, you're not well enough."

"There's nothing wrong with me that getting away from here won't cure. If he doesn't want to see me I'll come home.

But at least I'll have made the effort to do what I should have done years ago."

William and Kate argued hard to dissuade her but James, listening, couldn't understand why they were bothered. "Let her go," he said. "Why interfere, it's up to her?"

"You don't understand."

"No, I don't. All I see is you two trying to run her life the same way your father did. Leave her alone and worry about the farm instead."

"That's the trouble -- she won't decide anything."

"Let her go to Scotland. If she sees this man it may help make her decide what she wants to do. She can't run the farm alone but she seems reluctant to let it go. Leave her to decide."

"She wants to drive, it's a long way."

"She's capable, leave it. Don't interfere."

But he was curious, the writer fascinated by a story of pathetic romance — and he couldn't see the ending. She'd made him breakfast after he'd done the milking and they were alone when he said: "I think you're right to go but will you be okay on your own?"

"Why wouldn't I?"

"I could come -- if you wanted -- if things are fine I'll leave you to it."

"Can you get away?"

"It's only a day, two perhaps. Wait till next week, till the new man starts and Jack can keep an eye on my place. You don't know what he may be like, Elizabeth, you could get a shock."

"I know," she said quietly.

"I'm not expecting much. I wouldn't be surprised if he hates me. You couldn't blame him." She reached across the table to refill his tea mug.

"But it'll be strange here when William goes back. I shall be alone, in control — for the first time. But I don't think I want to be here, too many bad memories. But if there's nothing for me with Graham, then I don't know what to do. But I couldn't blame him," she repeated softly.

"What happened -- it wasn't your fault."

"But I could have gone to him."

"You could. But you had William and Kate to think about. It can't have been easy."

"It wasn't. But I know now, have known for years, I made the wrong decision. I should have gone and taken them with me."

"Perhaps but tell me, do you want me to come?"

She nodded. "If it makes you feel better -- and them."

Watching her move round the kitchen as he ate the large breakfast she'd cooked, he realised how she'd changed. She seemed rejuvenated, as if she'd lost those twenty years of unhappy disappointment. She had a sparkle now, a new sharpness, a lightness that had changed her, the hair was different, the clothes were different and it was hard to believe she was the same woman who'd stopped him seeing Kate. In his mind's eye he pictured her as the girl she'd been, he watched her, fascinated, wondering how she'd allowed all these years to pass without a rebellion. He realised how much he had come to like her and it struck him then what an impact people had on others, how they made them change, like Kate, already a different person for knowing him.

He smiled as she brought him toast. "It would be good to see you happy," he said. "But don't build up your hopes."

"I won't. But whatever happens it'll do me good." She raised her hand, hesitated, then stroked the dark lock of his hair, untidy from milking, clear of his forehead, as if he were a child. "You're a kind man, you've been kind to Kate and to me, I can see why she clings to you."

He frowned at that, unsure what she meant. He ate a slice of toast in a hurry then got up saying: "I must get on, get home, there's a lot to do there."

Kate's anger when she heard the plan was a shock, it caused an unpleasant scene, the first real row they'd had.

"What's the matter with you?" he said. "You got me into all this, I'm even doing the bloody milking! From the first day you arrived with the damned horse, you've dragged me into your family turmoil. Now when I'm trying to help your mother, you don't like it."

"But you'll be away overnight with her."

"So?"

"It's a long time."

"What's the problem? I'm not going to share a room with her."

"That wouldn't surprise me. The way she looks at you ."

"What is this? You think I'm into the mother and daughter bit? I suppose I could." He was laughing.

"It's not funny. It's just, you haven't seemed to want me so much recently. Maybe you're tiring of me."

"What? Silly child -- we've all been busy and distracted, we haven't had much time for it, have we? I want you, don't worry. But if it bothers you why don't you come as well?"

"I can't get the time off."

"They'd let you, surely -- your father's just died."

"You know I want to keep the time for when I need it."

"For Harry, I know."

"Look, I really like your mother, she's a different person now. But I'm worried for her. If it goes badly with this Graham she may need someone there."

Kate nodded. "I expect you're right as usual, I hope it works out for her. She deserves something after all this time."

"You're not really jealous of your own mother, are you?"

"Well," she paused. "I've seen the way she looks at you, sort of hungry, her eyes kind of linger on you. William's noticed too, he said something."

"She's lonely, that's all. She's probably thinking of Graham when she looks at me. She's different now, full of feelings she's repressed all this time. I'm only going to drive her up there."

He changed the subject. "You can't stay here while I'm away and certainly not at the farm without William. Better stay with Pat for a night or two."

"And leave this place unattended?"

"Jack will keep an eye on things and we'll take the dogs there."

Chapter seventeen

The drive north took much longer than he expected, in his mind he'd thought, turn left at Carlisle and we're there. But it was a long way on motorway then dual carriageway hugging the coast across the breadth of Galloway until they turned inland. They'd started later than he wanted, Elizabeth fussing what to wear, which surprised him. Before Ted's death he'd always seen her in dowdy country clothes, uncaring how she looked but she had changed so much and now he waited, curbing his impatience. It was nearly lunch time before they left and by early evening they were still a long way short of their destination and dusk was falling.

She talked a lot on the journey but he had only half an ear on what she was saying, wishing she would be quiet, keyed up as he was trying to listen to the car radio. NATO planes had begun air strikes on Serb positions around Sarajevo -- the world had at last decided to intervene in Bosnia. He tuned in to every news programme, trying to catch the latest details.

The thought of finding a remote farmstead in the dark and an uncertain reception made him insist they stop for the night and start fresh in the morning. Elizabeth wanted to press on but he turned off near Castle Douglas and they hunted for half an hour to find somewhere to stay. Eventually they followed signs up a wooded drive which brought them to a small stone-built Georgian building which had seen better times. But it had a board outside welcoming non-residents to eat and it had rooms available. By now she was anxious and inclined to bad temper.

"It'll be easier to find the place in daylight," he said. "If we went on now it would be very late if we found it at all, you don't know what facilities he has, even if he invited us to stay. It's not fair on him or us. By the way, did you write to him, as I suggested?"

She shook her head.

"Why not? It was the sensible thing to do."

"I don't want to be sensible and I didn't want to give him the chance to say don't come."

Kate sounded cross when he called, unable to hide the anxiety in her voice when he told her about the hotel. "So you haven't even got there yet?"

"We set off too late."

She asked about the rooms in a way which revealed real jealousy and it dawned on him what she must be thinking. It shook him but he restrained his reaction saying only to himself: "Does she really think I might shag her mother?"

He considered this turn in Kate's attitude, as he showered before supper, surprised and a little flattered that she should be jealous of her own mother. Certainly his own attitude had changed, thinking of her now as Elizabeth, a person in her own right — and an interesting person.

Before supper as they talked comfortably together it occurred to him for the first time that she might think of him a little in that way, she certainly reacted to him and seemed to glow with the attention he gave her.

He quickly realised she wasn't used to alcohol, he'd bought her a sherry while they studied the menu and was surprised how soon it was gone.

"Would you like a refill?" he asked and she nodded, saying: "This is a real treat, I haven't been out like this for years, not since -- "

"Those stolen evenings with Graham?"

She nodded: "You always seem to know what I mean, even if I only half say something."

He shrugged: "It doesn't take too much working out. I presume Ted wasn't one for eating out?"

"No, I could count the times and those were early on. In recent years it was very rare. Our social life was mostly supper with the Sterlings. But we weren't really friends with them, not close friends, not comfortable. Ted just assumed I'd cook, every day. That's what I was there for."

James smiled. "Your life's going to change a lot, whatever happens up here."

"I hope so. I hope I've got enough time left to get a bit more out of it. I know I should be grieving but I'd be a hypocrite if I pretended."

She tossed back the rest of the second sherry and whispered: "I know it's wicked to admit it but when I knew he was dead, my heart really did leap. All I could think was that I was free. That's terrible, isn't it."

A waiter came to take their order before James could answer. "Would you prefer red wine or white," he asked her.

"Whatever you think." The choice was limited so he went for a bottle of South African white which might not be too dry for her.

He ignored her empty glass and didn't order another sherry, sensing the fragile state of her emotions which could easily rise to boiling point. He didn't want tears at the table.

She went on: "You must think me dreadful. It's the sherry, I expect, it's going to my head."

"Don't worry, food and an early night is what you need, tomorrow could be a long day."

"I'm fine, life's looking up." The sarcasm was against herself.

"Don't blame yourself for how you feel. It wasn't your fault Ted did it, you stuck with him all those years. If you feel released, it's quite natural, it's no different to getting divorced.

People change, they can't always stay together. Death is just another solution."

"You make it sound easy."

"Not easy but understandable, don't dwell on his death, try to look ahead. Have you thought what you'll do about the farm?"

Through the meal he put options to her for the future, trying to establish if she was willing to leave the house which had been home for so long. It seemed she had no special love for it, too many associations in her mind with bad times over the years. Her main concern was whether William might want to come back to farming, an idea James thought very unlikely. William appeared to him an urban creature doing well in a sphere which made plenty of money and gave him plenty of time. Why would he want to tie himself down with farming?

"I expect I should sell up and be done with it and give most of it to them," she said at one point. Then: "Do you think you and Kate will get married?"

He looked away, avoiding her eyes, but said truthfully: "I haven't really thought about it. I don't think we've looked that far and I don't know if I'm the sort for marriage."

Elizabeth swirled the wine around in her glass and seemed to be studying it closely, her face glowed and she slurred her words. She reached across the table and touched his hand saying, rather too loudly for his comfort: "You know Kate thinks you're wonderful?"

"Does she? Not that wonderful I'm sure."

She nodded. "Oh yes, no one like you. I know what she means. It's your eyes, you have such dreamy eyes."

He looked at his watch in embarrassment, it was only nine thirty, he could do with getting her away to her room before she got too carried away. She continued so all the room could hear: "She cares a lot about you."

He said they shouldn't talk about Kate, that it wasn't fair.

"Why not, she's my daughter, I want to see her happy."

He got her out of the dining room into a quieter lounge where they had coffee but he found his patience slipping when she persisted in trying to discuss his relationship with Kate. He went to the bar for a whisky, and she said: "Nothing for me?"

"At the risk of being rude I think you've had enough to drink. Have some more coffee."

"About you and Kate," she began again.

"Look, what Kate and I do is our affair. I really can't discuss it with you, it's not right."

"Maybe you don't care about her."

"Of course I care." He spoke sharply and she got the message to leave the subject. She became subdued after that and then sleepy and he suggested she go to bed. At the door of her room she turned to him and said, stroking his shoulder: "You really are a very sweet man."

"Mm -- I'll see you in the morning."

At breakfast she was different, apologising to him and apprehensive about the coming day. With the time for actually seeing Graham now so close she was afraid.

"It's so many years, we might not know each other.

"You will. But if he doesn't want to know -- then we go home again and that's an end to it. At least you'll have tried."

As they drove she grew increasingly despondent and when they turned off at Newton Stewart, heading down the peninsula she said: "Oh God, am I doing the right thing?"

"You'll find out very soon," he said, thinking it was as well he'd come.

She had the directions and they followed a single track road which headed off into hilly moorland. A few miles from the sea they turned onto a stoney track across a cattle grid, dropping into a shallow valley with a single storey stone cottage and barn ahead of them. Dun coloured shaggy cattle with well-grown calves turned their heads to watch them from very green fields. In another field several young bulls stood reflective, hock deep in the grass.

He drove slowly towards the cottage looking for signs of life and parked near the door. They waited but no one came so he got out and looked around.

"It all seems very quiet," he said to her, "not even a dog barking." He left her in the car and got out to approach the door but his knock brought no response. Everything was still but peering through the window he could see a fire in the hearth burning brightly behind a guard.

He returned to the car. "He must be out somewhere although there's a Land Rover here. If you wait in the car I'll walk across the fields the other way and see if there's anyone about."

She agreed in silence and he left her, frowning in anxiety, staring at the door.

Beyond the cottage was a yard with a gate opening onto fields enclosed by low grey walls, like the low grey cottage, with sheep and more cattle grazing. The land rose in a gentle slope from the farmstead, a sea of grass moving in the breeze — he'd never seen such lush green grass. He decided to walk to the horizon. Somewhere a dog barked. The sun was shining and the land seemed warm and welcoming. If he found no one they would have to go away and come again. He shrugged and began to walk. As the land rose he could see more and heard the dog bark again. Looking to his right, three fields away he saw a man at work, walling, piles of stone around him and a dog lying nearby, sometimes moving off when something caught its attention. James walked towards them, if not the man himself at least he might know where they could find Graham Milburne.

The collie saw him before the man looked up and bounded towards him barking. He greeted it with a pat and walked on. The man turned, watching his approach and he knew at once he'd found the one they sought. One eye was drawn down, pulled into a scar across his cheek and the bare head was adorned with a fine growth of hair, greying fast and faded from its youthful glory but unmistakably red. But he was surprised because the face was nothing like as disfigured as he'd been led to expect and the handsome man he'd been could still be traced.

"Who are you?" said the wall builder.

"Mr Milburne – Graham?"

"Aye," the accent wasn't Scottish. "That's who I am, who might you be?"

He wanted to break it gently so said simply: "I've come up from Shropshire."

"Aye? To see me?"

James nodded and Graham said: "It's a long drive."

"Yes."

"Why come here? Are you alone?"

"I've someone with me."

"Aye? Does it concern me?"

"Yes, an old friend – Elizabeth Patterson -- remember?"

The man stared at him then ran a hand through his hair, in a gesture of shock.

"She, here? — Of course I remember."

He looked unsteady, as if he might fall and James hurried to take his arm. "You all right? Sorry if I've surprised you." He led him back to the wall and helped the older man sit on the stretch he was rebuilding.

"You certainly have, it's a bit of a shock. What's she doing here, what's happened?"

James had planned to let Elizabeth make the explanations but he had to answer such a direct enquiry. He said, choosing his words with care. "Things have changed with her, there was an accident."

Graham burst out: "Is she all right, has she been hurt."

"No, she's absolutely fine. It was Ted, her husband, he's dead."

The man lifted his eyes and stared at James with a look of disbelief. "Dead -- how?"

"An accident, he was shot."

"Who? Who shot him?"

"He was alone, they think he tripped, they found him dead."

Graham opened his mouth to speak but stopped, a strange brief smile flickered across his face and he remained silent, gazing across the fields towards his cottage, absorbing the news.

He nodded towards his home. "Is she there?"

"Waiting in the car."

"She came to find me," whispered Graham, to himself not James. "After all these years, she's come at last. Is it true?" he asked.

"True that she's here and a widow. Will you see her?"

"Aye -- I'll see her." He stood up. "Best get down there then." Calling his dog he thrust back his shoulders and set off, striding across the land towards the waiting car.

James followed but hung back as they neared the cottage. Graham Milburne walked past the parked car without a glance and made for his door which he opened and went inside. Elizabeth made a move to get out but James had hurried to the car and shook his head to stop her. "Wait," he said through the open window. Graham reappeared in the doorway, staring towards the car, he started to come forward but hesitated, then stopped.

"Now Elizabeth, get out now and go to him."

James watched the man's face as Elizabeth approached, the damaged eye hadn't totally wrecked it and he saw it working through shifting emotions and for a moment thought he was crying. She halted a few yards in front of him, uncertain what to do but he stepped forward saying quietly: "You, here — is it really you?"

She didn't speak so he took her hand, led her into the cottage and closed the door. James contemplated the closed door, wondering what he should do but his presence was patently not required.

Some time later Graham came to the door and beckoned to him. "You'd better have a drink before you leave," he said.

"Thanks." He followed into a low ceilinged room, poorly lit but warmed by the fire where Elizabeth sat with a glass in her hand, looking as if she'd been there all her life. Glancing at her he had no need to ask the question in his mind, she was obviously all right.

"Would you like a wee whisky or some tea?" Graham asked to which he replied: "Both I think," stunned by the joy in Elizabeth's eyes as she turned to him and smiled.

"I knew I was right to come," she whispered as her man returned with the whisky. When he'd gone to the kitchen she stood up and put her arms round James. "It's wonderful, I knew it was right. Thank you so much for bringing me."

"I'm glad for you but what's happening now? He said: 'before I leave'."

"Well, you have to get back, don't you?".

"Yes but — "

"He wants me to stay — and I'm going to."

"Here," he glanced around. "It's not much, not what you're used to, are you sure?"

"James!" she took his hands. "I've waited twenty years for this, surroundings don't matter, it's him I want. We'll be together and nothing else means anything. It may not last but for now I'm here with him. And listen, I want William to put the farm on the market, at once. Get it sold, then at least I'll have some money. Here -- " She handed him a slip of paper, seeing his look of surprise. "The phone number — yes, he's got a phone. Get William to ring me as soon as possible, I want him to arrange a power-of-attorney."

James was startled. "Are you sure?" She seemed to have everything worked out.

"Quite sure."

"But what about Kate? The farm's her home."

"She won't want to be there, you know that. She'll be with you, won't she? And she'll have her share of the proceeds."

He didn't know how to answer her. He waited in silence, still wondering, when Graham came back to stand by the fire looking down at Elizabeth as if he could not believe her presence. He was embarrassed to be there, uncomfortable, impinging on their intimacy, apparently unchanged by the years of separation, as if it were just yesterday they had parted. Now he was the unwanted witness to their happiness and he knew they were impatient for him to be gone.

"I'll go then, when I've drunk this, " he said and she nodded.

Graham said: "Aye, best be gone, it's a long drive you have."

After that they took no more notice of him, absorbed by one another, hardly speaking, just contemplating their mutual satisfaction. He left them together by the fire.

He drove back thinking of all the practical considerations that Elizabeth was ignoring, transport for one, he'd seen only a battered Land Rover at Graham's. Wondering too what Kate would say when he told her he'd left her mother in the wilds of Galloway in a dark croft. He reminded himself it was not his problem.

He went straight to Jack's, assuming Kate would be there with the dogs, pleased to see her car in their yard as he arrived. He could hear Bobbie barking in the barn, as he recognised the sound of the car.

"Won't be long, boy," he called making for the house. Jack was at the door before he got there, and Kate appeared behind them, looking pleased but worried. "I'm so glad you're back," she said, "did everything go well?"

"I think so, at least your mother thought so."

"Is she with you?"

"No. Can I come in?"

"Sorry," said Jack, "course you can."

"So is mum back at the farm?"

James took a deep breath, and sighing said: "No, she's in Galloway."

"You mean she's stayed there — with him?"

"Yes."

"So you found him."

"Yes. There was no way she was coming back with me so I had no choice but to leave her."

Kate appeared stunned, hurt and James could only say: "It's her life, it has to be her decision. I'll tell you about it later -- everything okay here?"

She glanced at Jack and he saw the anxiety that passed between them. "Problem?" he asked.

Jack answered: "I'm sure she'll be back soon but your little bitch Tess is missing. I let them out first thing this morning, like always, they never stray but when I came out of the parlour she wasn't here. Bobbie was in the yard on his own."

Frowning James said: "Maybe she's gone home, she'll probably be there when we get back, she'll be hungry."

Kate said, her voice sounding worried: "I went over when I got back but there was no sign of her."

"She's probably rabbiting," Jack said. "She'll surely turn up, I bet she's over there now."

"I hope so, I'm very fond of that little dog." He pushed aside the unpleasant idea and foreboding that had come unwanted into his head.

But Tess was not there and they went to bed hoping she would be back by morning, both clutching at the idea she'd gone off after rabbits or even a deer. He was down at first light hoping she'd be out there waiting but in his heart he knew she wouldn't be. And he was right. Something bad had happened to the little yellow bitch. She never went far from him or Bobbie. He feared the worst, she must have been taken. The sick misery of panic set in.

Searching for her was a hopeless task in wide open hill country like this, impossible to search every small valley, so many places she could be. But he had to try, his mind frantic with possibilities, there was no way he could sit at home and wait. He had to do something.

He spent the day in the Land Rover, driving up and down rough tracks he normally only covered on foot, whistling and calling with no response. Late in the afternoon he was back on his own land, scanning the landscape from a stoney knoll when the raucous cries of corvids caught his attention and he saw a cloud of black birds circling and crying above woodland two fields away. Something was attracting their excitement. Back in the vehicle he followed the track which took him nearest, a small copse straddling the boundary between his land and Jack's. He hurried through the trees, a horrible premonition growing inside him, fearful of what he would find.

The cacophony of screeching rose louder at his approach and the birds which had settled took off with indignant cries and flapping wings. He entered a small clearing where three carrion crows squawked in fury as they fought over something hanging from a low branch of sycamore, the centre of the crows' attraction. Jackdaws and a pair of magpies hopped nearby watching, afraid to get closer.

The carcase of the yellow dog swung round and round as the birds ripped at it, tearing pieces from the belly. Tess hung, a barbed wire noose deep in the flesh of her neck, one bloody, torn paw above her head, hooked in the wire where she must have scrabbled in a frantic attempt to free herself. The birds flapped away on his arrival but remained circling overhead, calling complaint at the disturbance. He could just reach her head but the wire was tight and without cutters he struggled to free her. The barbs tore his hands as he untwisted the wire but he didn't care and eventually the ravaged body dropped at his feet.

He knelt beside her among the dried leaves and stroked the ruined head, eyes and tongue already gone.

Tears ran freely down his cheeks, dripping over his bloodied hands as sobs wracked him. He muttered again and again: "Oh Tess, poor Tess, why did you have to pay like this? Why did I leave you? I should've known something like this would happen."

He rang the police but knew it was pointless. They could do nothing. He knew exactly who was responsible for the vile act but there was no way he could prove it. A woman constable came out and listened and went with him to the spot in the wood. He showed her the tree and the dried blood on the leaves. She looked upset as she examined the dead dog and the bloodied wire but could only tell James what he already knew — without a witness or an informant they could never make a case. All the girl could say was: "Well, it's certainly no accident and if she was sheep chasing they'd have shot her. Nasty business Mr Lambert, I'll keep the case open and if you get any inkling of someone knowing anything, let us know."

He buried her in the garden watched by the spaniel and Kate who was as distraught as James. She'd been almost hysterical when she saw the body and heard how James had found her.

"It's all down to me," she wailed. "It's just the dreadful, evil kind of thing he would do. He was always cruel, I told you, and he's grown up even more wicked -- evil. Oh James, what else will he do? He can't have me and now he won't get our farm either. He'll have his revenge somehow and this is the start of it."

He didn't answer because she was right, it was down to her and his entanglement with these families. Shovelling soil into the hole to cover Tess his thoughts were bitter — he'd come back from Bosnia to leave horror behind, to live a peaceful, easier life, write and make a living.

But there was only more horror, right here, in this quiet, beautiful stretch of the English countryside. His idyll seemed destroyed, enmeshed in the labyrinth of other people's lives

He stayed a long time by her grave in the garden, thinking about the little yellow dog and the joy of her and the spaniel, together and with him. Not for that long but long enough to make memories which hurt when he thought of them. Just a dog — but she didn't deserve an end like that and as he squatted, gazing at the small mound of soil that covered her he was both angry and afraid.

He promised himself he would be ready in future, ready to protect himself and those around him. He thought about Kate and the horse knowing each time she was out of his sight on Harry he would be afraid again. He rose to his feet, hands clenched into fists to mutter: "Bye Tess."

Years after, when it was all over, he would recall that moment, pondering why he acted as he did, what prompted him suddenly to think of the gun, to go upstairs for it. What impulse made him take the shotgun, still dirty from the aborted pigeon shoot all those months ago, into the utility room to find his cleaning kit.

He watched himself in hindsight, taking out the rods, fitting them together to slide down each barrel cushioned by the little squares of soft oiled cloth. He'd lifted the barrels to check each shining shaft in turn and remembered how the metal gleamed.

He'd gone back upstairs, unlocked the cabinet and placed the shotgun inside. Then as he turned the key he paused and reopened it, taking the gun again in his hands. He laid it on the bed, studying it a long time, then he went to the window to stare across the yard, his face creased in a frown.

He sighed, made up his mind and glanced again at the weapon before locking the cabinet. From his wardrobe he picked out a jacket unworn for years and carefully wrapped the pristine gun in its folds before kneeling swiftly to push the bundle under the bed

Chapter eighteen

The entire village knew Elizabeth had gone away and those who didn't soon found out. James could never understand how word got round so quickly.

"Chinese whispers," he said to Jack.

"That's the trouble with a village like this. I've told you before — you can't fart in Derrington without someone knowing."

"But we were discreet about the Scotland visit, I was only gone one night."

"Well, they know. I expect Rod or Tommy'll have said something in the pub."

The village knew about the dog as well. The news of the callous killing shocked them, rocked their gentle complacence, it wasn't the kind of thing that happened in their village. Nothing was said out loud but in whispered conversations behind closed doors everyone thought the same — young Sterling had done it to get back at Lambert and the girl. Who else would have done such a rotten thing? In the pub people moved tables to get away from him and his cronies, uncomfortable to be associated.

Towards the end of the week after James got back Rod the cowman rang Jack to tell him the Sterlings had been nosing around the farm the day Elizabeth went. He'd seen them in the grain store, examining the new corn.

"They were quick off the mark," Jack said. "Why didn't you say something before or tell Mr Lambert?"

"I didn't like to, didn't want to cause any more trouble. I didn't know if I should say anything."

James heard all this at Jack's, trying to keep away from Sedge Farm. He resented even more being inveigled into managing the place with William in London and Elizabeth gone. And there was no question of Kate being there on her own. But with only the dairy man and young Tommy he needed to be there to keep things going.

William promised to come, he was arranging leave to spend time at the farm and deal with everything. In the meantime Sedge Farm was already being advertised for sale by private tender.

The local paper and the Farmers Weekly were on the bar in the pub, open at the right page and Richard had an unusually busy lunch time trade as several farmers congregated to talk about the sale.

William was expected any time and James and Kate idled in the Sedge Farm kitchen, wondering if they should eat something or wait for him to arrive. Kate had peeled potatoes but James said he wasn't hungry and they should wait.

"Okay, I don't mind waiting," she said. They heard a car on the gravel. "That'll be him." James went to the window to see a taxi leaving and turned as the door opened to reveal Elizabeth standing there.

"Mum! What are you doing here? How did you get here?"

"Is something wrong Mrs Patterson?" James asked, reverting to formality.

"Everything's wonderful. Don't worry, I'm not stopping — not long anyway."

Kate said again: "How did you get here?"

"On the train, it's very easy." She looked tired but somehow enlightened. James studied her face and saw that all was well.

"You look good," he said.

"Thank you. I'm a bit tired — takes longer by train but it's an interesting journey."

Kate watched her mother and noted the solicitous way James brought a chair for Elizabeth. He caught the frown as she saw her mother's smile of thanks. But she was bursting to begin the questions and only hesitated as James gave the slightest shake of his head and busied herself making tea instead.

"How is Graham?" he asked.

"Excessively well," she replied. "He is, always was, such a lovely man, so kind."

"You're going back, then?"

"Of course."

"It's working out?"

"Oh yes, very much so," she paused, seeing Kate's discomfort. "It's all right Kate. Don't know what he's told you but the croft is lovely. A bit small and it needs a few things to bring it up to scratch but nothing I can't easily deal with."

Kate frowned: "But mum —"

"You can come up and visit, you hardly remember him, do you?"

The girl shook her head. "You were very tiny — so long ago, yet now it doesn't seem so long."

"So why -- " Kate began.

"Why am I here? I've come for my car and some clothes and a few favourite bits from the house."

James had seated himself at the table opposite Elizabeth, staying out of the conversation but watching in fascination what passed between mother and daughter. Elizabeth had changed after Ted's death but now she was different again, her skin clear and blooming, eyes bright and a bounce about her which enchanted him.

Kate insisted on practicalities. "What about all the furniture, mum, all the stuff? What shall we do with it all?

"I told you. I've come to take my favourite things, most of

it I hate anyway, what I can't get in the car I'll have sent up. You must take anything you want — and William. The rest can go in the sale, let whoever buys the place sort it out."

"We put house and contents in the ad," said James.

"Good. Get rid of it all."

"Isn't that a bit drastic?"

"No. Get rid. Close the book."

The sound of another car on the gravel made them all look up and this time it was William, relieved and happy to see his mother though his face fell, daunted, when he realised she was returning to Scotland.

He began at once to try changing her mind, see reason as he called it but she laughed at him. "William, you are my lovely boy but you will not alter what I'm doing. I love this man, I've loved him since you were this big," she held her hand a foot or two from the floor. "And now I've found him again I don't intend to lose him -- not this time."

Her son seemed embarrassed and began to speak again but they all turned to the window at the sound of another vehicle, this time a heavier crunch. James looked out: "It's Bill Sterling's Range Rover."

"What the hell do they want?" William said, his face darkening.

Elizabeth said calmly: "You know what they want. They want the farm."

"Mother!" William went to her, put a hand on her shoulder.

"Don't worry, they won't get it."

James opened the door to them, father and son, the younger glowering when he saw them all there together. He glanced at James then quickly away. Elizabeth stayed in her chair, pulling the short jacket she wore more firmly round her shoulders. She sat very upright and James watched a hard, bitter look transform her expression as she faced Bill Sterling. A look that meant business. "What do you want here? Why have you come?"

"About the farm, Lizzie. I've come to make you a proper offer — sort it all out."

Elizabeth appeared to be weighing him up. She said nothing for more than a minute while he stood literally cap in hand, his tall figure stooping as he waited. He moved to draw up a chair beside her but she said: "I didn't ask you to sit" — the tone sharp and cold.

"Lizzie," he began.

"Don't call me that! I've always hated it. Leave my house Bill and take that creature with you."

"Elizabeth, be sensible. The place is on the market and we want to buy it. You know Ted always meant me to have it if he sold. Your William won't farm it. We'll give you top price, you know that."

William stepped forward. "You should leave, Mr Sterling. We've already told you, you cannot match the price."

"What d'you mean? I'm probably the richest man in the county, I can match any price."

Laughing, William said: "I doubt that. But it doesn't matter how much you're worth, we won't sell to you or any of your proxies."

Throughout this exchange James was silent. He'd followed them in, closing the kitchen door behind them waiting with his back to it, his attention caught by the cricket bat in the corner. He did not expect violence from the father but knowing what the son was capable of, he was mindful of his own resolution to be prepared. Kate was looking hard at him and he gave her a brief reassuring smile but fixed his gaze on Steve who stood just behind his father, shuffling his feet, eyes on the floor, looking at none of them.

"Be sensible, Elizabeth," Sterling began again. "We've know each other a long time, aways been friends, you —"

She burst out: "Friends! We've never been friends! I've had to put up with you all these years, but you've used us, you used Ted and now he's dead because of you. You and your evil, vicious bastard of a son, I don't want you here and I won't let you get this place."

"But surely," he tried again.

"What is it you don't understand? This farm is mine and it's not for sale to you."

She stood up, glaring at him. "Now get out."

Sterling seemed puzzled, shaking his head as if unable to accept she meant it. He started to speak again but suddenly his son moved close to Kate, shoving his face very near hers.

"You're gonna regret this," he growled and for an instant she quailed in front of him but then thrusting back her shoulders she stared into his face.

"You heard my mother, get out of our house." William moved to Kate's side, raising a hand as if to push Steve away but he spun round with a vicious glare at James. "And you," he shouted.

"Enough," his father said as James stood aside to let them pass. At the door he hesitated and turned again to address Elizabeth.

"I'm sorry you decided to go this way. It's a pity."

James went after them to the door. Reaching out he grabbed Steve Sterling's shoulder: "I know what you are," he said. "I know what you did. You may be the one with regrets."

Steve shook the arm away angrily, following his father. "We'll see pen man. You won't keep her for long."

The venomous hatred in his face was chilling but James had seen it before and knew what he had to deal with.

William had heard and looked anxiously as James came back . "You okay?"

He nodded. "Find a bottle, will you. We need a drink, at least I do. Are you all right Elizabeth?" She and Kate both looked shaken and Kate trembled as he hugged her, stroking her hair. "It's over, they've gone."

"Is it? Will it ever be over, I heard what he said. He means it, James."

"If he carries on like this he'll be arrested. You can't go around threatening people these days. There are laws you know. I can't prove what he did to Tess but there are other things he's done to intimidate you and me. It's a pattern of behaviour and we'll get him inside if he carries on."

"Do you really think so?" William asked.

"I hope so." He took the glass William offered and sat down with a sigh. "You really mean it Elizabeth, about the land?"

She looked surprised. "Do you doubt it? After all that's happened and what they did to Graham, between them, I won't sell if there is any chance of them getting it."

He turned to William. "Why are they so desperate to get it?

William smiled, staring a moment. "You're a farmer's son and you don't understand?"

"Not really, not this obsession — because that's what it seems to be."

"You're right there. It is obsession, pure greed, for land and the power it brings. It's not just about farming, remember land is a finite commodity, they don't make it any more. When land comes on the market it triggers something in all of them but with the Sterlings it's as if they think they have a right to it."

"It's so unreasonable, horrible, how does he get away with it?"

"He's a bully and for too long no one's stood up to him. He's got money and land and that gives him influence and opportunity to push everyone else aside. The only person who tried to stand up to him was Graham Milburne and you know what happened to him."

"Jesus!"

"It's not just here, it's always been the same. All through history, land causes wars, people die for it." William paused, glancing at his sister. "Our father died because of it, I suppose, though we'll never be sure."

Leaving William with his mother he took Kate home, glad to be away. She was very quiet during the short journey and his mind was fixed on the unpleasant scene and its implications. He assumed she was upset by the incident and thought no further. She should have been at work and he wished she was.

He wanted time alone, not only to catch up on neglected work on his own farm but time to think, get things in perspective. He was exhausted by his involvement at Sedge Farm and longed for the sale to be over so he need never go there again.

She sensed he didn't want to talk and that was fine as she nursed her thoughts about him and her mother.

An ugly doubt had lodged itself in her head and she knew also that the death of Tess had driven a wedge between them.

As he parked she said: "I think I might take Harry for a short ride, see how he is now, I need to get him back into work."

She saw his frown. "Is that a good idea?"

"What d'you mean?"

"Well, with all that's happened and that nutter threatening us both, do you think you'll be safe riding the horse on your own?"

"If I let that stop me," she said fiercely. "I might as well give up. If I can't ride Harry he's won."

"This is getting a bit much, Kate. When I let you bring him here, I didn't bargain for all this."

Her face contorted and he thought she would cry but she looked away, hiding the desolation sweeping through her. He was again the man she had first met, aloof and uninvolved.

"I should never have asked you," she said, "but I didn't expect all this. I would never have involved you if I'd dreamed this could happen. "But," she reached out to touch his arm, tentative, uncertain. "I thought you wanted me here. You did, didn't you?"

He'd been looking away from her, his eyes fixed on a small flock of birds perched in a holly tree, wondering if they were fieldfares, early arrivals perhaps. He turned, feeling all her vibes of anxiety and uncertainty as he met sorrowful eyes.

"Yes, I did want you here. I still do, I suppose. I care about you but all this has spoiled it, hasn't it?"

"Has it?" she whispered.

"I think so, at least for now. I don't know where we go from here."

He put his arms around her, kissing the top of her head. "Don't look so miserable, we'll sort something out, somehow. Ride Harry if you want, it may cheer you up. But be careful where you go."

"I was only planning a short ride on the road, nothing exciting."

"Okay."

He watched the girl and the horse leave the yard, thinking again how handsome they looked together; hard to imagine a lurking menace in the sunny early autumn afternoon.

The sale of the farm had created plenty of interest and the excited agents reported information requests from a surprisingly wide area, a holding such as Sedge Farm being not that common on the market. The high quality of the land and the desirability on the house and buildings would attract attention not just from farmers but from businessmen and others eager for investment.

James kept out of the way now William was running things but Jack came to see him and Kate, hoping to get a more sympathetic hearing. He stood uncomfortably in the kitchen, making inconsequential comments and drinking tea until James said: "What is it, Jack? What have you got to say that's causing you so much trouble."

Jack grunted, screwing up his face in embarrassment, fiddling with his cap. "It's difficult, none of my business really, but I said I'd have a word if I could."

"What about? Come on, you've known me long enough now. If I can help I will but you need to spit it out."

"Well, it's the lads, Rod and Tommy, Tommy specially." He paused.

James sighed: "What about them?"

"Well, they're worried, see, for their jobs. When the farm's sold, they'll likely be laid off. Specially since you've found a new manager."

"Mm. Maybe but they may equally well be kept on. But I can't do anything, you need to speak to William, he's organising everything."

"Well, I thought, Kate being the daughter and you and she close, maybe you could bring some influence. And they say Mrs Patterson likes you."

James grinned. "Do they! Is that what they say?"

Neither man noticed the expression on Kate's face as she turned hastily away.

Jack peered at him anxiously. "Rod should get a job easy enough, he's a good cowman but Tommy's not been at it long and he's still got a lot to learn. They may not want him."

"I'll see what I can do."

William, whose attitude despite his origins was coloured by London life, considered Galloway as something akin to another planet, its countryside and people quite alien. The thought of his mother spending the rest of her days in such an outlandish corner of Scotland outraged his feelings. He came up to see them, hoping to enlist their support in trying to 'make her see sense', as he put it.

James said nothing while he poured a large measure of whisky into a tumbler, added a splash of cold water and handed it to Kate's brother. He waited for him to speak but when he seemed quiet and undecided said: "You like a malt, don't you? You could always go up and see them, there's a distillery not far away, the most southerly one in Scotland I believe."

"Oh come on! You can't seriously imagine she'll want to stay there, it's impossible."

"Why?"

"A small scruffy cottage — that's what you said — how can she live somewhere like that?"

James shrugged. "But if that's what she wants — anyway, I'm sure she's got ideas to improve the place. From what I saw it certainly needs a woman's touch. I wasn't there long but it seemed cosy."

"But it's such a comedown," William took a long sip of the whisky. "She's our mother — we can't let her do this. Kate, what do you say? You can't be happy about it."

James leaned against the aga, warming his buttocks against the doors, studying them both while he waited for Kate to answer.

She looked at him as if for guidance but he shook his head. "Don't look at me. You know what I think. And it's nothing to do with me."

"Let her go if that's what she wants," said Kate and he looked up sharply at the harsh tone. "She seems determined to stay there with him. I can't remember him, what sort of guy is he?"

William butted in. "It doesn't matter what sort of bloke he is, he lives on next to nothing in the back end of Scotland. I'm not prepared to let her do it."

"How you going to stop her?' asked James.

"I don't now but somehow we've got to."

"She'll have plenty of money when the farm is sold, enough to keep them comfortably."

"So he wants her for her money," William almost shouted. "We can't let that happen."

"William, it's not like that," Kate said. "You can't accuse him of that. She went to find him remember, it's all her doing"

"Yes," James said softly "and if you'd seen the expression on his face when he first set eyes on her, like he was seeing a vision, you wouldn't say stuff like that."

His words were aimed at Kate more than her brother as he continued. "He seems a very gentle man, well spoken, probably from a good family. Of course he's had a rough time and his face is badly scarred but not enough to change him for her. I suspect there's a lot more to him than a croft in Galloway."

"Mum said he escaped there to get away from people, after what happened, after what our father did to him." Kate frowned as she looked at William, repeating: "Yes, what our father did. I'm sorry Will but I can't support you in trying to stop her."

Her brother sighed, looking troubled. "But is it enough? All right, she's found him again but all that was a long time ago. I can remember a bit about it but surely they don't still feel that way, not at their age."

"Why not?" Kate said.

"It's absurd."

"Not absurd," James said softly. "From what I saw they were and are very much in love. I had to get out of the room, there was such a current between them, like electricity, a tension so tangible I couldn't watch them. They'd forgotten I existed."

"But she's nearly fifty," William insisted loudly.

"So? She's a woman in love — you should be glad for her — both of you."

"I am," said Kate. "Haven't you noticed the change in her," to William "how well she looks, how good? James has. It's literally taken years off her. Can't you see that?"

"She certainly has a new assurance, she surprised me with the Sterlings, I've never seen her like that. And you're right, she does look younger and really quite attractive."

"Don't sound so surprised William," James laughed. "She's been released. She's her own woman now and bloody good luck to her I say."

William went very quiet, he seemed bewildered, confused. He left them and walked over to the window staring out at the gathering dusk fighting with his own thoughts as if unable to decide what was right.

When he turned back to them he asked: "So you both think it's the right thing for her, we should let her go?"

"What else can you do?" James said. "There's nothing for her here, except Kate, but that isn't really a choice for her, is it?"

"So what should I do?"

"Help her, make it easy for her and let her know you're happy about it. If you try to stop her, William, you won't succeed and all you'll do is push her away from you."

She was enthralled by his description of her mother's rapture over Graham and asked more about the place in Galloway, easing the inhibitions which had come between them after the horror of Tess and the clash with the Sterlings and in bed she cuddled close to him. They lay entwined, warm and sticky from love and all the joy in her which had eluded him came flooding back.

From the wall he watched her drive down the lane, the little car pulling in to let the postman pass. He walked across to meet the red van and save Eddie getting out with the sheaf of mail. He shuffled through them and picked out a long white envelope addressed in Louise's handwriting with the Wiltshire postmark. Wondering why his sister had written rather than call he put the rest aside and opened it.

Inside was another envelope, several times redirected until it had found its way to his sister in Wiltshire. Only then did he notice the stamp, blackened with overlaid post marks. It was from Bosnia. His hands trembled as he tore it open and drew out the letter, couched in stilted, broken English — a letter from Esma.

Chapter nineteen

"But why must you go?" Kate's anguished voice made him look back from the doorway. She sat on the edge of the bath, shivering, chilled legs bare, half covered by one of his shirts she wore for bed, swamping her slight frame.

"Why must you go all that way just to look at a grave? I don't understand."

"No," he said. "You don't understand and I can't expect you to."

"But why?"

"I have to go. I have to — to see them and the grave. I can't explain it but I must. I just have to."

He'd spent the evening putting off the moment of telling her about the letter from Sarajevo, from Esma, the letter that told him that after all these many months they had at last located the spot where Katya's body was buried.

The letter was written in poor English, often with the wrong word or grammar, making it difficult to follow. But it told him that once the NATO bombing had brought the Serbs to heel and the ceasefire came into force it had been easier to get around the city and search for the grave.

They had hunted through the lists at the new cemeteries, eliminating each possibility until at last they found the place. Arif and Esma thought they must tell him, knowing he would want to know. And he did. But for him and Kate it couldn't have come at a worse time. He'd waited until she came home, trying to find the right moment.

Through the entire evening together he'd looked for an opportunity to speak but couldn't summon the words to begin.

Now, stupidly, he'd come to her as she was running a bath and blurted it out all in a rush.

"Kate, I'm sorry — I need to go back to Bosnia."

It had gone on from that, he'd tried to explain, tried to make her understand but here she was with a bath of tepid water behind her looking up at him with those large wide eyes which reminded him so much of Katya's. It was an awful coincidence, their eyes so similar, especially when they were sad and then she said the worst thing.

"I suppose Katya is so special because she's dead."

The words were out before she thought what she was saying. She watched his face change, he went white and his features contorted as if in pain. He stood up and grabbed her, raising his hand as if to hit her but when she cowered away in fear he stopped, staring wordless.

After a moment she said quietly: "I just don't understand."

"I know." He dipped his fingers in the water.

"You'd better run another bath, this water's nearly cold. Or just forget it and go to bed."

"It'll be warm enough, I'm too tired to worry," she said, her voice edged with incipient tears.

She had her bath alone in cool water while he went outside in the chilly night prowling the yard with the spaniel trotting beside him.

He stood in the familiar spot looking down at the village and Bobbie dropped to lie at his feet. Since Tess had gone he stayed close to James, who knew he missed the boisterous company of the little yellow bitch.

When he returned to their room she was huddled against the edge of the bed and as he slid in under the quilt she seemed to shrink further away from him. He lay on his back with his arm stretched out on the wide space of cold sheet between them.

Rueful thoughts of the previous night's love scorched his mind and kept him from sleep. Was it only last night he thought that they had delighted in each other, shared love with all the old passion and delight. Sadly he remembered how she'd looked at him, gazing into his face with so much love before she kissed him.

Then the memory blurred into another vision and it was Katya with that same look of love which left him in a torment of sadness and confusion. He didn't want to leave Kate and he didn't want to make the journey back to Sarajevo but it was something he had to do. If he failed to go he would never rest, never be free of the guilt of not going back. He knew it was pointless, that there was nothing to be gained for any of them, it would not help Arif or Esma. But they had written to him, expecting him to go. And for them his going might be a comfort even if it only proved his love for Katya, proof that what they had together was more than a passing infatuation.

There was no question in his mind about it and maybe the going would bring a little peace. But he knew it would not bring peace for Kate. He sighed, wondering if she was asleep or just pretending, but he didn't reach out or attempt to touch her.

He knew how bad it was for her, how fragile she was in this whole turmoil since her father's death, uprooted from her family and increasingly dependent on him. He wanted to make her understand it didn't change anything, he wouldn't be away for long, he would come back. But the memory of Katya had come between them.

"You'd better go home while I'm away," he said in the morning as she hurried to leave for work and paused to look at him, frowning.

"I thought this was my home — with you."

"Maybe it is but you can't stay here alone."

"When are you going?"

"The agency's fixing me a flight, tomorrow or the day after.

No civilian planes going in there yet — though the fighting seems to be over. I won't be there for long," he struggled to reassure her.

"I can't go home," she said. "I'd be on my own and that's worse than here."

"William's there."

"No, he's going back to London any time and Mum's off to Scotland today."

"I'll ring him. The farm's his responsibility, he needs to know I can't be there. And the agency man needs support."

"But he doesn't live in," she said. "The farm will be empty."

"Oh Kate — it was your home, it must be sad for you." He reached to touch her arm but she snatched it away. "I'm sorry, I didn't expect this, it's come out of the blue. I don't want to go but I have to. Please try to understand."

Her face was pale and strained and he saw she'd been crying. It hurt him to see her like this and though she turned away from him he put his arms around her, hugging and kissing her hair.

"Kate, sweetheart, please don't take it like this, it doesn't affect us, it's just something I must do. I care about you, you know I do but this is something I have to finish."

"You never say you love me. You don't love me, you're in love with a ghost," she said, trying to push away from him.

"That's just silly, please try to understand," he repeated. "I'm confused, I don't know what I feel now about the thing with Katya but going might help. I need closure. I need to end it and move on. But I can't. Maybe this will help me, to see her grave. It might, you know, it might be like closing the book. Please don't be so angry."

Still now, locked in his embrace, she rested her chin on his shoulder. "You're right, I can't stay here. I'll go to Pat's — Sheila won't mind. You won't be away long?" The voice was timid.

"No, not long, I promise."

He let her go, shaking his head and becoming practical again.

"You'll be safe with Pat, I won't worry if you're there but we'll put the horse in livery, I'll ring Thompsons and take him over there this morning."

"They may not have room," she said.

But he answered firmly: "They will. And this time I'll put Bobbie in kennels."

"Jack will have him," she said.

"You think I'll risk that again? And it's not fair on Jack. He'll go to kennels, somewhere secure that bastard Steve won't dare try getting at him."

"Do you really think he'd do something like that again?"

"No doubt about it, of course he would if he got the chance. But we won't give him the chance. But listen Kate — keep your mouth shut. Don't tell anyone else I'm going away and I'll tell the Wilsons the same."

He saw her worried stare and softened his words.

"It's just, people are careless in what they say and the fewer people who know, the better. Though word will get round soon enough, I expect."

He'd rung the agency before he told her and got hold of Milton, the man who'd arranged his book contract -- the book he kept trying to forget.

The reception on the telephone was frosty, including the mention of the considerable advance James had already received — and spent.

"I will do it," he said. "I can't get a handle on it yet, too soon."

"It's coming up two years and I'm the one getting all the ear ache. It's okay for you hidden away in the hills."

"Sorry. I just called because I need to go back and I'm hoping you can fix me a flight."

"To Bosnia?"

"I have to. The girl I knew there — they've found her grave. I need to go -- and it'll help me with the book," he added as an afterthought.

"What will you be doing there?" The voice was eager now.

"I'm not sure. Visit the grave, spend some time with the family, do what I can if they need any help — come home. There's nothing to keep me there."

"We'll want something for getting you there. Can you get to Srebrenica?" was the next question.

"I don't know."

"Well, get yourself there. We need good copy on that, it's a big story and we don't know half of it. Looks like it's much worse than they thought. They've begun to find grave sites, all over the place, it's going to be mega. They say it could be years before they find them all. There's a lot to come out of there yet," he said.

"Right. I'll try."

"Keep in touch, Jim."

Sarajevo airport from the air looked much as he remembered it, the runway sited along the river valley with the hills rising either side, late afternoon sun sparkling on an early covering of snow. It was still closed to civil aircraft but now the fighting had ended there were already signs of rebuilding.

As the plane dropped towards landing he saw the scale of the damage in the neighbouring suburbs, acres of ruined buildings with skeletal vehicles among the detritus. Some way in the distance a horse drawn cart was drawn up alongside one of the high rise wrecks, men laboriously loading rubble onto it by hand. Hoists and cranes had sprouted on rooftops and piles of brick and stone littered the streets.

On the ground he spotted a wrecked tank on its side at the far edge of the airfield and remembered the United Nations tanks on site the last time he was here. Blue-helmeted UN-

PROFOR troops cradled their automatic rifles, restraining alsatian dogs on chains as they hustled him through the buildings and onto a military plane to leave Sarajevo behind.

Arif must have been watching for the taxi, its progress slow as the driver avoided potholes, broken drain covers and other debris on the cobbles. James saw him from far down the street waiting on the pavement. When the car stopped he rushed forward to open the door before the driver could move, his face bright with excitement.

"We did not expect you, we did not think you would come. But we hoped," he said.

He stood back to gaze at James with a look in his glistening eyes which was of simple love. The only word. Then he clasped him close, kissing both cheeks as if unable to believe he was really there. James was overwhelmed and tears came freely, out of control.

"I'm sorry," he gasped. "I can't help it, it's so good to see you."

Inside little had changed though the gaps in the walls which had let in snow and wind were blocked and a stack of concrete blocks beside a pile of sand indicated the start of repairs. "It all takes so much time," Arif said, "and it is still very hard to get materials. Slowly we are getting there but we are a long way from normal life."

"But the cafe is open," James said looking around him at the tables and chairs back in position with a few customers drinking coffee or small glasses of slivovitz.

"Yes, we are open!" a cry from the kitchen and there was Esma in her apron rushing to greet him. She knocked over a chair in her hurry to hug him with even more enthusiasm than Arif.

"Oh James, it is so wonderful you come. We wrote but we did not believe you would come back and it is some time now since the letter. We did not think you would come," she said again.

"I had to," he whispered into her grey hair as she clutched him so hard, reluctant to let him go. When he could step back he said: "The letter arrived only a few days ago, it's been going from place to place to find me. I came as soon as I could."

Customers had gathered round to welcome him back to Sarajevo, some he knew and the rest soon discovered who he was and why he was there. Neighbours had been quizzing the taxi driver and a small crowd collected outside and pushed through the doors to join what quickly became a party.

James was stunned by their eagerness to see him and struggled to keep up with their questions and expressions of pleasure while Esma sat him down with a plate of her speciality stew of lamb and beef, bright with yellow potatoes, peppers and fresh green coriander. On a separate plate she presented two of her delicate savoury pastries.

He'd eaten little on the plane and he looked at her in amazement, thinking of the meagre meals they'd shared when he lived with them. Reading his thoughts she said, laughing: "At least now we have good food and I can cook again. Enjoy it James and look for better times. Here," she put a bottle on the table "we will drink a toast to your return and we'll raise a glass for Katya."

She saw his smiling face change and the tears so close as he met her eyes. "Don't be sad — maybe she was too lovely to live. But you are here and that tells us what she meant to you. So we honour you, James — for her sake."

They put him in the room he'd shared with her. He said nothing, not wanting to offend but wondered if they had any idea of the effect it had, being in that room, lying in the same bed. He lay staring at the ceiling or at the window over the street which had curtains now. He'd drawn them back and each time a car went by its lights shone into the room. There was no street lighting, many repairs were needed before the streets would be bright again but he was back three years or more when they were dark and no cars passed and the only light was from a flare bursting overhead or a shell exploding.

The nights he spent with her there were so real to him that he stretched out his hand across the bed to feel for her. It was so strange to be in that room without her beside him.

He touched his chin, surprised by a trickle of water on his neck and realised tears were streaming down his face. He began to sob, turning over to bury his head in the pillow, unable to control the violent weeping and trembling that shook his body.

He had wept in that church when she lay dead on the floor but not like this, not this devastating flood of loss sweeping over him. He hadn't expected such an impact simply from being in this room again.

He'd thought about it on the flight, wondering how it would be but had not anticipated this overwhelming sense of loss.

He struggled to control his sobbing, afraid to be heard but he couldn't stop and sometime after midnight he heard the door open and sensed rather than saw someone in the light from the landing. He raised his head saying: "What is it? What do you want?"

"I heard you — for so long you have been crying."

"I'm sorry," he mumbled. "I didn't mean to disturb you, I just can't seem to stop. It's this room."

She came to sit on the bed next to him. "Ah, I am sorry. We should not have put you here to sleep. We thought you would like it."

"I do, in a way. But I have this sense of her being here, all around me, as if she is close. But I can't touch her — I can't get her back."

Esma held his shoulders gently, as he trembled and her touch calmed him.

"She was very special," she whispered, "like a daughter.

We miss her too, very much, and our sons. This wicked war has taken a terrible price from all of us."

James sat up beside her, drawing deep breaths as he regained control. "Perhaps we were wrong to write," she said.

"This is very hard on you, very difficult. I see now how much you cared for her, we were never sure. These things happen in war," she hesitated. "We never knew how much it meant to you, being with her. We know now."

Shaking his head as if to clear his thoughts he said: "I wanted her to be my wife, we were going to England. I loved her, Esma and I love the memory of her."

She didn't answer but drew his head against her shoulder, stroking his hair until the trembling stopped. After she left he remained on his back, staring at the window, unable to sleep as he trawled his brain for small intimate memories of Katya.

He leaned against the cafe door, waiting for the taxi, his eyes absorbing the aspect of the street, the many empty window spaces dark without glass, or some with shards like jagged teeth; large ragged holes in walls and several shops still boarded up, glass fronts gone and broken rafters showing through the roof.

Arif had ordered a car and the same one came at mid morning bumping along the street again to take them to the cemetery. It was a big day for the couple. Esma had brought someone in, a neighbour's daughter who was glad to work and helped more often now the cafe was rebuilding its business as the city struggled to return to normality. The girl would open up the cafe and serve simple meals until Esma returned.

The taxi driver climbed out and opened the door respectfully for them all to get in, directing James to the front seat beside him. He'd hardly slept at all, his pale face revealing the traumas of the night. Esma had made him breakfast but he could face nothing but coffee and a small bun. He told himself it was just a grave, just one spot among thousands but for him it was a special spot and after last night he wondered how the moment of actually seeing it would affect him.

From the plane the whole panorama of Sarajevo had been laid out below revealing how the landscape of the city had changed. Much of its green open space was submerged by ranks of white grave stones, the whole made more dazzling from above by the fresh snow which softened and blurred the area into one mass of white.

The clustered neat ranks reminded him of war graves he'd seen in France and Burma though without the precise regimentation organised by the War Graves Commission. The area of the Olympic site, which he and Katya had passed through as they left the city, still had the remains of its proud buildings, twisted wrecks of metal, battered from shelling. The bobsled track had become acres of graves, one vast cemetery straddling the hillside, climbing towards the base of the higher rock faces.

Now at ground level amongst them he saw how closely the graves were packed together, side by side, neat rows making best use of the space. Some had the white pillars of Islam, others the more familiar headstones and crosses of Christian burial.

The taxi driver took them uphill towards the mountains on a lane made narrow and oppressive by the ranks of silent graves so close on either side. He sat in silence glancing at row upon row. Sarajevo's original cemetery had long spilled over and all across the city these new sites presented a harvest of the dead.

The temperature in the open air was very cold. An icy wind scything from the east made him shiver but without a word he followed where Arif led between the rows, Esma walking behind. He wondered how they could find one single grave in all this mass but they must have been there many times because they walked with confidence straight to a grave that to him looked identical to those around it, a white pillar stood tall with a flat white stone beneath where wilted flowers lay under the snow.

He stood before the pillar and read the memorial aloud to himself, whispering the words. Her name he could read, but of the rest he could pick out only the word Michel, the young man who was so briefly her husband. Below there was something written in Arabic script.

He raised his head and looked at them questioning, his eyes roving over the acres of Muslim memorials.

"I don't understand," he began. "She wasn't Muslim, why is she here?"

Esma looked up at him. "God sees no difference," she said.

"No, but — "

"Her papers showed Michel's name, her husband, so she was brought here. Does it matter where she lies?"

He shook his head. "No, she's among friends, after all." He stared around the vast cemetery: "So many dead, when you see it like this it's hard to comprehend -- so many gone."

Esma sighed: "This is only one of the new cemeteries from the war. There are new graves all over the city, all over Bosnia. It is why it took so long to find her, we searched through many sites."

"I'm amazed you found her, it must have been horrible for you."

"It was difficult, the records are confused, not complete."

"I can believe that," James mumbled, shivering again.

"She was our daughter, our son's wife. We had to find her."

Arif, who had stood a little way off, moved closer to the grave to speak to him. "It was very hard to make progress but by chance we found the priest, the one who was with you in the church when she died. He told us where her body was taken but even then it took so long to find anyone who knew where the bodies were put after that. There were thousands, you see."

"Yes, I do see. It must have been hell."

The old man nodded and spoke slowly. "It is cold, James. We will go back to the taxi and wait for you. Give you a little time alone with her."

From England he'd brought a wreath of poppies, which seemed to him when he thought of it to have more meaning and would last longer then any hothouse flowers he might bring. And as she was a victim of war, it seemed appropriate.

He knelt in the snow, the cold biting into his knees as he studied the grave stone, struggling to make some connection with this desolate hillside spot and the woman he'd loved.

He tried to pray but nothing came to him as the thing to ask or say. It all seemed alien and far removed from the body lying on the church floor. He had expected to be moved or saddened in this place but with a shock he realised he felt nothing.

"You're not here my darling, are you? There's nothing here of you. Last night in the room, that's where you are. I found you there, I could almost touch you."

He moved the dying flowers and laid the poppies in their place, their petals red against the snow clad stone.

The taxi driver didn't speak much English so when he tried to ask him if he could take him to Srebrenica he merely shrugged, waving his hands as he drove.

"Srebrenica, Srebrenica," James repeated without effect and he turned to Arif. "Ask him for me, will you. I can't make him understand."

Arif looked troubled. "Why do you want to go there? It is a bad place. You know they are uncovering many bodies."

"Yes, I do know that. That's why they want me to go, they have asked me to find out more and write about it. I hoped this man would take me."

Arif explained to the driver in Bosnian telling him James worked for a famous newspaper in London but the man shook his head and spoke rapidly.

"He says the soldiers will not let people through unless they have permission. There is much work being done, it is very difficult — very unpleasant."

"Tell him I have a press pass. Tell him they will let me through. Ask him to take me, I will pay well. Tomorrow perhaps?"

Arif asked the question and the driver shrugged and nodded.

The old man looked at James. "He will take you, tomorrow."

Chapter twenty

The scene in the valley was strangely peaceful. The large white mechanical digger which had been biting into the earth and creating a furore of engine and steel against the voices of men directing the driver, had stopped. It stood silent as the team of men paused to stare at the area of opened ground, a new lumpy surface exposed by the digger, awaiting their more cautious attention.

In the stillness the only sound came from a flock of rooks flying overhead and wind moving the slender branches of nearby trees.

The team of men were clad in blue overalls and he watched them step down into the wide trench and begin with gentle deliberation to scrape away at soil and debris.

It was cold with a dusting of snow, misting strange forms and lumps in the pit which as the men gradually cleared away the covering soil took shape as arms and elbows, knees, shoulders and skulls. Two of the team worked together to pull the first body clear of the rest, lifting the corpse with intense care, as if the man were still living and their caution might save him. They half carried, half dragged him to the edge, others came forward to help lift him clear and he was carried some yards back and laid face up on the muddied turf to be covered with tarpaulin.

Two more workers chipped away at compacted mud with pickaxes and shovels to ease apart bodies which seemed to cling together in the earth.

He saw the process repeated over and over as each body was uncovered, all male by the remains of their clothing but some were small, just boys, probably less than ten years old. Each was lifted clear and laid out beside the rest in a neat and growing line. He noted how respectfully the bodies were handled, with a gentleness they may never have received in life.

He walked slowly down the line, studying each body, all in advanced stages of decay but with clothing and enough skin and flesh on the bones to attest their humanity. He saw that some, not all, were tied hand and foot, some behind their backs and several had blindfolds still tight around the skull, which in almost every case showed a gaping hole at the back.

Hearing the digger engine restart he turned to observe as with great precision the driver extended the trench at the far end revealing more burials to be uncovered. As they freed another body from the tangle of dead limbs he saw beneath it the corpse of a small dog, its pale yellow and white fur still recognisable despite the clogging soil. The yellow fur reminded him instantly of Tess and he realised with a shock he had hardly thought of home and Kate since he first sighted Sarajevo from the plane. Shaken by instant guilt he made a mental note to try to contact her when he got back to the city.

He walked some way from the death pit into what were to his farmer's eye, well cultivated arable fields, some in the distance with the remains of crops. But much of the valley was disturbed, the land churned up by what he took to be tank track marks and the wheels of many other vehicles.

He felt the soil soft beneath his feet and stooped to pick up a handful, crumbling it through his fingers. It would be fertile he thought, rich loam in good land in a peaceful valley among wooded hills now revealing an erupted crop of horror.

A couple of hundred yards away his taxi waited on the road. The driver must have seen him and flashed the lights, clearly wanting to be away. It had taken them nearly four hours to make the journey from Sarajevo, delayed in turn by damaged roads and a succession of UN checkpoints where each time he needed to convince different American officers that he had a valid reason to be there. But his press pass opened the way and nearing Srebrenica he got into conversation with a helpful young lieutenant who directed him, not to the town itself but away to the area around Potocari where the Srebrenica citizens had fled as the Serbs advanced. He'll have to wait, James thought, waving at the driver as he turned back towards the grave site.

A few hundred yards from the dig close to the road a couple of cabins were the base for operations and he made his way towards it. He knocked and opened the door but paused before hesitantly walking in. In the warmth several officials and two UN soldiers were drinking coffee and he gladly accepted the offered mug. He explained his presence and asked for directions to other sites in the area.

"How much can you take in one day, fella?" a bulky US army sergeant asked him.

"Now I'm here, I'd like to see as much as possible, though it's a bit overwhelming."

"You've no idea," said a young man who glanced up from scanning a list. "What we're finding here and at other sites are secondary burials. The bastards dug 'em up and took them wholesale to new sites to hide them. Three years of killing, we're finding sites all over eastern Bosnia. This work could go on for years."

"You got a driver?" asked the sergeant. When James nodded he said: "Okay. If you want I'll come with you, take you some places. Save you time."

The taxi driver wasn't happy, he wanted to get back to Sarajevo before dark and started to argue. But a stern look from the sergeant shut him up. "Just drive," said the soldier.

The taxi was driven fast, too fast for James but he knew it was the driver's way of protest. He said nothing, though the wheels frequently screeched as they avoided broken carriageway or obstacles. He watched the passing landscape of the Drina valley, farmland and woods, a pleasant place to spend your life in normal times.

"Stop here," ordered the sergeant and they got out and walked across fields to another site where men were digging. This was a smaller pit and with only a few bodies, wrapped in plastic, lying to one side.

"This was an execution site," said the sergeant. "There were a lot of these all up the valley. But many of the bodies have gone, moved en masse to more hidden sites like back there. You know what happened I presume? The Serbs rounded them up and loaded them in lorries and brought them to places like this," he looked around him. "Peaceful spot, you'd say. Then they were shot and buried."

They went into the village of Potocari itself. "They all came here, you know, for safety. The whole place was supposed to be a safe area, UN designated. They were supposed to be protected but those Dutch bastards just stood back and let the Serbs come in."

He stood in the village where a fenced compound had been set up to protect the men, women and children who had fled as the Serbs advanced earlier in the year. Up to 25,000 people had come here seeking refuge with the Dutch troops of UN-PROFOR — the protection force.

He'd heard about it at the time, so many rumours, accusations and counter accusations flying about but no one knew why the soldiers had done nothing and allowed the massacres to take place without apparently lifting a finger, let alone a gun in protest.

When the world first got to know what happened he like so many others pondered one question. Would it have been different if they'd been British troops? They'd never know. He looked at the sergeant.

"D'you think your boys would've done it different?"

"Who knows? But I sure don't think we'd have let those rapes and child killings go on before our eyes and done fuck-all to stop it."

The sergeant waited in silence while James walked around the area of the compound, still littered with tell-tale signs of cramped conditions for humans beings huddled together behind a fence.

He'd heard all the stories, the Serbs doing exactly what they liked in the town, the Dutch standing by doing nothing, the continuous sound of shots from outside the compound, the sweltering heat and insufficient food and water for the mass of people.

How the Dutch soldiers had been unwilling to confront the Serb forces, watching and doing nothing as men and boys were separated from their families and prevented from getting on the buses that came to move the refugees.

Later they were taken away in groups, shot and scraped away with a bulldozer into hastily dug mass graves. Blue helmets turned away as young girls and women were raped the other side of the fence and babies and small children were brutally killed. The Muslim population of Srebrenica was herded and treated like animals. In the wider district Serb forces were setting fire to houses and haystacks at will, all in an area designated as safe.

The walls of buildings told the story, pocked and broken by bullet and shell holes. The passage of time could not conceal the truth of what had happened there.

He went back to the car and the sergeant directed the driver out of town, towards some low hills a few kilometres away. On the outskirts of a village they stopped again and followed on foot the line of a fence which led to what looked like a quarry, ahead of them a large opening, perhaps a cave or mine.

"They're using this as a makeshift morgue," the sergeant explained "Have a quick look, don't stay long, the smell ain't good."

James walked a little way inside, gasping as the stench hit his throat and clasped a hand over nose and mouth. He walked a few paces further. On either side of him were piled three deep two rows of plastic body bags sealed with wire. He looked ahead down the length of the passage where all he could see were identical parcels of human remains.

He just looked at the sergeant, the question in his eyes.

"All found in mass graves out on the hills. Stored there till they get round to trying to identify them all," the sergeant said. "You did well to go that far in. But it gives you an idea of the scale of all this."

"Will they ever put a name to them all?" he asked. "The numbers are beyond belief. How will they ever do it?"

"It'll take years, literally. But they will do it. People are coming forward all the time, women mostly, looking for sons, husbands, brothers. The majority of bodies we find are male, very few female among them. We get details of where they were last seen, where they were taken from and they give DNA samples. And sooner or later we'll have a match to every last one of the poor sods. The missing persons units are only just beginning to get to grips with it all but they're getting better organised and doing a great job. But it's a long, slow, painstaking process."

He planted his large hand on James' shoulder. "Seen enough?"

He nodded. "I think I've got the picture."

"Right. We'll head back. There's one more site we'll pass that you should see."

Again there were the cabins of the recovery team, two large diggers this time, a wider area of ground uncovered. Here skulls and individual bones were laid out on the soil where they'd been found, each with a small red label stuck in the ground next to it. He walked to the edge near a skull which seemed to gaze up at him from its empty eye sockets. The back of the head was missing and he watched in appalled fascination as a helmeted man moved towards him and placed a number beside the skull.

"Big forensic team here," said the sergeant. "All experts with skeletal remains. I think that guy's from Finland."

"Thank you for taking the time," James said. "I'd no idea of the scale of it. Away from here, nobody has."

"You'll be able to do a good piece."

"Yeah, but who'll read it and who will care?"

The sergeant shrugged. "Well, you can only try."

It was long after dark before they were back in Sarajevo. He wasn't hungry and had only one thought in his mind, to contact Kate. The cafe telephone was still out of action so he set off on foot to the Holiday Inn where he could make international calls.

Trudging through the slushy streets he was struck by the realisation of how little he'd thought about Kate and home since he left. His head was so filled by the images he'd seen, struggling to come to terms with it and grasp the simple fact that human beings could behave like that in late twentieth century Europe. People who'd lived together, side by side as neighbours for generations could turn so savage, could carry out wholesale slaughter, in an attempt to wipe out a whole nation. It had happened so recently in Rwanda where tribal fighting had created a dreadful horror, choking the river with the ghastly remains of the dead. But here in this beautiful, bountiful country it was hard to believe.

He remembered talking of it with Katya, the rapes and killings -- not just rumours — perpetrated by both sides in this complicated tale of destruction. She despaired of it all and feared her country would never recover from its self-inflicted wounds. She hadn't lived to see the worst of it.

He paused on the street corner, examining a row of shattered buildings, their upper levels roofless, jagged with the familiar black spaces, once windows. Walls all over the city were pockmarked with bullet and shell holes but this line of what were once shops was totally desolate.

The Holiday Inn was bright and welcoming, partly repaired, though on one side the gaping holes of blown out windows still displayed the effect of the repeated shelling it had withstood. Now it offered warmth and a full menu but he recalled the last time he was there. If only they had got through the tunnel he and Katya would be safe in England now.

But that hadn't happened and all he had left was the site of her grave and memories to keep him from sleep. And Kate. It was late, nearly ten thirty and in Shropshire it would be later still but he called the Wilsons' number, uncaring if they were all in bed. It rang and rang and he imagined the sound in their hall where the telephone sat on a little table, the extension in the kitchen clanging too. It was late — maybe no one would hear but he let it ring on hoping someone might be roused by the noise.

After several minutes it was answered — Pat's voice, startled and sleepy: "Hello? What is it?"

"It's me, James. I'm sorry to ring so late."

"We're all in bed. What's wrong?"

"Nothing, I haven't been able to call before. Is everything all right there, is Kate okay?"

"Apart from worrying about you."

"Nothing's happened?"

"No."

"Can I speak to Kate?"

"She's asleep."

"She'll be upset if you don't wake her. I'm sure she'll want to speak to me."

"I suppose so — though she's very upset with you."

"I'll risk it. Please get her."

"This is a crazy time to call," Kate's voice was angry. "Why now when we're all in bed? Where are you?"

"Still in Sarajevo. I'm sorry, it's not easy to ring from here, things are only starting to get back to normal. I just wanted to know you're okay and say I'm thinking about you," he lied.

"Nothing's happened if that's what you mean. I'm still here with Pat."

"Good," he hesitated. "I miss you."

"Do you?"

"Of course."

The line went quiet. "When will you be back?"

"I'm not sure. I'll probably try to get a flight the day after tomorrow."

"Why not tomorrow?"

He sighed. "It's not that easy to get on a plane and I still have things to do. But it won't be long."

She almost whispered into the phone: "I miss you James."

"Good -- better get back to bed. I'll see you soon."

He thought about her padding along the hall and back upstairs to bed — and what he hadn't said, what he should've said, those two words: "Love you."

The night air felt better after the warmth of the hotel and he walked quickly back to the cafe. But glancing up he saw the sky had cleared, revealing a three-quarter moon high overhead, the bright orb gliding in and out through the striped cloud of a mackerel sky. The cafe was still thronged with drinkers, some eating a late supper. He watched them through the new glass door. Esma was busy around the tables, she'd told him she didn't care how late people wanted to eat. It was her delight to be able to serve them again, she said she'd cook all night if needed.

He pushed the door to enter but paused, looking up again at the moon which seemed brighter and showed a shimmering bronze halo appearing to carry the moon fast through the cloud streamers. He felt the wind rising.

The wind made him think about home, about Shropshire and the many times he'd stood out in the cold night gazing at the stars and the moon. He couldn't see much expanse of sky in this damaged street but enough to make him marvel as he always did. He and Katya had star-gazed in this very spot, clasped close for warmth and he'd looked up several times with Kate from the hilltop, once on a special evening when a harvest moon rose, huge and golden, to climb free of cloud over the crest of Wenlock Edge.

Kate loved it. She'd spent all her life in the district but told him she'd never looked at the night sky or any of the landscape around them. "No one ever told me to look up," she'd said.

He remembered it clearly, her face alight with the joy of new experience and she had turned to him, kissed him and said: "You show me things I never thought about, so much more in the world than I was ever taught. I'm so glad I got to know you."

Her delight entranced him then and remembering it now brought the idea of her very close. It was as if they were both there beside him, Kate and her namesake, so alike, yet different. It was cold standing in the street but he was reluctant to break the spell by going in. He stayed put conjuring the images of two women, shivering, watching the busy moon.

But Esma must've seen him through the glass because the door opened and he heard her voice through his dream.

"James, why are you out here in the cold? Come in, get warm, have some food."

The halo had gone from the moon when he looked again and he sighed and went inside.

He was grateful to Esma, he'd had to borrow currency to pay the driver, a much larger figure than he'd expected. But then he had kept the man and his car occupied all day and dragged him round places the fellow would not have gone by choice. She'd opened the till without hesitation and handed him the cash without a word. He hoped to get funds wired from London next day.

The full cafe was noisy but he was glad business was so good for them, it made him feel better about leaving. Steadily if slowly Sarajevo was coming back to life, starting to be the vibrant colourful city it had been. Esma sat with him as he ate, more hungry than he realised once he got started and she watched with deep satisfaction as he tucked into her dishes. With the dark red local wine in a carafe beside him he began to relax and looked at her with affection.

"I shall never forget my time here with you. A sad time and a bad time but very special for all that."

She said nothing, watching him down the wine, refilling his glass as soon as he set it down. He smiled at her: "Thank you," he whispered.

She sighed. "Will you come back to Sarajevo?"

He stopped eating, resting his chin on clasped hands to look at her. "I don't know, Esma. We must see what life brings."

"Is there a woman for you at home?"

He smiled and nodded. "I think so. She's young, very sweet with eyes like Katya. I am confused about her."

"Do you love her?"

"I don't know."

Esma studied him. "Being back here has made it harder, no?"

Again he nodded. "I feel Katya all around me here. So close to her. I know she's dead but in that room upstairs it's as if she is only just out of my reach. It's a weird feeling."

She put her hand on his, gripping it. "I am sorry. We have made it more hard for you, putting you in that room. But she is dead and you must make a life for yourself."

In that room he lay awake again, not thinking of Katya but of what he'd seen that day. Fatigue affected his body but his mind lingered on the images of evil that played through his head as he struggled to find the line, the peg to hang his story on. Serbian revenge on the Turk, age-old hatred from centuries back, bubbling beneath the surface, awaiting an opportunity. He couldn't understand how the Serbs could so lack humanity and compassion to act as they did. There were faults on both sides but the Serb determination was fuelled by Karadic and Mladic and their desire to annihilate the Bosniaks. To them they were sub-human, to be eradicated, cleansed, the men murdered and the women violated in the cruellest way, and children killed like kittens.

Killed like kittens -- that sparked another tangent and unwanted into all this drifted the image of Steve, his face a mask of bitter fury as Elizabeth told his father they would never get the farm. The way he'd bullied Kate, the motorbikes on the hill frightening the horse, the missile thrown at him, the attempt to pull her off the horse. And the little yellow dog dangling from the tree, such cold deliberate cruelty. Cruelty, and all the wickedness humanity could conjure was there just beneath the surface, under the veneer of decency, evil waiting for its chance. He wondered if Steve was any different from the Serbs with nothing to restrain them. With nothing to hold him back, how far would he go? What was there, under the skin?

In the morning he walked back to the Holiday Inn to write his copy in the press room. The place was quiet, with only two other desks in use and his words flowed well, the phrases he'd rehearsed in the darkness coming back to him with intense clarity. He was pleased with what he'd written and read through it with satisfaction, making only a few changes.

He printed it out and faxed it to the agency then copied it onto a floppy disc. He held the disc in his hand a moment, looking around the office, with all its new equipment laid on for him and other journalists. It surprised and pleased him and he realised the enormous possibilities ahead in the huge changes the technology would bring. He knew what he'd written was good and as he stared out over the city he began to realise something else. Could he really stop being what he was? He sighed, knowing the farm on the hill could not hold him for ever. His thoughts in turmoil, he pocketed the disc and made his way back to the cafe.

The parting with the old couple was painful. Arif stood back, silent, his face set but watching him with an unnerving intensity. But Esma, quiet all through breakfast, could not conceal her distress and when the taxi came — the same driver who'd had a very good week's takings — threw her arms around him and held him so tight he thought he might suffocate before she let him go.

"It has been so good to see you," she said. "So good you should come — all this way. We are so grateful, so glad."

"It's me who should be grateful," he said. "You've treated me like a son. It's been wonderful to be here, if sad."

"How else would we treat you?" said Arif. "You are the nearest thing we have now to a son."

He bowed his head. "I will try to come back," he said before the driver closed the car door.

They stood as when he arrived, staring after the vehicle as it disappeared down the street. Arif put an arm round his wife and led her inside. "We will not see him again. He will not return."

Chapter twenty-one

A bitter wind that he knew so well was blasting the yard as he left the car and the ground already glistened with gathering frost. He shuddered, thinking of the snow on the ground in Sarajevo. But the cold felt harsher here on the hill and he hurried into his chilled and empty house.

He'd driven straight home from the airport and stood with an empty feeling, bag on the floor beside him, wondering what he was doing there. At least the kitchen felt warm and he went gratefully to the aga, shivering. He'd thought of going to the Wilsons, part of him looking forward to seeing Kate but then the idea of having to talk to them all, answering questions, he didn't want to face that. Suddenly this farmhouse which he'd grown to love and see as home seemed peculiarly alien. He'd expected when he got on the plane that he'd soon forget about Sarajevo and think happily of getting back to Shropshire. But all through the flight his mind was back there and Esma and Arif were more real to him than the Wilsons down the lane.

And Kate. He turned, pressing against the heat, to look towards the sitting room, trying to imagine her there, wanting to want her there. But somehow he couldn't bring up her image. He moved from the kitchen to switch on the heating and bring some comfort to the place. He ought to ring her, tell her he was back but something made him hesitate. The place felt lonely and he wished Bobbie was there but the spaniel was still at the kennels and it was too late in the evening to collect him. He'd go in the morning.

He thought about food and decided he wasn't hungry, the sandwich he'd eaten while driving was enough. But he poured a tot of whisky and swallowed it straight down. He took another and picked up the phone. As expected Pat answered, sounding happy to hear him.

"I'll get Kate," she said. "She'll be thrilled."

But Kate didn't sound thrilled, just anxious, asking at once "Where are you?"

He let out a long breath before answering. "I'm here, at home. Got back a while ago."

"Oh." He detected a mixture of surprise and resentment in the single word and the unspoken question which he answered.

"I was tired. I didn't want to cope with all the Wilsons. It's been a long day."

"I'll come over then, right away."

"If you like. But it's getting late and it's cold outside. You needn't turn out tonight, tomorrow will do." He winced at himself, knowing it was the wrong thing to say.

"You don't sound keen to see me." He heard the hurt in her words.

"Of course I am. But the house is cold — the heating's off and it's been a hard trip." He paused. "It's strange being back."

"I don't understand."

"Don't suppose you do. I'll tell you about it, don't worry."

"I thought you'd want to see me — I've missed you so much."

"I do want to see you, of course I do but — it's hard to explain — I just need a bit of time on my own. Look, tomorrow's Saturday, I'll pick you up and we'll collect Harry and Bobbie."

"If that's what you want."

"I'm tired and I can't get warm. I'm going to bed and start fresh in the morning. I'll see you then."

He avoided the ordeal of drinking coffee with the Wilsons, saying he had arranged a particular time at the kennels. This was untrue but for some reason he couldn't explain to himself he was reluctant to meet them all and talk about Bosnia. He felt a strong need to insulate himself from the affairs of the village and particularly Sedge Farm.

Bobbie of course was ecstatic to see them both and the dog's pleasure broke the ice between them which was almost tangible from the moment she got in the car. Bobbie made a great fuss of her and she laughed happily to see him while James spoke to the kennel owner who explained the spaniel had lost some weight in the few days he'd been there.

"He hasn't eaten much at all," the woman said.

"That doesn't surprise me, he's never been in kennels before. But at least he's been safe here."

That was another reason for not speaking to Jack Wilson, he didn't want to explain about Bobbie and the kennels — the truth being that he couldn't trust them to keep the dog safe. He knew from their attitude that they failed to understand the depths of Steve Sterling's malice.

Driving home he kept hoping she'd say something but he wasn't in the mood to make conversation and the way she sat in the car made it clear she was upset. At last he took a deep breath and said: "Kate love, I'm sorry about last night. I didn't mean to upset you, I was just so tired — I didn't want to be bothered with anyone, not even you."

"I got the message," she muttered.

"Sorry, but it's good to see you, I have missed you."

"Have you? Honestly? You didn't even kiss me when you picked me up. When you called I was so happy, so longing to see you."

"I know and I'm sorry. I feel very unsettled right now. I'll be fine — we'll be fine." He reached across to take her hand

and touch it to his lips. "Let's go out to eat tonight, be nice to each other again. Would you like that?"

She looked at him with a vague smile and nodded.

"I'll take Harry out when we get home."

Busy round the farm and with the horse, who seemed pleased to be back in his own box, the tension eased and he watched her ride out on Harry as he had done many times before.

He lit a fire in the sitting room which was blazing well by the time she returned. He watched the flames licking at the wood, curling around each log like a caress, the orange tongues reaching for the chimney. It was a fascination he'd had since childhood, a cheering blaze, the fire with a life of its own. The room felt good again, warm and cosy, the house more like home and he started to relax. Kate's cheeks were bright with cold when she came in and he got up to take her near the fire with a warming arm round her.

"You're freezing," he said, touching her face. He drew her closer and felt her tremble, unsure if it was the cold or being close to him again. He kissed the top of her head and held her face against his shoulder, snuggling her to his own warm body.

"Nothing like a proper fire," he said. "Does that feel better?" She didn't answer. "I am sorry about last night. I did want to see you but I didn't want to see the Wilsons. I know that sounds ungrateful but I just couldn't face them. I have missed you and it's lovely to have you here now in my arms again."

She leaned away from him, searching his face. "Do you mean that?"

"Of course I do. I'm sorry I had to go. I didn't like leaving you."

"But you had to."

"Yes."

She started to speak again: "James, you never say — "

He smothered the words by kissing her. Holding her close he looked out at the gathering dusk. But what he saw was a snowy slope with tall white tombstones and the dark room above the cafe. And Katya's face. He sighed and bent his head against Kate's, clasping her more tightly to his chest. "Oh Kate forgive me, I do care about you, you know I do."

He struggled to catch what she said, muffled so tight against him. "But you never say you love me, not once."

He raised his head and sighed again and spoke almost a whisper. "No, I've never said that. But there's a reason. It's too easy to say it but theres's no point in just the word, I have to mean it. I'll only say it when I mean it, when I'm sure.

"And you're not sure."

She tried to pull away but he held on to her.

"No, that's not what I'm saying. To me love is a big word. I suppose what I feel for you is love but I need to be sure."

She pushed away from him and frowned, confusion and something like anger mixed in her face.

"And when might you be sure," she asked. "How long do I have to wait?"

"I don't know."

"I really don't understand you. You want me here — or I think you do — and you like making love to me — or maybe you don't any more. Is that all it is?"

He sat down looking into the fire, as if the answer might be found in its glowing depths, uncertain what to say to her, uncertain what he wanted.

For several minutes he was silent while she waited, still frowning, for some attempt at explanation. When he looked up at her she was surprised to see his eyes brimming with tears.

He wiped his hand across them and said: "Come and sit. I know you're confused but I am too. I can't explain it to myself. Going back there, it's like opening an old wound. I thought I'd got over it. Do you want me to tell you about it?"

"Well yes, it might help us both to understand, though I don't know why you have to analyse everything so minutely." Then she added: "I suppose I've been a fool about the sex thing. Perhaps you've been too good a teacher."

He smiled at that and took her hand, drawing her down to sit beside him, perched on the arm of the chair.

"There are so many graves in Sarajevo," he began. "I knew there would be a lot but I never imagined the extent of it, that's why it took them so long to find her. The cemeteries seem to dominate the city — there were so many dead. And it's the same all over Bosnia.

"But it's much worse than that because now they're finding all these mass graves. Victims from earlier in the war, many of them have been dug up and reburied, bodies broken up and scattered. They think there are many more to find and the work will take years."

With her hand held tight in his he told her what he'd done and seen during the days he'd been away, trying to explain the impact of being there again.

"Being in the cafe, in the room I shared with her — it's brought Katya back to me, I felt so close to her. I can't expect you to understand, it's the most peculiar sensation."

"But she's dead."

"I know she's dead, I saw her grave. I left poppies there. But it doesn't stop me thinking about her."

"You did love her?"

"Yes, I did. And there was no doubt about it. We were coming back here to England, to be married. But you know what happened."

Kate had watched his face as he spoke, turned away from her, looking always at the fire. She remembered what he'd told her and imagined them on the mountain, the sound of the shot and Katya's blood weeping over the snow.

"I don't think I can compete with a ghost," she whispered.

"I'm not asking you too. I just want you to understand why I'm so uncertain what I feel or want at the moment. And this place, this village — all your family's complications — I don't need it, it just adds to the mess."

"Yes, too many complications."

He nodded. "And there's another thing. When I wrote that piece for the agency, when I read it back, I realised how good I am at what I do, or did. And I think I want to go on doing it, maybe. You see, I'm not sure. I don't know what I want. Does that make sense?"

She didn't answer, stunned by the implication of his words and what it meant for her. Trying to stay calm, after a moment she said quietly: "So will you leave this place?"

"I didn't say that. I don't know. That's the point, I need to think it all through. But apart from anything else I must get on with writing the book, you know, the project I keep putting off. The agency won't do much for me until I fulfil that contract."

"I suppose I knew deep down you wouldn't be permanent. You're not that sort of man are you?"

He laughed, a harsh unhappy chuckle and tugged her onto his lap. "Oh Kate, I wish life were simpler. I love this place and I love having you here and starting work again doesn't mean I'd have to leave you or the farm. But I have to sort it out in my head. For a start I could be away for long spells — I wouldn't want you left here alone."

"I'd be all right."

"What, with the Sterlings threatening you? I don't think so."

"Oh James, I completely forgot." She stood up. "We've got a buyer for the farm, William rang the day you went away."

"I suppose that's good news."

"They want to complete as soon as possible."

"Good. Is the agent keeping it quiet?"

"I don't know, why?"

He left his chair quickly and started to pace around the room. "Because once the Sterlings realise they really aren't getting it I think there'll be trouble."

"Bill wouldn't do anything serious, surely?"

"The father might not but I wouldn't put anything past your ex-boyfriend. Ring William. Tell him to make the agent keep it totally confidential."

His mind suddenly focused on Sedge Farm and the fresh trouble it could bring so he didn't see the expression of misery on Kate's face as she went out. She was gone a long time, fussing with Harry he supposed and it occurred to him to see if the pub was still open. He left her a note.

He studied the vehicles in the car park, checking for any that might belong to the Sterlings. There were none he recognised. Richard behind the bar looked up surprised when he walked in.

"Didn't expect to see you," he said. "Thought you were in Bosnia."

"Who told you that?"

"Jack Wilson."

"Christ! This place. I asked him not to spread it around. Did everyone know I was away?"

"Don't know. I didn't know it was a secret."

"It wasn't — but the less people know less harm gets done."

"That's a bleak thought. We're not that bad."

"No, course not — but I like my privacy."

"And you a newsman." Richard chuckled. "Anyway, what can I get you? Good trip?"

"It wasn't pleasure," he said quietly. "A pint please."

The pub was busy, Richard stayed open all afternoon at weekends and he studied the different groups of people, looking for anyone he knew but there were no locals. That was good. He put the question he'd come to ask. "Have I missed anything?"

Richard set the pint glass on the bar and James took a long swig. "I expect you know they've got a buyer for the Patterson place."

"Kate just told me."

"That's given them something to talk about, all dying to know who's bought it."

"So it's common knowledge?"

"You bet."

"So much for confidentiality, how long have you known?"

"Couple of days. Don't know what you expect, James but you won't keep a thing like that quiet for long. Word soon gets round."

"That's what I was afraid of. The agent was supposed to keep it quiet."

"Not them -- big feather in their cap, selling a place like that."

"But they'll grab their commission quick enough. Fuck it!" He slammed his beer down in fury, slopping half of it across the bar.

"Steady on. That's not like you — what's the matter?"

"Think about it, Richard. You've warned me enough times about the Sterlings. This deal should've been kept quiet till it was done and dusted."

"Why? D'you think they might try something."

"God knows. But you know how much they wanted that land." He glanced behind him, seeing curious faces alerted by his angry voice and the glass slammed on the bar.

"Calm down, man," Richard leaned over to put his hand on James' arm. "Have another drink."

He shook off the restraining hand saying: "No. I don't need another. Sorry, not your fault — it's this bloody village."

He barged out through the door leaving Richard with a worried frown working across his face.

In the kitchen Kate still wore her boots and outdoor jacket, waiting for the kettle to boil. She didn't speak to him when he came in but reached for a second mug. He went through to the sitting-room and she knew by the way he walked, from each emphatic footfall that there was trouble.

She followed him with the tea. "James, I know you said about going out this evening but I don't want to. I'm not in the mood and I can't be bothered with all the hassle of getting ready."

He shrugged without looking at her. "Just as well probably." Then he swung round to her. "The whole damn village knows about the sale. How could your brother be so stupid? He should've insisted on confidentiality clauses."

"I don't know. I left it all to William. He's handled everything. I'll call him now."

"Yes, warn him. And then I'll ring the police."

"What?"

"Maybe I'm paranoid — but I don't think so."

The fire had died down and he began to riddle the ashes, poking so fiercely he lost half of it. He shoved a handful of kindling on the glowing embers and piled more logs on top.

"There's a load of messages on the phone," Kate called.

"I know. I haven't got round to them yet. Have a look while you're there, ditch what you can."

A chill had crept into the room with the fire so low and he slumped back shivering into the armchair to watch the flames recover. But there was only smoke from smouldering logs. He needed to think, angry that already the problems around Kate's family were dragging him in again, angry and uncomfortable, a discomfort edged with fear.

He didn't raise his head when she said William wasn't in but she'd left a message. "There were three calls from the agency, I left them on and a message from someone in France called Jenny about coming over."

"What?"

"Who's Jenny?"

"I've told you about them, friends, they live in southern France, I stayed with them that time just before you first turned up."

"It's quite an intimate sort of message," Kate said slowly.

"That sounds like Jenny."

"She seemed to know you very well."

"How can you tell that from a message?"

"As I said, it sounded intimate."

"I don't want them here at the moment, any of them. It's not a good time. We don't need visitors."

"Were you close to her?"

"Oh God -- she was my friend's girlfriend, we had a bit of a thing, shared a flat — for a very short time. It's nothing for you to worry about."

She came to stand in front of him, blocking the burgeoning fire. He didn't look up at her. "Are you jealous?"

"Well, yes. Do you blame me?" He didn't answer. "You come back in a strange mood, obsessed with a woman who's dead. Now there's another one with claims on you. And you talk about leaving — where do I fit in?"

He saw her eyes clouded with doubt, mouth pouting with uncertainty. "I've told you Kate, I need time to think. That's why I'm so angry about this sale. It distracts me from my own concerns and — don't you see how it creates danger. But I'll tell you about Jenny, she won't let go, she exaggerates everything in her life, what she doesn't know she makes up."

"Just one on your list is she?"

"I'm thirty-six I like women. I'm not a saint, I've been around, I've met a lot of attractive women and I've had sex with some of them."

"And I'm just another on the list? How soon will you tire of me. Or have you already?"

He got up and grabbed her arm, shaking her in exasperation.

"Just stop it. I'm not tired of you. I want you very much but I need time and worrying about what that fucking awful family might do is something I can do without." He took a mouthful from the mug of tea. "The bloody tea's cold now, great."

He left her, calling over his shoulder. "I'm going to ring the police, put them in the picture."

There was no reply from the local police station, half the time there was nobody there, and the duty officer at headquarters sounded uninterested and told him not to worry. He'd hoped to speak to the young woman constable who'd come about Tess's killing, at least she knew the background and might take notice of his fears. He wondered how soon they might get back to him.

Through the night he registered each passing hour by the clock beside his bed, trying to sleep but aware of the knot of anxiety like a physical ache in his gut and unable to resist the impulse which urged him to get up and check yet again. Each time he went back the bed had gone cold because there was no Kate to keep the warm place in the middle. She had chosen to sleep alone in the spare room.

His bedroom window on the hill gave a clear view over the valley and although Sedge Farm was masked by a stand of poplar trees he knew its precise location. It was fire he feared — the obvious and easiest act of revenge and vandalism. So he stood shivering to peer out into the darkness, each time expecting to see flames or smoke rising behind the trees. The moon was nearly full so smoke would show up like cloud in the dusky sky. But there was nothing.

Before dawn he looked in at Kate, comfortably asleep and went out to his car, scraping a layer of ice from the windscreen before he could move. Down in the quiet village only two homes showed a light.

His arrival triggered the security lights but everything appeared normal when he drove into the yard at Sedge Farm.

The dairy was ablaze with electricity and black and white heads swung round in turn to eye him suspiciously as he appeared in the walkway between the two rows of standings. The rhythmic thud of the milking machine dominated the shed with the steady sound of cows munching from the line of troughs. Rod the cowman looked up surprised from attaching the cluster to another udder and stood up as he finished.

"What's brought you here so early, Mr Lambert? Anything wrong?

"Just passing, thought I'd look in. Any problems?"

"Don't think so, the cows are happy, they're more settled now they're in for the winter."

He looked around the large shed, with more than a hundred milkers in there the heat they gave off made it almost cosy. He pushed aside the dark thoughts in his head.

He watched Rod at work, moving from cow to cow as the milk was drawn off, flowing away through the pipes to the bulk tank.

"Have you moved into the cottage yet?"

The man looked up again. "Yes, last week. It's worked out well. William did a good deal for me, the new owner wants to keep me on to run the herd and offered me the cottage so there's someone on the place till they move in."

"I heard that."

"I'm well pleased. I think you had a hand in it?

"Well, I did speak to William, told him you're worth keeping."

"Thanks. I appreciate it. I'm on three months trial but I should be all right. It means Rachel and I can get married at last."

"Your fiancee? She's not here yet."

"No. Thought we'd better wait till the owner arrives."

"So you're alone here."

"For now. But it's okay. The agency man comes in each day."

James frowned, wondering how to warn without alarming. He glanced again down the contented row of backs and said: "The cows look content. Well done, but keep your eyes open."

"What do you mean?"

"Just watch out for anything unusual. Remember not everybody is as pleased about the sale."

Rod stood upright and left the cow he was working on. "What are you saying?"

"I'm probably getting paranoid. I just don't trust the Sterlings."

"Them as wanted the farm?"

He nodded. "Keep your eyes open. Don't hesitate to call me — or the police."

"I hope you're wrong."

"So do I."

Back home Kate hadn't come down and he assumed she was still in bed. He made tea and took some to her. She was awake but frowned at him, a furrow of worry above her eyes. "Where did you go? I woke up and you weren't around? What's happened?"

"Nothing. I was restless so I went over to your place. Rod was milking. The new owner wants him to stay, given him the cottage. Did you know?"

"I think William said something."

"We need to talk to William. I assume he hasn't rung."

"It's a bit early for him."

"You should call him as soon as you're up. Shall I feed Harry?"

"Thanks. D'you mind?"

"I wouldn't have offered, would I?"

Feeding the animals occupied him but didn't stop his thoughts. Circumstances were ganging up, one thing after another. He didn't want Jennie here, something he didn't need, as if she had a claim on him though they were merely passing friends who'd slept together. It was nothing more than that but how could he make Kate understand. And the public interest in the farm sale, he knew she thought he was worrying needlessly about the Sterlings but the gnawing fear inside wouldn't be stilled.

He thought of Elizabeth out of it all in Galloway, tucked up with her rediscovered lover, oblivious of the issues her departure had created. She knew Bill Sterling better than anyone, perhaps she could allay his fears. He took it into his head to call her, imagining her in that cottage luxuriating in bed with her man on a Sunday morning. He suddenly envied her. She'd made a decision and stuck by it, finding a freedom she'd never known.

Kate was on the phone to her brother, he could tell by her replies that William was annoyed by the early call. "I know it's Sunday morning but James is worried. When can you come?"

She ended the call and turned to James. "They've got a posh lunch today and he's tied up tomorrow. He says he's coming Wednesday for the completion."

"Not till then?"

"He says you shouldn't worry, he can't see a problem. Once the sale's complete that's an end to it."

"That's the point. They'll be trying to stop the sale going through. Why can't he see that? I'm going to ring your mother, see what she thinks."

Graham answered. His quiet, slow voice expressed no surprise at hearing him. He simply said: "I'll fetch Elizabeth."

She sounded thrilled to hear from him, asking questions about Kate and him. She said nothing about his visit to Bosnia and he realised she wasn't up to date. When she paused long enough he asked: "You know they've sold the farm?"

"Is it definite?" he detected surprise. "William said there were several possibilities but I didn't realise it'd got that far." She paused.

"Yes, completion is on Wednesday."

"Good. At least I think it's good. We'll all be better off with the money."

"It'll certainly give Kate more options," he answered slowly. "I didn't call about that. It's something else."

"You sound worried." She was ahead of him. "I know why you've rung — you think the Sterlings might do something. Is that it?"

"Yes," he whispered.

Chapter twenty-two

His anxiety was dismissed by both Kate and William saying there was no way the Sterlings could halt the sale. He struggled to clarify his fears, wondering if he had it all out of proportion. Was he exaggerating their animosity -- perhaps? Yet he saw more than ambitious determination in Bill Sterling's make up, something beyond the normal expectation of behaviour in a rural community, a sense of ruthless entitlement. And in the son there was something worse, a brutish cruelty and disregard for the rules of decency that once out of control might stop at nothing. He knew too well how far people would go to get their way.

He couldn't understand the obsessive craving revealed in their lust for the land or was it just they hated to be thwarted in anything? He thought it could be simply that — that all his life the father in particular had come to expect to get or take whatever he wanted. And the son grew up with his father's attitude, made worse by that streak of depravity. He feared them. Thinking about it he admitted it to himself for the first time. He did not doubt his own ability to cope with them one to one but he'd already seen enough to expect some devious act of vengeance.

He knew Sterling and his associates had been crossed over the water scheme and though it was years ago the bitterness lingered. The sale could stir up all the old resentment. Yet Sterling was a wealthy man with a lot to lose and it was hard to imagine he would do something stupid enough to get in trouble with the law.

These thoughts trawled through his head throughout the day as he tried to stay busy and calm. Three more days until the farm no longer belonged to the Pattersons. He found no comfort with Kate who was nowhere to be seen, out on the horse or over at Pat's, to avoid being near him. And all because he could not — or would not as she thought — say the magic word. She appeared unable to understand, as if she would rather he lied to her, even if she knew he didn't mean it. He tried to find her and several times during the day caught glimpses of her disappearing through a door or round a corner and once at the bottom of the stairs he tried to catch her arm and draw her to him but she pushed him away and hurried back upstairs to get away.

He called after her: "Kate, we can't go on like this --" but the door closed with a bang and he turned away with a sigh.

His loneliness at night made little difference as he maintained his vigil watching the dark valley for signs of trouble.

The day for the farm completion came and with Kate at work he waited alone trying to write and making calls to the agency who'd been pleased with his Sarajevo piece. They wanted more from him on the search for mass graves and the work of identifying the bodies. But they were also pushing him harder for the book he'd been paid for.

William drove into the yard in mid afternoon as the rain began, a cold slash of sleet sweeping over the valley. He hurried to the door looking pleased with himself as James came to open it.

"It's done. Finished. The farm isn't ours any more," he said. "Thank God."

"Amen to that," said James. "Did everything go smoothly?"

"Yes — all straightforward. They came in person and seem very pleased but they're not moving in till new year. They're leaving Rod to run the herd and keeping the temporary manager who'll come in daily."

He noticed the look on James' face and asked: "Why are you so worried?"

"I'm just expecting the worst. Stupid of me, I expect. Come on." He led William towards the kitchen. "We must have a glass to celebrate."

"Why not," William said dropping his bag. "Can you find me a bed?"

"Oh — I expect so." He heard the hesitation.

"Problem?"

James rubbed a hand across his face to hide his embarrassment. "Well, Kate's using the spare room."

"Had a row?"

"It's complicated. She's been upset since I got back and then a girl I used to know rang from France and that made it worse. I tried to explain we were never close, it was nothing really, you know what I mean but she's got it into her head that I've got a crowd of women in my past and she's just another in the line."

"Ah." William watched James pour two tots of whisky. "And is she right?"

"What d'you mean?"

"She's my sister. I wouldn't like to think she was just your latest lay. I thought she meant more to you."

"She does! It's difficult — I don't know what I feel about her. Did she tell you I've been back to Sarajevo? That was hard and all this going on here has got me so confused. It's difficult."

"Do you love her?"

"Damn it William, that's the issue. Because I don't say it -- because I haven't told her I love her she thinks I don't."

"So say it."

"I don't want to say it if I'm not sure."

"It's only words, man."

"No! No -- it's not just words, it has to be true. I loved Katya, the girl in Bosnia. I know I loved her. I was bringing her back to get married. Kate knows that, she knows all about it."

"And now she thinks she's fighting a ghost," said William. "Is that it?"

"That's about it. We go over the same ground again and again."

"Anyway -- cheers." He clinked his glass against William's and slumped down at the kitchen table, resting his chin on his clenched fingers. He looked up at William: "I just don't know if I want the commitment. She's a wonderful girl, she's here with me but maybe I'm too old for her. I helped her with the horse, that's how it started. I'm very fond of her but I'm just not sure.

"And all this trouble with your family and the Steve thing. I don't need all that and I'm not sure it's finished yet."

William studied him but said nothing. After a while he continued: "I bought this place for peace and quiet. I'm supposed to be writing a book and you need thinking time for that."

William said: "If I can help at all, just say — but it doesn't sound the sort of thing I could help with."

James shrugged. "No. Enough of that, let's go through and be comfortable."

William flopped into an armchair near the fire, relaxed and at ease.

"So when do you get your money?" asked James.

"It should be in the bank by six o'clock. Then I've got to divide it between us. Three way split, that's what Mum wants. I'm not even sure if Kate's got a proper bank account. My sister will be a wealthy girl, it's a big farm and we got a good price."

"I'm not interested in her money. My share of the family farm will come eventually when my mother goes, though not yet I hope. I'm not rolling in it but I'm okay and I wouldn't dream of hanging on to Kate for her money, that's not me."

William gave him a knowing smile. "Many would but I've seen enough of you not to think that. You're a good bloke but you probably dwell on stuff too much. Maybe that's no bad thing. You've been good for Kate and good to her."

They were comfortable by the fire while outside the sleet had turned to hail and the temperature was dropping towards freezing point.

"What time will she be home?" William went to look from the window surveying the bleak yard in the fading light. "It's turning nasty out there. She won't be able to ride, will she?"

"No, it'll be too dark. He's been turned out today, I'll get him in soon."

William said: "That horse means a lot to her, he was such a lovely foal. We had the mare at our place with him, it was easier that way. She bought him almost as soon as he was born, at least the deal was done."

"But the Sterlings were virtually blackmailing your father over it, that's why I let her bring him."

"Has it been a nuisance?"

"No, not really," he grinned. "There were a lot of compensations."

He went on about the horse. "I like the animal, he's a good horse and she's good on him. That injury, earlier this year, it put him out of eventing for the season but hopefully in the spring she can get him going again. I think they could do very well."

"Do you mind doing all that ?" William sipped his whisky. "Are you happy being involved?"

"I quite enjoy it — something different. That's not the problem."

"Would you like me to speak to her?"

He didn't answer but moved nearer the fire, leaning back against the iron canopy. "Whoa, that's hot," he said. "What can you say? Tell her to get back in bed with me and forget it all? I don't know. I miss her in my bed William, I know that."

"Tell her that."

"It's not enough. I know she likes to be with me but she needs more." He swallowed the last of his whisky. "She'll be home soon. I'll go for Harry, it's nearly dark." He started from the room then turned to say: "Well done on the sale. Thank God it's gone through."

Kate hadn't recognised her brother's car and she laughed with pleasure when she found him. "I didn't expect to see you here," she said. He folded his arms around her in a hug, brushing icy drops from her hair and shoulders. She shivered. "It's bitter out there."

"Your face is red, you look really well."

"Thanks."

"Big day today," he said.

"What? Oh! Was it today? I'd forgotten."

"Had you really?" he asked

"Yes, I knew it was Wednesday but I haven't thought of it till now."

"We're wealthy now Kate, you, me and mum. When everything's settled it's left us with getting on for two million between us. How about that?"

She frowned as she peeled off her damp coat. "So much? I didn't expect that much."

"It gives you plenty of options."

She nodded. "Yes but I don't know what I want apart from being here. Where's James?"

"Fetching your horse," he smiled. "You've got him well trained."

"He likes Harry, he's very good with him. He's a rider himself."

"But you're not happy, I can see that." He put an arm around her again. "You and him not getting on?"

"It's been difficult since he came back. You know he went to Bosnia to find the grave."

"He told me."

"He's been so strange this week and he worries about the Sterlings. He's convinced they'll do something."

"Surely they wouldn't be so stupid."

"Not Bill but Steve's capable of anything. He rang mum and she said the same."

"But now the sale's gone through it's not us they'd be hurting," William said, thinking like a rational man.

"But people's minds can work in a funny way. It might not make any difference," Kate said.

The phone rang while James was making supper, chatting to William as he worked. They heard Kate answer it and her end of the brief conversation.

"I'm Kate." Pause. "I live here, oh."

Then her footsteps as she came into the kitchen, thrusting the phone at James. "It's Jenny again."

"What? Hell, what does she want?"

He went off with the phone and though both pretended not to listen they caught the murmur of his voice, rising in exasperation.

He came back looking angry and ignoring William said to Kate: "You know all about it, so don't blame me for this."

"Why did she ring?"

"I don't know. She's got some idea in her head. Is that bad timing or what?"

"And?"

"And nothing. I told you about it. It's in the past, you know that."

She turned away.

William watched them through the evening, the atmosphere stiff with embarrassment, the two of them edgy, wary like dogs waiting to fight.

He made lasagne and they ate it on their laps and talked politely in stilted discussion between long pauses about the farm and the sale and their mother.

When Kate went to fetch cheese he took the opportunity to say: "Looks like you'll be on the sofa William, I'm sorry. It's quite comfy and it's warmer down here. We have another bedroom but it's full of Kate's stuff from the farm. There wasn't much she wanted but when it's all together it takes up a lot of space."

William smiled: "I don't mind, I've slept on plenty of sofas in my time."

She returned to hear the end of that and glanced at them both without speaking.

They stayed drinking together with the TV in the background until James switched to the news at ten o'clock. "I'll just watch the headlines and then get you some bedding."

"Thanks. I'm tired, it's been a busy day."

When James disappeared William looked at his sister.

"Is it so bad? I thought you two were good together?" She sat beside him and he leaned across to plant a brotherly kiss on her cheek. "I don't like to see my little sister upset -- you should be pleased tonight, you're a wealthy woman."

"I know. But the money doesn't mean a lot in itself."

"Doesn't it!"

"You know what I mean, you need to be happy in other ways."

"And you're not?"

"Well," she looked away, unwilling to meet his eyes. "I was happy, in spite of all the problems but now I just don't know about him, what he feels about me. I didn't realise there'd been so many women in his life and I have this awful feeling I'm just one more."

"He told me. It didn't help that woman ringing earlier."

"No."

He took her chin and turned her face towards him. "And what do you feel about him?"

Her face clouded and he saw tears welling up in her dark eyes. "I can't imagine being without him, not now, he's so different from anyone else I've ever known. I can't bear the thought of leaving him."

William breathed a long sigh. "Trouble is sis, you haven't known many men have you? Stuck with that oaf. And this place isn't exactly full of likely lads, is it? Maybe you should move away."

"What? I want to be with James and this is my home, the sort of life I want is here in Shropshire. I don't think I could live in London, like you."

"I do miss it sometimes but my work and my life are there now. I can see there might be a time when I'd want to come back. But the farm's gone — though I never saw myself as a farmer. If things had been different I might've kept the house and just sold the land."

"Too late for that," she said.

He took another sip from his glass, saying: "I don't often drink whisky, it's going to my head. Time I was tucked up. But listen Kate, with the money you'll have you've got plenty of options. It will make a difference you know."

"Yes, I suppose it will. Look William, you go up to bed, I'll sleep down here."

"No need for that. I'll be all right."

"I really would rather you went upstairs, this isn't big enough for you and I'll be fine on it."

When James came back with a sleeping bag and blankets William had gone and Kate was huddled on the rug by the fire.

"I sent William upstairs."

"Oh, will you be okay down here?"

"Of course."

He stood waiting but she didn't turn. He switched off the television and made up the fire, setting the guard in place and said: "William did a good deal over the farm, you're a wealthy girl."

She nodded. "So he tells me."

"Aren't you pleased?"

"I suppose so."

"Kate -- " he began but the determined set of her hunched back deterred him. He bent, touched her shoulder and felt her recoil. Frowning he stepped back and left her. Before he closed the door he called quietly: "Good night." But she didn't answer.

So the farm sale was done. It had new owners who had nothing to do with any of them, Sedge Farm was no longer of concern for William and Kate, or for him. Yet he couldn't relax, couldn't resist the nagging anxiety that made him leave his bed to strain his eyes towards that spot behind the poplar trees. He tried not to do it and slept for a while until he woke with the clock by the bed showing ten minutes after three. He lay on his back wide awake, willing himself not to get up.

He turned on his side, his arm feeling the empty bed and thought of Kate alone in the sitting room. He didn't like her being down there away from himself and William. It was a totally irrational fear, that someone might enter the house and find her there alone and vulnerable. It was the same as his anxiety about the farm and it only increased the more he thought about it. The night was cold but he began to sweat and threw off the covers to lie naked on the mattress. Thinking of Kate in danger made him think of her in another way and become very conscious of the accustomed effect she had on his body. Ashamed of his hardness he shook his head and got up to check for any activity in the darkness. The valley seemed at peace and he sat on the bed, contemplating what the idea of Kate did to him. It was too vivid and his anxiety for her too real.

The house was undisturbed and in silence he went downstairs. The evening's fire had sunk to a scarlet glow but the room was still warm and she was half uncovered, head on the edge of the sofa, bare arms drooped to the floor. He moved on tiptoe to stand in front of her, studying her as she slept, peaceful and untouched, beautiful. A pang of longing rippled through him, a longing more than physical and he couldn't help but kneel beside her and with one finger push back the hair from her face.

He waited but she didn't move and steadying himself on the sofa arm he leant forward to kiss her, stroking her temple with his lips. Content that she was safe he was about to rise and go but couldn't resist touching her bare arm where it hung relaxed. She stirred then and he remained motionless wondering if she would wake. Helpless he touched her again and now she woke, startled from her dream, eyes so frightened he thought she would scream. He clamped a hand over her mouth whispering: "It's me, don't be scared, I just came to check on you."

She sat up staring from wide eyes still blurred by sleep. When he removed his hand she said: "What? What do you want?"

"I -- nothing. I was anxious, that's all."

"Go away, I'm fine. I was dreaming."

"A good dream?"

"Not sure, I can't remember. Go away, I don't want you here."

He stayed on one knee beside her, a hard push would unbalance him. "Kate, please, talk to me. I miss you so."

Drowsy from sleep she looked at him unthinking and shivered. "I'm cold now. I was so warm and comfortable."

"I'm sorry." He squeezed his way onto the sofa beside her and wrapped her in his arms though she struggled.

"Kate I'm sorry I've upset you, you mean so much to me," he whispered. "I hate us being like this."

She didn't answer but closed her eyes and tried to snuggle back down under the covers but his body was in the way and she pushed at him, trying to force him away.

"Go away," she muttered. "Leave me alone. I don't want you here."

"Do you really mean that?" He stood up and stared down at her, desperate to touch her. He hesitated a moment then pulled her up to make room for him to sit properly, so she was forced to lie with her head against him. He stroked her face and ran his hand under the covers to find her breasts. He felt her body tense for an instant then relax as his fingers found the right spots. He moved so he could feel further down her body and when his hand slid between her legs she brought her thighs together, trapping it. He waited until with a sigh she relented.

"Do you want me to go?" he whispered. "It's nice here -- I was cold alone in bed."

She licked his chin with the tip of her tongue, saying: "I don't really want you here but my body does. You've taught me too well. I've learned what I need. I don't want to want you but I do."

"I would miss you so much if you went away. My head's in a mess, I don't know what to think. I think I love you but I'm not sure. I need time to get things straight."

"Don't say any more, just do it. Make me feel good."

Chapter twenty-three

Three weeks until Christmas, the weather was kinder but the ground around the farm was soggy. The short days meant Kate could only ride at weekends or on a free afternoon and Harry was mostly in the paddock. He watched in disgust as the horse galloped around each morning, kicking up his heels in the joy of being out, rapidly turning the grass into a sea of mud. Rain filled the marks of his shoes making a quagmire of the area around the gate and by the fence. He thought ruefully of how neat and tidy his land had been until Harry arrived, understanding very well the fixed attitude of most farmers against having horses on the land, they made such a mess. But at least the sheep mitigated to some extent the damage from the flying hooves.

But the horse's enjoyment was worth seeing and he considered the muddy mess a small price to pay to please Kate. Since the farm sale was completed she seemed happier and more relaxed with him and content to leave things as they were.

There had been no repercussions so far after the sale and neither of them went much into the village so had no contact with Bill Sterling or his son. Pat told them any gossip but the only information of interest was from Jack who mentioned to his daughter that Steve Sterling was spending a lot of time in the pub with his motorbike friends, swearing and creating an uncomfortable atmosphere for the supper customers.

Richard had warned them twice already and was threatening to bar them if they didn't quieten down. Kate laughed when she heard but he frowned, glad they didn't visit the pub more often.

Jack Wilson said: "It's just bravado, he's trying to look big after they lost out on your farm."

He'd come over on the tractor with a load of hay for Harry, better quality horse hay than James had made on his own land.

"You're probably right. He's showing off so the family doesn't lose face. Trouble is I can't see Richard being able to enforce a ban on them. He might need to get the police involved."

"He won't do that," Jack said, grunting as he threw a bale onto the stack in the barn. "Too much unpleasantness, Richard wouldn't like that."

"Maybe. But his best trade is the people who come to eat. If Steve's crowd gets too rowdy the sort of people Richard likes won't come."

"I shouldn't worry," Jack said. "If they get too out of hand he'll tell Bill. He wouldn't like his son barred from the pub."

Elizabeth rang from Scotland early one evening while Kate was still outside. He asked how life was treating her in Galloway and she responded with a detailed account of the changes she'd made to Graham's cottage. She sounded exuberant about it — and happy.

"You sound good," he said. "I'm glad it's working out."

"The money's helped of course. Graham has struggled up here, been living on very little. He's much more like his old self."

"I suspect it's you as much as the money," James said quietly.

She asked about Kate and questioned him on what they were doing and brought Christmas into the conversation. He realised she was angling for an invitation.

"It seems such a long time since I saw her," she said.

He hesitated, on the point of asking them to visit, but thinking better of it said instead: "I'll get Kate to call you. We were talking about you both just the other day."

"I hope she has kinder thoughts about me now," Elizabeth said slowly. "She has good reason for a grudge after all that's happened."

"We all know why you were forced to behave as you did."

"I think your mother wants to come for Christmas," he said when Kate appeared.

"Really?" The surprise made her frown as she pulled off her dirty boots and left them by the door.

"She rang earlier. I send you'd call her."

"Does she mean stay here?"

"I don't know. Suppose so."

"Would you mind? Both of them?"

"I've no problem with Graham. It's up to you, we have a spare room."

He handed her a mug of tea.

"I don't know what to think," she said. "Do we want them here?"

"It's up to you. I don't mind, she's your mother."

"And you do like her, don't you?"

"Yes, she's surprisingly good company."

"I need to think about it," said Kate. "I'll ring her tomorrow."

He wondered what she would decide, understanding a certain reluctance towards her mother from the time when both parents seemed in league against her. He didn't want any new disruption in their relationship which had settled back into a groove, comfortable and comforting, enjoying each other not only in the physical sense.

She appeared to take no great interest in the considerable amount of money which was her share but he soon discovered it had opened her mind to the wider possibilities of life. She admitted she'd never stretched her brain but he always told her she was far better than she let herself believe. But now she was constantly asking questions, almost as a child would ask her father but having never had that relationship with her father it was as if a damn was unblocked and the torrent of queries poured out on him.

He began to believe he could be happy with her, at the farm as a base, taking on selected commissions for the agency who'd indicated they would use him but hopefully he wouldn't be away too often or for too long. He pictured Kate in the days ahead, successful with her horse and maybe when she had achieved all that she might turn to other desires.

He imagined her with a child — would she want that? Probably yes if he did. But did he? He probed his deepest longings and began to believe it was all meant to be, that there was a future for them in this cosy dream of normality.

He had relished the prospect of spending Christmas alone with her. The image of a relaxing day with just the two of them alone with no interruptions was very enticing. But he didn't say this and when she informed him she'd invited Elizabeth and Graham to come he brushed aside his disappointment.

"It'll be nice to see something of them and find out what they do up there. What about William? Are you going to ask him as well?"

"I don't know. He might not want to come and we haven't enough room for them as well."

"He might have other plans but you should ask him. Don't want him to feel left out."

"But we haven't the room."

"I'm sure he'd find somewhere to stay, he's not strapped for cash, is he? Richard has rooms at the pub."

A couple of days later there was gossip in the village about a bust-up in the pub with different versions of what had actually happened buzzing from family to family. Jack Wilson made a special visit to tell them his version which was that Steve Sterling had attacked his own father when Bill had come to shift him from the pub.

Jack reckoned Steve had gone for Richard over the bar and Bill had held him back. James and Kate heard this tale in disbelief, thinking it unlikely Steve would go so far. William got the story from Richard when he rang to ask about a room for Christmas. The pub was already fully booked but he'd found a room close to the village.

In a long phone call William told them what he'd heard from the horse's mouth. The pack with Steve had their girlfriends along and they'd ordered a meal, pushing two tables together in the corner. Steve bought the first round saying casually: "On my tab."

When the food arrived two of the girls tried only a mouthful each before complaining about their salmon, claiming it was undercooked and when Mark the chef appeared to talk to them they began shouting abuse before he could open his mouth.

The talented young cook was slender and gay with blond highlights in his auburn hair. Steve laughed and said loudly: "Fucking shirt-lifter, you should learn to cook."

The room went quiet as customers stopped talking and eating and turned to take in the commotion. Behind the bar Richard looked furious.

The chef retreated with the offending fish and a little later the waitress returned with two fresh plates. The girls didn't say thank you but tucked into their food and the party carried on, laughing at crude jokes between mouthfuls.

Then one of the youths pushed his plate aside saying: "Don't know why you bother with this place, Steve, the food's fucking awful."

"Yeah. You're right, Tone. It's handy — that's all. I'll tell him about it."

He went to the bar, pushing between two regulars chatting on the stools. He leaned across to get as close as possible to Richard and said loudly: "I reckon you owe us a round for that meal. My mate's steak was tough as his boot."

Richard glowered at him "It didn't stop him eating it. Julie's just cleared his plate, looks like he licked it clean."

"He said it was tough and that's good enough for me."

"Well, tough to you. You'll get no free drinks tonight!"

Tony came across to join him and whispered something. Steve shrugged and sauntered back to the table while his friend ordered another round for all of them, again no money changed hands.

The noise from the corner grew more raucous and the couple right in the corner began groping each other, egged on by the rest. It got to the point where the girl had unzipped his trousers and had her hands inside.

The diners sitting nearest swallowed their drinks and left in a hurry, causing others to look across to see what was happening. Several people grinned but most turned away in disgust and the pub rapidly began to empty.

Richard strode across to the youngsters.

"Right. That's enough! I want you lot out now. And I don't want you back. And you Sterling, you settle your tab before you leave."

"No chance, grandad. Who's gonna make us? Not you." He stood up and pushed Richard who staggered back.

"That's it. I'm calling the police."

"You won't do that."

They all ignored Richard as he retreated behind the bar and went to the phone. It wasn't the police he rang but Bill Sterling who listened in silence to the angry publican. "I've rung you first but if you don't sort it I'll call the police. My pub's almost empty, because of them. I won't have it."

Ten minutes passed -- enough time for another pair to begin undressing each other -- then the door flew open. Bill Sterling strode in followed by his tractor driver Len, a heavily built man in his late thirties, who was often the butt of Steve's jokes because of his stammer. Without a word Bill grabbed his son by the neck of his fleece and hauled him to his feet.

"What the hell d'you think you're doing, you stupid young sod?"

"Just having a bit of fun, dad. No harm done."

"No harm. You've emptied the pub. I've never heard Richard so angry. And what are they doing over there? Get them out of here."

He nodded to Len who pulled the tables apart and dragged the rampant youngster off his girl and across the room to the door, jeans sinking round his legs. The rest of them scrambled for the exit, two of the girls tugging their clothes into place.

Bill, only slightly taller than his son, was still holding him by the arm. Steve began to struggle. "Let me go. I'm not a child."

"You're behaving like one. You're a bloody disgrace, it's no wonder Kate couldn't bear you."

Suddenly the situation changed, the mention of her name turned Steve's face red with fury and he lashed out at his father, thumping him hard in the belly. Winded, Bill let him go and Steve threw another punch which caught him on the cheek.

Bill felt his face and saw blood on his hand. "You little bastard, hit me would you!"

Richard had come round from behind the bar as Bill went to hit his son. "Don't Bill. Don't make it worse." They stood two feet apart and Steve moved to swing another blow but Len had come up behind and grabbed his arm, twisting it up behind his back as he propelled him to the door.

"That's for you, master Steve," he growled as he shoved him down the steps.

James listened in silence as Kate repeated the story. He raised a wry smile because she found it amusing but the bit where Steve's temper burst out at the mention of her was not funny at all. The resentful anger was still there, bubbling away inside him like a volcano waiting to erupt. He started to say something of this to her but stopped and kept the thought to himself.

She heard the sound of a motorbike in the distance, the rising growl of its engine indicating it was coming her way. She'd set out with Harry on a longer route on her afternoon off as the start of a programme to bring him gradually back to fitness now his leg had recovered.

The afternoon was cold but at least it was dry and as she trotted up a farm track several miles from home she was enjoying the ride. The horse was happy too, full of it, bouncy and really well. Kate was thinking about Christmas, surprised to find she was really looking forward to spending time with her mother and getting to know the man who had unintentionally made such an impact on her life.

She hadn't seen the croft in Galloway where Elizabeth had chosen to live, having only James' description to go on. It was an area she knew nothing about and she'd thought she might stay with them some time in the future. Her mind was full of plans and arrangements for festive catering, determined to do her share of cooking and hospitality. She'd made a Christmas cake, the first one ever but it was overcooked so when she got home from this ride her next task was to make another. There was still enough time for it to mature and James had told her to feed it with brandy.

The noise of the motorbike was much closer, approaching at speed and she realised it must be on the track behind her but she couldn't see as the way at this point ran between high hedges. Harry's ears flicked back and she stroked his neck to reassure him. "It's okay fella, just a bike. It'll slow down when they see us."

The track went steeply downhill and she heard the engine noise very close behind. She glanced back to see the quad bike bearing down on them fast and waved her arm to ask the rider to slow down but instead the bike roared louder as it accelerated. Harry started to sidle in fear, half turned towards the oncoming menace, then he broke into a canter, running from the roar literally at his heels. She struggled to hold him, relaxing the reins a little to ease him before shortening them and he was beginning to listen when the rider blew his horn, a screaming klaxon chasing them.

Harry bolted. The bike kept coming and as the track widened it swept passed them and she saw who it was. "Enjoy your gallop, Kate!" he yelled as he went by before disappearing round the sharp bend ahead.

Harry was moving at top speed and pulling on the reins only made it worse. She slackened them trying to reduce the pressure and make him realise the danger was gone but as he got to the bend she knew he was moving too fast to make it. The hedge gave way to railings there, the site of an old gateway, with a ditch in front. Unable to make the turn Harry paused then launched himself at the rail. He managed to clear it but it was an enormous jump and he landed steeply and stumbled, throwing Kate over his head.

She lay on her face in the mud, struggling for breath while the horse galloped on across the field. She hurt, the pain was in her chest and back, the wind knocked out of her when she hit the hard ground.

For moment she panicked, unable to breathe, gulping for air. She gasped in fear which eased when she got breath back in her lungs and raised her head to see Harry some distance away, head down, his flanks heaving but looking at her.

She kept still till she found the will to move and begin gingerly to test each limb in turn. After some minutes she decided she wasn't injured and sighed with relief that she was only winded and filthy but nothing broken. She sat up and called the horse who raised his head, ears pricked. There was pain in her ankle but it took her weight and slowly she hobbled towards him. He watched her approach and when she called his name again he answered in a soft nicker of recognition and began to come to her. Anxiously she looked at his legs, caked above the knees with wet mud but there was no blood mingling with it. Both reins were broken, one missing and the martingale swung between his legs as he moved but she could detect no sign of injury.

They had landed in a large corn field, still unploughed and she scanned the boundaries before spotting a gate at the far side, the furthest from home. She made a lead from the neck strap and began to trudge across the stubble, the horse walking quietly beside her.

The gate brought her out onto an unfamiliar stretch of road. She looked both ways trying to work out where she was but was disorientated because she'd come there via the field.

Standing together on the tarmac she began to shake with cold and shock. Harry too was trembling and she put her arms around his neck to comfort them both while she tried to think what to do. She had no idea which direction to take so set off to the right from the gateway. The afternoon was turning colder and without the energy to walk fast enough to keep warm she began to shiver uncontrollably.

After about half a mile the verge widened where a stack of logs awaited collection. She slumped down onto a length of oak and burst into tears. Harry waited quietly beside her, ignoring the stale grass around the logs, his head hanging to the ground. She couldn't collect her thoughts to think how to get home, before long the short afternoon would fade into dusk and the winter night. Her only idea was to keep walking until she arrived at a house and hope someone was there to make a phone call.

She thought about James and the time at the beginning when he'd come looking for her, anxious, although then he hardly knew her. But this day he would have no idea where she might be, having gone much further than she intended.

She'd sat too long on the log and her feet in rubber riding boots were numb with cold. She could feel them but they hurt when she stood up and she wondered if she would be able to walk at all. But she hobbled on along the tarmac despite the pain.

She forced herself to keep going, sunk into a dull despair and fear as to the outcome of this nightmare. The road was quiet at that time of day but several cars and lorries passed in both directions speeding away from her without a second glance. Sometimes she tried holding out her arm to attract attention but the drivers had neither time nor inclination to stop. She began to feel indignant that no one noticed her plight.

"I'm sure I'd stop if I saw someone in trouble," she said aloud to herself. But most people would see nothing unusual in a girl leading a horse. And flying by in a car at speed they wouldn't know they were seeing a crisis. They'd have no notion of what had happened.

The road she followed ran straight between fields for several miles with no sign of habitation. As she put one foot in front of the other in the failing light she began to be seriously afraid, the grey muddy horse in the darkness would not be easy to see. She tried to stay on the verge but in many places it was too narrow between the road and the ditch. The headlights of passing vehicles dazzled her in the growing darkness and the horse was startled as they came up behind and whooshed past.

A line of cars approached head-on and she scrambled onto the verge as two more came speeding behind her. A smart Jaguar going the other way slowed down as it passed and she saw its brake lights flash red further down the road. Looking back she watched it stop and back into a gateway before returning. It passed her slowly and pulled up a little way ahead.

A woman got out of the passenger door and walked towards her, her elegant cream boots smeared by the muddy grass. "Are you in trouble?" she asked.

Kate nodded, her mouth too numb to speak clearly. "We had a fall," she mumbled.

"Are you hurt?"

She shook her head. "Bridle's broken, can't ride him."

"Can we take you somewhere?"

"Can't leave him."

"Couldn't you put him a field?"

"Can't leave him," she repeated. "Can you get to a phone box or a house and ring for me?"

The driver joined them, a large wide-faced man in a leather coat. "We can do better than that," he said. "Come here." He motioned her to the car and leaned in to pick up a phone from the central console. "Only got this last week, bit of a toy I thought but this is just the situation they're meant for. What's the number?"

"It was him," she said. "It was deliberate. He made Harry bolt." She was swathed in blankets by the fire, clutching a hot water bottle.

"Are you sure you're not hurt?"

"My right arm aches a bit, I must've landed on it. But it's not broken, I can move it. That was a big hedge he took."

"For fuck's sake! You could've broken your neck." He studied her grimly. "Then he'd be facing a manslaughter charge. You're sure it was Steve."

She sighed and nodded. "He shouted at me as he went by — and laughed. I'd know that laugh anywhere."

He'd rushed out with the trailer to find them when he got the call. The Jaguar couple had waited with her in the car, wrapped in a sheepskin coat, holding Harry through the window. Kate was sobbing again when he arrived, mostly overwhelmed by their kindness. "It's shock," the woman said as he looked in at Kate. "She was very cold."

"And frightened," the man explained. "The traffic was just whizzing by, nobody bothered to stop." He paused. "She wouldn't say what happened. I get the feeling there's a bit more to it."

"I'll find out," James smiled. "But thank God you stopped. It was kind."

"The wife's a rider," he said. "We could tell she was in trouble. And fortunately I had this." He waved the phone at James. "You should get one. Takes a lot of the sweat out of life."

"I've thought about it," James said. "Just haven't got round to it. It'd help with my work as well."

"You wait, before long, everybody'll have one."

They stayed to help load Harry into the trailer, the woman holding him while he did the ramp. They weren't local, down from Cheshire to see friends.

The driver, grinning as he introduced himself because his name was Harry, said before they drove away. "I'm glad we came along, the traffic's fast on this straight bit. They could easily have been hit."

"We owe you a drink," James said. "If you're round here please call us."

"We will. This is my number if you need it."

"Thanks again," he said as Harry got back in his car. He watched them drive away and told himself he'd go into town in the morning and buy a mobile phone.

Chapter twenty-four

"The problem is Mr Lambert, like before, you don't have any proof." The young woman constable who'd come out when Tess was killed looked at them with genuine sympathy, after hearing the details of the quad bike incident.

"But I saw him. He was laughing and shouting at me as he went by. He deliberately frightened the horse," Kate said.

James butted in: "She could've been killed. I drove down that track to look at the hedge they went over. It was enormous."

"I believe what you say," she told Kate. "But he'll deny it and it's your word against his without witnesses."

"What about the couple who stopped? They saw what state she was in and I know they were suspicious."

"Yes, but all they know is she came off the horse. They don't know what happened."

James stomped round the kitchen, face scrunched between his arms in fury.

"There must be something you can do. You know what he did to Tess. You saw her, you saw the tree and the blood on the ground. She's not making this up. He could have killed her."

"I hear what you're saying but to make a case you've got to have proof."

"That bastard's capable of anything. He attacked her a while ago on the horse, he tried to pull her off in the lane and his motorbike friends chased them on the hill. I warned you what he might do when the farm was sold."

"But nothing happened. And all this stuff is circumstantial."

"So he gets away with it?"

"All I can do is log it. Without proof he'll laugh at us."

"So we just wait for the next time? What does he have to do before you people take some action?"

The girl's face was full of concern but she said: "I know there's history here but don't you think you're getting this out of proportion. He may not have realised it was Kate, perhaps he did it without thinking — if it was him. It's hard to believe he'd be so vindictive."

Kate laughed. "If it was him? You don't believe me! I've known him all my life, he's capable of anything. He's banned from the pub so he's got a grudge against his own father now. Can't you warn him or something?"

"That might be possible, I'll speak to the sergeant." She was edging towards the door and James went to open it for her.

"You need to understand, he's obsessed with Kate and bitter about not getting the farm. He has a nasty, vicious streak."

As she left she frowned and said: "Do you think Mr Lambert, that you could be just a little bit paranoid?"

He didn't answer but as he watched her drive away a surge of exasperated anger rushed through him. He swung round and grabbed a plate from the table, smashing it away from him to the floor.

Kate looked down at the shards of china and said: "That won't solve anything."

"It made me feel better. I could kill that bastard."

"Don't say things like that."

"Why can't they see? He'll do something really bad, I know he will."

He glanced at Kate. "Am I paranoid?"

"No." She slumped onto a chair, resting her chin in her hands. "I did think so. When the farm was sold I thought you were getting things out of proportion but after what happened yesterday I think you're right." She looked up at him, her face pale, eyes bright with tears she struggled to control.

"I'm frightened. I didn't think he could scare me any more but after this I'm afraid to take Harry out. I don't know how he came to be on that track, it's nowhere near their land and I don't usually ride there. Is he watching me?"

"I don't see how he can. It may be just bad timing or perhaps someone spotted you going that way and told him."

"What do we do?"

He sighed. "Not sure. But you must stick to the roads in future and I'll follow you."

"James, that's crazy."

"Just for now. You can't ride much this time of year anyway. You'll have to be patient."

He'd called the police as soon as they got home but they couldn't come till morning. She insisted before anything else on making sure Harry was comfortable then he made her take a bath.

He stayed with her and watched her undress, noting the dried mud right through to the skin in places. Most of one arm was purple, blackening as the bruising came out and her elbow tender to his touch. But otherwise she was unhurt.

"You were lucky," he said, helping her into the bath, seeing her wince as she put weight on the arm.

"Let me wash you."

She sat quietly in the water while he knelt beside the tub, soaping all over her body, and lying back to enjoy the hot water as he gently rinsed her. He smiled, kissing a shoulder. "I didn't expect a treat like this, so the day's not all bad."

"You'll be in here with me any minute," she laughed.

"No, better not, I don't want to hurt your sore arm. I'll go outside, that'll cool me down."

He dried her with warm towels and that took a long time because he had to touch and caress every bit of her. Afterwards he made her sit by the fire and drink tea.

Caring for her took his mind off the reality of the perils ahead. The reaction from the police when he explained what had happened told him they were unwilling or unable to help. They couldn't come till tomorrow — that meant low priority and when the woman officer arrived he knew it was just routine.

He'd hoped for some action but when he considered it calmly he realised she was right — he couldn't prove Steve had strung Tess up to die or that he'd deliberately frightened the horse or even that it was him on the bike. But it left them on edge, wary of another incident and the culprit free to do whatever he could to damage them. He doubted if Steve would even be interviewed.

The horse at least seemed untroubled by his ordeal and was content each morning to be led out into the paddock. Kate fed him and cleaned out before work and he would go to him about eight thirty when Harry would be munching on a net of Jack Wilson's good hay.

The horse had a knack of peering over his shoulder when he arrived before grabbing another mouthful as if to say: "You can wait while I have a bit more of this."

He leaned against the wall before putting on the head collar, looking into the brown gentle eye. He rubbed his fingers over the velvety muzzle and Harry would push against his hand for more.

"It's down to you, boy, all this. If you hadn't come I wouldn't have any of this shit. I don't know where we're going with it."

He'd put three cull ewes in the paddock, waiting for the market, their breeding days over and Harry had five minutes fun hassling them round the small field before he put his head down to graze. James stayed long enough to be sure he wasn't hurting the sheep but the horse was only fooling and it was too cold to wait

Watching the horse made him think again about the incident — no way was it an accident. The moment in the pub story when Steve exploded into vicious temper at the mention of Kate's name tied in too well with a man riding a quad bike close enough to terrify a horse into bolting. The same man who'd string up a dog with barbed wire and probably stay to watch its slow and painful death.

They'd attempted to shrug it off, concentrating on preparations for Christmas. Kate tried to hide it but he knew she was afraid and her fear made him angry for being unable to do anything about it.

Katya was back in his head recalling her fears in Sarajevo, fear that made her desperate to get out. He couldn't believe he was back in another nightmare.

He saw again that scene on the mountain and thought of lying alone in the room above the cafe and the bodies he'd pulled from the pits where they'd been dumped like refuse, soil cleared from their faces by gentle fingers, each duly labelled in the search for identity.

He didn't want to go back, it was too painful, even seeing Esma and Arif again would twist the memories. But he knew if he wanted his career to survive he must conquer his reluctance. Bosnia and places like it were where the stories were. The horrors making the news there brought him back to home. He couldn't help but link Steve with the Balkan agonies, the same careless cruelty of evil done with so little thought. It was hard to believe something bad could happen here in this quiet countryside but he'd seen the secrets unearthed in the pretty valleys of northern Bosnia. He knew from years of covering bad news how evil can erupt in the most unlikely places.

The phone was ringing when he went indoors but he was too late to get it. Somehow he wasn't surprised as he listened to the caller's message and recognised Milton from the agency, wanting a word urgently he said. He hoped it wasn't to nag about the book but it might be an assignment offer. Was that what he wanted? He picked up the phone but replaced it again, needing to think first.

Then Elizabeth called. She sounded full of it, friendly and excited about Christmas and her elation cheered him, he was glad her life had changed.

She sounded happy. She was happy. She wanted to know what she could bring to make less work for them and laughed when he told her about Kate's cake.

"Graham knows a man who produces really good geese," she said. "Would you like one?"

"I love goose. I've ordered a turkey but we'll have both," he said. "Even a big goose won't feed all of us but the two meats together will be delicious."

"Will you be able to cook both?" she asked, thinking of the oven.

"Don't worry, we'll cook the turkey the day before."

There was a short silence as if she hesitated, then she said quietly: "I'm so looking forward to it, James. You're sure it's all right?"

"Of course, why wouldn't it be. Kate's really pleased and so am I."

He imagined her in the low roofed stone cottage with few luxuries around her, though now she could afford to buy anything she needed. But she didn't need much, he reflected, now she had Graham.

Milton hadn't called about the book -- the agency wanted him back in Bosnia to report on the fresh NATO initiative, particularly how it affected people trying to recover from the conflict. They wanted him because they knew he monitored events in the Balkans, especially the progress of the international aid effort.

The latest UN resolution in early December had authorised a new force with fewer troops on the ground to implement military aspects of the peace agreement. They called it the Implementation Force.

The new group had a one-year mandate to enforce the peace agreement. It interested him because it involved troops from many different nations, not just NATO members and he wondered how it would all work out.

"Will you do it?" asked Milton.

He hesitated, considering the implications of another spell in Bosnia, not least how Kate would react. But if he didn't accept they would offer it to someone else and probably not ask him again. It was no good saying he'd think about it, the news business didn't work like that.

"When do you need me to go?"

"Soon as," Milton said. "You don't sound keen. There are other people we could ask but we'd like you on it, your stuff on the graves search was good. You seem to get the smell of the place."

"Thanks. I was close to people there."

"I know. That's why you're good."

"Flattery."

"You have an insight, you understand the place, it's the colour we need, bring to life what's happening there."

He said: "I'll go — but not till after Christmas. You can't expect that."

"The new force — IFOR they're calling it — takes over on the twentieth."

"I know," he said. "It'll take them a while to get sorted. And there's a lot of countries involved, it'll probably be a bureaucratic nightmare. I'll go straight after new year, will that do?"

"Okay. I'll get back to you if the boss doesn't like it."

He can please himself he thought as he replaced the phone, doubts already creeping in and dreading the idea of telling

Kate he was going back. But his real persona, the writer who could draw out the crux of an issue and paint it for his readers in words that brought it alive, imagined this new challenge. He knew he would go, had to go, couldn't give up what he'd struggled so hard to achieve.

He peered out at the grey December day, contemplating how to tell Kate. Black clouds curtained the valley, hiding the far hillside and large drops began to spatter the yard, harbingers of heavy rain. The sky was dark for midday and it felt cold enough for snow. He decided to say nothing to her until the family were gone. Telling her would ruin Christmas and she could do without another threat hanging over her.

He was feeding the sheep when Elizabeth and Graham arrived just before lunchtime on Christmas Eve. Since Elizabeth came back into his life Graham had abandoned his isolation and got to know his neighbours and two of them had agreed to feed his cattle over the holiday. Happy his herd was in good hands they'd set off early and made good time. They were waiting in the car when he came back on the tractor, irritated to see them so early and wondering how to feed and entertain them till Kate came home.

His jaundiced attitude to the festivities meant his hold on the Christmas spirit was slight but he forced a smile and made them feel welcome.

William and Annie didn't turn up till after six, which James considered civilised. He had to admit that William was never much trouble and fitted in comfortably with whatever was happening. James envied his knack of relaxing in any company, always apparently at ease. But they were all surprised after supper when Graham suddenly said: "Why don't we go down the pub for a couple of drinks. I really fancy a pint."

James turned round sharply, in the act of supplying them all with another drink: "I'm not sure that's a good idea," he said. William looked wary and Kate was startled, shaking her head but Elizabeth said: "Why not? I think I'd enjoy that."

"But mum," Kate began "when you went to Scotland it was the talk of the village for weeks. If you two go in there together it'll be a sensation."

"Do we mind that?" She looked at Graham who shook his head. James had seen a new assurance in the man, very different from the character he'd met dressing the stone wall.

He said: "It'll be heaving, Christmas Eve's always a busy night. Can you be bothered with the hassle? What about you?" He looked towards William for support but he shrugged, saying: "If mum wants to go, we don't mind."

"I won't come," Kate spoke up.

"Oh come on, it'll be fun," Elizabeth laughed. "Give them something to talk about. It'll keep them going all over Christmas."

William was first through the door. The Fox had a two door entrance, making customers close the outer one before the second opened into the bar. His mother was next followed by Graham. Behind them James couldn't see inside but he heard the loud buzz of celebration and the sudden hush as Elizabeth entered. Every head was turned towards them as she led the way through the crush. Richard had seen them arrive and called across: "With you in a minute, Mrs Patterson."

All the tables were occupied so there was no chance of sitting down but they found a space in a corner where they could stand together clutching their drinks.

James groaned. "I hate it when it's crowded, I like to drink in peace."

"I didn't expect it to be this busy," William was studying the crowd, nodding to people he recognised.

"I warned you, Christmas Eve's a big night. You should see it at new year." He scowled as his raised elbow was knocked by a man carrying two pints and a glass of wine, spilling beer down his shirt.

Jack Wilson pushed his way across the room thrusting a hand at Graham.

"It's good to see you back in here after all this time," he said and Graham smiled.

"Thanks, Jack. It's good to be back, I used to love coming in here."

"And you Elizabeth," Jack said. "You look well, really well. I'm glad to see you home for Christmas."

She hesitated before smiling back at him. "It isn't home any more but thanks."

He'd hoped they'd be satisfied with one drink given the discomfort of standing in a constricted space but both Elizabeth and Graham seemed unconcerned by the noisy throng with conversation only possible by shouting. Strange for a man who'd spent years on his own in the back of beyond. They grabbed a table when one group left and people kept coming to greet them like long lost friends.

He was surprised at the welcome but Kate, who'd given in and come as well, said many people had known about the relationship and understood why it happened. He gave up trying to talk and resigned himself to a long evening, sinking back onto the bench with his hand round the remains of a pint.

The crowd thinned as the diners drifted away but after ten more people arrived to drink before church at midnight. When the door opened again Bill Sterling walked in with his son behind him. Richard saw them at once and waited with his arms folded, face set in a frown. "What's he doing here?"

"Two pints, please," said Sterling.

"Not for him Bill, you know he's barred."

"Oh come on Richard, it's Christmas Eve. He's with me. He won't do anything while I'm here."

"No," Richard was emphatic. "I won't serve him, not till he's apologised. I need a proper apology and an assurance about his behaviour. Till then he's barred."

Bill looked astounded.

"Come on, Richard, you can't mean that."

"I do mean it. It's my pub, I'm busy enough and I'll say who gets served. If you want a drink you're welcome but not him."

"It's Christmas Eve, man!"

"I know and it's a time for goodwill so if he apologises he gets a pint." Behind his father's back Steve was muttering and the words "fucking old fart" were distinct through the hubbub.

"Be quiet," his father roared but Richard had heard enough.

"Are you staying or going?" he demanded.

"I'll stay for a pint," said Sterling.

Richard pulled a pint and set it down. Most of the pub had heard the exchange and the noise subsided as heads turned to see what would happen. William whispered: "That was brave."

James nodded, watching closely as Sterling began to drink, back turned on his son. Steve stared a moment then swung round and began forcing his way through the crowd to the door.

He glanced across the room and saw them all there, saw James watching him and paused, as if puzzled to see Elizabeth and Graham. But then his gaze moved to Kate, laughing as she raised a glass to her lips. His face contorted into the same ugly look they'd seen so often and he swore in their direction, the words indistinct in the renewed cacophony.

A brightly twinkling Christmas tree stood in its usual place near the door, a pile of gaudy parcels round its base. Steve had already pulled open the door but stepped back to kick out at the presents, scattering them across the floor. Then he lunged at the tree, yanking it with such force it fell headlong into the crowd who were left scrambling clear, feet crunching on shattered baubles and lights. Bill Sterling rushed forward bawling at his son but the door slammed and Steve was gone. Sterling watched the lights of the quad bike disappear up the lane.

None of them were late to bed at the end of Christmas Day, celebrating with food and alcohol showed its effect by mid evening, and that jaded somnolence familiar at such times hit them all at varying stages. William and Annie were ready to go soon after ten, Annie seemed especially tired, causing James and Kate to speculate if she might be pregnant.

Graham too appeared suddenly worn out as if the unusual sociability had sucked his reserve of confidence and the weariness in his face emphasised the scars from his old injury. He was comfortable beside Elizabeth on the sofa near the fire with a glass in his hand, the good malt whisky he'd brought for James. They were sharing a nightcap while Kate watched the end of a TV drama.

"It's been a good day," Graham said in a reflective tone. "Good to come back here and see the place but I don't suppose I'll come again."

"Really?"

"It never does to go back, better to leave things as they are. You've given us great hospitality and I'm grateful but I reckon Beth and me are better off and happier far away from here."

He hadn't heard her called that and Elizabeth too looked up in surprise when he said it. Graham had lapsed into a kind of reverie and she glanced at James who was observing the other man with curiosity.

"We're both tired," she said.

Outside the night had turned very cold, the sky clear with a bright moon dimming the stars. He helped William clear the ice from his car and when he came in they'd all gone upstairs.

He snuggled for sleep with his arms around Kate, drawing warmth from her, pleased she was happy after a good day. Any constraint towards her mother had disappeared.

But sleep wouldn't come, too many images buzzing in his unquiet brain and the persistent niggling fears. He thought about Tess again, drawn back repeatedly to probe at the hurt, unable to be rid of the image. He fell asleep imagining the cries of the circling black birds.

Kate moved out of his grasp pulling the quilt with her and he woke feeling chilled. The clock showed something after three so he must have slept. The familiar feeling of unease crept over him and reluctantly he went to the window as he'd done so many nights before. The moon was a touch off full and in its pale light buildings and trees across the valley stood out in black relief against grey night. His eyes traced the dark line of the hedgerows marking the field boundaries against the grey frosted grass. By now he knew Sedge Farm well, it would be all in darkness at this time unless the security lights were triggered. He knew every tree and roof between his hill and Kate's old home.

He looked that way from habit and snapped wider awake when he saw what he most feared, what he'd been expecting on all those other nights. Beyond the line of poplars the outline of a roof was sharp against an orange glow which expanded as he stared.

He grabbed the binoculars and with a closer view saw a plume of smoke rising as a dark mass into the sky. Suddenly the farm was bathed in brightness as the floodlights were triggered.

Standing naked by the window he shivered in the freezing night yet felt sweat in the palms of his hands and his armpits. He snatched up a dressing gown and ran downstairs to the phone.

The terrified bellowing of cattle guided him as he raced from the car towards the main barn which was well ablaze. It held the bulk of the harvest -- the grain store, most of the straw and some hay. The tractor shed was across the other side but nearer, butted up against the wall was the lower roofed building where the young beef cattle were over-wintered, bedded on deep straw. The big yard lights showed dark smoke billowing from the barn, turning black and thicker as the plastic wrapping of the silage bales started to burn. An acrid stench in his throat made him cough as he ran.

There was no sign of the fire brigade but he saw Rod struggling to open the big gate in the side of the shed to get the cattle out. A depth of straw litter was blocking it and he looked for a fork to help clear it. The steers had gathered in a tight bunch furthest from the fire, milling together in panic. They would have to be driven closer to the flames to get through the gate to safety out in the pasture.

The dairy cows were housed beyond the milking parlour, within easy reach of flying sparks and ash. They were disturbed by the distress sounds from the others but fastened in their cubicles couldn't move far. Their building was safe for the moment. He heard Rod shout: "Thank God there's no wind."

The still night was a blessing, wind would quickly spread the blaze around all the buildings.

It seemed forever before they heard the siren of the first fire engine driven fast past the house into the main yard. He and Rod were now behind the steers trying to make the frightened beasts go forward but they were afraid to pass the roaring inferno in the barn. A fireman with a hose came in and shouted above the din: "Shall I try this?"

Rod nodded and a pressurised blast of water rained onto the cattle. They began to run from such an onslaught and with shouts and wild arm waving the three of them chased the animals outside.

Seconds after the cattle got out a loud roar alerted them and they both leapt back as a massive rush of flame swept through the building, making the whole barn a mass of fire. The firemen were training several hoses on the blaze with no effect, the heat was so intense it fed on itself.

"Oh Christ, the calves!" Rod screamed and rushed towards the lower end of the barn. He followed and watched the cowman wrench open the stable door on a small lean-to shed. They used it to house the young dairy calves taken from their mothers at days old to be reared for beef. A dozen or more were loose housed in there, fed on bucket milk and pellets.

One wall was already burning. Inside it was stifling hot, the air so thick with dense smoke they could barely see but James, with his sweater shrouding his head, stumbled over two dark shapes in the bedding. He found the heads and felt quickly inside their mouths. Both were alive but barely conscious. He shouted for Rod and together they dragged the little bodies outside where they began to cough and splutter in the cleaner air.

Back inside they found three still on their feet. They struggled to move the frightened babies, shoving them towards the door but close to the wall, where flames danced in the creosote soaked wood, another three bodies were down in straw that had begun to burn around them. Rod got close enough to look but shook his head. It was already too late to help them.

Part of the dividing wall collapsed and now long tongues of fire were reaching into the smaller shed. A fireman appeared at the door and ordered them out.

"Part of the main roof's gone and the whole thing'll go any time. You'll have to leave 'em. It's too dangerous. All we can do is stop it spreading to the other buildings."

Minutes later they watched in awe as the entire structure of the barn collapsed in a roaring crash to become a raging heap of flame.

William's room at the bed and breakfast overlooked the road and he was woken by the sound of sirens and the sensation of heavy vehicles shaking the building as they raced through the village. He listened, trying to judge where they were heading but he knew at once with a dreadful certainty what was happening.

Annie was awake and about to get up but he said sharply "No. You stay here. If it's what I think it is you'll only be in the way."

A sense of guilt took hold as he hurried along the lane to his old home where the scene of devastation shocked him into bitter tears. He found Rod and James in a far corner of the yard and stood watching, utterly dazed, as they fitted hurdles together to make a pen for a group of shivering, mewling calves. They'd saved five, the rest were charred lumps smouldering into ash in the blazing wreckage.

Chapter twenty-five

The only thought in his head was water, or anything to ease the dryness in his throat, raw from the effects of smoke and heat. But the sight of Kate huddled in a blanket at the kitchen table, trembling and sobbing in near hysteria unnerved him completely. Her mother hovered around, uncertain what to do and he stood riveted near the door, staring at the girl.

She turned her large dark eyes on him with a frantic appeal as if he could instantly reassure her, Elizabeth caught his eye, shaking her head and whispered: "I don't know why she's in this state."

He ignored the mother and went to Kate, pulling her up to close his arms around her. "It's all right, I'm here, nobody's been hurt. Calm down. It's not that bad, stop crying."

"But the animals," she sobbed. "The poor calves and the cattle, so terrified, burnt to death."

"How do you know that?"

"William's here, he told us."

William appeared from the other room and saw the angry glare from James. But he shrugged: "What could I say? I had to tell her. First thing she asked was about the calves. She'd been watching it all since you left. She could see the barn burning and she knows where the calves go."

He seemed unconcerned at his sister's distress and said before disappearing again: "I just hope the new people had it well insured."

"You should've been more careful," he snapped and turned back to Kate. "Come on, you're not even dressed. Let's get you upstairs — I'll help you."

He spoke as he might to a child and at that moment he felt awkwardly old beside her.

By the time they got upstairs she'd stopped crying but still trembled, asking for details. He helped her dress, trying to be calm and play down his own reactions.

"Was it him?" she asked. There was no need to say the name.

"I'm certain of it," he paused. "But proving it's another matter.

"We waited with Rod to see the police and help him move and rehouse the stock."

"How many dead?" she asked.

"At least four calves -- not sure how many were in there — and three of the dairy cows, the smoke and fumes did for them." He didn't tell her he'd found them in the building already starting to swell.

"Rod was in shock. He couldn't tell the police much. Just that he heard a quad bike go fast past the cottage. That's what woke him and then he saw the fire, already taken hold."

He thought of Rod staring at the smoking wreckage where flames still flickered along the blackened beams, idly intent on a burnt fragment of plastic bucket, which he kicked about in the ash as he waited. He'd listened with a stunned expression while James spoke to the police, telling them exactly what he thought and they wrote down what he said.

"That woman constable was there again. At least she seems to be joining it all up — she said it could not be coincidence."

The police girl had met his eyes and said: "I know what you're thinking, Mr Lambert. I'll talk to the inspector."

Rod was staring at him. He'd snapped out of his reverie and said in a dull voice: "You came to warn me — that morning. You were expecting this."

Frowning, he said nothing but after surveying the wreckage one more time he'd nodded slowly at Rod and walked away.

Kate listened intently as he described the scene, missing out the worst bits and sat patiently as he knelt to fasten her trainers. She seemed distracted and nodded when he said: "Ready to go down and face them?"

He saw her frown, as if she had suddenly made a decision and as he moved to go she caught his arm and slumped back on the bed.

"No, come here. There's something I need to tell you, something I should have told you long ago."

"I've tried to forget it all these years." Her forehead furrowed in concentration as she spoke, her voice a whisper, as if it was hard or painful to recall. Then she stopped speaking at all as if dredging her mind, grasping through memory to things and times she'd left hidden. He wondered what was coming.

He said very gently. "You don't have to tell me any more. If it's something best left alone then don't talk about it."

"We all buried it, tried to pretend it didn't happen. But this has brought it back," she mumbled at the floor.

"Something about Steve?" She nodded.

"You've told me how cruel he was as a boy. Nasty things like the hide and seek."

She lifted her head and laughed, a bitter shallow laugh. "He did much worse than lock me in a shed."

"Oh, bad?"

"Very bad."

"You don't have to tell me."

"No but I need to. You have to know what he is."

"Take your time, we're not going anywhere." He moved away a little, not wanting to crowd her. He took her hand, touched it an instant to his lips and then held it as she began to tell him, slowly and quietly what had happened when she was twelve years old.

"Dad always had a dairyman for the herd, he sometimes did the milking himself but there was always someone in charge of the milkers. That was his specific job, like Rod.

"Eddie he was called. They had the cottage, where Rod is now -- two children, a little boy, Timmy, about seven, and Penny, my friend Penny. I was twelve then and she was two years younger but she looked nearer my age. She was a bit tubby, you know, not fat but well covered, well developed I suppose. We were good friends, they lived on our place so naturally we saw a lot of each other."

She seemed to lose her thread and paused. "Their mum worked part time. It was in the summer holiday so the children were often at home alone."

"Kids that age shouldn't be left on their own," he interrupted.

"Yeah, well. A lot of things happen in life that shouldn't. We spent a lot of time together, she'd come over or I'd go there. There was one morning I called round for her — can't remember what we were planning — and Steve was there, in the kitchen. Just making himself a drink, he said, it was nearer than going home. He left when I turned up and I didn't think anything of it at the time. But after that I noticed he was in and out of there a lot and Penny began to seem uneasy, sort of strained.

"We had a camp thing in the woods -- spent a lot of time there, we'd take a picnic and just muck about. It was good fun but suddenly Penny started bringing chocolate and cans of coke and those big packets of crisps. She loved Crunchie and Mars bars. She said Steve had given them to her. Timmy thought it was great because their mum didn't often buy stuff like that.

"Sometimes she'd say she had to get back because Steve was coming over. I think she liked the attention. I suppose I was a bit jealous of her spending time with him instead of me."

She paused and smiled at him.

"I was very innocent at that age, you know about that."

"You were a child, maybe Penny was more aware of boys than you."

"Maybe. I had no idea what was happening but I went in one morning and he was there, with his hand inside her jeans. He looked at me and laughed then left without a word. She told me how he'd started to play about with her, you know, cornering her in the cottage and round the farm, touching her breasts — she had much more in that department than me — feeling in her knickers, stuff like that. She said she didn't like it any more but didn't know how to stop him. He kept going a bit further.

"I told her to tell her mum but she wouldn't. She was frightened she'd be in trouble. It's what always happens isn't it? Kids are afraid, made to think it's their fault, like it's them who've done wrong.

"Her mum came back one time for something she'd forgotten and he was there but he got out of it with the coffee story.

"He kept on, came most days through the holiday and soon he started doing other things, he made her wank him off and eventually he got her into the bedroom — and he raped her."

Kate stopped. "She was only ten. He hurt her."

"The little shit!" James growled. "How old was he then?"

She thought a moment. "About fourteen, I think."

"After that he did it every day, often more if he found the chance. I didn't know till after. He went every day when her mum was out. I knew something was wrong, she went quiet, sort of withdrawn and she didn't want to see me. I knew she was frightened but I never thought it had gone that far. I didn't know much about that stuff — grown up stuff. I was a bit green, didn't realise kids could do it."

"It depends," said James.

"Anyway, I was missing the fun I'd had with her and Timmy. I thought I'd upset her in some way and went over to try and sort it out. Went straight in like I always did and caught him at it — he had her pinned against the kitchen wall. He wasn't bothered, he just said, 'so what, she's only the cowman's daughter, what's it matter'. But he was angry at being caught.

"He hit her as she pulled her jeans up, thumped her several times round the head. And he tried to hit me but I dodged away."

"He threatened us both, saying what he'd do if we told anybody but I said I would tell my dad and his dad."

"And did you?" he asked.

"Yes, Steve went and I took Penny home with me and told mum. She looked horrified, then kind of afraid but all she said was, wait till your dad comes in for lunch. We kept Penny with us. Dad listened, didn't seem surprised and didn't say much, just something about being careful how we handle it. I remember saying 'aren't you going to tell the police?' Mum said we ought to.

"But he said. 'We can't.'

"To be fair to mum she made dad ring Bill Sterling and he came over and I told him what had happened. They tried to shut me up but I said it all. He listened and stared at me and looked at Penny — I can picture it now, he looked at her with such contempt, as if she was nothing. Then he laughed and said 'you're a fine pair of little liars aren't you. He wouldn't do that, he's not old enough. We'll see what he has to say.' "

The mere thought of that day made her angry and she raised her voice as she went on. "I shouted at Bill and my father smacked me round the head but I yelled at him 'I saw him doing it! He raped her and he's been doing it all through the holiday.' "

He looked incredulous. "So they didn't believe you? Either of you?"

Kate shook her head. "Mum did. She took Penny to the bathroom and examined her so she knew damn well it was true. Her knickers were wet from him —plenty of DNA if they'd done anything about it. And her face was all bruised where he hit her. It was undeniable. Then I heard them talking in the kitchen.

"I heard Bill Sterling say: 'You know what happens if you tell anyone. It'll be you that ends up inside.' "

" 'That's blackmail.' I heard dad say those words.

"Sterling said: 'I suppose it is but I saw you aim that gun, remember. It was me got you out of that and you owe me. You'll go on owing me. It's simple, Ted, you drop my boy in it and you go in as well.' "

She was speaking softly again and he strained to hear the words. As they tailed off he said quietly: "Well, that explains many things but what a burden for you all this time. No wonder you loathe him. But how did they ever come to think you might marry him? Knowing what he was like."

"My father had a way of avoiding reality, he only saw things as he wanted them to be."

He'd listened to her story with growing alarm and a renewed sense of dread; the word psychopath came into his head. Was it too strong a label for Steve? He watched Kate recalling the moments that spoiled for ever her relationship with her father. She was calm, there were no tears but she looked as if she had confessed her own sins.

"You poor love," he said. "But what happened to Penny? Did you tell her parents?"

"She didn't want to but I told her mother and I think now, maybe I shouldn't have. She spoke to dad about it and went to see Sterling but the pair of them just refused to countenance it at all, said it was silly kids' talk — all made up.

"Bill threatened Eddie, told him if they went to the police he'd make sure he wouldn't get a job in the area and he'd get no reference. Bill told Dad to get rid of him and they offered him money."

"And your father did as he was told?"

"Sterling was always the stronger character, dad was weak but they kept each other's secrets very close."

"So the man lost his job and his home and the child had her life ruined," James said.

"Yes and I lost a friend. She was a sweet girl and we had fun together, kids' fun, till that happened."

"Did you keep in touch?"

"For a while but you know what it's like. They went to Devon. Eddie got a job there, he was a good man with cows. Dad gave him a glowing reference which was something. And Bill Sterling gave him £5000 to be gone quickly. It was awful."

"So you were left living next door to a rapist."

"Dad had to do his own milking for several weeks, it took ages to find someone as good as Eddie. But worst of all, Steve started getting interested in me and they all encouraged it."

"What!"

"I couldn't believe my mother. She knew what happened, she knew it was true. Yet she let them get away with it. She said something about dad being in a difficult position which I didn't really understand then because it was all about Graham."

"And this is the woman downstairs right now we've been entertaining for Christmas. No wonder she looked so frantic — and I'd begun to admire her."

"Now you know why I felt like I did."

"I'm surprised you wanted her here at all."

"I'm older now and I know what happened so I can understand. But it spoiled things."

Elizabeth, pale and anxious, was still hovering in the kitchen when they went down.

"Is she all right?" she addressed him rather than asking her daughter directly.

He studied her expression, looking for signs of guilt and noted she wouldn't meet his eyes, like a child discovered in a lie.

"She's what you might call stressed," he said. "She's been telling me a story about the psychopath you wanted her to marry."

Elizabeth gasped: "You told him?"

"I thought it was time he knew the truth about Steve."

William was there and James caught his eye. "Did you know?"

William shrugged, with his habitual response to conflict. Through the open door he saw Annie, ostensibly watching TV but by the set of her head he knew she was listening — and tense.

"You don't understand —" Elizabeth began but he raised his hand to silence her.

"Leave it. You told me before about their hold on your family but this is something else. I didn't know we were dealing with a psychopath."

"That's a harsh word," said Elizabeth.

"You defending him?"

"He was only a boy."

"Old enough apparently — rape is rape, whatever the age."

"He…" At that moment Graham appeared.

"Don't say any more," he told her and to James: "This is news to me as well."

He looked at Kate, eyes soft with sympathy. "I'm sorry, girl. I had no idea how bad it was." Pausing he glanced at Kate's mother and said: "We're leaving — now. Get your stuff."

Elizabeth seemed about to resist but he said: "They need some peace."

Surprised, James saw another side to the man, an impressive authority coming through, redolent of what he'd once been.

As Elizabeth disappeared he spoke to James. "I'm sorry. I knew the pub was a mistake, bad idea — like this whole visit. Brought nothing but trouble — I knew Sterling covered for Ted but that business — no. You won't see us here again."

After a moment's reflection he asked: "Will you shake my hand?"

"Of course. You're a victim of that family, just like Kate and the other poor kid."

Word of the fire spread quickly with a sense of outrage that such a thing should happen on Christmas night. Not just the church goers but everyone was appalled at such an act — it seemed a sacrilege — that the peace of Christmas should be so abused. And when it became clear that Steve Sterling was the main suspect the village waited in suspense.

For once the farmers didn't say much, even to each other, but none were surprised at the rumours — they all knew how much the Sterlings wanted that farm.

By mid morning on Boxing Day everyone knew it was definitely arson. There were no footprints or wheel marks on the frozen ground but the police had found two empty petrol cans near the barn, flung there as if in contempt by the culprit. They were with the forensic team.

When the police arrived at the Sterling home Steve wasn't there. They questioned Bill Sterling who told them his son had gone to bed early, the worse for wear after drinking all through Christmas Day.

"He ate his Christmas dinner then slobbed out in front of the tele, slept all the evening and went up about eleven — he'd been drinking all day. I doubt he was capable of going anywhere after all that booze."

The woman constable was there with an inspector. It was she who asked Bill: "Are you sure he was there all night?"

"Well, I didn't go up to check but I saw him go upstairs and I saw him come down very late this morning."

"You didn't look in when you went to bed?"

"No, why would I?"

"What about you Mrs Sterling?"

"No — but I think I heard him in the bathroom."

"And did you both sleep well?"

"I'd taken my sleeping tablets," said Steve's mother. "I slept right through."

The inspector studied them both. "So you have no way of knowing if your son got up and went out in the night?"

Bill Sterling shook his head.

"I see," said the inspector. "And where is he now?"

"I've no idea."

When the phone rang in the middle of Boxing Day afternoon James sighed wondering who would bother them on a bank holiday. But his stomach lurched as he recognised the voice of the policewoman he now knew as Evelyn.

"I shouldn't really have called you," she said, "but I thought you should know. They've found DNA on one of the cans. Whoever started the fire must've urinated there and it splashed on the can so they'll be a total search of the ground — and there's a fingerprint. So when we find a suspect we should be able to match it."

"A suspect?" he queried.

"At this stage I can't tell you any more but we're still looking for Steve Sterling."

There was silence on the phone then she said: "Look — please don't tell anyone I've called you. I shouldn't have but given all that's happened I thought you had a right to know."

"Thank you," he said. "It's good of you. I won't let on."

Kate was outside with Harry and he walked across the yard in the icy air to tell her. Small flakes of snow were drifting on the wind and in the failing light he saw clouds closing in to bring that peculiar heaviness that comes before snow.

"It was kind of her to ring," she said when he told her. "It must've spoiled her Christmas too, having to work today."

"Yes," he sounded puzzled. "It was very careless of him, I'm surprised."

"Why?"

"Well, was it deliberate, a token of his hatred and frustration or did he simply not think that far and needed to go?"

Kate laughed, that bitter sound again: "Do you really think he thought that much about it?"

"It was so careless to spatter the can."

"That's typical of him — and his arrogance wouldn't let him think that far."

"Assuming it was him."

She looked surprised. "Do you doubt it?"

"Not really and the fact he's missing says a lot. But that's not proof, he could be just hanging out with his friends in Telford."

They could only wait. They kept at home together and heard nothing from anyone. He was starting to think he'd dreamed it all and the whole episode of the fire was a nightmare. But he knew it was real and the images of the dead animals came into his head unbidden, along with little Tess.

As always it was the Wilsons who knew what was happening and when he heard Jack's voice on the phone, full of expectant excitement he waited tensely for the news.

"Someone rang the police," he said, "they didn't leave a name -- well you wouldn't, would you if you're shopping someone, and round here it pays to be cautious." He rambled on for a moment about the need to be wary of the Sterlings until James interrupted.

"Okay Jack but what's happened?"

"This caller just said he'd been seen, Steve that is."

"Right."

"Cops were there within the hour, at Sterling's. They've got him James. Took him into custody on suspicion of arson.

"What d'you think of that?"

"Relieved. After the way he's been behaving."

"Of course he's denying it, reckons he just went off to see his mates and get over his Christmas hangover."

"He certainly wouldn't admit it," he said. "But the DNA will tell us. How do you know all this?"

"Oh, y'know -- I know someone who knows someone who works for the police. Stuff gets out. Thought you oughta know — might make Kate feel a bit better."

"Thanks, now it's wait and see."

"Yeah," Jack sounded doubtful. "But I'd lay money Bill's already got some hotshot lawyer on the job."

Next day the evening paper had the full story about the fire and that farmer's son Steve Sterling had been charged with arson. He had appeared before the local magistrates and was remanded for trial at Crown Court at a date to be decided. Everyone knew the DNA test was positive

As Jack predicted he was represented at the lower court by a top barrister who hurried down from London at Bill Sterling's behest and tried with all his skill to get bail.

Wpc Knox, Evelyn, stood up in court to tell the magistrates that police were opposing bail because of the seriousness of the offence and the defendant's threatening behaviour plus other matters under investigation.

Throughout the brief hearing Bill Sterling sat on the public benches with an expression of dazed confusion clouding his face, as if he could not believe what was happening. He saw his son led away to be locked up and remained in his seat as the court cleared until an usher came to tap his arm, telling him it was all over for the morning.

Chapter twenty-six

In northern Bosnia James stood among a group of journalists and photographers watching in silence as a fair-haired girl in white overalls made her way along a line of corpses, pausing by each to turn the skull on its side and reveal the gaping hole in the back of the head. The bodies were laid out beneath a bank of dark rich-looking soil excavated from the newly discovered burial pit.

At the end of the line was another less tidy row of body parts and individual bones, with a number of skulls, clustered together.

The bodies were mostly skeletal but their rotting clothes and remnants of skin and flesh clinging to the bones indicated their humanity. They hadn't been long enough in the earth to rot completely and on some brows and around the eye sockets sections of skin retained a semblance of facial structure. The same bitter wind he had known before in this part of Bosnia whined across the valley and lashed the watching group with a fine sharp snow that blistered their faces with stinging cold. The girl walked back to them, lowering her face mask to speak. James thought she might be Swedish.

"We have found more than forty here so far," she said, "but that does not include the body parts, human remains from bodies probably broken up in the removal process. They will be difficult to identify."

She pointed to another site a few hundred yards away, marked by white pegs. "We think there is another site over there. We start digging tomorrow. And there could be more."

James opened his mouth to ask a question but the woman next to him was quicker and enquired in an east coast American accent: "Do you get a lot of information? Who is it that tells you?"

"All kinds of people, some are Muslim, those who escaped and survived, women who saw bodies being dug up and taken away, and sometimes it is Bosnian Serbs, farmers and country people who saw the machines in action, digging and reburying.

"And they think it is safe now to say something — not all the Serbs agreed with what was happening but fear usually keeps the mouth quiet."

He listened to the ongoing explanation of the work carried out under the auspices of the implementation force, embroidered with technical terms which were to him a long-winded way to say "we are dealing with the bodies" — labelling each with what details they had in the attempt to discover identities.

Basically he knew the story, thousands of people, mainly men and boys murdered in cold blood here in northern Bosnia and dumped in mass graves, many later dug up and moved to be hidden in more remote sites.

His mind wandered, thinking about the land around him, about farming in this fertile valley, its blanket of snow muddied now by digging and the tracks of large vehicles. He noticed a line of bushes not far away, hawthorn probably, like at home, where a flock of small birds fluttered among the leafless branches.

They'll be waiting, he thought, hoping the human gathering might leave some morsels of food. Beyond he spotted a small orchard of what looked like plum trees. It was an area whose business was producing food in the time honoured way on land now corrupted and disturbed by this obscene crop of decay.

It was an area whose business was producing food in the time honoured way on land now corrupted and disturbed by this obscene crop of decay.

He didn't want to be there, wished he'd never agreed to take this job and found it hard to concentrate thinking all the time about events back home. He couldn't free his mind of Kate, worrying about her and how she was coping without him. She had insisted that this time she would not be forced out of what had become her home, she didn't want to stay with the Wilsons, kind though they were and with Steve Sterling locked away on remand he felt it was safe to leave her. The early January weather had turned mild and he'd driven away from the farm in sunshine, satisfied she would be fine on her own for the short time he planned to be away.

He'd been back in Bosnia only one night, flown into Sarajevo but taken with the group straight up to the area north of Tuzla. He was uneasy, troubled by guilt because he was relieved to have an excuse not to visit the cafe. The strange reluctance was because of what had happened over Christmas and the new commitment he felt to Kate. He must decide if he would go before he flew home, knowing already he didn't want to be drawn in again to the family and the atmosphere he needed to forget. Perhaps there would not be time.

Guilty too because he wasn't doing his job properly. He was paid to be there but it was the same story repeated — more pits, more bodies — he puzzled how he could ever relay the enormity of it, express the horror of mass murder in this pleasant, rural landscape.

He ceased listening and the girl's flurry of information washed over him as he let his mind wander, remembering Steve's fury on Christmas Eve when he wrecked the pub tree. He wondered how that mind worked, aware in himself of an uneasy sense of something unfinished. The guy was locked up, safely out of the way but he knew that wasn't the end of it, the story continued. It couldn't be that easy, there was more to come. He wasn't paranoid. He just knew there would be more to come.

He edged away from the others, eyes on the area of white pegs set out beyond the plum trees. Walking back past the line of bodies he tried not to look at them but a sudden movement made him glance down to see a small brown mouse had crept out from one of the eye sockets on the nearest skull. It sat cleaning itself on the forehead. It must have sensed him pausing and for a second stared up at him before diving back inside the skull.

Fascinated he waited but it did not reappear. It startled him that he felt no sense of disgust that the tiny rodent should make a home in a man's head but rather an odd thrill of satisfaction that life goes on in whatever form.

He strolled on among the plum trees, composing in his head how he would describe the mouse incident then took the recorder from his pocket and spoke into it, though knowing he wouldn't quickly forget the image. He studied the lie of the land, around the pegs, an area of maybe a hundred yards long and half as wide, covered in muddy corn stubble.

At least one crop, maybe two had been grown here since the land was disturbed. He noted an unevenness, some sections slightly raised which had defied the attempt at concealment. But the ground had been levelled sufficiently to go unremarked from a casual glance. The searchers would not have noticed anything in this valley without information — that was what he wanted to know, who were the people who told the researchers where to look. How did they know and survive to tell what they knew?

Frowning he stared at the small white stakes stretching across the field, the line of plums marking the boundary to his right. Moving parallel to the trees he found himself in a small copse of scrub and bushes and ahead a winding line of spasmodic growth which he guessed followed the course of a stream or perhaps the river itself. Flurries of snow came intermittently snatching at his face like cold fingers and he wished he'd thought to wear a hat. He looked back to check the group wasn't on the move but they still stood grouped around the blonde girl.

Plodding on through the copse he decided to go as far as the stream and then turn back but something moved again at the edge of his vision, this time something larger than a mouse -- a flash of red.

With one hand shielding his eyes against the thickening snow he saw a figure watching him, then move quickly away, sharp and active like a teenager. He began to run, calling: "Wait! Please wait."

The red hooded figure stopped and turned to face him. A girl peered at him from under the hood, a girl with slender legs and rubber boots. "Perhaps you can help me," he began but hesitated. Wondering if she understood him.

She studied him a moment before asking in near perfect English. "You're with them?"

She jerked her head towards the group across the field.

"Yes, we're here to see what's been found."

Hearing his own words it seemed so inadequate to sum up the reality.

"Are you from London?" she asked. He nodded, it was near enough.

"You are going to tell the world what they did?" — a simple appeal in her face.

"If I can." He waited then went on. "Maybe you can tell me more, more than the official line?"

"What sort of things can I tell you?"

"Well, someone must have known what they did here, about the burials, someone told them where to look, so --" he stopped again, seeing her stiffen in expectation.

"Someone must have seen them." He hurried on, afraid she would run from him. "It must have been a big job, coming here with machinery, digging the pits -- and trucks to bring the bodies. It can't have been that quick and it must've made a commotion."

She watched him as he spoke, eyes slightly closed, shadowed by the hood so he couldn't see her expression. He waited, glancing back again to check the group was still there, not leaving him behind.

He would have to leave soon, they'd be moving on. "I haven't got long," he said. "I have to go soon."

She gazed across the field towards the open pit "You want to know who showed them the place?"

"Yes, if you know. Do you?"

"I told them. I showed them the place."

James gasped. "You saw it?"

"Next to our plum trees. This lovely piece of land, polluted."

Across the field he saw the group begin to move, heading back to the minibuses. "Shit!" he muttered.

She saw his desperation. "I will tell you about it. But you must go."

"Yes -- no!"

"You could stay and listen."

"But how would I get back?"

"My cousin has a taxi. Go. Tell them you'll catch up." It was a command. She had a strange authority and he did as he was told.

Beyond the trees the land dipped to the river and revealed a small stone built farm, with an elderly Zetor tractor among other implements parked around it. He followed her across the stream on a narrow plank bridge and as he set foot on the other side a loud shot rang out, the sound of heavy gauge which made him jump and cringe, nearly falling backwards into the water.

"It's okay, only my uncle shooting duck."

He breathed in deeply and she took his arm to steady him as he laughed at himself. "Sorry, I'm a bit jumpy these days. I don't much like guns."

The room, the only ground floor space, with a kitchen through the door behind, was dark. A single bulb dangling from the ceiling left some of it in shadow but it felt pleasantly warm, heated by a tall iron stove. A large pot of something aromatic stood on top.

The place was badly ventilated and he coughed in the thick atmosphere but after a few moments began to breathe more easily as he got used to it. The room was sparse with little in the way of comfort, a wooden table and three chairs, a sofa, which looked old and uninviting and a couple of small armchairs. In the corner he noticed a pretty stool with what appeared to be newly upholstered top. The girl saw his gaze and said: "I did that, it is very old, it was my great grandmother's and I used it as a child. I have remade the top."

"You did a good job."

The kitchen area was small and bare, with a brown clay sink and wooden drainer. A single tap hung above the sink with an electric geezer on the wall for hot water. Again she saw him looking.

"Yes, we have hot water — when the power is on but for a long time there was none. But it is better now."

He watched her put the kettle on a small stove and noticed the gas bottle.

"Sit down," she said and he went back into the room and found a place in one of the small armchairs. She brought him a mug of coffee saying: "It is tinned milk. We have a cow but she has not calved yet."

He drank the coffee gratefully, relaxing into the chair but sat upright and alert as the outer door opened. An elderly man entered carrying a shotgun broken over his arm and a brace of duck slung across his shoulder. The grizzled man who looked older than he probably was, peered at James, grunted and moved into the kitchen where he began to pluck the birds over the brown sink.

The girl inclined her head, "My uncle."

She went after him and spoke in Bosnian then came back and explained to James.

"My uncle speaks very little English but he says you are welcome."

Outside darkness had fallen. He went to the door and peered out searching for any sign of light but there was no life anywhere and the night had brought a deeper grip of cold. He shivered and hurried back to the comfort of the stove. The coffee had been welcome and he realised how hungry he was, with nothing inside him since breakfast.

He glanced at the big pot wondering what it held. The girl who seemed to know what he was thinking moved the pot to the centre of the stove and he heard it begin to bubble. She watched him eyeing it as the increasing heat released more tantalising aromas.

He looked at her. "I don't know your name."

"Nadija, are you ready for supper?" She asked with a smile.

He nodded eagerly. "What is it?" he asked, guessing at some kind of stew.

"You have a saying in English — pot luck." She giggled. "It is a good saying. Most of our food comes in this pot."

She fetched a large spoon with a long handle, lifted the lid and stirred. He asked again: "What is it?"

She brought a spoonful to her mouth to taste then offered it to him. "A little more salt I think," she said. It tasted good and stirred the juices in his empty stomach.

"Today it is mostly rabbit but some lamb, my neighbours killed a few sheep last week and brought us half a lamb."

"It tastes as good as it smells," he said, his appetite spurred by the taste.

"We're lucky," she said. "We have plenty of game here, rabbits, ducks sometimes a hare and deer in the woods further over."

He sat again and watched her set the table with a clean cloth which surprised him with its pristine whiteness and he thought he must be careful not to spill anything. A large loaf of crusty bread waited on a wooden slab in the centre.

The uncle came to join them and when he was seated she gestured James to sit and they waited in silence while she dished up a large bowl of steaming potage for each of them. James ate eagerly and tried to make conversation but she was quiet, saying only: "My uncle does not like talk at the table."

When the old man had finished he pushed away his bowl and Nadija rose at once to remove it, returning with another wooden board holding a large round cheese. She cut a slice for James who bit into it cautiously, then grinned with delight to find it delicious. With no refrigeration the room temperature gave free rein to its complex flavour. "This is wonderful," he said.

"We make it when we can, it is ewe's milk with nettles."

The uncle watched James eating the cheese, smiling as he noted the appreciation. He nodded to himself and rising slowly, went to the dresser near the door to fetch two small glasses, then from another cupboard came a bottle of slivovitz. He filled the glasses and pushed one towards James. " Y o u drink," he said in English, raising his glass in salutation. James clinked his glass against the other with a broad smile.

"To your hospitality," he said and Nadija translated.

The old man said something as he tossed back the spirit and Nadija said: "He says he doesn't know who you are but if you are English it's good and he is pleased to see you here."

"Tell him why I'm here."

"No," she said quietly. "We won't say that. It's better not."

"Don't you drink?"

"Not in front of him. Women should not, he says."

"You're not Moslem, are you?"

"No but he is old-fashioned." She glanced quickly at him. "No, my family is not Moslem and they should have been safe. But they were in the wrong place at the wrong time — it happened to many of all faiths in Bosnia."

The uncle refilled the glasses and toasted James again and when his glass was empty, he rose from his chair, grunted, nodded to them both and disappeared to bed.

They remained at the table, talking about the war, its impact on so many and after a while she began to ask him about Britain — just as Katya had done. Her voice and the intensity of her questions took him back to his first visit to Esma's cafe when he met Katya. This girl too was lovely, enchanting, but it was not the same. Looking into her face he analysed his own reactions, knowing at once she did not stir him as Katya had done. But more than that she made him think of Kate and as she spoke he wanted it to be Kate's voice and her at the table beside him. It hit him for the first time that he missed her and frowned as a physical surge of yearning welled inside him.

Nadija noticed the change in his expression. "What is wrong?"

He shook his head. "Nothing, I'm just tired." He studied her, trying to assess how frank this perceptive girl might be with him, then leaned across the table so his face was much closer to her and asked. "Are you going to tell me what happened?"

She nodded. "I will tell you but you must not use my name. Will you promise that?"

"Of course, I can use any name, that doesn't matter."

She began carefully, as if weighing each word. "I was a student at Sarajevo but I used to stay with my uncle in Srebrenica for the holidays. That was before it all began but that summer when the Serbs came I was with him. When they came with Mladic at their head it was as if they were something different, as if we were lesser people. We were unimportant, not quite human, I shall never forget it.

"I was lucky. They simply took over the town and rounded people up, mostly the Moslems. I was caught up in it but I managed to stay out of the compound. They raped me but only once and I stayed alive. I told them, there were two, to my shame, that I wasn't Moslem, that I was Christian and they laughed and let me go. So I was fortunate and still here to tell you about it."

She stopped. "I felt ashamed -- I felt I had betrayed my Moslem friends."

"Fortunate!" James searched for signs of anguish in her face but she was serene and calm as she talked.

"Yes, fortunate, I am alive when so many are dead. So I am lucky. And I came back here, home, to be with my parents."

"We stayed here quietly, my father running the farm. You have another saying I think, 'keeping our heads down'. That's what we did, trying to stay out of trouble. Then one night I was outside and I heard the noise of engines and saw lights beyond the trees. I crept across the fields and hid among the plum trees.

"I saw them. Big machines digging a pit. The soldiers dragged rotting bodies off the trucks — I could smell it — lugging them over the ground and they threw them in anyhow, like so much rubbish at a tip, their arms and legs all jumbled together. It was horrible. They were in a hurry, rushing to cover them, a bulldozer pushing soil over them. In the middle of it another soldier came hurrying to them through the trees, he passed very near me, pointing here, to this house. They hadn't realised the farmhouse was so close. Four of them set off back with him and I waited, afraid — I knew what was coming."

She looked down at the table, away from his searching eyes. "The noise of the rifle was very loud in the darkness. The bulldozer had stopped — waiting — and very soon the soldiers were back, dragging the bodies of my parents. They threw them in along with the others and the bulldozer began again, filling the pit and scraping the earth to make it flat and hide what they'd done. Then they worked in a line to scatter seed over the place."

"They killed the witnesses?"

"Yes."

"So you were left alone?"

"Yes, alone. If I had not gone out to watch my body would be in there with them." She paused, thinking about that night but went on.

"My uncle came back here to take over the farm, rented out his house. He is happier here, it was his childhood home."

"So you are waiting for the second site to be opened?"

She nodded. "They are in there, my mother and my father and when we find them we will bury them properly."

"How many bodies d'you think are in there?"

"I don't know — many, maybe two hundred, I don't know."

The annihilation, the total denial of the self — that was the true wickedness. Buried like animals — it made him think of the foot and mouth outbreak when as a young boy he'd watched on TV the burying and the burning. He remembered being upset by the images of carcases heaped together, rigid legs stuck up pointing at the sky and asking his father why they had to be killed.

He sighed, overwhelmed by the evil of it and with respect for this girl and her search. He took her hand, eyes seeking hers and when she met his gaze he said.

"You are a very brave girl, I am full of admiration for your courage and determination. You'll be there when they open it?"

"Of course. I watch every day to see their progress. I am lucky, as I told you."

He laughed: "Lucky indeed."

"So you have your story, a good story, yes? About a lucky girl -- but you will not use my name? I trust you for that."

"No, I won't use your name, you will be Katya."

"Katya?"

"Yes, she wasn't a lucky girl."

She said again, "I trust you." And smiled. "But you haven't told me your name."

"James."

"A good strong English name."

He smiled and asked: "What now? I'm very tired."

"You will stay here tonight, you can sleep by the stove. I will bring a mattress and in the morning we will take you back to Tuzla."

He lay awake beside the iron stove, glad of its heat as the temperature dropped. Once he went outside to pee, reluctant to disturb the house and uncertain where to go. He tried to dabble his fingers in the water butt but found it frozen hard under a clear bright sky.

He warmed his cold fingers over the stove and lay down again, trying to sleep but kept awake by thoughts of Kate, overcome by the longing to be with her and a drastic urgency to get home. Back to her. He thought about her warm, soft body nestled close to him but also her character and courage. There was a new yearning in his thoughts of her perhaps driven by a fear of losing her. Get back to Tuzla in the morning, send some preliminary copy and get down to the airport. His mind buzzed with paragraphs for his story and planning a longer feature sent him at last to the edge of sleep. Half awake he heard soft footsteps and opened his eyes to find Nadija beside him.

"Are you okay? Do you need anything?" She stooped over him wearing a gown of some soft fabric which hung open over the tops of small firm breasts. Dazed he stared up into her face, then lowered his eyes to the inviting softness below her neck. For an instant he was tempted and moved a hand to touch her but there was no surge of desire, picturing instead Kate's form curled up in the bed. He drew back his hand and heard her murmur again: "Is there anything you need?" as she pressed her lips on his forehead.

He closed his eyes, shaking his head and heard himself say: "No, I'm fine thank you. There's nothing I need. Just sleep."

Chapter twenty-seven

He bought flowers. He'd never done that before, not for any woman — not unless you counted the poppies on the grave. But that was different. He'd never bought flowers for a girl-friend. He thought of it as he drove away from Heathrow and came off the motorway into a smart Buckinghamshire town to find a florist.

He knew the winter selection of home-grown blooms would be limited but was amazed by the choice of flowers from Holland and much further away. Asking what he wanted the assistant offered him dark red roses, from Kenya, she said when he questioned her.

But such a cliche was quite wrong for Kate, she would surely laugh at him. He looked around and spotted a delicate, unassuming little arrangement of early bulbs with small irises and crocus, set into soft moss with strands of a flowering shrub adding a delicate scent. He held the tiny flowers of the shrub to his nose and drew in a deep breath to taste a sweet aromatic scent he knew but couldn't place.

It was just right for her and he set it carefully on the floor of the car, cursing the traffic back to the motorway. The winter day was grey and depressing, a light rain falling to make the motorway a misery in the continuous spume from lorries. The bad visibility slowed him and the journey took much longer than it should, making him curse and drum his hands on the steering wheel in frustration. Then he began to worry she might not be there, she could be at Pat's or out somewhere.

Since Steve was locked up she'd been less anxious and took pleasure in life again; now he wanted to make her happy, really happy he hoped, by telling her his news. But then perhaps she wouldn't take it as he wished, might feel insulted that he'd condescended to say he loved her. But it wasn't like that. He hadn't wanted to give her false assurances of love when he wasn't sure himself.

But now he was. He was. And he needed to get home and hold her and tell her.

When he saw the yard was empty he realised with disappointment he'd rushed his journey for nothing and it would be at least an hour before she was home. Deflated he made the best of it by planning how to handle what he wanted to do.

He carried the plant arrangement with care into the house and placed it in the centre of the kitchen table. He paused to consider, then from the cupboard fetched a bottle, a cremant de Bourgogne, a favourite fizz from a case brought back from the French trip. He preferred it to champagne which was inappropriate and banal in this context. He set it to chill in the fridge.

Kate arrived at last and rushed past him with a brief greeting to change and go out to Harry, passing the table without a glance. He followed to the stable unable to resist hugging her quickly as she worked, kissing her on the cheek. She turned to him surprised, a startled look of uncertainty.

"Missed you," he said. "Don't be long."

It pleased her, saying that, and she thought about it as she swapped Harry's rugs and filled his hay net. Brief as it was she sensed a change, something different in him.

He'd made tea and she washed her hands in the sink before taking the mug.. She turned and saw the flowers.

"Who's been giving you flowers? They're lovely, what a pretty arrangement."

"They're for you," he said softly.

"Who from?"

"From me."

"But you've never brought me flowers."

"Well, today I did."

"Why?"

"Why?" He repeated. How to explain — now she was here and the time had come he found the words eluded him and the planned speech had gone from his head. He opened his mouth to speak but instead reached for her hand, stroked it and raised it to brush the fingers with his lips.

"I need to talk to you, let's go through."

She almost jumped back from him, pulling her hand away and shocking him with the dread in her face. "Oh, what now?" she said, expecting the worst.

"Don't look like that sweetheart, there's nothing wrong." He took her hand again and led her after him to the sitting-room where the fire already blazed with a cheerful golden heat.

"Oh James, for Gods sake, what's happened?" She began. "Or what's going to happen?"

"Oh Kate, do you think that badly of me?"

"When you say you need to talk it usually means something I won't like."

"No, no! It's nothing like that." He saw the fear still in her face. "Kate," and clasped her to him, smoothing the dark hair and kissing her face and then her mouth.

"Kate, I just want to tell you, listen. This time while I've been away I thought of you all the time. I missed you so much. I wanted you there with me."

She tried to speak but he put his fingers on her lips.

"No, just listen, please. It's never been like that before. There was a girl I met there — I'll tell you about her — she reminded me of you and of Katya too. She was lovely. I stayed at her house with her uncle." She frowned but he ploughed on, determined to say it all.

"She came to me in the night -- no, don't look like that, I'm just trying to explain. I sent her away and she was very sweet about it but I knew -- I knew I just wanted you. I needed you so much. But looking at her made me realise for the first time that what I was feeling, this awful longing was -- " he paused again. "It was love. It was like a burst of sunlight."

He stopped, watching her changing expression as she heard him in disbelief.

He rushed on. "It's hard to explain but it was like when the sun comes out in a grey sky and makes everything clear. You know? All this time I've agonised about what I felt and knowing how much you wanted me to say it and I couldn't because I wasn't sure. But I am now, Kate. It just hit me."

He was holding her shoulders, bending to look into her eyes while she stared at him in wonder. "Do you really mean it?"

"Of course I mean it. Would I say it after all this time if I didn't?

"Darling, dearest Kate, I just had to get back here to tell you. I love you Kate. I know it now. I love you, I love you, I love you and I need you. Oh my sweet, kiss me, tell me you love me."

"You know I do. The first day we spoke I think I fell in love with you."

"But you were so distant then."

"I didn't know you, I was scared. But you were the sort of man I'd always wanted to meet. It was like you'd dropped from the sky."

She put her arms around his neck and pulled his head down to kiss him, clinging to him, snatching at him with her open mouth and James felt all the pent up passion of the past few days, urging him to do what he'd thought about for hours and days.

Frantic he began to undress her, holding her breasts to his face in cupped hands and pulling her down beside him. She was eager for him too, but she stopped and laughed when she pulled off his boxers and eyed his body.

"I've never seen you quite like that," she whispered.

"I've been wanting you so much." He pushed her back with a long sigh releasing all his suppressed longing and slid inside her, a profound sense of relief exploding in his head.

They lay together for a long time, entwined, making love again and again, Kate nuzzling and clinging to him, wanting more.

Satiated they fell asleep and he was first to wake, feeling chilled, the fire had burned down and he watched her as she lay, a slight smile curving her mouth.

"Why did I ever doubt what I felt?" he whispered, tears in his eyes. Eventually he roused himself and took his languid body into the kitchen to fetch the bottle and two glasses.

She woke up as he wrapped her in a blanket and took the glass he handed her, meeting his eyes with a smile. They didn't talk but sipped the bubbling wine, while the flames grew stronger, rekindled with fresh logs.

Rapture. That was the word. He wrote it in his diary. A new exquisite delight in each other as if Kate, now assured of his love, was somehow freed from her last inhibitions and they entered a time of joy, unable when they were near to keep from touching one another.

His longed-for words were like a miracle for Kate and changed her world. The knowledge of his love gave her a new sense of security. She'd been in love with him from the start but always there'd been doubts and the fear it couldn't last.

Each time he was away or doing something without her she was afraid he would return and say it was finished. What she knew of his history and the other women in his life had compounded her insecurity but now she knew by every look and touch that what he said was the truth.

They began to go out more, no longer troubled by being seen together and meeting friends he didn't know. One evening she said: "Let's not bother cooking, let's go to the pub. Richard's got a new chef and he's supposed to be something special. I haven't eaten there for years and then it was with mum and dad. Let's go and find out if he's any good."

He'd thought a moment before saying: "Why not?"

The pub was busy but Richard found them a table — thrilled to see them. Most of the customers were visitors, too early for the drinking locals who would come later. But there were a few from the village and one by one they came across to say hello, all saying much the same — "good to see you".

After their meal a couple who had horses came to the table to ask about Harry. James listened as she talked, her face alight with excitement as she explained her plans for the horse and the systematic fitness programme she'd already begun. She'd arranged flexible hours at work which meant some very long days but gave her precious time to work him as the days lengthened.

The February days were mild and she felt safe and free to ride Harry wherever she fancied. With a happy smile James went to the bar for another round of drinks.

Richard came to him at once saying: "I can't tell you how pleased I am to see you two in here like this."

"Thanks," James was surprised. "Good of you to say so."

"No, everyone feels real bad about it all. Nobody realised the dreadful things he'd been up to."

"We try not to talk about it," James said. "She won't forget about it but I hope time will ease things. Please don't say anything to her."

"Of course not. But that bugger will surely get a good long spell inside. I almost feel sorry for Bill. He hasn't been near this place."

James sighed: "At least that shows some sense of shame."

Richard nodded. "Brought it on himself really, didn't he? Let the lad do anything he wanted, wouldn't believe what he was, covered up for him. He always had a nasty streak."

"I'm trying to forget him," said James.

"Of course, I'm sorry. But you two look really happy, it's good to see." Richard put the drinks on a tray, holding it out to him. "This round's on me."

"Thanks very much," James smiled. "We are happy. I know now what I want."

Richard gave him a knowing look. "Like that is it? Sounds promising."

"We'll see. And that's between you and me, right?"

"Right. I hear a lot of stuff I don't pass on. Don't worry."

The sensation over events at Christmas had simmered down but it was still discussed quietly when snippets of information came to light. The full toll of what Steve had done before the fire was out in the open and caused genuine shock at his campaign of cruel intimidation. The story of Tess's death had sickened the toughest farmers.

The wrangle between the new owners of Sedge Farm and their insurance company reopened the topic. The farm was covered at the time of the arson but the insurers were trying to lessen their liability because the main house was not occupied at the time. The owner, now revealed as one Thomas Lawson from Essex, was engaged in the battle with the loss assessors both my telephone and frequent visits to the site. The damage ran to many thousands and until they could agree a figure there was no prospect of a start to rebuilding.

In the background the Sterling family kept a low profile, neither Bill nor his wife were seen locally and Mrs Sterling had taken to driving nearly thirty miles to shop in a town where she wasn't known.

But everyone knew Bill had the same top barrister working behind the scene in an attempt to get Steve released on bail. He was held on remand a long way from home and the police vigorously opposed any suggestion that he should be freed before the trial.

Jack Wilson always found out what was going on, almost before it happened and he kept James informed of developments. But they'd all agreed on a code of silence when it came to Kate, fearing any suggestion of Steve on the loose would freak her out and put her back into the state of nervous fear which had affected her after the fire.

The warmth and friendship they'd found in the pub had an impact on James, he'd been surprised and encouraged and for the first time felt he belonged in the village.

It unleashed in him a spurt of effort as he began seriously to work on the Bosnia book. His features on the aftermath of the conflict and the ongoing search for victims had been well received, especially the story of Nadija — known in print as Semira — not Katya, he'd thought better of that — and her hunt for her parents' remains.

She'd been in touch to tell him they were found where she'd expected them to be in the latest pit uncovered, the one the Serbs were digging on the night she heard her parents slaughtered.

He found the words to tell her story in simple phrases that revealed the depths of her anguish.

He gave it to Kate to read before submitting it. "This is the girl I told you about, an amazing brave young woman."

She absorbed it in silence then said: "She must have loved her parents."

"Don't all children?"

She eyed him with a strange expression and said in a small sad voice: "There was a time I'd have been glad to see my father dragged away."

"You don't mean that."

"Don't I?"

He'd described what Nadija told him, how she waited and watched as the digger bucket carefully scraped away the soil to reveal the twisted bodies before the workers took over to pull them out one by one. She'd spotted the colour of the cloth and jumped into the pit to wipe away the dirt from the rotting body of her mother, clad in the remnants of the dress she'd worn that night.

It was a traumatic piece to read and brought home the horror of the facts and the ongoing outrage as more sites were discovered. He was proud of it, he'd done the job he went for and he knew it was good. But his name in print had made him much better known and increased the urgent demands of the publisher who'd paid the advance.

But now he felt more able to do it, as if rocks that blocked his way had been cleared and when Kate was either at work or occupied with Harry he shut himself away, keyboard bashing on the Mac he realised was well out of date.

More often he sat at the kitchen table scribbling with a soft pencil on an A4 pad — finding the words flowed more easily through the pencil in his hand whereas the technology somehow got in the way and stemmed the flow of inspiration.

Content with herself and their life together and focused on the horse Kate was happy to leave him alone until he appeared, relaxed and at ease, satisfied with the day's achievement. She knew at once if it had gone badly, if he'd been distracted or interrupted because he was irritable and tense, his shoulders hunched with the look she knew so well when he was stressed.

But it was coming. Just as well because he was getting serious grief from the publishers, who'd waited a long time for the book. Writing took time he kept telling them but the early chapters he'd sent were not what they expected. They wanted a more personal angle, about Katya and him, and especially about her death on the mountain. He had touched on it but was unwilling — no, he found it impossible — to go there in the way they wanted.

He'd argued in several telephone conversations that his own story was not relevant to the overall picture of what had happened in Bosnia. But to them the love story was what would sell the book and they were insistent. He knew they were right, knew it would provide the spin to hit the bestseller charts but he found it unthinkable to recreate that raw and painful time.

He was trying not to think about Katya but her image invariably brought him back to Kate. It was always one or the other, the two were so closely linked in his mind. Katya died as they tried to leave Bosnia to come home to England and be married. He'd wanted that more than anything but now he compared it with the situation with this younger but equally beloved girl.

His thoughts of the one made him more sure of his love for the other, tangled ideas that confused him.

So many times in his life people had told him: "You shouldn't dwell on things, let it go, you need to move on. Forget it, move on."

Move on. He wanted to but he wasn't made that way. He couldn't help it. As a small boy he'd found it hard to get over things, bad things stayed in his head, images which wouldn't leave him, like the unborn leverets he could picture years later as if they were there on the bench in front of him.

He knew he analysed it all too much but that was the way he was. But now he was sure. Sure what he wanted and needed. He wanted Kate as his wife. If she would have him.

He was desperate to ask her but afraid she might refuse. He hoped and thought she would want him but he couldn't be sure and he couldn't bear the possibility she might reject what he most desired. It had to be the right moment. He didn't want the soppy down-on-one-knee business but just to ask her at a time when they were both at ease, relaxed and happy. Those moments came more often now but always something happened to prevent it.

He lay with her one night in his arms, passion drained, both luxuriating in the joy of physical repletion, total satisfaction. He'd taught her well and she loved him in every way, nothing between them was unacceptable and on this night his soul brimmed with love for her, for all she was and would be for him.

Her head rested on his chest and he stroked her hair and her naked back, relishing the texture of the smooth skin. Now, now was the moment. He moved his head to kiss her hair and murmured: "Kate." She didn't respond so he touched her cheek and whispered again: "Kate sweetheart, I want to talk to you."

But she just snuggled closer against him with a small grunt of pleasure and straining his head back he saw her eyes were tightly closed. She was fast asleep. Sighing he frowned — the moment had slipped away again.

She slept through the rest of the night without waking and in the morning he had to rouse her for work, it was one of her long days. He sat beside her for several minutes reluctant to disturb her, watching her gentle breathing, lying on her side with one arm upwards across the pillow. He wanted this to go on into the future, he thought he could be content with her and his work and he realised in another revelation that what he felt was joy -- he was happy. He couldn't remember a time when he'd actually said to himself "I'm happy." He knew it to be at best a brief and ephemeral state of mind but for that moment he understood what it meant.

He ran his fingers up her arm, harder when she did not stir and then lifted the arm and ran his tongue along the inside of her elbow and gently pulled her fingers. She opened her eyes and looked up at him.

"It's you. Is it time to get up?"

"Yeah, sorry, you'll be late if you don't hurry."

"Don't want to hurry, want to stay with you. Come back to bed." She reached up to pull him close.

"No sweetheart, we mustn't, you need to be there."

Gently he pushed her aside , kissing her forehead. "Last night was pretty special for me, what about you?"

She smiled, not in the least abashed. "Oh yes, memorable, wonderful, you're wonderful."

"We both are. I love you so much."

But he moved clear of her, with a grin. "Get up now or I shan't be able to resist you and then you'll be very late."

He was smiling and humming some tune as he led Harry out into the paddock for his rest day. Kate's system worked well and the horse looked grand, lean and glossy in the March sunlight and nearly fit enough to compete. He was a handsome horse and James never tired of seeing Kate on him, especially togged out in her dressage gear. They made an impressive picture for a judge. He remained leaning on the fence for several minutes, musing on pleasant images while he watched Harry enjoy the first touches of new grass.

Reluctantly he forced himself back inside to work but the euphoria evaporated when he noticed the answerphone flashing. He hesitated before listening to the message swearing out loud as he did. "Fuck." It was the publishers again.

"Get back to us at once. We need you down here to sort out this book."

He listened to it again, a male voice, probably one of the directors, not the girl who usually called. He needed to think before he spoke to them. He stared through the window, visualising the snow in Sarajevo and Katya falling after the shot. He could almost hear the crack of the rifle. Outdoors the sun was shining and he went back into the fresh air to feel it warm on his face.

The grass was coming through as a green haze on the fields and the tulips Kate had planted in the border in front of the house were colourful, heads bobbing in the breeze.

He didn't want to go to London, not right now. He needed time to think about the book, what he could and couldn't put into it. He knew exactly what they wanted, the graphic facts of what happened on the mountain — the night in the hut and the blood on the snow. But he didn't want to write that.

He heard the phone ringing again but didn't hurry to answer and it stopped with no message. He found it was Jack and called back.

"Glad you caught me, I was just going out but I didn't want to leave a message. Thought I'd come over."

He had an inkling of what was coming. "It's about him I suppose."

"Yes."

"What now?"

"There's another bail hearing coming up. Bill's barrister's determined to get him out and my contact reckons they might do it this time."

"What? Surely they won't let him out," he shouted down the phone.

"Don't shout at me, lad. I'm just telling you, thought you should know."

"Do you know when?"

"Not yet, we think a week or two."

"It's months to the trial date, if he gets out we're back to square one."

"There'd be conditions — any trouble he'd be straight back inside."

"Do you really think conditions will have any effect on Steve Sterling?".

"No, he doesn't seem to take notice of anything."

He sat down to think about it and on impulse rang a contact from the London days, a criminal barrister who'd helped with stories in the past. His opinion was that given the circumstances it should be unlikely Sterling would be bailed. "But you never know, strange things happen in my profession."

The answer was not reassuring but he tried to dismiss his fears as paranoia.

Jack's call had darkened the sunny day and he reflected bitterly that only hours before he'd told himself he was happy.

He tried hard to push away thoughts of Steve Sterling but it was impossible not to think of him. Was it his upbringing, with no parameters, which made him as he was, or was he just born bad?

James believed in evil, he'd seen enough of it and he knew the human animal, given the right opportunity, could allow the most basic instincts to take over and take satisfaction in the process. He knew how quickly the darkness creeps in, just a spark in the mind, worming its way to turn a man into a beast. The serpent in the womb, always there, under the thin veneer of decency.

The young man was brutally cruel, unthinking and above all, jealous and the jealousy was the greatest danger to them. He saw clearly that to have a future with Kate they would have to go away, there could never be a good life here as long as Steve was around.

He'd grown to love his small farm and the comparatively unspoiled backwater it was part of, a time warp in some ways. He liked the people and was captivated by the landscape, its sheer beauty and variety — though he knew its beguiling scenery could be deceptive.

He glanced towards the crag and called Bobbie. The spaniel bounced towards him, ever eager for a walk though these days his tail didn't wag so often and he would lie moping, waiting for James to notice him. He missed his dashing games with Tess.

He thought yet again of Tess dangling from the wire and wished he had Steve here alone so he could punish him, hammer his face to a pulp, hurt him as he'd hurt the dog. The image of him raping the plump child and the face of Nadja in the trees waiting to find her parents, were all aspects of evil which brought bad thoughts.

He hated to wish for a death but since the fire he'd found himself several times contemplating the idea of Steve not being around. If something happened to him — if he were dead -- that would end it. He shook his head to dislodge the ugly thought and smiled at Bobbie. He didn't want to wish that -- knowing too well the saying, be careful what you wish for. The dog jumped up to plant paws on his stomach and he ruffled its head and rubbed around the ears.

"Come Bobbie, let's go." The spaniel ran ahead as they walked to the top fields and the open hill, hoping fresh air and exercise might help him think.

He enjoyed the walk but it did nothing to make things clearer and when he returned he couldn't settle to work and stared at his pad in despair. And there was yet another message, this one from Milton. He called him back.

"Bloody hell, James. What're you playing at? They've been trying to get you for two days, they want you down here."

"I don't want to."

"Listen. Let me spell it out. They've waited a long time for you and they want the goods. I'm having a job to stall them, if you don't cooperate they'll want their money back. Can you pay it?"

He sighed: "No."

"Well, you better get the hell down here and sort it out. What's the problem?"

"It's too personal, they want too much."

"It's gonna cost you if you can't do it — or won't."

"Okay, okay. Don't hassle me. Call them — say I'll come next week."

"Next week?"

"Make some excuse, tell them anything. I need to think."

"You better think hard, man, you've had long enough in therapy."

"What d'you mean?"

"That's what it is, isn't it — this farm thing? Time out -- but you need to get back in the real world."

He listened and there was a long pause before he said quietly: "Maybe I don't want to." He paused then added: "Make me an appointment mid week. Tell me when, I'll be there."

He fetched Harry in and fed him, longing for Kate to be home but it would be two more hours before she was due so he organised the supper and opened a bottle. When she came through the door he grabbed her as if she'd been gone a month, holding her so hard she pulled away to breathe as he said: "God, I've missed you today."

"What's the matter?"

He explained about two of the phone calls and his dilemma over the book but he didn't mention the real problem, what Jack and told him; no point in upsetting her.

"It's not so bad, is it? Couldn't you do what they ask?"

"Maybe, but I need to get my head round it. It's difficult."

He saw by the way she looked at him that she didn't see his difficulty. "I shall have to see them, go to London — next week I said."

"Okay. Will you stay over?"

"No, I'll do it in the day."

"That's no problem, is it. I can spare you for a day."

Chapter twenty-eight

Milton had made the appointment for the afternoon. He'd wanted a morning slot to get it over with and back home. But that was the time they'd set and he didn't want to make things worse by quibbling. It was the second week in April and spring had gone into reverse. An east wind howled around the farm bringing bitter air from the steppes of Russia and small hard grits of snow which stung the face with a frost as hard as anything in January. The hill was dusted with white.

Years later, when he recalled that time, mixed with other scrambled memories, he would think of the drive through the lanes to catch the London train — the hedgerows across the valley draped in white where the blackthorn was in blossom.

Blackthorn winter — April is the cruellest month the poet said, knowing too well the truth behind such old saws of country lore.

The sight of blackthorn in flower would always bring back the events of that day as clear as if he watched it on a screen. On some bushes the blossom seemed especially plump and white and he marked the places thinking they might bear the best sloes in autumn. If it wasn't blighted by frost there would be an abundance of fruit. He'd always meant to make sloe gin and perhaps this year he might get round to it.

But something about the small pale flowers among the sharp thorns on leafless branches chilled him through, making him shudder despite the heater and he turned up the temperature, shivering, wishing he didn't have to make this journey.

Waiting for the train he wanted it not to come, his reluctance growing as each moment passed.

An odd irrational fear took hold, almost a foreboding which he couldn't explain and with it an urgent desire to speak to Kate. He felt in his pocket for the phone, little used so far, and called home.

She'd gone out on Harry before he left but she might still be about the house before leaving for work. But there was no answer though he let it ring a long time. He was still cold with the sense of dread hanging over him. He saw the train arrive and with a sigh switched off the phone. He opened the train door, looking up and down the platform in a ridiculous hope that Kate might appear but there was nothing. The guard blew his whistle, checking all doors were shut as with a last look James stepped in and slammed the door behind him.

At home the phone was still ringing but it was Pat trying to contact them. Her father had just come off the phone and hurried to find her. She'd never seen him look so worried.

"What's up Dad?"

"You need to get hold of them," he jerked his head up the valley. "They've let him out. He's got bail."

"What? Steve?"

"He came home last night. We must warn them."

"Surely he'll keep his head down now?"

"You'd think so -- but I doubt it. If I know him he'll be looking for trouble -- for revenge."

"Shit! James has gone to London -- Kate told me yesterday." She ran into the house and tried the call but after a few minutes rushed out again to her car.

"I'll go over, try and find her."

"Stay with her Pat, better safe than sorry."

But Kate had already left and Harry was happily munching hay in his box, rugged up snugly against the cold. Pat gazed around the yard, marking how it had changed since James came, neat and tidy, flowers growing, a place that was cared for. She smiled to herself, thinking the two of them might make a go of it now. Then she remembered why she'd come and like her father the thought of Steve Sterling on the loose wiped away the happy thought. He was a threat to anyone in the community but especially these two, fuelled by his bitter jealousy.

She looked in again on Harry, stroked his glossy neck and murmured nonsense to him. She'd known him from a foal, when Kate first bought him and she'd never seen him look so good. She knew how hard her friend had worked to get the horse to where he was and what he meant to her. Pat was glad she'd found someone. James supported her ambitions for Harry, so different from the thuggish Steve who saw the horse only as a weapon.

The train got him to London too early for his three o'clock appointment and he stepped out from the station into a wind as cold as Shropshire whipping the city streets. He found a cafe and nursed a mug of coffee while he tried to plan what he could say to them. He knew he would have to give way, make concessions but there were aspects of his personal story he just didn't want to put in print. Couldn't put in print.

The coffee was too strong and he was inhaling cigarette smoke from the tables either side, hating the smoke and the acrid air he was forced to breathe. But he needed somewhere to wait out of the cold, determined not to arrive early. He intended to be five minutes late -- he was the writer, important, not someone to be summoned like a lackey.

But when he entered the warm, plush office with its elegant easy chairs, antique furniture and stylish watercolours on the walls he found his plan had backfired. The pretty pleasant girl he knew in reception greeted him with a smile to say:

"Sorry, Robert's been delayed at another meeting. He sends his apologies. I'm afraid you'll have to wait. He'll be about an hour."

"For fuck's sake, I can't hang around waiting for him. You better make me a time for another day." He made for the door.

The girl grimaced and half rose from her chair.

"Hang on. It's not my business but I think you need to wait." She stopped and took a deep breath. "They're really not happy with you."

He studied the girl. "That bad is it?"

She nodded, saying eagerly: "You can wait here, I'll get you a drink."

"No, I'll come back. Don't want to stay here."

He left the building and found another place to wait, this time a bar where he allowed himself a whisky -- and then another. There'd been a time when he loved London, the bustle around him, the sense of being where the action was. He enjoyed the lifestyle, so much choice of everything at his fingertips, just a cab ride away.

He'd never noticed the noise or the crowds as he revelled in the whirling activity, or the smells, fags and diesel fumes, all part of the mix, the way it was.

Now he hated it, he was a stranger, surrounded by an invasive hubbub in an alien atmosphere. It was another country where he didn't want to be. Buried in the countryside his London friends called it but these days it was what he needed and he longed to be back on the train heading west.

Back just after four he was forced to wait again. Robert, the main director he was seeing, was still not back and arrived eventually at almost four thirty with a vague apology.

By now he suspected it was deliberate and followed the other man into his office with a grim expression, looking at his watch. It had stopped.

He stood still in the doorway and reached for the phone to check the time. It had been off for hours. Some days he never switched it on at all. Only a few people had the number and he hadn't yet acquired the habit of relying on it. He turned it on.

"When you're ready James," Robert said, irritation showing -- not a good start.

He listened as the publisher launched into a tirade about the history of the deal, the money they'd paid, the long wait to get anything on paper. Basically it came down to an ultimatum: finish the book or return the cash.

"Time to make up your mind. You've got an angle no one else can do. And we need that."

"You're asking a lot, I don't think you understand. I loved that girl, I was going to marry her. It was devastating, it's wrecked my life, how can I explain? So much pain."

Robert grinned when he heard the plea, leaning forward across the desk so his face came close. "Exactly -- that's what'll sell. I'm a publisher -- people don't want war stories or a travelogue. They want a human story -- your story."

"I just don't know if I can do it. It's hard."

"You can do it. You must -- or give us back the advance."

"Can't you give me more time?"

"I don't think so. You've had time enough. We've been very patient."

James went quiet, staring at the wide old-fashioned desk where Robert sat waiting in his large leather chair. Then with a sigh he began to speak in a quiet defeated voice. "Katya and I were coming back to England -- " but he stopped -- the phone was ringing in his pocket.

"I thought you were turning it off," Robert said with an angry look.

He ignored him and stared at the phone, a stab of fear as he saw his home number.

"Sorry, I need to hear this."

He left his chair and crossed the room, knowing she would only call if it were important.

"What's wrong?"

"He's out. They've let him out."

"Oh God! Are you alone there?"

"Pat's here, she says she'll stay till you get back."

"That's something, try not to worry. I doubt if he'll try anything," he lied.

"Get finished outside and then lock yourselves in. Lock all the doors."

"When will you be home?'"

"I'm not sure, I'm still in the meeting. I'll get the earliest train I can. Stay calm, Kate. He surely won't want to cause more trouble."

"You don't know him, not like I do."

"Okay. I'll cut this short."

He swung round to Robert, who'd half risen, listening with curiosity. "I've got to go -- I need to get back."

"You can't just walk out of here, nothing's settled."

James moved towards him and said very softly: "I'll do it your way. I'll write your fucking bestseller. I'll bare my soul for you but right now I've got to go."

He went to the door but turned again. "Then I'll write you another story, about a psychopath.

With only a few moments to spare at Euston a long queue of taxis stopped him getting close so he left the cab and ran through the entrance onto the platform in time to see the back of the departing Birmingham train. The next would be another hour.

"Fuck," he said aloud and two middle aged women turned to stare at him as he clenched his fists in furious frustration. For ten minutes he paced up and down the platform wondering what to do. The next train meant changing at Wolverhampton which made the journey longer but he had no choice. Waiting was the only option and to calm himself he found a bar and another whisky. He tried to ring Kate but she didn't answer.

"Call me," he left the message, struggling to keep the anxiety out of his voice.

The whisky steadied him and he ordered a sandwich but when the girl brought it he couldn't get it down. The rising sense of fear had suppressed his hunger and he found himself squeezing the whisky tumbler tight in his hand as he tried to rationalise it all. No -- Steve wasn't fool enough to risk landing himself back inside as soon as he was out. He wasn't that stupid -- or was he? The image of pure hate in his face at the pub on Christmas Eve belied that comfort and he dreaded that the prize of vengeance would outweigh common sense.

He stared up at the big old-fashioned clock over the bar, willing the time away and with twenty minutes to spare he was back on the platform. The station was bright and warm but outside the cold light was fading into an early clouded dusk.

He tried Kate and she answered, sounding relaxed. "Everything's fine. Don't worry, Pat's here. It'll be okay, he wouldn't try anything while she's here."

He frowned at that, thinking the presence of another girl wouldn't stop Steve doing anything. But he only said: "Good, just stay put till I get home.

"Don't worry, nothing's going to happen."

"Love you," he said and heard her say: "I know."

As the train trundled west James glared with growing impatience through the glass at the urban sprawl dim in the fading light, while in Derrington Steve Sterling and his three friends rode up to the farm gate. Steve jumped off the quad bike with a grin.

"Over there," he said, nodding towards the stone wall and watched as they dumped the three bikes out of sight from the house. He unstrapped a heavy sledgehammer from the quad's carrier.

"What's that for?" asked the youngest lad.

"You'll see."

The other boy frowned. "Maybe this isn't such a good idea, Steve. You don't want to end up back inside."

"Something I gotta do," he said. "You just do what I say, right? Come on."

The others glanced at each other, shrugged and fell in behind as Steve strode boldly across the yard to the loose box where Harry quietly munched his hay. He switched on the light and went in, dropping the hammer by the door. The horse was startled by the strangers in the sudden glare, snorting as they crowded in. Steve grabbed the head collar hanging outside and approached Harry who snorted again and tossed his head away, unnerved by the rough handling, otherwise he didn't struggle as the collar was put on.

"Here Gaz, hold on to him," he thrust the rope into the boy's hand. "Hold him tight."

"What you doing?"

"Putting an end to her bloody nonsense -- see how you like this, Harry boy!"

He swung the hammer twice, testing the distance, then made a wider swing with all his force to smash the head into Harry's leg below the knee. The youths gasped at the sound of splintering bone. The horse screamed and reared, tossing Gaz aside but as he came down Steve swung again and caught the other leg. Harry collapsed into the straw, shuddering and squealing a high-pitched agonised whinny. Steve's face was a mask of wicked pleasure as he lifted the hammer above his head and brought it down again and again on the horse's legs until Gaz, appalled, grabbed his arm.

"Christ man, are you mad? You never said you were planning something like this."

Steve smiled, a weird look in his eyes as he wiped the blood splashes from his face. "She'll never ride him again."

"Fucking hell! What've you done! Let's get out of here."

The three of them started for the door but Steve bawled. "We haven't finished. You're not going. You're staying with me. You back out now and I'll fix you all. You know it. Trust me -- I'll have you."

At that moment the front door opened and Kate rushed out, with Pat calling her to come back. They'd heard the sound of Harry's screams, which had subsided into a pitiful rumbling groan.

Steve turned to face them, laughing in near hysteria. "I knew that'd fetch her out. Grab them, quick. Bring 'em both."

The train was held up on the last stretch of the journey and he emerged from the station in a panic of anxiety, unable to raise Kate on the phone. By this time it was completely dark and very cold and he let out a stream of oaths at the windscreen already obscured by a thin film of ice which took precious minutes to clear.

He drove home too fast, oblivious of the icy roads until the car went into a skid on the hill. But he righted it and slowed down on the last bit. The bikes were there by the gate, clear in his headlights which he shut off in instant reaction as a wave of fear engulfed him. He sweated despite the cold and started to run but saw the light in the barn, a bright oblong around the big double doors. His ears caught an eerie and horrible sound which he knew at once must be Harry and he half turned that way. But the front door was wide open, light from the house casting a bright swathe across the yard. He started towards the barn but stopped again, hesitant, then turned and ran to the house and up the stairs.

He unlocked the gun cabinet, then remembered the weapon was under the bed. He stooped and pulled it out, still wrapped up clean and oiled in his old jacket. He yanked open the top drawer of the tallboy to grab a handful of cartridges, spilling the box across the floor, then rushed down the stairs, the gun broken over his arm, shoving cartridges into the breech as he went.

He strode across the yard and heard a woman scream — not Kate. All the time in the background was the sound of the horse's whimpering agony.

Wrenching the big door open he went in and halted in shock at the scene, for an instant stunned before the meaning of what was happening hit home. In the barn's dim light he recognised the two lads holding Pat near the straw stack. They had her by the arms between them, struggling to restrain her as she fought to get to Kate. It was she who'd screamed. He saw their gloating obsessive faces as they watched what was happening on the floor. One of them had his free hand inside his trousers.

A bale of straw had been thrown down where the light was brightest and Kate was stretched over it, her arms pulled forward and down by the third youth. He stared at them incredulous, all the horrors he'd seen and the worst things he'd tried to shut away encapsulated in this act of bestiality.

The youth knelt in the straw beside Kate's head as she sprawled face down, naked apart from a torn shirt round her neck. Steve was leaning over her, head upright and thrusting hard as he raped her.

James screamed: "Get off!" in a voice he didn't recognise as his own. He stepped forward, snapped the gun closed and fired over their heads, both barrels one after the other. The noise of the pellets rattling against the ceiling beams was very loud in the sudden hush.

They let go of Pat and the one holding Kate jumped up in fear. But Steve bent over Kate and whispered something in her ear before he pulled himself away, unhurried, clutching his jeans. Then he stooped to hit her, a contemptuous swipe across the buttocks as she rolled over into the straw scrabbling to cover herself. She stared at James but didn't speak, Harry's the only voice in the silence.

Steve turned to face him, still waiting near the door, a triumphant grin lighting his face. He laughed loudly.

"Told you I'd have her. Should have done that a long time ago but you got in the way. She's a good fuck, better than I thought. I've had plenty of time to think about it in that filthy prison. Three times in half an hour -- not bad, eh? I've been storing it up for her."

Everything after that moved into slow-motion, or so it seemed.

James felt in his pocket for cartridges and reloaded. Laughing, Steve started towards him and repeated: "Told you I've have her. You don't scare me with that. I know you won't use it -- you'll only scare yourself."

He kept moving forward, slowly, fastening his jeans and James raised the gun, pointing straight at him. "What you gonna do, pen man?" Steve sneered.

"I'm going to turn you in for rape and what you've done to the horse. They'll lock you up for years on top of the arson."

"No, you're not," Steve laughed. "You haven't got the balls to shoot me. I'll just take the gun."

He took a step nearer.

"Stop right there."

Steve laughed again. "Who d'you think you're kidding, Jim boy. You won't shoot me, you haven't got the guts. Soft you are, soft -- they tell me you can't even shoot a pigeon."

He said nothing but tightened his grip on the gun as Steve kept talking.

"I've spoiled the girl's little hobby, that fucking horse has been in my way for years. But I've done for it now."

He came forward, face contorted with sneering hate and stretched out a hand for the gun.

"Me and the lads are going now, done what we came for."

The thought of the horse more than anything pushed James over the top into blind rage with the realisation that this dreadful act had been planned, premeditated and carried out in cold blood with not even the excuse of impulse.

"You fucking bastard, you're not fit to be alive."

He noticed his own breath as he spat out the words, a shimmering wisp of haze in the cold air.

"Well, I am," Steve growled and James stepped back. He looked beyond him at Kate, collapsed on the floor, her bare skin red and bruised. Steve lunged to snatch the gun and he closed his eyes, eased his forefinger back and squeezed the trigger so gently it was like no pressure at all.

The blast caught Steve full in the chest, spattering James with a fine spray of blood as the force at short range twisted the body and threw him backwards into the straw.

There was a shocked silence broken by Kate's frantic voice whispering over and over: "What have you done?"

He knew at once what he'd done, blood ran freely from a ragged hole in the chest, the head, tilted to one side was covered with the spurting gore. He bent down and pressed two fingers against the neck. There was nothing. Steve was dead.

He shook his head and looked up at them all, watching him, appalled. One of them, the boy Gaz, was crouched spewing into the straw.

As if nothing had happened he gestured with the gun at the two who'd started to scramble past him to the door.

"Stay where you are," he bawled and they cowered back.

"Get up!" he shouted at Gaz. "Move back."

He herded them towards the poisons store at the back of the barn and said curtly to Pat who was hugging Kate.

"Fasten the door." He watched her drop the bar which secured it.

He glanced at Kate but couldn't meet her eyes as she turned her anguished gaze on him. He looked away from the trail of slime trickling down her thigh but took off his fleece to hang it round her shoulders.

"Put it on." Then he snatched one of Harry's blankets from the rack and wrapped it around her. She leaned against him a moment but he couldn't touch her.

"Take her indoors, Pat. Look after her."

He passed Steve's body without a glance and went quickly across the yard to Harry's stable, calling Jack's number as he went.

"Jack, get up here fast and bring your gun -- for the horse. Don't ask -- just come -- now."

He couldn't call the horse by name, somehow it distanced him from the savagery. Harry was quieter now, the groaning sunk into shudders, his breathing heavy and laboured. James squatted beside him, fondling his head as they waited for Jack to come.

He went outside when he heard the truck. "What's going on?" he demanded but James just shook his head and the farmer followed him to the loose box, his face paling with shock when he looked in.

"Are you sure?" he asked, staring down in pity at the animal. "Christ, I never thought he'd do anything as bad as this. Is there nothing else we can do?"

"There's no vet could put that right, the bastard's done a good job."

He knelt again to stroke the horse's head, straightening the forelock and rubbing the soft velvet skin of his nose. "Good lad, Harry," he whispered. "It'll be over soon. You'll be all right now."

He got up with a hand over his face to hide the tears. "Do it, Jack. Do it now."

He turned away as Jack dropped to his knees, gun in hand. He too stroked the silky elegant neck before he put the muzzle against the forehead and pulled the trigger. The sleek grey body shuddered and a back leg kicked at the bedding, then he was still. James gazed at the dead horse, Jack numbed into silence beside him, neither able to take in the horror of it.

In only his shirt he shivered in the cold and trembled as he put a hand on Jack's shoulder to murmur: "Thanks."

Jack watched him go out to the car beyond the gate and noted the quaking shoulders.

He climbed in, teeth clicking, his body racked with shudders from the cold and shock. He started the engine to get warm and sat in silence for more than ten minutes, staring at the house and yard, unable to control the trembling. The rising moon was already halfway up the sky, clear now and bright with stars, illuminating the place he'd come to love.

He'd just killed a man. He'd seen men die, several times, women too and children. But this was his doing, no longer an observer but the perpetrator. He hadn't intended the death but somehow it seemed meant to be.

He waited till the trembling stopped. When he came out of his reverie, he stirred and shook his head, sighed and smiled ruefully, remembering the words he'd said so clearly in front of five witnesses: "You're not fit to live." That would sound worse at a trial.

Stuffed by his own words. He shrugged.

He looked again at the house, the moon seemed to be watching it. Kate was in there -- Kate,
poor Kate. But he couldn't go to her -- he knew there would be a different path for them now. The spell was broken -- it could never be recast.

He left the car and looked across the valley at the dotted lights from homes and farms nestled in that bowl among the hills, all unaware of the drama waiting to unfold. How it would shock them.

Turning his back on the scene he took the phone from his pocket and summoned the police.

Afterword

Twenty years later he sat among the press corps at the international criminal tribunal for the former Yugoslavia in The Hague to witness the sentencing of Ratko Mladić to life imprisonment for genocide and crimes against humanity.

The previous year he'd been there when Radovan Karadžić was given a prison term of forty years for war crimes including the 44-month long vicious siege of Sarajevo and the 1995 massacre of more than 8,000 Bosnian men and boys at Srebrenica.

The Mladić trial had lasted more than four years after they finally caught up with him in northern Serbia. James had been in The Hague several times listening to evidence from some of nearly 600 witnesses, many of them survivors of the atrocities.

The man they called the Butcher of Bosnia looked a broken, pathetic creature standing in the dock but he retained sufficient arrogance to swear at the judge who said Mladić's crimes "rank among the most heinous known to humankind and include genocide and extermination". He had faced eleven charges and was convicted on all but one.

James served two years for the killing. He was charged with murder which he denied but subsequently pleaded guilty to manslaughter. The judge, despite hearing the full toll of Steve Sterling's crimes, ruled that the death could have been avoided.

Prison at least gave him plenty of time to write, though the book was much changed from the original synopsis, coloured as it was by events.

He couldn't bring himself to sell his beloved hill farm, hoping he might one day go back. He leased the house and gave Jack the use of the land. On his release he went back to press work based for a time with his mother in Wiltshire. Kate, who'd gone to William in London to start a new career, went once to visit him in jail when he was moved to an open prison where he worked with the animals. But it was an unhappy and difficult meeting, with the memories too raw and he could find little to say to her. He never saw her again.

In the succeeding years he returned to Bosnia many times, to observe the ongoing and now highly organised search for the missing. Bill Clinton's brainchild the International Commission for Missing Persons, was established in June while James waited for his trial. Designed to deal with the aftermath of this new holocaust no one then could conceive how long their operations would continue.

He watched and wrote about the long arduous task over the years as more burial pits were unearthed and the painstaking work of identifying the thousands of bodies. He went back to find Nadija and stayed some time with her. She lived still with her uncle, looking after him and running the farm between them. But she had a new role with the ICMP liaising with the Bosnians on identification work. He found this strangely pleasing, in some sense reassuring.

She seemed thrilled to see him, unfazed by his record, showing him proudly the improvements they'd made to the old farmhouse which was lighter and brighter now the power was more reliable. He still slept on the mattress by the iron stove but found comfort in the darkness when she crept under his blankets to wrap her warm arms around him. Her uncle never moved from his room at night and made no comment on his presence.

In Sarajevo he was based again at the refurbished Holiday Inn but went often to the cafe to let Esma spoil him like a son and to the cemetery with flowers for Katya.

He made a life but was, as ever, essentially alone.

Printed in Poland
by Amazon Fulfillment
Poland Sp. z o.o., Wrocław